Ter'Avan Trilogy, Past Powers: Book 1

Heir To Sorcery

Book 1 in the Ter'Avan Omniverse©
by

D.C. Soas

WorldofTeravan@gmail.com

Cover art & design by D.C. Soas
Maps and character artwork by D.C. Soas
The artist signature is the trademark of D.C. Soas

ISBN 978-1-7348466-1-4

Contents

Dedication

D.C.

To Soas. Your perfect amount of crazy is a paradox. To our publisher for wishing upon a new light in the sky. To Stefnie, my first fan can never be forgotten. To my beloved, without you these worlds would only hear one voice and never pass into the hearts of others.

Soas

To D.C. for putting up with me and my antics. To others in my life. You know who you are and why I remain a crazy, happy hermit.

Foreword and Preface

(Like we can tell those apart)

D.C.

Well, I should imagine I will have more to say than Soas. These books are from a world similar to our own. This will become apparent as time goes by. I hate spoilers. So I will not divulge any here. Suffice to say, this world has grown parallel to our own and has had influences from Earth. Yet, it is not Earth. Sayings are odd at times, as if they have heard them but never got them right. Perhaps, Earth heard the sayings from them, from Ter'Avan?

The story has been created from reading translations of the original Ter'Avan language. Some words will not translate and are left in an italic format. I apologize if the translations are not perfect, but they truly are the best Soas could do. We worked on this together to create a story from the histories that we have. So suffice to say, this is not a true story and still a work of fiction. I enjoyed created the cover art, sketches, and maps for the book. In book 2, I hope to create sketches for new characters and some for those not depicted. I hope to create new sketches for the ones already introduced. One character has already requested a drawing with better clothing. I absolutely agree. So, I turn this introduction over to Soas. I fear to wonder what Soas will say. Please let it not be the cookie recipe he wanted to add.

Soas

What is when there is not why, but when there is not why to try. So try to why is when is now, and try to now when there is a why. Simple as that, the meaning of life?

Maps of the World

map 1 of 2

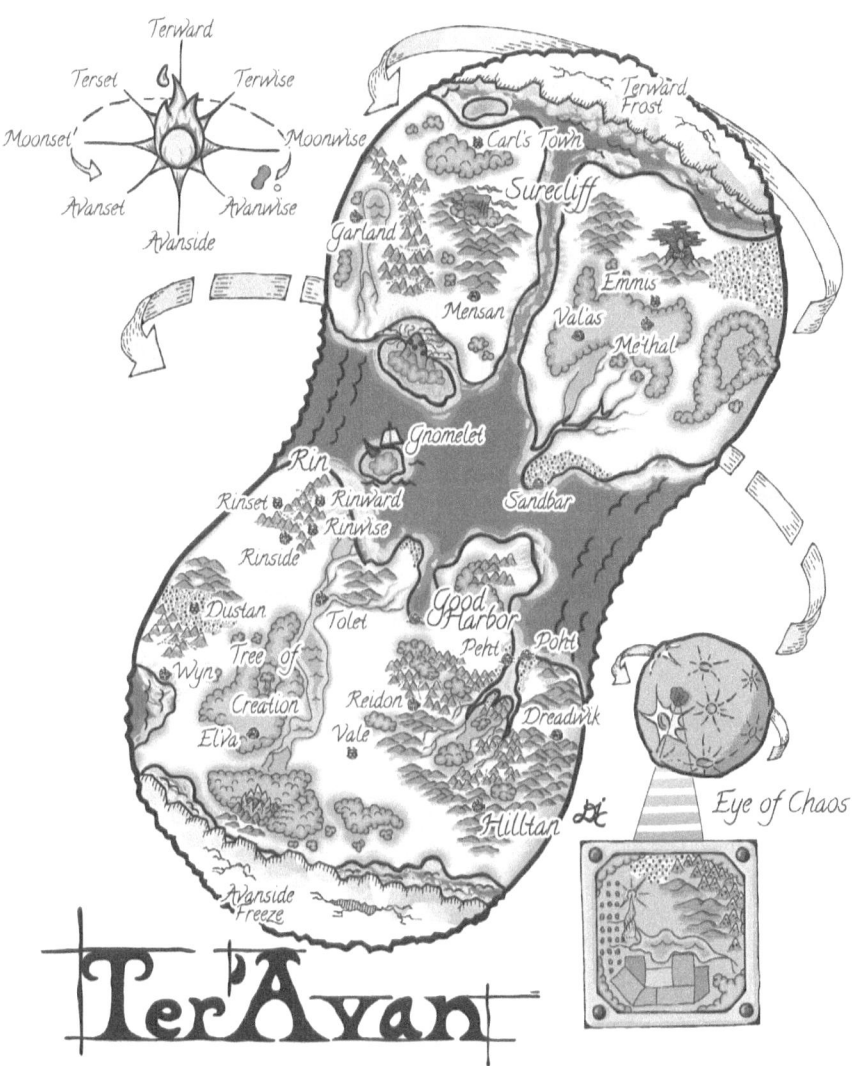

Terward

Tersel   Terwise

Moonset'   Moonwise

Avanset   Avanwise

Avanside

Terward
Frost

Carl's Town

Surecliff

Garland

Emmis

Mensan   Va'as

Me'thal

Gnomelet

Rin

Rinset   Rinward

Rinwise

Sandbar

Rinside

Dustan   Tolet

Good
Harbor

Tree of

Peht   Poht

Wyn

Creation   Reidon

Vale   Dreadwik

Elva

Hilltan

Eye of Chaos

Avanside
Freeze

Ter'Avan

map 2 of 2 Yes, the other side!

This is Soas. The maps look like they took time to craft. D.C. Do you know what sunlight is anymore? Oh, your computer is unlocked.

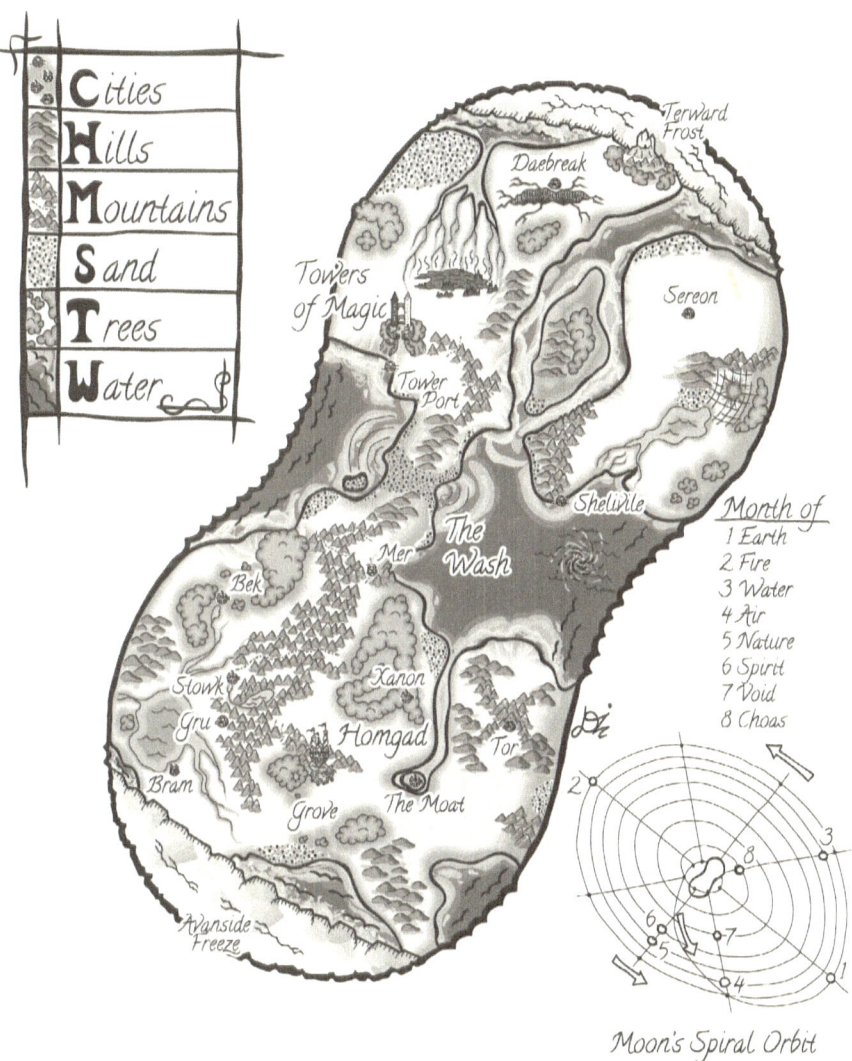

Cities
Hills
Mountains
Sand
Trees
Water

Terward Frost
Daebreak
Towers of Magic
Sereon
Tower Port
Shelivile
The Wash
Mer
Bek
Xanon
Stowk
Gru
Homgad
Tor
Bram
Grove
The Moat
Avanside Freeze

Month of
1 Earth
2 Fire
3 Water
4 Air
5 Nature
6 Spirit
7 Void
8 Choas

Moon's Spiral Orbit

5

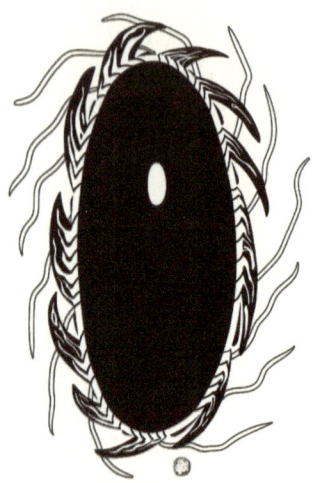

Chapter 1: Home Never Seen

What now was one, what now was two.
What now was three, but now untrue.
What one takes two, and leaves but none.
What one returns, from two made one.
Thus, by claim of dragon, thus to hearken call.
Thus, by future's peril, thus one to save all.

Three AM, known as the witching hour. Few within this sleepy town would know this secret whispered in the night. Most of the town-folk were of the ruff-and-tumble farmer type, more ready to grab a beer and climb into a pick-up truck than stay up at night and look for the unusual. Few would think mysterious things were afoot in the dead of night. The last of the neon signs quietly clicked to sleep when the distortion formed. A silent pulse blasted down the narrow alleyway. It tore free loose bricks and flung paper along like frighten birds. A chill wind sprang from a singular black bead that hung mid-air. The bead lengthen like a cat iris, until it formed a long oblong of black energy. The portal waved back and forth vigorously until it finally snapped into an oval suspended a few centimeters above the ground, and as tall as full-grown man.

A figure stepped across the void. Pain registered on his face as he held his battered, pointed hat in place. As the figure emerged, the void pulled away from him slowly. Its shadowy tendrils clung and stretched until it snapped loose and back into the black plane. From the void's dark recesses, the shadows screamed in his ears as other howls of fury echoed around him. The void closed with a silent snap to swallow the man's hat. Black wavy hair hung in loose curls as the man pulled the hood of his cloak over his head.

The cloaked man was dressed in midnight blue, the edge of the cloak skimmed the ground, as he straightened. Under the cloak, were robes of black and shimmered in the moonlight. Leather boots, grey with age, hugged his feet. His beard, black with streaks of white, stuck out from under the recesses of the hood. His face blended with the shadows of the night. The figure reached into the brick wall with his right hand as if it was soft clay and pulled out a pole of unwieldy brick as high as his shoulder and cumbersome enough to drag at his arm. He gave two hefty taps with the stone pole. It transformed from the ground up and replaced stone with the gnarled lighter form of oak.

Momentarily overcome by the effort of transformation, he gave a shuddered sigh and reached into his cloak. He pulled out a jet black cat by the scruff of his neck and set it on the ground and pet it fondly. The cat begun to purr and traced a figure eight around the old man's legs as the man took in his surroundings.

At last, the old man spoke to his cat. "It seems we have barely arrived without harm Daylow. I certainly hope the *tempra* will hold for a return with our guest." The cat, Daylow, gave a curt meow and clawed its way up to the man's shoulder and promptly fell asleep within the folds of his hood.

"It seems you have no fears," he chuckled. "Well and well. I say, lets be off before my power grows any weaker in this flamed world. I would, if I had time, like to see more of this place again. I wonder what kind of games they like to play now. What do you think Daylow?" He pondered this as his curiously eyed his surroundings.

The cat split open a single golden eye and spoke in a strange whisper-like growl. "Mercadio would you please hurry, I feel suffocated in this world. I can barely sense anything." Daylow closed his golden eye and fell back into his blissful catnap.

Mercadio snorted as he strolled out of the alley while he spoke to himself. "Just trying to rouse a conversation Daylow, no need to get your fur in a knot. Ouch! Watch the claws you ashing feline, else I tire of your dox ways."

The cat growled a reply without opening his eyes, "I am not dox nor ashing, just annoyed. Now go." Mercadio grumbled but did not reply. He focused his thoughts back to his goal. He must reach the heir before the competition got to him. With that thought in mind, he quickened his pace and disappeared into the night, the soft clack of the wooden staff was the only indication of his passing.

As soon as Mercadio and Daylow left the alley, a small red ball of fur, no bigger than an eye, rolled out of a crack in the wall. It settled to a stop as black mist faded from its furry body. It twitched and rolled out of the alley. As it reached the mouth of the alley, a barn owl swiftly swooped and plucked it up with its beak. The owl flew into the night with the ball until it suddenly squawked and dropped the lost prize on a passing flat rooftop.

The little ball of red fur remained still as a small trickle of blood oozed out of it to form into a pool. The blood continued to slowly ooze out until it was enough to have filled a deep tub. The ball gave a single shudder as the blood ebbed its flow. With a burst of speed, cracks of white tendons shot through the puddle of blood and begun to whip around in the air like hungry snakes. Bone fragments sprouted like crystalline flowers to form into a rib-cage, skull and other bones. The puddle pulled itself into the center, twisted upon itself, until it formed a large cocoon of blood, meat and bone. The cocoon shrank upon itself, sprouted skin and feathers and made deep popping and shifting noises. Minutes later, a large blood-red barn owl roosted on the roof top above the other houses, shopping buildings, and trees. It blinked its great white, milky eyes and shot into the air. In a nearby tree, the barn owl watched as the unnatural bird took flight. It fiddled with its beak and a small hole that had been freshly punctured.

He dreamed the same old dream again. The Mountains were great and purple in their height. The moon twisted slowly in the air got larger and larger as it trailed across the sky. The air was sweet with flowers and the great green land stretched out underneath him. He looked around in stunned silence. He always liked this dream; in fact he loved it. Even though he had never remembered seeing a place like this in real life, it always felt like home. Yes, he always liked this dream, even though it always scared him. He knew what will happen next. The grass that sparkled with dew begun to became dull and grey. The sky slowly filled with storm clouds. The wind turned chill and made his nostrils hurt as he breathed. He pulled the collar of his shirt up over his nose to cover his face. He turned to see a dark shadow fall over the land. It looked unnatural against the growing darkness. This shadow was liquid and twisted as it felt on its surroundings. It whipped in the air like a snake and turned to face him. He turned and ran. He pushed hard. The cold took his heat with every step. He knew he must get away from the shadow at his back. He tried to cry out for help, but could not get the words to come forth. He looked behind him to see a pair of golden eyes look out from the shadows. He tried to run harder, pump his legs and arms as fast as he could.

A low hum started to build in the sky. Before, the moon had looked innocent, but now it shone with a bloody tint. It had stopped its track through the sky and now was steadily getting larger. The front of it started to glow red as it hit the atmosphere. Great rending cracks sprang across the surface. The hum suddenly dropped into a deep deafening moan as the atmosphere buckled downward. He screamed, but it only came out in a gargled whisper as the pressure pushed into his lungs. He couldn't run any further. He stopped and panted as he struggled to work air out of lungs, but he couldn't exhale. The liquid shadow coursed over his legs and chilled them far greater than the air ever could. It was like the vacuum of space feed on his soul. He knew he was going to die this time. This time the dream was going to take him. It was never this bad before; it was alive. A huge explosion of sound from the moon's impact on the atmosphere finally reached the land. It blasted everything he could see. Snow and trees tore from the mountains. The grass whipped at his face and embedded into his skin. Sound muffled to a pitched scream in his ear as his hearing deafened. He slammed his hands over his ears in defense, but it was a futile gesture. The sound resonated through everything, including his body. He felt liquid poor from his ears. It was probably blood, dear god, he hoped it was only blood. His vision wavered as the air heated around him, yet the shadow that pooled and climbed chilled him with deadly icy cold.

Then he saw it. At first, it was a blurry red dot against the burning sky. It grew large on the horizon until it took on the shape of a huge red owl. The owl was not just big; he was at least the size of a house!

He gasped and felt terror run through him. *Great! Not only am I going to die in fire, cold and a moon sized fist, but I will be a final snack for a monster bird as well. My imagination sucks.* The sky was a web of burning lightning as the moon was only moments from impact. He could already feel the crackle of static in the air and a weightlessness as the heavenly body came to kiss its mother. The bird passed overhead and made a grab for him. He closed his eyes from the sight of the big beak so close to his face. He still had his eyes closed as he felt claws gentle snapped around his arms and lift pull him from the liquid shadows. He summoned enough courage to opened his eyes and see that the owl did not eat him as he thought. It flew him away, but to where? The sky made a crackle noise like shattered glass. He looked around to see where it came from but could not find the source. It cracked again, and a third time. The dream evaporated. He woke slowly and confused.

He blinked and looked around for the noise that was now somewhere in his room. It cracked again. He heard chips of window fall from behind his window shades. He got out of bed and walked to the window and pulled the blinds up by the string. On the other side, a large red barn owl stared back at him with blind white eyes, eyes that looked aged by death. He jumped back and blinked in confusion. There was definitely and owl. The eyes had a white glaze, not red. It was just a stupid brown and white owl with blinded eyes. *Darn dreams are getting to me. No wonder it was hitting the window, the poor thing has been blinded. It could be trying to find a safe place to roost? I can bring it in a call a bird rescue in the morning*, he thought to himself.

His hand slowly moved to the window latch. His thumb brushed the lever as the owl twisted its body nervously around but kept the head focused on him. His thumb moved the lock with a small click. The latch opened at the same moment as a light turned on, and he heard his father scream a blood chilled "NO!"

He turned to see his father in his doorway. The hall light illuminated his father's face, stretched in a horrid mask of terror. Behind him stood a dark figure wrapped in a dark blue blanket pulled over his head. Under the hood glowed a pair of golden eyes. His dream screamed at his mind. They were the same pair of eyes that was hunting him from the liquid shadows. His blood turned cold as the sensation swept from his head to his feet. As he heard the owl fluttering into the room behind him, he saw the figure raise a stick at his face. Something black like liquid shadows leap forth. He didn't know what to do. *What can I do? What!* He closed his eyes and braced himself.

∞∞∞∞

Mercadio felt the heir. He was close, but his magical sense blurred like a fog to the point of useless. *I do not think I will locate him until I am extremely close. Nothing looks the same.* He held up the piece of old swaddling. He closed his eyes. *Yes, he is this way.* He turned and jogged off into the park. Daylow was still asleep, generating heat like a kettle stove on his shoulder. Mercadio was at a walking jog. His eyes scanned back and forth. *I hope he will come peacefully. If not, I will do what I need to convince him.* Mercadio grimaced at the thought.

He was looking at his surroundings when he noticed the red bird flying in the same general direction overhead. Mercadio swore under his breath and aimed his staff at the bird. A terrible black writhing bolt of lightning swept out of his wooden staff towards the red bird. The bird dodged the bolt smoothly and dived into the canopy of trees as a second bolt blasted through the sky. It ripped leaves and limbs and scattered them like straw. Out of the tree came a reply of loud mocking hoots.

Fully enraged, he ran full bore ahead. He spotted the red bird dive towards a simple white shingled house. He was about to fire again when he realized that he might hit the heir. He needed him alive. Daylow had been jostled awake, his golden eyes stared death-like up at the second story window.

"He's there. Take him Mercadio, kill the bird."

"I know you fuzzball, I was trying to aim at the bird. It is not normal, I think it is a *drethcon*. Those ashen parasites, I'll kill it yet." He heard a hiss from in his hood and gave a sharp growl himself.

Mercadio reached the house and pounded on the door. A light glowed from the front window. Time seemed to pool into a stagnant puddle as he saw the silhouette stand up and come to the door. A man hesitantly opened the door and looked at Mercadio with fear and suspicion. Without hesitation, he lifted his palm and spoke a word under his breath. A light flared in his hand. Around the man's head a crown of light appeared and shattered. The man's eyes widened as he whispered Mercadio's name. The man turned and ran for the stairs. His feet took them two at a time. Mercadio followed behind him at his heels. The man reached the top he flicked on the hall light and yanked opened a door. Mercado saw the poor man's face go pale as he shouted "No!"

Mercadio reached the door a moment later as the boy turned towards him. He lifted his staff towards the heir and brought forth shadow lightning. His only thought was the hope his mark was true.

Something cold and charged whipped past his head. He heard an awful squawk behind him. He threw himself to the side. His head slammed into something with a solid thud. *Ouch! Was that the nightstand?* He opened his eyes to see the dark figure loom directly over him.

"Fine time to be sitting down boy." the figure spoke. "Get up and out of the way Delex."

He was still recovered from the knock on his head. Delex numbly obeyed as he nodded and crawled on to his bed. His father stood speechless in the doorway. He saw the figure reach the bird and lift it to his study desk. Delex noticed that it was the red color he thought before. The owl was in a crumpled heap of broken meat and feathers. Blood oozed from numerous places from the feathers. It looked like a smaller version of his dream owl. The dark figure pulled out a knife started hack at the owl until he split the chest open. Delex didn't know what to do. He struggled to make sense of it all. His hands reached the lamp on the night stand and swung it towards the dark figure. He heard his father cry out again but it was too late. The lamp crack over the cloaked man and followed him to the floor. Delex's hands, numb from the shock of the blow, dropped what was left of the lamp. He bent down to see how badly he hurt the man was when something black jumped out from under the hood and attached itself to his shirt.

Two golden eyes stared back at him. It was a sleek pure black cat. He was about to throw it off when the cat struck. The little paw hit him square in the face. The blow felt like he had smashed face-first into a wall, and then the wall punched him. Stars whirled in his vision almost comically as his eyesight tunneled into a moonlit speck. The last thing he saw was one of the cat's golden eyes locked with his and a not so cat-like feline smirk on the cat's face. He heard his father's muffled voice say something he thought might have been his name. Darkness like liquid shadow, took him.

Delex woke up suddenly. His father was over him with a damp cloth to his head. "I was wondering when you were going to come around. You took a nasty blow from the cat. I saw your head whip back. Well that will teach you to mess with a familiar." His father chuckled nervously.

Delex was confused. *What in the world was that?* As he thought to himself, his father spoke again. He had a serious look on his face. "Son, I haven't been fully truthful with you. I think you need to know that-" He couldn't finish his sentence. Tears welled in his father's eyes.

Delex noticed the cloaked figure in the corner of the room. The hood was down. The man wore a mask of annoyed pain of his face. His face looked weathered and darkly tan like he had been outside most of his life, but in his brown eyes still held the vigor of youth. His hair was wiry and black with a few strands of white streaked through it. His hair came down to his shoulder like it gave up growing any farther. His beard was another story. He gripped the staff with one hand and held a bag of frozen peas on his head with the other. He glared at

Delex as he rubbed it over the spot Delex hit him. After an uncomfortable long silence, he spoke. "You, my boy, are more trouble than you are worth. Why in this world did you let that thing in? I hope you know it escaped after it reassembled itself." The man in the large comical robe glared and spoke again. "My name is Mercadio. You boy, I know as Delex. I knew your father and helped raise you until your foster father came along." He waved a hand at Delex's father. "Jim here helped raise you until now, but now you must listen. Go ahead Jim, it might be better if you explain."

Jim, his foster father, his father in Delex's eyes, sighed. Delex spoke before he could. "I saw that owl in my dream. It grabbed me in the dream dad!" The gnarled hobo raised an eyebrow in curiosity. "Who in the world is this old guy to come barging in with that demon-cat. Those eyes were in my dream as well, and I was none too happy to see it. Don't trust them dad. I think they are here to kill us." His hands where clenched to his sides. His face still hurt and may even bruise. *Bruise for a cat's slap! What in the world was that cat!* Delex eyed the knife on the floor.

Jim noticed his son's attention and quickly grabbed the knife. He handed it back to Mercadio. Delex stared at his father in disbelief. His father sighed and sat down in chair. There was a tremor in his voice. "Delex, son," he stood back up and paced a bit and put his hands around his son's shoulders. "I need you to listen. Mercadio was not trying to kill you. He was trying to save you. I saw the owl. It raised a talon towards your face. It was about to go for your neck." Delex froze and looked around for the owl, "It isn't here son. It flew off after you hit Mercadio."

"But how? It was in tatters. It was sure as dead."

"It was a *drethcon* boy. A poorly aimed shadow lightning would not kill that creature," Mercadio scoffed.

Delex turned to the man named Mercadio and spoke with venom in his words. "Don't call me boy again. That bird was good as dead. It was not a deadcon or whatever you called it.

Who the- No, what are you!" He stood up ready to jump on the man again. Jim got up and caught his shoulders. The cat gave a small hiss from the shadows.

"Settle down! Now sit and shut up!" Jim's grip on his son's shoulders tightened. Even though Jim may be in his sixties, his strength had not left him. Jim finally let go and flicked the lights on in the room. Delex sat back down and rubbed the numbness out of his shoulders. "Now listen because I am not repeating it. You always knew I am your adopted father. I told you I did not know about your parents. Well son that was a lie. Mercadio here can tell you more, but you must know now that you are not a normal person."

"Thanks dad," Delex pouted. Delex's heart skipped whenever Jim talked about his parents but soured when he realized that the cloaked man knew them. He did not trust this man any more than he could beat him with a lamp. "Why didn't you tell me that you knew my parents? Who is this man?" He pointed and accused Mercadio.

Jim shrugged,"I didn't know, son."

"How could you not know? Are you telling me you have had amnesia until now?" Delex could feel the back of his neck get warm with anger. He waited. If he pushed too much his father would only get cross again and close up.

Jim looked into the night. As he spoke he sounded much older and worn. "It was a spell son. Mercadio had cast it on me when you were young. It was complicated Delex. You were, you were troublesome, not normal, amazing. We had to do something." Jim turned to him with a small smile.

Mercadio dropped the peas. The cat pawed at them playfully. "When you were young I knew Jim here. I am the one that brought you to Jim. I amended the records to create your adoption. Jim, I found by accident when scrying for a suitable father figure. You my boy are a sorcerer."

Delex's blood felt like ice. His mouth would not work. It did not sound familiar at all to his childhood memories, but for some reason it sounded like the truth. When Mercadio said

'Sorcerer' the way he did, he felt a pulse thump within him. Mercadio continued. "You, my boy, are not from this world. You are from a planet called Ter'Avan. I brought you here to protect you until you were old enough to protect yourself and time passed on our world. Many dark things were after you when you were a child. I brought you here when you were only five years old. Less than week ago was your real birthday. Happy birthday Delex."

"My birthday is not for another two months."

"Now boy, Er, I mean Delex. Your real one celebrated last week on my planet. You should be twenty-three now in Earthen terms but over there. Well, you will see it is a bit complicated." Mercadio rubbed the back of his head again as Delex gave him another glare. "Any of ways, to spear the point. You father and mother died in a battle against an extremely evil man. I rescued you and brought you to Earth to live." Jim had sat down in a corner and held his head while Mercadio spoke.

"I visited with you for a time. You and Jim had your memories changed to keep you safe. Also, it helped suppress your magical abilities. We noticed, in time, you tended use magic accidentally. So we had to change yours and Jim's memories to keep you from spreading the muck. Naturally that would not look kindly on this planet." Mercadio chuckled at the last statement.

Delex sat in confused wonder. *I am a sorcerer? I could use magic? A different planet? What does this all mean?* He arrogantly asked. "So what am I going to do now, have a successful career in Vegas? You still have not answered my question; who are you?"

"I, my boy, am Mercadio, First Wizard to the two towers of magic, keeper of arcane knowledge, and leader of the counselors of the black gift, unequaled in Craft and Cast. Does that help?"

Delex nodded dumbly. He actually started to believe this guy. From the look on his father face, he was not kidding. Mercadio continued his lecture with a serious voice. Jim got up from the floor and sat down beside Mercadio to look at Delex. "We must be brief now I have wasted too much time as it is. I must take you from this place back to Ter'Avan. Your life has ended here, if you do not come with me, then your life will end in literal."

Jim looked at Delex, as his eyes filled with tears. "Mercadio will change my memory, so I will not remember you. He has left me a charm to use on others that you knew. If not, those creatures will come back and use us to trap you."

"What creatures?" Delex stood as his fists tighten. *Forget my dad? No fricken way.*

"As I said, that my boy was a *drethcon*. It takes on the form of living creatures it touches but it slowly robs them of their life. As long as the real owl lives it can feed off it in body and mind. But the *drethcon* will sap the owl's life until dead unless the *drethcon* is killed. The only way to kill it is to kill the host and destroy the *drethcon* as it revert to its natural form. Or if you can catch the copied form, you can destroy the heart." Mercadio pantomimed the gruesome procedure with a hooking motion. He pointed dramatically at Delex's chest with his staff.

"That and other creatures will be sent to kill you and anyone that knows you. Don't worry, as we speak my familiar unleashed a prepared spell of mine of great magic to help disguise you in this world, permanently. You father will be safe and the ones that knew you. Your records on this world will no longer exist. Jim will need to find the spots the magic did not reach. We must be short now. The magnitude of this magic will draw creatures, if there is more."

"No," Delex spoke the word with a calm whisper.

"What boy?" Mercadio said in shock.

"Delex son, you must believe him." Jim urged.

"Don't call me boy, and no," Delex said. His jaw muscles clenched in renewed anger. "Why should I believe a single word? You may not know this. But in this *world* we have a thing called proof and sanity. So where is your proof so called wizard?" Delex said the last with a grim smirk on his face. Behind him Jim had gone quiet and looked to Mercadio for help.

Mercadio simple smiled. "Well and well. You are as smart as I hoped you would be, yet bullheaded as an ox arguing with a rock's shadow. Here boy, here is your proof." Mercadio's hand swept up in a flash in front of Delex's face while he spoke in a weird voice. Light sprang forth from his hand. A crown of light appeared around Delex's forehead and shattered.

Delex staggered to the floor. Memories flooded his mind. He remembered Mercadio when he was young. He remembered the secret lessons in the basement. Jim was there. He overlooked it all, a smile of pride on his face. He remembered not being very good. An image came to mind of a cat with a hateful glare and brilliant pink fur. *Who was that? Oh, yes! It was Mercadio's cat. What was the name? Yes, it was Daylow*. He remembered having a friend over. His friend had taken ill. It was his fault; he knew it. The child had lived but the incident meant Delex could not perform anymore magic until he was safe to train. He was too young. He will have to have his memory changed. Delex was only five, scared, and alone on an alien planet. A flood of memories blinded his mind. There was too many to go through right now.

When he opened his eyes he saw his stepfather and Mercadio in a whole new light. Over powered by emotion, he cried. It was true; he was a sorcerer, a being of magic. Unlike a wizard who had to learn magic, it was in his blood, it was his blood. If was all of him. The world suddenly felt dulled. His simple world, and he knew that he could not stay here any longer. He looked away. He tried to fight the depression that tried to drown him, but it gnawed at his stomach. "I know now, when must we go?"

"Now son, I am sorry but now." Jim gave him a hug and whispered in his ear, "I love you my boy, you are always my boy." Delex's heart felt like it was about to fall apart.

"Don't I have enough time to say good bye?" Delex pleaded with his father. His life felt like sand spilled from his gripped fist.

"No son, this is the goodbye. If we are to live, you must go. If you don't hurry, more things will find their way to us. The *tempra* residue remains connected to both worlds as it fades. They may find a way to detect it and come back." Jim said with a heavy heart.

Delex nodded numbly and let them herd him out of the room. Delex didn't pack. Mercadio said they could not waste time. He would provide everything they need. Delex grabbed his coat and load it with apples and oranges. Before he knew it, he walked with his father Jim and Mercadio towards main street. The cat vanished once again. Delex suspected that it prowled somewhere close. They went down past the park that he grew up in, past the high school where he got his first kiss, and ducked into the alleyway between the pawnshop and the gas station that always smelled like a wet fridge.

Delex stopped and turned to Mercadio and spoke with a bit of steel in his voice. "I don't like this and I want to make a few things clear." Mercadio folded his arms patiently. A smug amused look played on his lips. Delex glared. "First I am not a child. I am twenty-three, a man. Second, I plan on coming back sometime, and if you try to stop me, I won't leave at all." Mercadio only nodded, his face a blank mask. "And last, I do not want to forget, you may have everyone else to protect, but by my blood I will not forget my dad Jim."

Mercadio nodded and spoke calmly, "Well and well. I will not stop you if you chose to come back, nor will I remove your memory. Furthermore," Mercadio smiled lightly as he spoke, "I will not cast magic over you to compel you against return." Mercadio smiled like a wolf. Delex didn't think of that one. He wondered what else the man could do, but decided not to provoke him.

An angry squawk penetrated the night. Jim and Mercadio turned suddenly. Jim spoke in a whisper, "it healed, and it's coming." Mercadio nodded and aimed his staff down towards the sound. Something fluttered behind Delex. He ducked but not in time. The red owl had fooled them and circled around. It had clipped him in the ear. Mercadio spun around and batted the bird to the ground. Jim, a bit heroic, leaped on the thing and battered it with a flurry of punches. Mercadio spun the tip of his staff in front of him in an oval arc. A black bead formed in midair.

"That's enough Jim," Mercadio said. Jim stepped back, his hands bleed from the fight. Mercadio shouted clipped words and the owl burst open. Where the bird's heart would have been, was a small ball of red fur. The fur begun to squirm and burrow its way out of the chest. Mercadio quickly crushed it under his staff as it wiggled to get free and sighed. "Now, it will remain dead." What was left of the owl quickly turned into blood and dried into blackish-grey ash.

Delex and Jim startled as a silent blast tipped them off their feet. The black bead suddenly snapped into an oval of starless night. It was like the same nothingness that Delex dreamed about. A cold wind swept down the alleyway. Loose debris sprayed out into the road. Mercadio stood ridged in front of the oval. He spoke something under his breath. Delex noticed that Mercadio's robes still hung limp despite the horrendous wind. Mercadio turned and shouted, "Time to go Delex. Jim," He gave a long look, "I left the device with you. Be safe Jim and make sure everyone forgets. I leave it in your hands. Too bad we did not have time to do it properly." He turned to Delex. "Now or never lad. Step after me." Mercadio turned and stepped into the oval and vanished.

Delex gave his stepfather, *no! His father no matter what,* one last hug and walked into the oval. He glanced back one last time. Everything within was black except for an oval that led into the alleyway. With a sudden snap it all went black. A noise came from where the portal once stood. I was a cross between a moan and tearing sound. He heard Mercadio whisper "That is unfortunate."

"Unfortunate? What's unfortunate?" Delex spun around towards Mercadio's voice.

A red light flared out from Mercadio's hand. It seemed somehow dim and lifeless in the dark. "The *tempra* is failing. The Earth side could not hold the magic."

"What does that mean?" Delex asked a little nervous.

Mercadio gave him an excited look splashed with fear. "It means lad we run, don't stop, never look back and follow. Fail, and be trapped between time and beyond death!" Mercadio turned and speed off in a morbid chuckle. Delex could do nothing but follow with the feel the liquid shadow at his back.

Chapter 2: To Trust a Thief

The darkness was like a lover's embrace. He didn't know if he was at a run or at a stop. There was no feeling underfoot. He only knew he had to follow the dim red light or else he would die. Mercadio stopped for a second to look back and shout over his shoulder to hurry. Delex was not in the best of shape, but he could run fast and hard when he had to. Yet, try as he might, this old man was like a machine. "Hey, come back! I can't see you!" He cried out when the bobbing light faded away.

The bobbing light abruptly came back into focus. Mercadio aimed his wand back at Delex. Something white and hot nearly hit him. A scream gurgled behind him and ended with a hiss. Mercadio motioned with his free hand at Delex.

"Come to me! Hurry!" Mercadio gave him a frantic wave. "I just thought of something. Hurry boy, oh dear!"

Delex thought to himself *oh dear? What is*- A thin flexible arm wrapped around his leg and yanked. His face whipped towards the ground. He didn't feel the impact. In fact, he did not feel any impact at all, but moments later his noise blossomed in pain. He could feel blood trickle out over his face. In the dim light a small greyish tendril writhed and licked at the blood. Delex felt the tug at his leg lifted him up and back. He cried out in terror. *This is not the way I want to die!* Other creature agile and fast crawled up his back and up to his captured leg. Delex squirmed harder trying to kick at the tentacle and the new creature. He heard rending sounds and suddenly was free.

He stood as fast as he could, but his leg was numb with cold. The thing that was on his leg moved to his back. Little teeth bit him in several places. Mercadio came to Delex while he spun around and around trying. He arms beat him in vain as his terror and the pitch of his screams rose in tandem. Mercadio stopped him and yelled fiercely "stop fool, or you'll hurt my cat!" *Oh! Daylow!* Delex felt a bit ashamed but that was soon overcome by a horrendous bellow from behind them again.

Mercadio shoved Delex behind him and spoke softly to himself. He withdrew sand from within his robes and threw it into the darkness. They were rewarded with an overpowered explosion of intense light he felt in his chest. Delex squinted in the sudden light trying to see the creatures, but could not focus through the afterimage. Everything else was still a stale black.

"That will scare them away for now, but we must keep going. Sooner than later they will get the courage to come again. We ran well Delex, the *tempra* is failing but it is now far behind us."

"What in the world are they?" Delex growled. "What are we running from?"

Mercadio turned to him slowly. The look on his face did not have the defiance that it had since he knew him, now or in the old memories. "Not in the world at all. Walk and catch your breath and I will try to explain." Mercadio started his lecture again. Delex quickly followed beside him. He looked sideways to Delex as they walked. "We are not in what we call normal time. We are not in a place." He shook his head. "None have argued with clear proof what it is. But, I think it is a tunnel between two places. I cast a hard and dangerous spell when I came to find you. It is called a *tempra*." Delex listened intently. With some of his blocked memories back from so many years ago told him if he listened, Mercadio would continue.

Mercadio gave a quick glance behind him. Delex's muscles tightened, ready to run. Mercadio looked to him. "Don't worry, they are still sulking back their trying to gather strength. I think I scared them almost as much as they scared you." He chuckled and continued. "You see, the *tempra* is a tricky creation. It links two places no matter the distance or time to each other." Mercadio lifted one finger on each hand and crossed them together.

"Even though destinations remain anchored, it does not mean the distance of the tunnel is. It could take us a few steps to get from one place to another, or even weeks of travel. Time has no meaning. It could take even longer to get from place to place in here then it would in real life."

"Why use it?" Delex asked. He was curious. Mercadio had a deep rich voice. Deep inside, he felt a knot of excitement. It was real magic, real honest magic. Though his memories were back, it did not stop his curiosity or to marvel at his new life. It was truly different seeing it than just merely memories.

Mercadio spoke with zeal. "Also with the *tempra*, you can cross dangerous places safely like the emptiness of space."

Delex snorted. This place did not seem that safe to him. Mercadio gave him a hard look. "Sorry, please go on."

Mercadio looked forward again lost in though. "The *tempra* has no bounds on time. We could go back or forward in time to any place. The danger within the *tempra* is the life. The *tempra* has its own intelligence and lifeforms. I haven't figured out why but when it links two places through a time and place it forms unique creatures. Perhaps they are the possibilities that could exist on both places through the timeline. A mixture perhaps? Farther the distance and more time between, the stronger and exotic the creatures. The *tempri* I have used on my planet, I mean our planet have never been this dangerous."

Delex and Mercadio walked silently for a time. He disappeared into his own thoughts as he went over the last few hours when caterwaul of howls and screams came from behind. The sound was proof the creatures where reformed for a second attack. Mercadio nodded to Delex and went into a light jog. He started again as if there was no lapse in conversation. "The *tempra* that we are in is falling apart. The creatures behind us are behind herded in our direction while the *tempra* slowly disintegrates. Slower ones vanish, into whom know where. I only know, when you are inside the *tempra* when it comes apart, you will not die."

"Well that's good isn't it?" Delex smiled.

"No." Mercadio grinned. Delex had noticed Mercadio had a bit of a morbid streak. "If you are trapped, your mind will be lost forever between time. Your body will unravel between both destinations." Mercadio made the red light split in half. Drips of red light splashed on the ground and dissipated.

Delex's smile wiped away immediately. "How do you know this?"

Mercadio spoke softly, his voice wavered. "One of my former students was too ambitious. He made a faulty *tempra* that was only from room to room. It broke as he entered. I was cleansing his splattered remains off everything for quite some time." For once Mercadio did not smile. "I tired to perform the same *tempra* and made it perfectly. I stepped within the *tempra*. I could hear his scream of insanity smeared around me. I wanted to save what was left, but there was nothing to grasp. I would have an easier practice peeling my shadow from the ground." Mercadio looked forward in silence. One red ball dimmed and went out.

Mercadio was silent for a while. Delex did not wish to disturb him. An occasional howl or grunt emitted from behind them, but they did not sound like they had gain on them. A light from somewhere ahead came into view. A roar of hate came from behind. Clusters of creatures scuttled just outside the light.

Mercadio yelled, "There! Hurry now I can feel the *tempra* weakening faster! The stronger silent creatures have crept upon us. They left the wounded and weaklings to cry out. With me, Fleet of foot now!"

Delex and Mercadio burst into speed. Delex felt like he ran through water. It was like the *tempra* was resistant. Delex pressed harder. Mercadio's story weighed fresh in his mind and the threat of eternity within the *tempra*. Daylow darted out from under Mercadio's robes and shot forward at crazy speed. As the cat hit the light, he flashed and disappeared. Mercadio was next to hit the light, it flared briefly and was gone. It was just him now, seconds behind. As he was about to hit the light, Delex was hit from behind in the shoulder cutting it deeply. The blow spun him around.

A single claw reached out of the blackness. The claw protruded from a bloody black and purple rope-like tongue. A large single eye, strangely human, nested within the palm. All of this surrounded a fanged mouth that dripped with steaming saliva. The mouth hissed as Delex spun and snapped so fast it blurred. The claw snapped from the tether and continued to crawl and squirm toward Delex. Another mouth in the palm spit the eyeball out and snapped and bit at Delex's clothes. The large maw's long glistening teeth stretched taunt on its cord. It snapped at Delex's face. He felt the wind's passage from the snapping teeth.

Delex screamed in terror and pumped his legs back and forth. He reached backwards for the light. The cord snapped and the maw lunged forward. His fingered grazed the line of light. Everything went a ghostly white. A deep chill slammed into him. He hit the ground in a jumble of bones. His eyes pinched tight from the sudden light. Someone shouted "Now Mercadio!"

A silent snap and a gust of icy wind lifted him off the ground. He hit the ground and skid across felt his skin open from numerous small cuts. He lay there with his eyes closed while he caught his breath. His hearing had gone. Someone stood over him and shouted at him, but a high pitch ring drowned everything out. Warm liquid dribbled into his mouth. His whole body jerked and felt light though it gained sudden mass around his chest. Warmth flooded him as his hearing came back. He opened his eyes. Mercadio, who stood over him, close a flask and tucked in back into his robes. Daylow lay on his chest fast asleep.

Delex lay in the grass and dirt with his eyes towards the sky of a new world. Wispy clouds blew across the sky. They had landed in a small clearing surrounded by trees. Delex laughed to himself. *It is just like ones in my fantasy role-playing games.* The sky seemed to be a dazzling blue like a sparkling clear spring. The air smelled sweet, like in his dream. Overhead the moon dominated the sky. It hung near motionless in the sky. He knew it spun, but it was not noticeable unless you watched over several days.

Delex smiled and said with a chuckle of relief, "Now what?"

A voice from behind him spoke. The voice was slick and tailored with a sense of mirth but cold as well, "Now, I rob you little bug."

He saw Mercadio spin towards the voice and point his staff. Mercadio gave an exasperated sigh and set the staff back to the ground and leaned on it heavily. His voice seemed weighed by stones. "Soas you dox troublemaker, why do you always insist on trying to stall my heart?"

Delex heard someone hit the ground as he spoke. "Merely keeping you and the rest of the wizards on their toes."

"My toes are fine thief, and none of your concern. How did you get into that tree? The barrier should have prevented all sorts of vermin from entering." He said the last with a snub.

Delex turned over to see to whom he spoke Soas looked to be a head shorter than himself. Delex only stood around 1.7 meters. On Earth where he came from, they called it five-foot seven. The newcomer's face had a clear light complexion. His face was round, though it came to a soft point towards the nose and chin. He wore a mischievous smile. His hair was a silver-white and pulled into a ponytail except for two long strands that hung to either side of his face. He clothes were leathers of either brown or black. He had a black vest opened over a light brown tunic that tucked into a wide black leather belt. His pants looked like they wear made of fine, dark brown leather. Black boots with belts around the ankles, came up to his calve and folded down in the usual fashion his saw at Shakespeare festivals. He had little knives tucked all around his belt in a row of sheaths. Delex noticed the eyes last, they were pure black except for a silver ring in the middle of the iris.

"Well boy let us have a look at you in this light. Soas, you stay back there where I can see you," Mercadio warned.

Delex stood up painfully. Mercadio stepped back and put a hand under his chin and held onto his beard. He examined Delex like some sort of artwork. Delex was a little shorter than Mercadio, but not as short as Soas. His hair was a sandy brown color cut short but long enough to sag over the top of his ears. His eyes were a startling dark blue with a light blue ring in the middle of the iris. He was of average build. His clothes had slices from many small cuts and bite marks. The liquid poured into his mouth had sealed the wounds and stopped his nose bleed. He lost his coat full of food in the *tempra* but in his hand was a greyish, pointed hat.

"Oh good you found my hat, how it survived, I do not know." Mercadio snatched his hat and rammed it over his hair. Mercadio looked back to Soas. "Well and well Thief, since you wise traveled, I assume from having to run from the law, would you know of somewhere to clean up and get supplies?"

Soas smiled impishly as he leaned on a tree. "I might, but my memory tends to get fuddle if not compensated." Before Mercadio could come back with a snappy remark, Soas interrupted with a lifted a finger. "Ah but curiosity is a great reward. If you let me tag along for a time, I will show you the best place for sleep and food in these parts."

Mercadio was red in the face but, he spoke calmly. "Well and well. Show us, and then you are gone."

Soas shrugged and grabbed a backpack down from the tree. He turned back to Mercadio and Delex. "If you two fine gentlemen would like I can get horses as well. It may take until tomorrow to get them."

Mercadio snidely remarked. "That will do. We will make camp tonight here. It is safer than traveling this late in the day."

"Good! Farewell until tomorrow! Head down the path, you will find a cottage." Soas darted into the trees and vanished from sight.

"Will he be safe?" Delex asked.

"Unfortunate for us, yes he will. Now come this way, and we will build a fire and get some food." He led Delex from the clearing to a small cottage nestled off a deer path. The cottage was a one-room shack with a bunk bed on one wall and a fireplace on the opposite side. Delex felt like he was on one of his scouting trip back home, but on his trips he never had a guy in a robe snap his fingers and bring a fire to life. Mercadio left the cottage to find more firewood. Delex took this time to look at himself. He was a mess. He saw a cupboard in the corner and opened it. Inside, was a deep porcelain bowl and a pitcher of water. He tore off a bit of his shirt and used it to wash his body and free of dried dirt and blood.

Mercadio came back in a little later with a large haul of wood under his arm. He stopped dead in his track and looked at Delex. "What? Do I look that bad?" Delex looked over himself and wondered why Mercadio stared.

Mercadio dropped the bundle of wood and almost fell from laughter. He used his staff to keep him upright between bought of laughter and shuffled over to Delex. Delex was a little annoyed. He couldn't find what could be so funny. Mercadio slowly regained control of himself between chuckles. He asked Delex, "all freshened up are we?" He burst out with another gale of laughter and sat down hard on the lower bunk bed.

Delex was mad, "what is it!" He looked around again and all over the cottage. "Is it my shirt? I had to tear it to wash up. Is my shirt that funny?"

"No my boy." Mercadio squeaked out. "It is what you were dipping it in." Mercadio fell back on the bed and laughed even harder.

Delex came over and waved the porcelain bowl at Mercadio who instantly backed away from it. He choked back his laughter but still had a large grin on his face. "That my boy is what we call a chamber pot." He snickered. "We use it to remove the wastes our bodies release."

Delex dropped the bowl in a hurry. Some water splashed out and hit his shoe. Mercadio curled into a fetal position and laughed into the mattress. The day continued with sour jokes about the bowl and instructions on how to take a bath. The mocking finally ended when Delex threw a piece of wood and up ended the bowl in Mercadio's lap. Mercadio apologized after he cleaned his robes and promised that in the future he would try to act more like a wizard. Delex doubted it.

As evening settled in, Mercadio left and came back shortly with a few rabbits freshly skinned for a stew. Mercadio was almost asleep when Delex woke him. "I need to ask you a few questions while we have the time." Mercadio nodded. Delex sat on the floor by the bed. "How come you speak English so well?"

Mercadio smiled, "well son, I do not. What you hear is our language. I taught it to your stepfather a long time ago. As for your understanding the words in English, I am not sure. Perhaps it is the sorcerer in you. I must say that your speech of our language, *Terrav*, is nigh perfect."

"My speech?" Delex asked.

"Yes, you have been speaking *Terrav* ever since you got here."

Delex thought that was weird but amazing. He leaned out from the top bunk. "What exactly is a sorcerer?"

Mercadio smiled at him. "An even better question. To begin, you are not like other life forms on this planet. Everything that is and was, is tied to one of the gods." Mercadio said with a grand gesture of his hands as he lay on the bed. "They are Ter'Avan the god of Earth, Forr the god of Fire, Seqoria the goddess of Water, Neroal the goddess of Nature, A'orria the goddess of Air, Sepria goddess of Spirit, Nulx god of Void. Nulx, has power over Darkness, Death, and Time. Lastly is Chaos, god of Chaos. Chaos is the only god that never had a given name, that we know. Now legend has it that your race, came from a ninth godling, a demigod." Mercadio shrugged.

"Now all the powers were all ready taken, but this unnamed godling befriended Chaos. Chaos helped him create your race, but when Nulx found out, he slew this unnamed godling. Chaos and Nulx have been bitter enemies ever since."

Delex lay back in silence. Mercadio went over and stoked the fire. Delex turned to Mercadio. "So, you are saying gods live on this planet, not just one?"

"Oh yes, eight gods in total. Their used to be more, but Nulx slew two of them and took their power. He was just the god of the Time or Timelessness, but he was clever. He killed the god of Death." Mercadio chuckled at the ironic statement. "Some say it was accidental, but after, that he became more powerful and even more insane. He then purposely slew the god of Darkness. After two gods gone, the rest of the gods joined forces and stopped him from taking any of their powers."

"Well, that would mean seven gods exist now, right?"

"No Delex, the god of Chaos was not there yet. When he came, he was a powerless godling. Nulx thought he could make him a servant, so he convinced all the other gods to share a bit of their power with the godling and make him a child of theirs. He was most convincing, playing on the big hearts of the other gods, while speaking in secret with the godling telling him that he would give him power if he would only serve him." Mercadio talked as he tossed more wood into the fire.

"So what happened?" Delex settled on his bunk and stared at the ceiling.

Mercadio came back to the beds and sat on the floor. "Well he finally convinced the other gods. He had to be the first since the other gods did not trust him. After Nulx shared a piece of his power, all the other gods shared. What happened startled even Nulx! The god of Chaos emerged. He refused to be Nulx's pet and claimed himself to be god of Chaos. He had the power of each god in him but made new. Now, this would be a small amount, but the combination of all the powers was exponential and made him into the most powerful god, even greater than Nulx. Since then, Nulx has slain any godling that appeared." Mercadio gestured with a swipe of his hand.

"That must have peed Nulx off." Delex grinned as he hung over the edge again.

Mercadio looked up and gave Delex a sidelong Delex hung upside down from his bunk. Delex retreated to his bunk. Mercadio continued. "I assume you mean angered him; but that was only the beginning. Chaos has been annoying all the gods for a long time, but Nulx seems to be his favorite target. If all the gods pooled their power they could overpower and destroy Chaos. All the gods except Nulx still see him as their child, and they do not like the idea of killing offspring. The good of it, thought Chaos is by far the strongest, his nature tends to defeat itself. Nevertheless, he has been known to cause a lot of trouble, like helping create your race. You are lucky though, after that unknown godling died, Chaos adopted your race."

Delex smirked, "That doesn't sound to great if you ask me."

Mercadio shrugged, "Perhaps it is not, but sorcerers once perform amazing things, things that seem almost impossible by wizard standards." Mercadio yawned. His long speech seemed to have tired him. "Well It is time to rest, tomorrow we will try to begin your training again."

Delex sat up quickly. "What do you mean my training?"

"Well my boy, tomorrow you are training as a wizard. You are still a little young, but I hope the sorcerer in you can help with that." Mercadio turned away and pulled his cloak over him like a blanket.

"Hey I am twenty-three, I think I could handle myself."

He heard the old wizard chuckle from within his cloak. "To be a wizard you must first be forty years of age. I started when I was fifty."

"That's ridiculous!" Delex exclaimed.

"If you say as such boy, but it is the rule of the towers. Now go to sleep, hopefully you have not forgotten everything that you learned so many years ago. By the way, you are twenty-four. Two-hundred and five if you count the *Tempra* difference."

Delex thought *two-hundred and five? It is way too late to open that box of questions*. His head spun from the reality shift and exhaustion. He closed his eyes and tried not to think about all the things that had happened to him since last night. He tried not to think about what he washed himself with earlier. *A chamber pot, why didn't I think of that?* He tossed and turned until the fire banked to embers, he drifted into a dreamless sleep.

He awoke to a lot of clanking noises. He opened his eyes to see that Daylow had overturned the pot of stew last night and was face deep in the pot. "Hey, you stupid cat! Get out of there!" Delex got up and went towards the cat.

"I wouldn't do that Delex," A voice warned from behind. He turned to see the old wizard stretch from his bunk. Mercadio stood up and strolled over to the cat. "Daylow if you are going to be so rude, go outside." He took the pot and threw it out the doorway. Daylow looked to Mercadio with what seemed like annoyance and padded out the door. Mercadio went out after him. Delex heard Mercadio talk to Daylow but could not understand the words. Delex thought he heard a second voice, but shrugged and put his shoes on.

Delex finished with his shoes when Mercadio came back in. "I know you were going to go after Daylow, but you must realize he is not a normal cat. He is much smarter than you think and more powerful. If you tried to treat him like a normal cat,

34

I fear we would see a reenactment of last night's fight. He is a familiar, a wizard's living arcane tool. You are thus warned."

Delex just shrugged and finished with his shoes. "I don't care right now. I didn't sleep well." Delex felt depressed. The realization that he had lost everything and everyone he loved could not be so easily replaced with the amazement that surrounded him.

Mercadio shrugged back, "Well and well, but it is your hide."

A knock came from the door. Mercadio opened it and grimaced. Soas entered with a large happy smile. In his hands he had a basket of eggs and raw bacon. "I thought since I did not see any supplies on either of you, I would acquire some breakfast for all of us."

Mercadio raised an eyebrow, "What do you mean by acquire Soas?"

Soas only smile again and shoved Mercadio from the doorway. He strolled over to the fire. "I mean I found them; It was fortunate too. They just happen to be where I was."

"And the horses, did you acquire those in the same fashion?"

Soas didn't answer. He pretended to not hear Mercadio as he busied himself with cooking.

Mercadio tried a few more times to find out, but finally threw his hands in the air. "I give up. But mark my words Soas," He pointed a finger at Soas who looked up quizzically, "If they catch you, I will be the first one to behead you."

Soas put a puzzled look on his face, "The first, you mean I have more than one neck?"

Mercadio grinned and lowered his hand, "No, what I mean is, with magic, a person can perform wonder things. I could reattach a limb, when it is slowly and violently, ripped from your shoulders." Mercadio rapidly blinked a few times with a quick smile.

Soas cringed. He was quiet after that. After breakfast, he decided it was best if he left to find a stream to wash the pots and plates. Delex kept himself busy. He cleaned the cottage and cleaned and placed fresh wood in the fireplace. When every thing was clean, Soas came in with a chuckle.

Mercadio sneered at him. "What is it now, did you find a way to steal the teeth from babies before they are grown?"

Soas smirked. "Better, I just saw you open a large black oval out there and walk through it."

Mercadio came to his feet "Repeat?"

Soas only smiled and motioned to them to follow him quietly. He led them to the clearing they came from earlier. In the middle was a black oval that was about to close. As they watched, something little and red shot into the portal. It suddenly wavered with a snap.

Mercadio sighed. "So that is what happen to it. I was wondering why the *tempra* was unstable. I hate those things. That also explains the hat. It traveled back before me, and we arrived with the hat, before I left." He turned away and started to head back to the cottage.

Soas stared at Mercadio like he was insane. Delex blinked rapidly. He barely kept up with that. *Sounds so wibbly wobbly, timey wimey.* He thought as he spoke to Mercadio. "I see what you mean about time in the *tempra*. Was that you leaving, to find me?"

"Yes it was, but it is fine since we did not interact. It could have gotten a bit messy. I now know how Soas scurried in here. The barrier was not up until the moment I left. This little thief guessed where I was going and arrived beforehand."

"Indeed I did, but that is of no matter. I have the horses packed with provisions, we are ready to go as soon as you are."

Mercadio nodded. "Lets be off, we need to go a great distance to get where we need to go."

"Where is that?" Delex asked.

Mercadio smiled. "To the towers of magic, Record and Practice."

Soas stopped in his tracks. "You can't be serious, that place overflows with idiots and insane people. It would be better if you just pushed your young friend off a cliff than expose him to such crazy overindulgent hedge magic wielding psycho-

36

paths."

Mercadio turned, his fists tight on his staff. "Those people you speak so kindly of are the best wizards in all the realms. They are my colleagues and friends. They are all great wizards and some of the best people I know."

Soas shrugged as walked by the others. He whispered to Delex, "My point exactly." It gave Delex a momentary chuckle. He had started to like this witty young stranger.

"I heard that Soas." Mercadio grumbled.

Delex chuckled again. He felt better since breakfast. His excitement grew as he thought about the new world. He wondered what kind of wizard or sorcerer he would be. Perhaps he could be as good as Mercadio. He saw Mercadio and Soas walk side by side as they went to the horses. Mercadio would snap at Soas now and then and Soas would come back with a witty remark. Delex smiled at the sight. He thought this trip might be more entertaining with Soas on board.

In no time, they were on the horses and out of the tiny forest of tress. Mercadio called it the Grove. The world opened into a vast prairie to the east and south. To the north was a large forest with mountains peaks behind them. It looked beautiful in the morning daylight. To the west he saw the mountains that surpassed his dreams. They were tall and craggy. The rock was a deep purple that went to a black tip. Snow dotted the tips like starts that twinkled upon the stone face of the mountains. The mountains marched in a line to the south. Delex took a deep breath of the sweet air. "Where are we?"

Soas was the one to answer. "We are near the home of Neroal, goddess of Nature and her boyfriend, the god of Earth. That mountain range hides her home."

Mercadio scoffed. "That is on the other side of the planet Soas. How do you even navigate off your-."

"Home, you mean the gods live on the planet?" Delex interrupted.

Soas grumbled Mercadio was correct then looked to Delex. "They might have some mighty ethereal home, but each god chose to have a place on the planet to call their own if they wanted to be alone. Except for Chaos, he decided to live on the moon."

"The moon?" Delex made a face of bewilderment.

Mercadio answered this time in a lecturer tone, "Yes, when the gods made a home for their self they took on one aspect of the planet and made a home of it. The other gods feared that Chaos, not having a single aspect, might take one of the other gods' homes. He decided to live on the moon because of the way it spun and orbited in the sky."

Delex looked up to see the moon hung in the sky in the northwest. *No,* he thought *Terset. We don't use compasses here. Dang I can't remember why.* "It looks different from in my dream, it looks larger. I didn't notice that before."

Soas smiled "That is because it spirals towards the planet then spins back out again. That is how we tell the months from each other. We see how close, what side, what phase shows in the sky."

Mercadio nodded "thank you Soas. No living person has ever returned from any of those places so get it out of your head. We must hurry, so I can get more supplies, and after that we are going to link up with a guard to help travel over the sea in safety."

"Why not me? I am as qualified as any to protect you and your gold. If I am paid for a bodyguard as well as a guide, I promise I will be on better behavior." Soas pouted.

This time Mercadio smirk like Soas. "No need Soas. My guard has skilled in protection or destruction. I would guess he would make a better guard than a thief."

"And who is this stone of authority to you speak of?" Soas retorted.

Mercadio smiled even bigger as he turned his head slowly to Soas. His face contorted with inner mirth. "Well my good thief, it is Blackus your beloved brother and master of weapons."

Mercadio chuckled for a long time as he watched Soas choke

and fall off his horse.

Delex leaned over and whispered to Mercadio while Soas caught up to his horse, "What's up with him."

Mercadio looked at him puzzled, "Up?" He looked to the sky.

Delex sighed, "I mean why is he upset?"

"They don't get along very well. Last time anyone saw the two together, Blackus had Soas pinned to a tree with daggers asking where Soas misplaced his favorite sword."

"Oh, will it be trouble to have them both?" Delex said with a bit of worry.

Mercadio chuckled. "Only for Soas. I fear he will be on his best behavior after we retrieve his brother."

Mercadio marked the rest of the day with laughter every time he caught Soas muttered to himself.

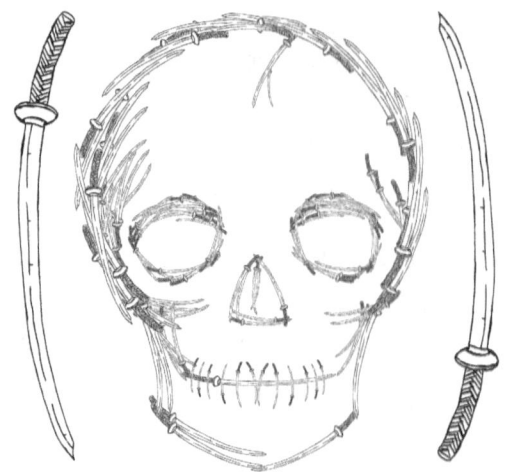

Chapter 3: Death in Many Forms

Mercadio continued to educate Delex. He muttered out the history and geography of the planet. As the day wore, on Delex became completely bored. Mercadio said, to understand magic you must understand the source, and the planet was the source.

Delex flicked a bug from his shoulder. "How does this relate Mercadio? Seriously, I do not see how dirt can make magic."

Mercadio sighed. "It is based on the being you are, and your relation to the planet."

"How's that?" Delex shook his head in confusion. "What kind of being?"

"Boy have you forgot everything?" Mercadio continued to call him boy. Delex grimaced. The wizard continued, "When the gods came to this planet, they created creatures suited to their taste. Most are dead now because of the War at the Chaos Tower. We call that the World Greed War. By good fortune, not all races perished." Mercadio took a breath. "Every god created a special few beings that represented them on Ter'Avan. We humans are the byproduct of Nulx's idea, the elves are-"

Delex eyes went wide. "What a minute, we are Nulx's creation?"

"Yes well, well, no. You are not-" Mercadio begun.

Soas mumbled, "More like stole the humans." Mercadio did not hear him.

"How can that be? I mean from the sounds of the guy, he is very evil. Are you saying-" Delex interrupted.

"Would you hold to silence and let me explain!" Mercadio interrupted. Delex quickly held his tongue under Mercadio's glare. "We were once his children, but when all the gods made there children, only two did not. The goddess, Water and god, Chaos. Water decided she did not want any children and only took what came willing to live in the sea and adapted them to live there. Eventually, she adopted the giants from Earth due to their awkwardness on land. She also accepted the pirates, and the gnomes after they were driven into sea."

"Why was that?" Delex lifted a curious eyebrow.

Soas grinned from the rear. "Well, they were having way too much fun."

Mercadio frowned at Soas. "They were inventors, but most of the time there inventions caused too much damage. When one of there invention burnt an entire old forest to the ground, and everyone in it, the elves banded with the other races of that time. They pushed the gnome race into the sea-" Mercadio looked him in the eye, "-to drown them. Water felt pity for them."

Delex looked at the wizard with wide eyes. *Giants? Gnomes? Sounds like something more and more out of a fantasy book at home. This is my home now. Earth won't remember me.* Delex came out of the sad thought to hear Mercadio and Soas start to bicker about if the gnomes deserved it or not and decided not to listen. Delex didn't notice they stopped until Mercadio smacked him in the head with his staff.

"Now where is the story, aye yes. Chaos saw what everyone had created and decided he did not want to create anything. The other gods, in a great understatement, showed little thrill. They were also afraid of what he may have created. He undertook far worse than that though. With his magic he stole the evil creatures made from Nulx, the humans, and removed Nulx's aspect. Nulx was furious, but that was not what made all the other gods mad."

"What did make them mad?" Delex asked. A godly feud had piqued his interest.

Soas spoke from the rear again. "Well for one thing Chaos made it so all the races could worship whatever god they choose. He made it especially easy for the humans. This really ticked them off, but that was not the end. After Chaos tore out the Nulx aspect, it left an emptiness that could be filled temporarily. This turned into the ability perform minor god-like acts, we call magic." Mercadio nodded to Soas' words.

"So you both are saying that Chaos stole the humans, made them good or at least not a jerk like Nulx, gave free choice to everyone and gifted them with magic."

"Yeah. Chaos thought it was funny at the time," Soas chuckled. Delex noticed Soas was in a better mood. Maybe he forgot that his brother would join them later. He smiled back to Soas, who grinned even bigger.

Mercadio pinched his lips in a frown and gave them both a look. "Any of ways, it proceeds that magic has ties to each god in some fashion. Each race could only use magic given to them. Now they can use many magics. Humans are the most adaptable. Yet I have seen some dwarfs and elves, and heard of one infamous gnome that performed great magics. Chaos's gift is unpredictable." Mercadio shrugged.

Soas pretended to snore in his saddle. Mercadio cleared his throat and glared. He ignored him and looked to Delex. "The only magic not on the planet is the magic of Chaos, which comes from the moon. It might be there due to all the others being on the planet, but that has not been proven since most cannot perform Chaos magic, and end up destroying themselves if they can." Mercadio looked at Delex. "How? Well the magic was to chaotic for most, that is; they could not control it like it needed, and it ravaged their minds and bodies." He said the last with a smile.

Delex shuddered. He noticed that his mentor had morbid ideas of what was funny. *I am going to learn how to do magic from him? Right?*

Mercadio reached for his staff tucked behind his saddlebag. Delex promptly snapped out of his inner thoughts. Mercadio nodded at Delex and continued. "Now, most humans had in them the magic of Nulx. Chaos stripped us of the magic. Yet we still are creatures that destroy. Our emptiness is more of an anti-magic and it shows on the land where large amounts of use live. The land changes and suffers if we do not tend to it. Other creatures attune to different magics. The elves reflect Nature. They mostly live in the trees and have a knack for forestry and wood. Magic from them is mostly Nature magic. Magic users that use Elven magic called themselves Druids. The land is least affected by their style of magical arts." Delex nodded as Mercadio spoke and tried to hide a yawn.

Mercadio still noticed the yawn. "I see I am boring you, so I will be brief." Delex was ready to fall out of the saddle. "Each race can cast magic. The magic they cast naturally draw from the god they attuned to, and sometimes a bit from others magics, but just a bit due to Chaos' meddling. Humans are special. We are empty vessels with no ability to perform magic without training, but with the highest potential. We can train ourselves to harness the magic around us and forge them into spells with great success, except Chaos magic. We can learn to cast as any other race can with given practice. Sorcerers are different." He gave Delex a steady look. "You must remember. You are not human. You are crafted in part by Chaos personally and your Godling. He entrusted in you great amounts of his essence. To what extent and what way, we do not know, but hopefully studying you will help."

Delex questioned, "Studying me?"

Soas pointed a finger at Mercadio. "Wisps of whispers! I knew it. You are going to use this boy as some experiment!"

Mercadio rolled his eyes. "Don't be so graveled. I am going to observe the boy and ask questions, that is all."

Delex wondered when he would get a say into how he ran his life. He was not sure if this magic thing was good or not.

"See! Look at the man, he doesn't like the idea either." Soas gloated, "It seems he would rather be free of the so called intellectuals."

Mercadio's eyebrows climbed a few inches on his head as he spoke to Soas. "Oh so you think we intellectuals are stupid eh? Well that's something coming from a whispen thief. Perhaps my life has been wasted in books. I should have stopped reading when I was young and instead joined a life in the circus or begged on the streets like some people acquainted."

"What did you say? I am a merchant-of-lost-goods. I do not beg you half-brained spell spouting stage-mage." Soas retorted.

"Stage-mage! How dare you-" Mercadio blasted back.

Delex tried to interject. "This boy or man would like to say-"

"Or perhaps too many book worms have crawled into your head while you fell asleep in the library and have made a nest. I better shove a parchment up your nose to make sure the worms get properly feed!"

Mercadio reached back for his staff, "I would like to see you try you undersized-"

Delex tired again. "Hey guys-"

"I have one right here if you would like to-" Soas waved a scrap of yellow paper from the back of his horse.

"That is enough!" Delex shouted. The other two looked at him. Soas pushed the latest item back into his saddlebag, and Mercadio almost dropped his staff as he slid it back into place. "Stop fighting over me. I decide if I will learn magic or not. I will not be an experiment. Soas, I am sure this is not what Mercadio meant." He frowned at Soas with disapproval. Delex was not finished. The heat of his anger continued to rise. He shifted his focus at Mercadio.

"Mercadio, I would have thought by now Soas could not goad you into a fight. You seem to know Soas' reputation.

Even a 'boy' knows this." Mercadio turned red in the face. Soas smirk and folded his arms in triumph. "And you Soas." He pointed a finger at Soas who lost his smile immediately. "You should know better than to get Mercadio mad. Remember he is letting you follow us out of the kindness of his heart."

Delex glared at them both. His anger had finally reached its flash point. "If you guys fight like this again, the first spell I am going to learn is a fire spell, so I can melt your lips together! PERMANENTLY!" Delex screamed the last word. He kicked the horse into a canter and got ahead of group.

Soas' face paled, which was a feat of its own. "Well I'll be a flamed, whispen, graveled, black-soot, son of a goat maiden," he whispered.

Mercadio looked at Soas in shocked of all the curse words Soas just spewed forth. Yet, he was more scared of the threat Delex said. Deep down under his cloak, his body flushed with goosebumps. He was not with a five-year-old child like in times past. He dealt with a sorcerer, a being whose magic could far outstripped a wizard. *Once he becomes a trained sorcerer-* Mercadio's mind refused to finish the thought. The goosebumps took a long time to settle. He glanced once or twice to Soas and noticed he rubbed his arms, legs and the back of his neck as they rode.

Silence was an unwieldy companion as they rode. Delex didn't want to look at either of them. They both kept their distance. Only Daylow dared come from out of nowhere and bothered him. Daylow jumped up into his lap and purred contently. Delex tried to ignore him. He remembered the warning from Mercadio, but found himself absently scratch and pet Daylow. As day turned into dusk, they made camp. By nightfall, everyone was in a better mood. No one spoke about the fight, yet in silence they all apologized. Night came swiftly.

The moon labored from right to left and was noticeably smaller. The soft glow lite up the surrounding grasslands.

Soas got out a small silver flute and played a haunting melody. Delex noticed Mercadio smile and hum along. His dinner lay forgotten as peaceful sleep took him in the wild grass.

The next day Delex was woken up by his stomach. Delex hurried out of his bedroll and blanket and rushed off to the bushes. When he came back, a plate of breakfast sizzled next to his belongings. Soas passed each person some eggs and bacon on hot plates. Delex thanked Soas and dug in to his food. Mercadio pulled out a roll of hard bread and some cream cheese. After breakfast, it was Delex's turn to clean the dishes. Soas helped him clean them. He showed Delex the best way to wash them with the least amount of water and what plants were good to dry and scrub metals. Delex chuckled and thought to himself again that it was almost like he was back camping in scouts.

They packed the horses and got ready to leave when Soas ask, "So Mercadio, where to now, if we cut thought the woods over there we can get to the nearest inn a lot faster."

Mercadio smiled. "That will be fine Soas. Besides, that is actually where I wanted to find Blackus anyways." Soas lost his smile as soon as Mercadio mentioned his brother's name. He mumbled to himself and ignored the others.

"We need to reach the forest by night fall, so we need to keep up at a good pace. Ready and right, lets move!" Mercadio took his horse into a light gallop across the grass. Soas followed behind him. Delex took up the rear. His backside still had not got use to a saddle. Pain radiated up his spine fifteen minutes into the ride. Mercadio took this time to quiz him on the lecturer from yesterday. He surprised Mercadio and himself. He remembered almost all of it. Delex only got a few points wrong about the gods and local plant life.

After his lecture, Delex's next lesson was to study his surroundings. Delex was more than happy to be by himself. He noticed a few things during the day. The moon came from the northwest and set in the northeast, opposite to Earth. No. *This is wrong, north is Terward, and south is Avanside. I am not sure if west and east exist here.* It looked different from yesterday. He remembered that unlike Earth's moon, this one orbited differently every day. Delex mentioned this to Soas after he rode back to Delex. At end of the day he told Mercadio what he observed.

Soas smiled. "Yeah, that is how we tell the different seasons and months. You see every month the moon circles closer and closer to the planet, until it launches back into the far orbit again. It is really neat to see the moon shoot back away again. We judge the month by the size of the moon, the day by what face is showing and what phase. In this month you will see the moon change directions twice, go from large, then huge, to tiny, hang in the air on one side of the planet."

Mercadio Chuckled. "True of word. Yet that is all merely an illusion of its orbital speeds. It makes a spiral, builds up speed then shoots back out until it slows and spirals back and repeats the process."

Delex asked, "how many months do you have?"

Soas raised an eyebrow. "We have eight, one for each god. The moon rotates about an eighth each month. From what I hear your foster planet's year is very close to ours. Our months have forty-five days."

Mercadio turned to Delex. "Yes your birthday is this month on the seventeenth. The month of Chaos, the eighth month. I think it was a Moonday. You are now twenty-four on this planet. Mercadio said the moon was in transition into its outer orbit. It would arrive in another twenty-three days. Today is year 1000 SP, the month of Chaos, the 24th, on Dawnday. If we wanted to be precise, you are around two-hundred and five years old. This is because the *Tempra-*"

Delex nodded and went back to his observations. After a time, his mind wandered back home. He wondered what his dad Jim did right now, and if he had forgotten him. Delex thought about his home until he noticed that it was late. The sun had set, but they had not reached the woods yet. Mercadio stopped to rest the horses. "It seems a bit farther than I thought. Perhaps we should camp here tonight." Soas was tired of riding and nodded enthusiastically. Delex's rear had gone numb from the constant riding. He just needed a good rest. The horses bickered and snorted their displeasure. "We need to rest our horses. Soas, if you will start camp I will find some wood." Mercadio asked.

Delex helped out as he could. He was used to a rough camp. He organized the gear and helped set the camp stew for the night. Mercadio had made it back with a load of wood, from where, Delex did not know. Mercadio would only say the wizards had their ways. Soas gave a derisive snorted.

Delex rested after dinner and looked at the stars in the sky. The moon loomed smaller, yet still far larger than the Earth moon. The night glowed in shades of silver. He noticed a green spot, small but visible on the moon.

Soas told him that is the Eye of Chaos was the true name of the moon. "This is also why this month is Chaos's month. Rumor has it that the green spot is actually where the dragons live after they left the planet. They have great magic, some says even greater than a sorcerer." Soas chuckled, "But that is not any good being so far away, and none know how to reach them."

Delex continued to stare at the moon when he noticed something in the sky. It was almost invisible against the black night except when it crossed by a small wisp of cloud. He lost it for a time but saw it again against the moon. "Hey Soas what is that in the sky?"

Soas came over and looked where he pointed, but there was nothing there. "I don't see anything Delex." Soas shrugged and when back to the dishes. "My guess is that those are stars, or all the dead sorcerers, unless you are talking about the moon."

"Dead sorcerers? What in the he-" His words died on his lips. "Wait! There was something black. There, right there!" Delex saw it emerge from behind a cloud. Now it was close enough it could not hide.

Soas rolled his eyes as he looked up. A surprised look went across his face. "Mercadio you better come quick!"

Mercadio looked up from the book poured over. His eye narrowed as he looked. "You better pack right now Soas. I think we have an unwelcome guest. Delex you get the horses and pack essential gear, food, water, tools."

Delex ran to fetch the horses and brought them back over to the camp. Mercadio and Soas mounted the horses. Mercadio turned to Delex "No time for the rest Delex get on the horse and don't look back." Delex got on the horse, but he took a quick look behind him. In the sky, the creature resembled a large bat but with the legs of a bird and the head of a scaled horse. His horse noticed too and almost toppled Delex off as it neighed and shot forward in panic. The other two shot forward to catch up.

"What is that?" Delex yelled. He could hear it behind him and knew it saw him. A terrible raspy shriek cut across the sky. Delex shrank closer to the horse's back. The horse bolted even faster almost tripping itself. Delex tried as he could to get the horse under control, but the yanked the reins from his hands. The horse won, and shot forward well ahead of Mercadio and Soas. He heard Mercadio yell after him but Delex could not lead the horse let alone control his own fear. Terror burrowed into his mind.

Black flapping wings and scales flew overhead. His saddle bags tore off horse and shot into the air. The creature gave an angry shriek and as it shot into the sky. It dropped the bag and bank sharply back towards the party. The creature was not alone. On top of it was a rider. As Delex looked at the rider he saw its head turn and stare at him. Two glowing eyes stared back at him covered in a black shadow. Fear hit him so hard he hid his face in the horse's neck.

The beast shrieked at him, but he did not know what to do. Mercadio's voice broke over the creature's roar as a light blazed in the sky. Delex looked up. The sky filled with small shooting stars, but they did not fall to the ground. They flew at the creature that attempted to dodge them. It pulled hard into the sky and became tiny within seconds. The stars followed, but then suddenly froze in flight and dimmed out.

Soas appeared at Delex's side and grabbed the reins. "Delex! Are you okay?" Delex could only nod. "Good! We are near the forest, we need to make it there. Whatever you do, keep your head down and trust me." Delex couldn't help, so he kept his head down as asked. *Some sorcerer I am,* he thought.

The creature bellow in rage hidden in the dark night. For now, Mercadio kept it at bay. Whoever that rider was, he was the match for Mercadio. He stopped any spell Mercadio threw at him. They had just made it to the outer trees when the horse's knees buckled underneath him. Delex cartwheeled over the horse's head and missed a tree by a hand width. He slammed to the ground and bounced. He felt pressure on his leg and a sudden break. He hoped it was a branch, and not his femur.

Soas was at his side in an instant. "Are you okay?" Delex nodded numbly and looked around. The horse's head was on his legs. Its eyes stared up at him, but they had a glossy look. The neck twisted in an odd position from the rest of its body. It twitched a few times and stopped moving. Soas helped Delex to his feet and got him on the back of the other horse. It was difficult. The horse bucked and danced as it ran, but he managed to hang over the side. Soas lightly spun into the saddle and spurred the horse deeper into the trees.

Mercadio shot past on his horse straddled backwards in the saddle. He green balls of light flew from him up at the sky. As soon as the green balls flew out, they blinked out of existence. Delex heard a terrible explosion. Mercadio made a lucky hit. The beast spun like a top and crash-landed into the middle of them. Delex spun in a cartwheel off the horse. Soas made a grunt of surprise. He heard Mercadio yell and curse. Bright lights flashed in his head. He heard the horses neigh wildly into the night as they fled. He was not sure how long he lay flat on the forest floor, but when he regained his sense, everything was silent; in fact it was completely silent.

Delex scanned the forest. He saw Soas spit dirt from his mouth. Mercadio hung from a branch that had speared his sleeves. Daylow lay in a content ball below him. A low chuckle came from somewhere behind him. Daylow's fur shot out in all directions. Delex followed the cat's glare. He made out a dark figure a few trees away. Cold pale eyes bore into his eyes. No one moved as they took notice of the dark stranger.

"I must congratulate you on crashing my steed. It will be a bit hard finding another healthy farg this time of year." The voice that came from the dark figure was cold as a whisper but carried a current of power. Behind him a huge mass of flesh lay impaled on several full-grown trees. Its mouth was big enough to bite a full-grown horse in half. "I had fun chasing you like frighten rabbits into the trees though."

Delex did not feel so afraid anymore. "You're the one that crashed that thing into the trees!" He shouted. A cold fury begun to build within.

"Lets not quibble over the detail Delex. Oh, yes. I know your name. I knew your parents as well, that is before they died by my hand." The dark figure laugh as he snapped his fingers.

"You killed my parents?" Delex said numbly. The words didn't register in his mouth. They felt odd on his tongue, like he spoke them in a different language.

The dark figure walked forward and passed right through a tree. Delex thought the dark looked like a ghost but more sub-stantial. *Like a hologram.* "Oh yes and slowly too, might I add. That is neither here nor there."

"Leave the boy alone Valash." Mercadio growled with sur-prised hatred.

Valash flicked his wrist. Mercadio eyes bulged. The wizard clasped his throat, unable to talk. "That's better, we do not want you to charm your spells with your voice." He raised a finger towards Soas. "Put the dagger back before I sheath it in your heart." Delex heard a clang and something hit the ground. "Close enough."

Delex felt an electrical heat rise from his stomach and spread towards his limbs. The burning faded away into a deep cold. "You leave my friends alone." Delex looked him directly in the eyes. "Or I'll kill you."

Valash waved him off. "Unlikely." He looked at Mercadio. "Haven't you taught anything to him about me yet? I thought better of you Mercadio." Valash clicked his tongue several times. He sighed deeply. "I tire of this. So we better cut this short, yes?" Valash pulled out a long blade out of his cloak. It looked like it was made of shadows. Where he held it in the moonlight, it disappeared completely.

"No!" Delex shouted. "I said I'll kill you!" He felt his whole body flush with goosebumps.

"No Delex! You don't know what you face." Soas shouted but suddenly crumpled to the ground and held his throat like Mercadio.

Delex felt something coil within him like a snake ready to spring. Valash still smiled when all the goosebumps on Delex's body flattened. Wicked light burst from his hands and streaked towards Valash. Delex spoke coldly to Valash. "Wilt and die." Red and black twisted light wiped out towards Valash. Valash tried to hide a gasp. The dagger immediately vanished. Valash caught both ropes of light in his hands. Pain shot down Delex's arms.

Delex collapsed as pain washed over his body and scoured every thought from his mind. He heard someone scream from down a tunnel. He slowly realized it was himself. The pain went away as fast as it came. The ropes of energy vanished. Delex shuddered on the ground. Delex eyes refocused to the sight of Valash over him.

"Well that was interesting, yes? You know, I was going to leave you alive. I could toy with you later and just kill your friends, but I see you have great potential, so I may have to kill most of you. I am so sorry." He mocked in a sad face.

Delex wanted to move, he wanted to struggle, but he still did not have control over his limbs. He could only stare in terror as Valash summoned the dagger. Valash raised his hands and cupped a ball of black energy around the weapon. "Say hello to your folks when you see them. Tell your dad his friend

Valash sends greetings, yes?"

Delex eyes widen. The hand pointed towards him, But he eyes did not see it. His eyes locked at something up in a tree ready to strike. It shot down in a blur in front of Valash and hid in the trees again. The smoky hand that held the dagger fell next to Delex. The dagger and black ball of energy dissipated harmlessly. Valash's face contorted in a mask of ugly hate. He spun around ready to shout and cast spells at the creature when it streaked by again. This time Valash's head came off. Before it hit the ground the entire body, hand and head lost form and blew away like smoke in the air. A single cry of rage echoed into the forest. The forest returned to its normal nocturnal sounds.

Mercadio quickly regained his voice. "You okay boy?" Delex nodded and stood up with Mercadio's help. Soas scanned around him with two daggers in his hands. He turned slowly in a circle and spun the daggers with ease.

"That was the great evil?" Delex asked as he rubbed his arms.

A soft deadly voice came from out of the forest. All three people spun towards a man that wore a black and grey robes with silver worked along the sleeves and legs. He was tall, taller than the rest of them. His face was pale like the moon. His eyes shone silver. His face curved in a graceful handsome almost pretty way and tapered to a pointed nose and chin. His hair lay draped over his shoulders to about mid-chest. A single woven braid hung past the small of his back. Leather shoulder pads attached to a cloak hung under his hair like an afterthought. "A shadow of your nemesis."

Two daggers flew from behind Delex towards the newcomer. With a blur of motion the stranger partially pulled his single edge blade from its sheath and deflected the first dagger with the hilt. He slammed the blade down in a fraction of a second. In the same motion he whipped his sleeve of his other hand in front of his face. The dagger bounced off the sleeve and left great sparks in its path. The stranger, not bothered by the Soas' attack, continued to speak. "His shadow has great defense against magic. To kill it, strike physically. You still will not harm the maker." He adjusted the sheathed sword back again under his cloak.

Mercadio came forward to speak. "May I introduce, the master of all weapons, the noble mercenary, commander of the Broken Moon Army and keeper of many deaths in all its different splendor, Blackus, the death bringer and temporary guard to Delex and I. Oh yes, and Soas' beloved brother." Mercadio smirked.

Delex heard Soas grumble from behind him. "I see you are doing well Blackus."

Blackus turned his head slightly to look at his brother. "I see you got down from that tree I left you on."

Soas cursed and reached back into his pockets. Blackus moved the handle of his sword out from his cloak, then casually moved the handle of another hidden sword out from the other side. Delex took a step back from the two as Mercadio step between them. "Now stop the both of you. Soas, Blackus, I do not want to see this happen so you both are going to play nice or else." Both men merely stood there, but both seemed to listen. "This Blackus, is none other than Delex, the one I said I would retrieve. Soas has decided to join us, so try not to kill him. Make it an order."

Blackus nodded and pushed his swords back under his cloak. Soas pulled his hands back out of his pockets and eyed everyone as he spoke. "Fine, I will play nice brother. I know your honor will have you do the same."

Blackus ignore him. "Come this way I will lead you to my camp tonight, we have a long way to walk tomorrow. You are a day early." Blackus motioned and disappeared into the woods. The other three retrieved what they could from the dead horse, but try as they might, they could not find where the other horses fled. An hour later, everyone was over the flight and much recovered. They had salvaged a mere fraction of their supplies.

Delex looked to Soas. "Soas, how did you find a horse and

all the other stuff that you got for us when we came to this planet?"

Soas smiled and turned to Delex "Well I-" He noticed Mercadio turned an ear toward them as them shoved items into packs. Soas changed his words. "I knew what Mercadio was up to, or in a general sense, so I had a few things prepared beforehand." He grinned to Delex and gave him a small wink. Delex grinned back. "Perhaps I will teach you sometime how to, er-bargain and haggle with people." He gave Delex another wink.

Delex laughed. "Sounds like it would be fun to learn how to haggle in this world." They both heard Mercadio give a loud cough and grumble as he went into the woods. They looked at each other and both started to laugh. The boys gathered the rest of their goods and followed. They whispered and snickered to each other as they went. Mercadio marched off at a brisk pace, his back stiff as a rod.

"I dare say Mercadio will have a few headaches in this journey. He has been trying to catch me at my merchant trade for a long time." Soas commented.

"He is not mad, is he?" Delex mused.

Soas shook his head. "Oh no. He and I had a talk yesterday. He did not like my 'influence' as he called it. We argued for a while, but we finally agreed that you are a grown man and of perfect mind to choose your own path. After we saw how you got angry at us, we decided to try not to interfere in each others affairs."

Delex nodded. *Good!* He thought, *I am glad they got that pile of crap sorted out. How long will it be before my name is not 'boy'?* Delex sighed. Delex hiked by Soas to the new camp. He listened to Soas give tips on how to 'find' items in the city.

"Never go for an easy mark. It is usually a guard in disguise or bad luck. Either way it is not as fun. More than likely the easy marks are just poor people scratching out a living to feed their families." Soas whispered.

"What do you look for?" Delex whispered back.

"You look for hired guards for one. Most of the time if someone wants something of value guarded he makes it known by a bunch of muscle following him around like trained apes. Most thief er- I mean merchants-of-lost-goods will shed away. I like these because of the risk. The real nasty ones are hard to spot and need no guards."

Delex questioned. "Do you ever steal from other merchants-of-lost-goods?"

Soas nodded. "I do at that, mostly the ones that pick on the poor. Someone has to teach those lowlifes that it isn't good inducing poverty on those that sow your field and make your clothes." Soas grinned at Delex. "Besides if you only attack the richer ones, there is less grumbling within the common folk. Most guards are poor themselves and tend to care less if a noble loses his spending purse."

Delex wanted to feel scared from the attack, but Soas' cheerful attitude helped wash it away. He started to really like this odd man and hoped to become good friends. Delex and Soas rambled on for a time until they caught the gleam of a small cook fire. Mercadio and Blackus were deep in conversation by the time they arrived. They stopped as the others came into camp. Mercadio smiled at Soas and gave Blackus a final nod. Delex noticed Soas glare.

Blackus had made a fern bedding while they searched for the horses. The flames dance but gave little cheer as they nestled into bed. Delex did not think he would get to sleep after he had been so close to death, but his body was weary and gave way to sleep before he wished everyone safe dreams.

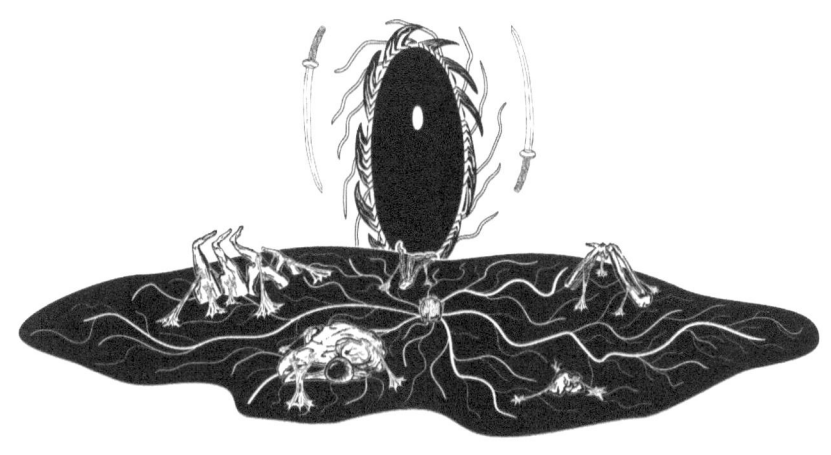

Chapter 4: Elven friendship

The mirror split in two and fell to the ground. It shattered across the dark granite floor. Valash sighed. "Ash that Blackus, always meddling, always around." Valash flicked his hand and the mirror used to project his shadow flew back into place perfectly whole. He extinguished the candle behind him and left the chamber. Valash walked along cold lifeless stone that shifted and wrapped around him as he passed along the dimly lit corridors. The passage glowed from a green moss that clung to the cracks in the walls. Not one of his servant saw him pass, or they simply ignored him out of fear. Valash clicked his fingernails together under his chin as he turned into another windowless corridor and ascended stone steps that led over a vast dark chasm that breathed a misty fog. One of his servants, a small pretty girl of about twelve, came down the stairs. She took one step at a time, foot by careful foot. Her focus drove away all thoughts and did little to warn her the dark master claimed rite of passage over the chasm. Valash took the stairs two at a time. His pace ate the space between them with silent grace. Her eyes strayed from the steps only see an aged claw crashed down across her face. The stunned girl spun over the edge in silent shock. Valash stopped to listen. Dreadful screams bloom and echoed in delicious disharmony. Valash grinned as the screams abruptly ended in a meaty splash. He gave the girl a comical shrug and continued up the stair. He felt much better.

He remembered he had slipped off those stairs before, several times now. He alone understood how deep, and what secrets lay under the fog. In fact, he went now to meet the man that continued to try to kill him. The chasm was only one of the many occurrences. Valash came into another corridor lit by torches that sputter and hissed in their holders. *Human fat will do that,* he thought. He chuckled at his private joke. He noticed that the corridor was uncommonly vacant. Perhaps his pets heard one of their own flutter off the stairs. He passed a series of doors on both sides. These are his experiment rooms. Rooms he used for pleasure, torture, prisoner cells, library, and other oddities. He came to a big double door made of oak and banned with rusted iron.

The doors swung out before him without a sound. Valash stepped into the room. The room was a vast chamber of rough rock and palpable fear. The walls hung no tapestries of previous glory. No lighting graced the walls or ceiling to welcome courtiers. The walls looked as if they chiseled to make room, then forgotten. The only decorations that made the broken hole of earth look like his throne room was the red carpet that led to his throne and two large braziers on either side which cast purple light across the chamber. Valash's braziers did not contain wood or dung. They contained bodies spelled by magic to burn slow and bright. He could still see the horrified faces on his most recent victims suspended in mage-fire. It was a good find this time. The bodies had burned for weeks yet still spoke of their final agonized moments.

Valash approached his throne with quiet reverence. A large tooth of rock grew down from the ceiling. The gnarled vein of stone came from the ceiling from the far side of the chamber to the center of the chamber. It descended into the floor in the rough shape of a curve. Valash shaped and tooled the stone into his throne of nightmares. It was the only part of the chamber carved into any resemblance of beauty. The rock looked like a large muscular arm skinned free of flesh. Stone tendons, veins and bones graced the stone in careful carvings. Daemons, imps and other corrupt creatures of the night carved in poses that crawled, twisted and fornicate along its length. More poses displayed the creatures digging and bursting from the arm. Their stone faces smiled forever in chiseled glee. Pieces of stone flesh hung from their fanged maws. The arm ended in a stone hand completely devoid of flesh. Its middle three long gnarled fingers cupped to form the seat of the throne. The thumb and smallest finger formed armrests. Valash smiled. It was beautiful.

These works of art that took many years to create. His artists were geniuses in their field. They did not start this way. When they were captured, they lacked the experience he needed to create this work of art, this throne. After years of torture to bring out the best flavor for his art, the survivors were ready to work his masterpiece. In the end it was better than he could have hoped for. The slaughter begun shortly after completion. Valash used his own hand and barrels of collected blood to paint his masterpiece. It was what the final touch. In the end, those brave artists not only made a work of art, but also became the work of art. It was beautiful.

Valash was so spell bound by this beauty that he did not notice the person behind him. When he finally turned to look, the man struck out with a dagger. The dagger ripped the flesh of Valash's throat in a deep ragged line. Valash smiled. The attacker's face snarl with hate, then quickly faded into a blank stare. Valash waited for the hole to mend itself, then strolled to his throne. The man stood numbly as he looked down at his hands and the dagger. Valash crooked one of his parchment-yellow hands at him and the man strolled towards him. "Why did you do that Moraphen?"

A harsh voice aged by grief answered back. "I do not know

master."

Valash nodded. He was strong willed. His charm was ever in need of repair. He could simply kill this man, but he was so much more useful as his pet. Valash took out a small vial from under his robes and handed it to his pet. "Drink my beloved Moraphen."

Moraphen nodded numbly and swallowed the contents in one gulp. The vial shattered as it slipped from his hands. Moraphen collapsed in pain. Valash smiled and watched with uncaring eyes. He waited until Moraphen stood a few minutes later. The look of evil was much stronger on his face. He held his body in a relaxed pose. Valash knew that was just a show. Under the black clothes were muscles tensed to kill.

"I have a boon for you." Valash chortled.

Moraphen nodded. "Indeed my lord, I await your command, and desire."

Valash cut his palm with his fingernail. He played with the tendons in his hand. His fingers twitched and writhed. "I need a toy retrieved, by the name of Delex. He travels with Mercadio and that little ant Soas."

Moraphen nodded curtly. "Your will done, by my hand. What are the orders?" He slipped the dagger into his belt sheath.

"Take him alive, I was going to kill him, but I think it is time I find a new body. Mercadio and Soas are nothing, do as you need with them."

"As you wish my lord." Moraphen pulled his blade slightly out the sheath and let it drop back in. It was a soldier's habit.

"One more person, I think you should know about. This is my boon I speak of."

"What is it my lord?" No expression played at all on his face. The question merely asked to please his lord.

"Blackus." Valash said. He watched for the response. The smallest movement played in Moraphen's hands. A twitch at the fingers. The eyes dilate ever so little. "Ah so you do remember, yes? He is there with them. I think you will have fun on this mission. I assume you know what to do with that one."

Moraphen nodded and turned to leave. When he was about to the door Valash spoke as he peered through the hole he dug in his palm. "One last thing Moraphen, if you can not find the child or if you kill him, then do not return. It would be better to take your life with your own hand, then have me do it with mine, yes?"

Moraphen did not turn to look back. He simply nodded, and departed. Valash smiled. He looked up at the arm of his throne and located a winged imp carved into the pose of fornication with itself. "Vex come forth." The imp begun to stir, it fluttered its wings as it extracted itself from the rest of the stone arm. It fluttered and settled in front of Valash. Valash pet it, and smiled to it. He listened to it coo like a baby and purr as he scratched its chin. Valash suddenly lashed out and gripped it around the throat. It squirmed, bite and scratch. Valash bashed it against the throne until it settled with a glare at Valash. "Vex, follow Moraphen. If he fails, then take him. You may eat your fill of him." The imp purred and cooed again with half-words of love. "Do not take him unless he fails. If you fail in this, then I know many poses that I can force upon you until the end of time. Poses that will not fit well with your bones and flesh. In the end, you will be shaped, yes?" Vex nodded. Valash released the little imp and it flew off while it muttered sounded close to 'Dada.'

Valash sighed. He sat there for a long time as he looked into the purple flames. The time has come at last. The time when he will be reborn was at hand! It was time. He would take the sorcerer's body and make the body his own. Valash left the throne room to find a servant to kill.

Blackus stood over Delex and shoved him lightly until he startled awake. As soon as Delex open his eyes, Blackus nodded tended to their meager belongings. It was still dark. Delex wondered if there was another attack, but by the calm in the camp he quickly reconsidered. Everything packed away quickly as they prepared to leave. Blackus came over to look at Delex's wounds. "They are not serious. You can walk the day; I will mend the wounds when we rest."

Mercadio lead them through the woods. Daylight filtered through the canopy as they marched. Delex was already covered in a thin sheen of sweat. The old man kept a hard pace. Delex liked to camp now and then, but he was not use to this road march. After about two hours, they took their first rest. Everyone received a ration of bread and dried meat. When Delex gave Soas a questionable look, Soas told him that they would not stop for lunch. Delex chewed on his meat and kept the bread for the next rest. Water was no problem. They followed a tiny stream through the forest. With every rest, they refilled their water skins. *At least we managed to salvage the essentials,* Delex thought.

Delex had a ton of questions to ask, but no one was in any mood to answer. Mercadio was irritable all day. Soas threw Blackus dark looks like invisible daggers. Blackus was oblivious to it all. His soul focus drove him to scan the forest for danger or signs of attack. The sun was close to noon when they took their third rest. Delex's feet hummed with pain. Blackus gave him a foul-smelling goo to rub on his blisters. It worked to dull the pain. The stench forced him to walk down wind of everyone else. It was about an hour after noon when Blackus slowed to tend to his boot. He put a hand under his cloak. "Company."

Mercadio held his staff ready. Soas sat down and to pick his fingernails with a dagger. Blackus stood and looked forward at nothing. Delex looked around but could not tell where any danger could be.

"I don't see anything." Mercadio grumbled.

"I saw a bush move." Blackus responded.

"Oh great, well I am sure nothing normal could have done

that. I guess we will be attacking the wind next." Soas snickered.

"I saw the bush move from where it grew." Blackus expanded.

Mercadio stiffen. "Elves." Blackus and Soas nodded. "They must be following us." Mercadio put his staff on the ground. Soas hid his dagger back into his clothes. Blackus still stood without a visible weapon. His hand still lay within his cloak. Delex was about to ask Soas what was going on when Soas motioned to him to stay quiet.

Mercadio spoke in a loud voice, "Noble Nature-children we bid you a good day." Nothing happened as far as Delex could see.

Blackus spoke in his quiet voice. "They heard you." moments later, Delex notice the bushes extend and rise. In front of them about 30 meters away, three people approached. All three were dress in green and brown. The clothes looked like they were made of moss and ferns intricately woven into patterns that formed pants, shirts and tunics. They were lightly armored on the chest, arms and legs. Delex though it looked like polished tree bark. Bushes and other plants adorned their legs, arms and back. Dirt and moss camouflaged every part of exposed skin. What skin he could see, was pale and greenish in tint and blended smoothly with the rest of their camouflage. The one on the left stepped forward. "I am Foran Darkwood. I know of that one." He pointed at Blackus, "and of that one." He pointed to Soas with the hint of a frown, "and of Mercadio. I do not know this one. It quivers like a scared rabbit."

"May I introduce in order, Blackus. He is the leader of the Broken Moon Army, and Soas his brother, annoying tag-along." The elves smiled and tried to hold their chuckles as Soas prickled. "I, you know as Mercadio, with my pedigree of titles. This young lad is my pupil Delex, and son to Doran."

The three elves took in a quick breath. The one on the right spoke. "It can not be Mercadio. Doran and lovely Zelexi are not with this world."

"It is true nonetheless Mossa Darkwood. He has been away to another planet. Now he is home to reclaim his birth right and avenge his fallen father and mother." The elves looked at Delex in a new light. Mossa gave Delex a small smile. It was that moment he noticed that Mossa was actually a girl. Delex gave a smile back. Mossa blushed and turned away.

The third elf spoke up. "This is great news Mercadio, this is powerful news. You must come with us and tell the elder."

Mercadio smiled. "We will at that. The dark one and his creatures harrowed us into the woods. It is good to see you here Wilor." The third elf nodded.

Wilor leaned on his spear. "I am glad to see you all alive then. We saw the monster dead in the woods and found two horses almost dead with fright. We came to investigate, but when we arrived the trail lead away."

Mercadio bowed slightly. "We are well humbled. You are talented trackers." Wilor gave a nod. Delex noticed Mercadio spoke differently to these elves. It was almost regal. Perhaps it was a culture thing. Wilor took out a deerskin bag with a cap on the end from behind his chest armor. He handed it to Mercadio. Mercadio drank from it and handed it to Blackus. Foran came to Soas with his own deerskin flask. Mossa walked over to Delex.

Mossa smiled sheepishly. "Drink. It will help you move swift through the woods. We can travel twice as fast as a horse but it will take your essence if drank in excess." Delex took a small sip. It tasted like grass mixed with coffee. Mossa motioned to him to drink more. He took a large gulp and handed it back to Mossa. She blushed and drank from it. "You smell quite bad Delex. Are you ill?"

"Ah, no, that is the goo Blackus gave me. It is for my feet. They hurt." Delex chuckled.

"Well and well. I suggest you remove it later, it is deeply unpleasant." Mossa crinkled her nose. Soas chortled from afar.

"Ah, yeah, okay." Delex turned red with embarrassment. Mossa giggled and went back to talk to Wilor and showed him the flask. Delex took that moment to throw a rock at Soas. Soas dodged the rock and curbed his laughter.

Foran came to Delex. He looked up and down Delex coldly then nodded. "You are fit that is good. The *Melthanna* will work well in you." Delex nodded. He started to feel an odd sense of energy flow from his chest into his limbs. "I see you like my sister. I do not know you of yet, but I give you permission to court. Anyone that is the pupil of Mercadio must be of noble character."

Delex looked stunned. "What are you talking about?"

"You gave the flask back, you accepted her gift and then gave your own as sign of affection. It matters not if it is the same gift or not." Delex looked around and noticed that Blackus and Soas still had the deerskin flasks in their hands.

"But it was hers, I mean she gave me a drink." He said in confusion.

Foran smiled slightly. "And you accepted her gift of friendship, then you showed her deeper friendship by taking of it and immediately offering it back."

Delex's eyes widened. The last thing he wanted to do was anger the brother of a pretty sister. "But I didn't know. I mean I am not from this world."

Foran chuckled, "But you are. You father was, your mother was. I see that she drank from it as well. She likes you." Delex looked like a scared rabbit. Foran laughed even harder. "I see you are innocent as a child. I will see what I can to help, but until then treat her nicely." Foran pleasantly patted a dagger on his chest.

"Yeah sure." Delex felt cold sweat running down his back.

Foran turned to leave but turned back "And if you make her frown, I will burrow a seed into your neck and grow a tree from your skull." Foran gave Delex a warm smile and went back to the elves.

Soas came up to Delex, "that was brave of you my friend, to offer back a gift to an elf. I admit she is a striking beauty, but you should never offer to royalty."

"What!" Delex whispered to Soas as everyone started to head into the woods. "Foran did not mention anything about royalty!"

Soas chuckled. "Yes, Foran and Mossa are the children of the elder."

After their initial meeting, they all speed deeper into the forest. The elves lead them at a brisk walk or so it seemed, but when Delex asked Soas how far they went, Soas just laughed and told him he will see. Delex doubted that he was faster than a horse, as the elves claimed. The woods still seemed thick. At every step he was at another tree. He could not believe that they could find a way through such dense trees. It looked like all the trees were so close to each other they form a wooden tunnel, but he could still see light shin down from the foliage. He looked behind him, but the trees did not look as close. In fact, it was like they moved a moment before. Delex was completely confused.

The elves stopped for the night. Mossa told him since they found them so late in the day, they will rest and move out tomorrow. If they had found them in the morning, then they could have been in the village within a few hours.

Delex blinked at her. "Huh? Why is that? We have been walking for hours."

Mossa chuckled. "It is the drink we gave you. *Melthanna*. It speeds your way through the woods. If we had found you sooner, we could have made better distance with greater speed."

Delex rubbed a shoulder. "I didn't feel like I was getting faster."

Mossa give a small silvery laugh, "oh silly man. Did you not notice the trees seemed closer? Did not every step be by a great oak, pine, or *Serridan*?"

"Well yes, I just thought that-" Delex stopped talking. When they entered the grove, that they were camping within, the trees were close, nearly touching. It was like they stepped into tiny house just large enough to fit them all. The trees were so close the looked like walls. As he looked around the trees seemed spaced apart like a normal forest, sometimes far enough the trees branches barely touched each other. The clearing could easily support 20 people. Mossa giggled at his shocked expression.

Mossa took his hand and held it. She spoke to him as if he was a child, but kindly. "The drink we make from our lovely *Serridan* trees allows us to walk from tree to tree without the space between. I will show you." She stood up and led him into the trees away from camp. She gave a cheerful wave to her brother. Foran continued to check his bow and quiver of arrows and let them pass without a word. He still gave them both a wary look with his yellow eyes. Mossa took them deeper into the woods. By the time they stopped, the camp was far out of sight. He felt a little awkward. Mossa still had his hand. She finally stopped and let go of his hand. She took out the deerskin flask and blushed as she looked at it, then put it to her mouth. Delex didn't see any change, but she smiled and walked to the closest tree.

Mossa eyes glittered like two green diamonds in the dim light as she moved behind the tree. She immediately reappeared from behind a tree to the left. A sly smile played on her mouth. It was over a meter away from the other. "We use this to cover great distances in our forest. It helps protect our borders and react to dangers."

Delex was stunned. Real magic, he watched real magic. Mercadio performed magic too, but it was mere lights and flame, but this was different, this was almost sensual. Mossa continued to move from tree to tree. Her green blond hair fanned out from behind her. She had cleaned off the dirt and now her skin shown like silk. Her silvery laughter could be heard from almost every direction as she moved around him. At one point she climbed a tree with ease. To Delex's utter surprise, she took her foot off the limb as if to walk right off the tree. She disappeared and reappeared on the tree limbs of another tree a good distance away.

"Even in the trees, there remains safety. No harm befalls me." She laughed and jumped off the tree and disappeared. She immediately walked in front of another one on the ground, perfectly safe. Delex had a large smile as he enjoyed her display. Her body moved like a breeze from tree to tree. Delex lost sight of her. He looked around but could not find her. He wondered where she went when he felt a smooth hand on his shoulder, and her breath in his ear. Delex was about to speak, but she put her finger to his lips and pressed close to his body. "It also good for sneaking up to someone and surprising them with a kiss." She moved her finger and placed her lips softly on his.

Delex sighed. Her lips were warm and yielding. He felt her tongue graze his mouth ever so slightly. Before he knew it, he had her in his arms with his lips pressed to her. Time lost all meaning in those kisses. Her lips were soft, like rose petals. Her mouth tasted like cinnamon bark and honey. He lost himself in the warmth of her embrace. After a time, he pulled away. "I'm sorry Mossa. I should not be doing this. I hardly know you."

She gave a small frown. "I know Delex. I should not either, but I feel a certain power in you, and it draws me like wolves to live meat. I am uncertain what came over me. I will go." She turned away. Delex grabbed her hand.

Delex watched her eyes as she slowly looked up to his. Mossa's eyes began to fill with tears. Even her tears were lovely. Delex spoke to her with simple truth. "I'm not ashamed, nor should you be. I, well, I liked your kisses. If I knew you better, I would lose myself, forever."

Mossa's eyes brighten like a bonfire, her lips curled into a small lovely smile. She gave him one last kiss. Delex's heart skipped another beat. *Surely,* he thought, *if she kissed like that again, I will be under her complete control.* Luckily, she put a slender hand to his face and giggled. "Lets go back to camp before my brother thinks ill of our absence." Delex nodded with a smile.

Delex and Mossa walked back to camp, the effects had worn off since she drank so little. Mossa listened with interested about his life. Delex told her about cars and planes and computers. She did not seem interested, so he told her about the planet. Her interest brightened up immediately. He told her about the sea and jungle and the Grand Canyon. He knew a lot about the Grand Canyon from an essay he wrote as a child. She listened, enthralled like a child, as she hung on every word. In short order, they were back at the camp. Delex saw Foran vigorously sharpened his dagger and talked to Blackus. Mossa rolled her eyes at him. Foran looked at them and gave a sigh of relief. Delex felt a sudden pang of guilt, but it was immediate swallowed by Mossa's smile. She left shortly after they settled their beds and went out to find berries. Soas came up to Delex with his crooked smile on his face.

"So you have a good time in the woods? Did Mossa show you any new bushes? Did she climb a tree?" Soas gave him a crooked smile.

"You're despicable Soas." Delex grumbled.

Soas laughed and splashed some water out at Delex from his water-skin. "That may be, but you're the one wet behind the ears."

Delex grinned and emptied his entire water-skin over Soas' head. Soas took it all with a smile on his face. After Delex shook the last drop in laughter over Soas' head, Soas launched at Delex and wrestled him to the ground. The male elves clapped and cheered them both on. The rest of the night filled with laughter and roars of encouragement for both participants.

They rolled in the dirt and leaves until both were completely dirty from head to toe. Soas' clothes had a mixture of dirt and mud and looked like a beggar rolled down a hill. Delex looked only slightly better. After about an hour of on and off horseplay Blackus got tired of the noise. Without a word, he grabbed them both and dragged them to the nearest creek where he deposited them both with a toss, headfirst. Blackus just stood there as Delex and Soas cursed and splashed, but in the end, Blackus came back to camp with two clean, wet and cold people in tow. Mercadio pretended not to notice. He kept his face in a book to avoid eye contact. Delex heard a few jovial chuckles float through the air from the wizard. Daylow opening grinned at them both. He swished his tail back and forth and purred loudly as he watched. That annoyed Delex more than anything else as he shivered and moaned.

As evening set, they had their dinner of berries and cooked bark and meat stew, Delex got ready to sleep. He noticed that Mossa's bed was next to his. When he settled in for the night and the campfire was out, he felt a slender hand reach over to his. He turned to see Mossa's deep green eyes sparkle at him in the dark. She leaned over and gave him a soft kiss on his hand and closed her eyes. Delex fell asleep with a content smile. Their hands stayed together through the night.

Delex and Mossa were first to wake. She took her hand back with a smile and went into the woods. Delex found the creek again and washed his face with cool water. Delex shivered by the time he came back but felt refreshed. Blackus had whipped up a warm cooking fire. Delex sat down to it eager to warm his skin. Delex thought that the elves would not agree to fire in the forest, but Wilor told him that they trust Blackus to his doings. After breakfast of sausages and mashed potatoes, they packed up everything and headed deeper into the woods.

Delex had become use to the taste and effects of the *Melthanna* and felt like he could climb through the trees. When he told this to the elves they laughed and tried to encourage him to try. Mercadio gave Delex such a horrible frown, he decided against it. Soas waled limb to limb as if there was a sidewalk under him, much to Mercadio's annoyance. With a bit of practice, Delex found that the tunnel of trees was a form of optical illusion. If he concentrated, he could see as normal through the woods. The only problem with that was the sudden shift of perspective with every step. Mossa told him that was normal. In battle, it was good to see your natural surroundings.

For now, he should switch back to the other way. A rapid headache on its way to a migraine and forced Delex to agree.

They arrived at the elven village close to noon. When they neared the village, the trees moved back to normal. Elves were dress in beautiful shades of brown, green, yellows, greys, and black. Many of them stopped to look at the strangers. Some even whispered to each other or hurried off to tell others to come. Foran bid them farewell to go see the elder and would come for them when it was time. Until then, they were all to be guest of the elves. Mossa told Wilor that she would lead them all to private guesthouse. Wilor gave a nod and went to converse with some other elves with tough looks. Delex assumed they were hunters or protectors.

Mossa led them to a tree with a hut that had grown into the tree itself. The tree house did not look like much on the outside. It looked like it was put together from dead wood and vines, but when they went within, the wood shone. The wood looked healthy and strong and smoothed to a polish. Mossa left, but came back soon with two other elven women. All three laid out a table of delicious meats and fruits. The elven women left in a burst of whispers while Mossa stayed behind and ate with them. Foran came by a few hours later and said the elder will speak to them all tonight. The elder knew most of their story so it will be a short visit.

"That is good Foran, thank you for your kindness. Will we have the horses that you found earlier?" Mercadio asked between bites of roasted chicken.

"Yes, and we will provision you as well for your journey."

"Well and well, we will stay here until it is time to talk to the elder. Thank you again Foran." Mercadio pulled a book from his robes and settled back.

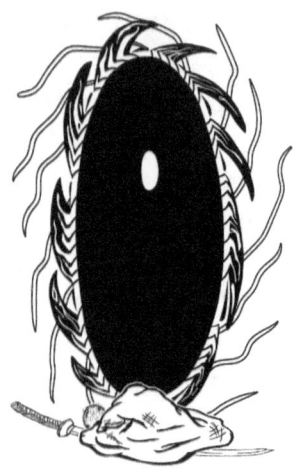

Chapter 5: Training in the Tempest

Mossa led them all up several rope ladders and across a few rope bridges as they went from tree to tree. They came to the Elder's house. This home rose above the others with a dominant circle chamber. It was so big, the span covered three trees growing a distance apart. It was tall enough to reach just outside the canopy. The outside of the Elder's house grew disorderly, like discarded bark, much like the other houses. Vines or crafted rope held in place old wood, jumbled together and collected from the ground. As they all entered, Delex felt his amazement rise like fire from his soul. The inside was as stunning as a sunrise. All the walls fit smoothly together with a seamless quality. The polished grain of wood glimmered like gold. Hand painted vines hung in stylized braids which were tied together into drapes and tapestries. The painted vines depicted vibrant murals of nature and historical elven leaders. Hand carved tables and chairs gathered in set on the sides of the great chamber. Large and small rocks magically tumbled artistically in place with vases, pictures, metal works on colored sands and other arts upon podiums and wall recces. Several round windows, set high on the walls, let the evening sky filter across the windows. More skylights adorned the ceiling in cut shape of leaves. Patches of sunshine shimmered through windows and skylights through glistening spider webs as the sun faded.

Delex didn't think he had ever seen anything so beautiful. Mossa turned to him and smiled. "I see you admire the sky chamber. In the day it glistens as gold, and night it shimmers as diamonds." Delex nodded as he turned in place.

The elder sat to one side and talked to a group of elves. He looked up and waved them over as he stood. The group of elves stood and bowed. They gave them all pleasant smiles as they departed. The elder rose to great them with an open smile. "Hello Mercadio, I see you have peculiar followings these days."

"Indeed, Selkroth Darkwood." Mercadio smiled as both men gave a friendly embraced.

Selkroth chuckled. "Are we not ancient Mercadio? We do not stand on ceremony here. Selkroth is fine, we can disregard the *royalic*."

Mercadio nodded. "This is Blackus as you may know, and his brother."

Soas prickled. "The name is Soas. I see the old man's mind is going, else he would have mentioned that fact."

"It is not, I just fail to see your significance." Mercadio retorted. Delex smiled at the two and rolled his eyes.

"I will show you something sig-" Soas started to jam his hand down the front of his pants. Blackus slapped his hands. Delex choked back a laugh as his eye bulged at Soas.

Mercadio cut Soas off and attempted to salvage the conversation. "Selkroth, this young lad is none other than Delex son to Doran and Zelexi"

Selkroth took a step back. "Surely Mercadio it can not be. I was one of Doran's friends I would have known if his son still lived."

Mercadio's raptor gaze pierced the elf lord. "Look at him."

Delex stood there nervously as the elf elder studied him. His stature seemed wooden as his green-blue eyes focus. The elder was a tall powerful figure in green robes. His hair was blond with green tips and hung lose around his thin frame. Delex noticed the ears. They truly did end at tips. He only now noticed, even when in the company of Mossa. To be fair, he was a bit distracted. Delex thought with amusement, *I wonder if I should ask if they live long and prosper? No Delex, don't be rude. Remember that sci-fi convention? No more black eyes.*

The sun's rays died away as it set over the trees. The chamber came to life with shimmer of white starlight as it flooded through the skylight and windows. They refracted a star-filled sky across the floor and walls. The elder's mouth opened in shock. "But how Mercadio? How can he still exist and be so young? He has not reached manhood." Delex frowned slightly.

"He was on a different world, safe in a different time. A short score of years had passed, not centuries. It is empty history, best forgotten. He is home now. I plan to take him to the towers." Mercadio patted Delex on the shoulder. Soas grumbled, but Blackus quickly backhanded the back of Soas' head so fast no one saw him move. Soas gave him a dagger look.

The elder walked over to Delex and took his hands. He looked with awe at Delex. "I knew your father as I would know these woods. If anything at all of him is within you, then you are a great man. I am your friend Delex, call on me your will, it will be mine as well." Delex didn't know what to say. He just stood there. He tried to say something like thank you, but what came out startled even him.

"How did he die?" Delex spoke softly.

Selkroth released his hands and took a step back. "He died by the hand of his best friend in a ritual battle of magic. He disgraced the rules and slew your father. They disagreed on the welfare of a specific knowledge of magic. He was a traitor to us all. We destroyed him at great cost, or hope we did, but he was a sorcerer. He had great evil magic at his command. To this day we still do not know how he has lived through these centuries."

Delex's eyebrows knitted. "Centuries, don't you mean decades?"

Selkroth looked at Mercado "I thought you told this boy Mercadio."

"I have not yet, I did not want to shock him." Mercadio sighed.

Delex turned to Mercadio. "Shock me how? What's so shocking?"

Everyone looked a little uneasy as Mercadio came to Delex. "Delex, You father died over 200 years ago. Your mother died shortly after when Valash came for her and you. It was their dying wish that you would be hidden before the battle not only through space, but also through time. That is why the *tempra* was so important. She was going to come for you if she lived."

"How? I don't understand." He looked from Mercadio to Selkroth.

Selkroth spoke first. "I am over 500 year aged. The elves have great life spans. Magic expands our existence. Mercadio is around 300 year aged."

Mercadio nodded. "When I met your father I was a young lad, and in time I tried to learn his magic. I failed since I was not of his race, but in the end I learned a great depth in wizardry."

"Like having a longer life?" Delex asked. He began to understand how Mercadio could have known his father.

"Yes. Wizards naturally have a life span that is longer than most humans." Mercadio shrugged. "When your father taught me. It enhanced this longevity. I should have died 100 or so years ago. Your father taught me many things about theories of magic. I was going to teach you those theories in hope it will help you find the sorcerer's way."

Delex paced a little. "I see. Why am I only twenty-four and not older? You said I am too young for magic school. Why not get me when I was older?"

Mercadio tapped his staff a bit. "I needed to get you at a

younger age in hope that the memories did not fade completely after I left you. I would be hard-pressed to teach you magic if you were an old man set in your ways, and harder to explain your lifespan to humans. I was guessing when to meet you when I made the *tempra*."

Delex voiced an angry thought. "Why couldn't you have brought me back to my father's time?"

"Valash would slaughter you as a child. It was a harder time. I barely made it through myself." Mercadio said with sad eyes.

"Well why not now? I can get older, I can get stronger. Why not later? Why can I not just see my mother?" Delex asked. There was an unmistakable longing in his voice he could not explain. He had no memories of his parents, yet it screamed at him from the dark corners of his soul.

"I will not, nor will you." Mercadio's voice was cold as stone.

"Why the hell not!" Delex was furious. He rarely swore, it shocked him that he did now. It seemed so simple to throw up a *tempra* and step through. Delex felt a gentle hand on his shoulder. Selkroth was at his side with a kind face.

"Delex, Mercadio never meet you except as a babe, nor did anyone else. You will not for, you were never there." The elf lord explained.

Delex shuddered. He tried to keep the tears away. His chance to see his mother and father fell out from underneath him by that one sentence. The prison of time snapped into place.

Selkroth looked to Mercadio "You should have told him, but that can not be helped now. Time to change the subject I think. Tell me what has transpired." Selkroth listened as Mercadio told him the entire tale from when he found Delex to the encounter with the elves. With the tale done, Selkroth was deep in thought. "I see why you did not have time. He plans to murder the boy. I will help you get through my woods as quickly as possible. You will rest in my village and leave in the morning." Mercadio nodded.

The party moved to another tree house that was close to the sky chamber. Everyone ate a small dinner with Selkroth and got ready for the night. Delex slept, but dreams plagued him with images of tall regal men and women that wore masks with no faces. As he approached to take off the masks, they would slide out of his reach. His nightmares continued all night.

In the morning they found that the elves had provided them with a few weeks travels worth of food and four fresh horses. The farewells were short. Some elves came by and offered them their wishes. Mossa gave Delex a kiss in front of her father. Selkroth nearly choked as his eyes bulged. Foran laughed so hard he fell into his father. She ignored her father and waved as Delex climbed on his horse. Wilor, the closest friend to Foran, lead them all to the edge of the village. Delex wished Mossa could have come.

Mercadio squashed that idea with one withered glare. "I will not be a chaperon to two teenage rabbits." Delex naturally took offense to that. Foran and Wilor fell to the ground in fits of laughter until they gasped for breath. Mossa stomped to Foran and Wilor and kicked them both in the head.

Selkroth stood dazed and embarrassed. "I am raising cattle." He rolled his eyes and waved as the party rode away. He could be heard as he shouted at Foran and Wilor to shut up and be more dignified.

After a few days ride, they finally came to the edge of the forest. Soas was beside Delex. Soas had taught him a clever barroom song. Delex listen and laughed when Soas' song finished with the puzzled barmaid and how she could mistake a wild boar for a paid tenant. "Oh, she slipped the pig a naughty jig in the drunken, darkened night. With a 'thank-you ma'am,' she left the ham and dreamed of bacon til morning light!" They both erupted in laughter. Mercadio looked up from his book and gave them both a furious glare.

Blackus was his ever silent self. His steady gaze swept over the horizon as he guided the party past the last few trees. He didn't smile or frown through during any of song. Mercadio was so engrossed in his reading that he almost fell off his horse several times when it changed direction too swiftly. Soas laughed and mentioned that the horses usually needed to go around trees not through them. Mercadio glared and went back to his book. Delex had his spirits back, but was nervous the first few days of travel in the woods. The elves had mended his wounds and given him grey pants, white shirt and a fine blue silk tunic. Silver scroll-work played up the sleeves and depicted different trees and flowers of the forest. Soas had given him a dagger from his collection and Blackus gave him a sword strapped to his belt. He felt almost like one of those medieval lords from the history books or a renaissance fair.

"Delex come here I need to talk to you." Mercadio put his book back into robes. Delex slowed his horse so Mercadio were side by side.

"More lessons?" He asked the wizard.

Mercadio huffed. "No, I need to show you something before we go to the towers. When your father and mother were alive, they had a house. I need to show you this house."

"Why? Do I have gold or something?" Delex snickered. He thought of a book series back on Earth. That resulted in a boy that became a wizard. He laughed to himself in his mind. *At least that boy left on a motorcycle and not a gassy horse the peed way too much.*

Mercadio pondered. "I am not sure; none have been able to venture into it."

Delex was curious. "Why show me it if I can't live there?"

Mercadio waved his hand. "You were young. Perhaps you did not retain proper memories. I thought you could see something your father built. With hope, it will show you a bit on the scale your magic can do."

"Sure, that sounds good." Delex thought it sounded wonderful. *To see something other sorcerers built, wow!*

Mercadio nodded "good, remember you said that. I hope it does not disappoint. It is still days away, but I will show you when we come across it. Now, since you mentioned, more lessons."

Delex looked at Mercadio and groaned. Soas looked at him with a grin. "What? I assume you know something of this house? Is it a tower or something? Quit grinning at me like that. What?" Soas just gave a mischievous laugh and quicken his horses pace. Delex rolled his eyes.

Mercadio knocked him on his head to get his attention. "No, it will be a time until we get there, so I think it would be best to try to get you casting. Now, when casting-"

Delex shuddered as he thought about the last time magic came forth from him. Valash used it against him. He was not sure if he could do it. Delex came out his thought and focused back to Mercadio.

"-so it is that simple. Remember that above all else, and you may not die. I will not repeat. I just hope you are a better student now then you were as a child. Doubtful Daylow wishes to be pink again." Mercadio finished. Delex heard a small growl from somewhere within Mercadio's robes.

Delex tried to ask Mercadio to repeat what he said. The look Mercadio gave him was so terrifying, he decided it was better risk casting and listen harder. He could probably ask Soas later. He always listened. *No doubt he* listens to find something to mock Mercadio about, He thought.

"Hopefully" Mercadio said, "in time you would be able to figure out the sorcerer way to cast. In the meantime I will teach what I know about the wizard way. With hope, you will also remember something of the sorcerer's way."

"You see dear boy, when a wizard casts, he pulls the magical essence into himself to manipulate the natural energies around him. The Air, Water and other essence we gather, shape and mold into a spell." Delex nodded. "We call this shaping, now pay attention to this. When you shape a spell you combine, in different amounts, the elements from the gods. To start a fire you would simply use Fire. You merely heat the wood. Now to make fire out of nothing you would mix Fire with Spirit. Spirit helps create, cure and heal. Fire helps light, destroy and heat. Now you mix Spirit and heat from Fire you get a fireball." Mercadio held out his hand. Delex saw a small black ball of flame.

"Why is it black? It looks pretty evil to me." Delex said with a frown.

"It has a bit of Void mixed in with it. Sorry." Mercadio concentrated and a black ball turned to the normal orange-yellow flames that Delex knew. "I do that at times. Now, the next lesson. Some things cannot combine well. Certain forces appose each other and those forces cancel the spell or explode when attempted. They are Air-Earth, Spirit-Nature, Fire-Water, Chaos-Void."

"Wait, hold on. Spirit and Nature don't get along? Sounds like they are on the same side." Delex questioned.

Mercadio nodded "Oh yes, it would seem. Air against Earth and Fire against Water seems pretty logical. Spirit and Nature are in disagreements. They both love life. Nature believes in life dying and returning to make room for more life. She is passionate in rebirth and a cycle of remaking. She does not think about good and evil as we do. Nature believes in luck and has little trust in karma. She doesn't comprehend good and evil, to her they are they same rock skipping over the deep pool of evolution. Spirit is adamant about good and evil, karma and judgment of actions. Spirit also believes in everlasting life, and does not believe death is a cycle, just another step. She hates the idea of doing one's life over to get another result. She only cares about making amends and rewards. They don't like each other. Their views are opposites and try to appose each other when they can. I personally believe Spirit could be smitten with Earth, but Nature caught his eye, not Spirit."

Delex had a glimmer of understanding. All those spells that Mercadio cast were different mixtures of energies. "So what about Chaos and Void? Is Nulx the Void?"

Mercadio waved up a hand "Oh well the usual as you heard. Nulx tried to make Chaos a servant. Chaos saw it clear as air. Nulx wanted a slave. Chaos has hounded Nulx ever since creation and finds Nulx the best to play his pranks on. Nulx has been trying to find ways to kill Chaos ever since Chaos was created. Nulx named Void magic himself. He is somewhat egotistical." Mercadio smiled. "Personally I don't think he can kill Chaos. Now listen, this is the third fundamental of magic. It is possible to combine powers that appose each other, but to do so, you must mix the power of Chaos."

Delex wondered something. "Well what about Chaos and Nulx or Void as he is also called? If they don't get along, how can adding Chaos power to the spell work."

Mercadio shrugged "Chaos is just that, unpredictable and of all magics. If that kind of spell had Void and Chaos magic in it, then you just add more Chaos. I need to stress though, any spell that has Chaos magic in it is fundamentally dangerous, flawed and unstable. Only the truly powerful of spell casters can perform these and even then, it can be deadly."

Delex and Mercadio talked all day about the different fundamentals of magic as they continued east. Mercadio showed Delex a simple wind spell, while Delex tried to control its power. Delex found out that the same formula of energy exists for different spells and it took a mental image of what you wanted to get the right effect. Wizards also had to use words, written images, and other craft to help.

Mercadio made a little flick of his finger and blew Soas' hat off his head. Soas caught his hat with a blur of motion and stuffed it into his saddlebag within a blink of an eye. Delex wondered were Soas even got a hat. Soas did not have a hat when he left the elves.

Mercadio rolled his eyes and told him to pay it no mind and try the spell on Soas' hair. Delex gave a small flick. Nothing happened. He tried again and again. He still could not do this simple thing.

"Hmm, perhaps we need to work on concentration. Close your eyes and focus on the idea of what you want to do, then search out for that power and form it into your image."

Delex flicked his fingers to no effect. "Did you learn this from the towers?"

Mercadio chuckled "Oh no, they don't teach this way. Their wizard way is in books and years of reading and study. Your father taught me this way, or tried. As I said though this is the sorcerer way, I do not know how much success we are going to have with me teaching you."

Delex tried again. He closed his eyes and pictured Soas' hair lift from the breeze off his back. He could feel the power around him but each time he tried to use it, the power slipped out of him.

The sun set in the sky when Blackus gave the halt. Delex had worked up a good sweat. Mercadio looked at him with a grand smile. Soas was mumbled to himself. "But I didn't do anything, not even the simple wind spell. I could have ridden up to his horse and blew on him with better results."

"You sorcerers are powerful, grandly powerful indeed." Mercadio did not look at Delex. He paced around Delex. "It took me two and a half years to sense the power around us and you do it in one day. I think he will be a great spell caster, oh yes."

"Hey I am standing right here. Mercadio listen. Hello? Fine then." Delex walked off towards Soas. Mercadio started to pace around the fire Blackus made instead of Delex. "Hey Soas why are you so angry?"

"I don't like being the target dummy of an untested spell casting race, that no one knows anything about." Soas gave Delex a sticky glare, "without offense."

"Hey don't look at me that way. You're just upset that you aren't teaching me." Delex poked Soas in the side.

Soas gave Delex a big fake laugh. "Ha! I could teach you better than that dox man. I can cast too, plus I have read the Book of Dragons. In that, it teaches about sorcerers and how to use their power."

"The book of what? Why didn't you say this before?" Delex chided.

"Well I was feeling jealous." Soas threw a stick into the fire. "I mean, we haven't talked in days and you look like a little puppy waiting for hand outs from its master. I don't think it would be a good idea anyways. I imagine mad men wrote the book and, I, well-." Soas sputtered to a stop.

Delex started to understand. "-And you didn't want me to get hurt." Soas nodded. Delex sat down by Soas and gruffly put an arm on his shoulder. "Don't worry Soas, if I have learned anything from you, it is good to take chances." Delex got a grin on his face. "While Mercadio looks distracted, why don't you teach me a bit about finding lost things." Soas' face bloomed with a wicked grin.

"Well, you do need a hat." Soas remarked.

****

"Has anyone seen my hat?" Mercadio was up in the morning with the content of his saddlebags strewn out around him. Soas had taken the morning to teach Delex more about the care of horse and tack. They got on the horses and looked away to contain their laughter. "I swear it was on my head when I fell asleep perhaps I put it away." Soas snorted. Mercadio turned and gave Soas a solid eye. "I see." Mercadio gave a smirk. "Soas would you be so kind to give me back my hat?"

"Don't have it." Soas said. His face was a mask of concealed laughter.

"I doubt your truth. Now give me it back before the sun burns my head." Soas and Delex laughed harder. Mercadio turned to Delex. "Ah, Soas has been teaching you his trade." Mercadio held out his hand to Delex. "My hat please." Delex shook his head. "Well and well." Mercadio spoke under his breath quickly and gave a small flick towards Delex. Delex was almost tossed off his horse as all his saddlebags and everything in it flew out into the air and hung there above his head.

Delex gave Soas a confused look. They stole the hat last night and put it in his saddlebag, but now it was not there. Soas gave Delex a small wink and pointed with a hidden finger to the ground behind Mercadio. Delex looked, but could not suppress his laughter. Mercadio turned around. Mercadio's hat scuttled across the low grass as it wiggled and bounced towards Mercadio. A small black furry tail stuck out the back and swished with energy.

"Daylow, You flaming cat." Mercadio took his hat off his cat and gave Daylow a look of shame. "Can't you keep your paws off other people's stuff? You two should have pointed my gaze." Mercadio reversed his spell and Delex's stuff returned to the saddle bags. The wizard hurried off to collect his stuff with Daylow in tow. Daylow gave them both a murderous glare.

Delex turned to Soas. "Wow You are good."

Soas winked and wiggled copper gear in his hand. With a flick it vanished. *"Darn tootin'!"*

Delex gave him a puzzled look. *That phrase was in English, but how? I heard it in English!* Delex memories been able to discern Terrav from English. That was not Terrav. Soas turned his face slightly away and gave Delex a quiet catty smile.

The rest of the day was the same thing as before. Delex still tried to get a hang of spell casting. Soas had tied a ribbon to his horse's tail for Delex to cast on. The wind had picked up over the night and made it hard for Delex to cast. Mercadio was hard-pressed to keep his hat on his head as the wind harassed the party. Delex and Soas laughed each time Mercadio's hat flew off his head, and he was forced to ride after it. He eventually resorted to spells to keep it in sight. After the sixth time, Mercadio stopped his horse.

"That is it! Now Delex, what I am going to perform, is frowned upon unless under grave need. This wind is getting so vexing. Weather control is dangerous." Mercadio got off his horse and scratched a circle around him with his foot.

Delex paid little attention. His concentration was on the ribbon that refused to waver in the simplest ways for him. Sure, the ribbon danced, but it did for the wind not from him. He was somewhat frustrated to know that the wind could do it, but he was still unable to move the ribbon.

"Now as I concentrate, try to see my spell." Mercadio put

his hands into the air and begin a low chant. Delex saw something bluish-white start to form around Mercadio's hands, but as soon as it formed, it shattered into little fragments and vanished. Mercadio recoiled with a flip and landed on his rear. His hat, miraculously stayed in place. Mercadio had a shocked look on his face. Soas did too. They both looked at Delex.

Delex looked back and forth at them. "What?"

Mercadio stood up in pain. "The storm is unnatural I could not stop it. The power in it is stronger than I. Delex I need you to keep casting that spell but this time try to stop the ribbon from moving."

"Yeah okay, why? Is that easier?" Delex asked, still puzzled.

Mercadio got that morbid look in his eye. "Well no boy, just that you have set the entire weather pattern around us into a maul-storm!"

Delex was taken back. "How? I haven't moved that stupid ribbon at all in any direction I tried? What is a maul-storm?"

Soas gave a nervous laughed. "Oh yes you have, you sent an entire storm at it, the kind of storm that only insects live through. Now concentrate on stopping it."

Dark clouds begun to form overhead into a thunderhead. As everyone looked, the clouds started to turn in a large disc that stretched as far as the eye could see. Blackus looked to Delex in perfect calm. "You should hurry." As always, his face showed no emotion.

Delex was stunned "How? I don't understand. I haven't even touched the outside magic. How could I have started a storm?"

Mercadio stuffed his hat into his saddlebag and pulled his hood up as a little shower begun to fall. "Well apparently you have. Think of that spell as a little drop. With every drop it got bigger. Now your spell is overflowing." He pointed to the sky as a funnel of air started to twist towards the ground. Two more swirls begun to form in the clouds as small dimples dipped from their centers. "Now concentrate as hard as you can! A maul-storm is forming! It is already reaching with one skyripper!"

The horse begun to neigh as the storm got worst. *I see, a skyripper is a tornado. Oh, crap! A tornado!* Delex Thought. *Okay 'skyripper' sounds way worse the tornado!* He concentrated harder to stop the ribbon as it danced around in the storm. The cold rain didn't help his concentration as it dripped down his back. He heard Soas mutter lost encouragement into the wind. Mercadio bartered the wind with a flurry of spells and counter spells against the storm. The tornado started to die down when a large clap in the sky startled everyone. Delex concentration broke as his horse begun to toss its head wildly.

"Blast and fire!" Mercadio yelled.

"What did you do Mercadio!" Soas yelled over the storm. He pointed to the tornado that punched the ground with an audible thump.

"I was trying to spin the storm in the other direction with my own wind. I think I just made it worse. We need to run!" Mercadio yelled.

Delex always did like storms, but this was a bit out of his league. A sudden image came to mind of his forgotten youth. He was four. Mercadio had him on a city wall as they watched a rainstorm. The four-year-old version had his eyes closed. He wished to know what it felt like to be a storm. Two more thumps reverberated through the air.

Something suddenly stirred in Delex. A hot and cold sensation flashed through his body. Delex felt it spin inside him. He looked back at the largest tornado as it came ever closer. The feeling inside became stronger. He felt like he could spin right off the saddle. He heard in the distance Soas and Mercadio yell at him, but he could not understand the words. Blackus said something too, but it was crisp and quiet as usual. Delex submerged himself in the feeling.

"We need to stop him! Three skyrippers, presently and now!" Mercadio shouted over the rain and hail that hit them from every direction. "I don't know what he is doing but that maul-storm is charging us!"

"I think he has felt the magic! I read somewhere the sorcerer feels it inside, unlike the wizard." Soas shouted back.

"What? Why did you not tell me this! Wizards have tried that and died! Soas by Fire I will kill you if he gets hurt! Delex snap out of it! You are making it worst!" Mercadio huddled in the saddle.

"He knows what he is doing." Blackus said in an emotionless voice. "Trust the man."

They both looked at Blackus who sat calmly in the storm. He looked unruffled as the storm rained and bashed hail off his clothes. His cloak barely moved in the air. His horse seemed calmer than the rest under Blackus' hand.

"Well I don't think we can stop him anyways." Mercadio groaned and looked to Soas. Soas shook his head.

It was power! It was the raw wind, the blast of freedom. Delex could feel the powers swirl wildly in it. He felt wind, lightning and travel from the power of Air. Spirit created even more air and caused the pressure to build. Destruction from Fire, powered the spell and gave it urgency and rage. Cold and moisture from Water feed hail into the storm. A touch of Nature gave in to neutrality. It would seek no favorites and give no mercy. Chaos twisted and turned in it all and put a balance through the magic. Delex briefly thought of Void, but there was no evil in the storm. It only destroyed but did not try to remove existence, nor was it polluted with Death, or Darkness. It was a storm of power!

Delex was vaguely aware of his friends. They held on for dear life. All four horses lay upon the ground crying in fear. Mercadio and Soas lay sheltered near the horses. Delex did not notice he had climbed to the ground. Even Blackus, stalwart as he was, bent on one knee. He grasped lightly to one of his single edged sword he pushed into the ground.

The power rushed around him. He became aware he had to stop the storm. He felt two different powers in the storm merge into a frightful dance. It was Mercadio's power and his own. He reached out with his mind and took a hold of the force of those spells. It felt slick and tailored like a weave. Delex started to tear at it.

"Mercadio! Mercadio! Oh! Rot oh Void! Blackus help!" Blackus turned to see Soas as Mercadio scream in his lap. "I don't know what is happening!"

Blackus shrugged, "It will pass, He will live."

"You flaming dullard! He is dying, something is killing him!" Soas screeched.

Blackus reached out and slapped Soas with his sleeve. The sleeve surprised Soas with a hefty metal weight. "His spells ripped apart, that is all. He will live."

Soas touched his face tenderly. "You! I will kill you! That is how you blocked my daggers, your clothes have woven magic metal! You got your hands on spell-weave!" Blackus did not answer Soas, he merely looked at the storm that immediately lost a little power. Mercadio stopped his screams and passed out.

Delex felt the magic fall apart in him. Now was only his spell. He could only feel Air, and Water powers now. He imagined it as part of his body and flexed it. The wind blew harder. He relaxed it and the wind died down even farther. He released it, and the wind almost stopped. Delex opened his eyes to see the clouds gone. The ground lay wet and beaten. The storm departed and left behind obliterated patches of barren ground where grass once grew thick and strong. Mercadio was on his feet but still unsteady, The wizard held his head with one hand and steady himself with his staff. He looked to Delex. "That is good for today Delex." Delex noticed it was the first time he did not say boy. He climbed on his horse and sprawled across the saddle. Blackus took his reins and rode at an easy pace. Delex voiced his concerned for his teacher, but Mercadio waved them away.

"It is okay son. You did well. I was unprepared for you to shred my spell. I will need to teach you how to unravel and counter spells properly. When you practice, you will not cause pain to your target. In some circumstances, you may even beguile them to believe their spell remains. You will even be able to counter much faster or even disrupt the spell before they finish." After Mercadio said that, he fell asleep on the saddle. Lines of exhaustion were visible on his face. Blackus led his horse.

The rest of the day faded in silence as Mercadio recovered. Delex did not feel to well either. At every meal he still felt hungry after he ate share. The few leftovers that they had we greedily gobbled down. Mercadio lectured him on the wizard way of casting. He was told not to do whatever he did the first yesterday and today. As he practiced, the weather stayed the same. Two days later of riding Delex finally made the ribbon twitch. "I did it!" He cheered loudly.

"With reliance." Blackus nodded with approval.

"And no murder storms!" Soas added. Both brothers looked at each other with the same small smile. Even Daylow popped out from where he hid and gave Delex a congratulatory purr and licked his nose. Then rolled into a ball on his saddle.

"I can't believe it. That spell took me months to perform as a young man. You have also stolen my cat." Mercadio rode in wonder and shook his head. Delex grinned at Mercadio. Daylow twisted so his back was to the wizard. Mercadio chuckled and the rode on. "The lessons have finished for the day."

The day ended in celebration. The night was ablaze with music as Soas played on his silver flute. Even Blackus was in good spirits and frowned to the beat of the song. Today was a good day for Delex. Today all fears of failure evaporated in one twitch of a ribbon.

Chapter 6: Green Time Dirge

Mossa was in the forest as she danced from tree to tree. They whispered to her about secrets no other mortal knew. They sang their stories to her, their past, their hopes. The day was flawless. The air was sweet with fragrant honey and soil. Lush deep woods of the earth were rich with life. Mossa skipped from tree limb to tree limb without a care. When she looked around, she found herself at the same spot where she had met Delex for the first time. Her hands went to the small deerskin flask that he gave to her. A soft smile played on her face as she thought about the memories that they had, and the hope for future ones.

"What are you grinning at elf?" A voice spoke from behind.

Mossa turned around and gasped, the flask she held dropped to the ground with a small squish. It sent *Melthanna* into the ground. The top of her elven ear turned down and flatten to the side of her head. A man clad in black from head to foot leaned by a near-by tree and eyed her contently. "Who are you?"

The man stood still as he watched her. Mossa notice that the forest had gone silent. It felt as if time had stopped and held its breath. "You know of me but you do not know me. I fought against the evil one for a time."

Mossa's hands trembled as she brought them to her lips. It has been 50 years. "No it can't be, Moraphen, but you are dead, all your men died against him."

"Yet I lived, and now I am back." Moraphen stood straight. His manner became more relaxed as he brushed the dirt off his back. "I did not die with the rest of my men, but I did die in my soul." He gave a small grimace at his own words. The taste was bitter on his tongue.

"You have changed, I see it now, but to me you are still elf-friend. Tell me what has happened to you." Mossa trembled inside, but her resolve held as she eyed this broken, changed man. She took a step towards him, but Moraphen stepped back.

Moraphen lifted a hand to warn her away. "Do not approach elf. I have been through Darkness. I now abhor the touch of goodness, like you."

Mossa took a few steps back. A cold chilled creep down her spine as their eyes locked. "Dear mother Nature, what has happened to you?" Her ears lifted slowly upright. It was almost noon, but the air seemed chilled and stale as she eyed the once Protector of the Realms. She gave out a silent prayer that help would feel this disturbance and come to her aid. "Moraphen, answer me please!"

"Where is the boy Delex, I need to find him; it is critical I find him." Moraphen demanded.

"Please Moraphen tell me, why do you not answer?" Mossa felt for her knife conceal under her tunic. She wished she had felt his presence earlier, but it felt like nothing was there. She could not feel evil from him, only around him. By the moon this was strange!

"I will not!" Moraphen hissed as his muscles tensed.

"Then I cannot tell you. Be gone from these woods, the alarm has already sounded and my brethren are approaching as we speak." Mossa said with a sweep of her hand.

Moraphen sighed and relaxed again. "Well and well. Come close and I will show you why." Moraphen fumbled for something in his backpack. Mossa hesitated and took a single step closer. "Come closer, it is an item that will explain everything. Please it is small but powerful, I must keep it secret only trusted eyes." Moraphen left his body exposed as his shifted through his pack.

Mossa did not know what to do. She stepped closer and tried to figure out his intent. She tried to glean meaning from his face. No secrets betrayed him. Yet, in his grey iris, not even the light of day reflected back. "Moraphen I am here to help. Show me what you will, then please come to the elder with me."

Moraphen nodded. His pose was calm, almost lazy. His eyes started to brim with tears. When Mossa got close enough to him, he struck out like a snake. A dagger conceal in his sleeve dug deep into Mossa's tender stomach. Mossa screamed in pain and surprise. "This my dear elf explains everything does is not?"

Mossa tried to reply but could not get a word through the pain. Moraphen rammed the dagger deeper and gave it a mighty twist. Mossa's screams finally tore from her throat. Leaves fell from the trees. Moraphen growled with pleasure. Her body lost function as it tore and rend from within. Moraphen's merciless hands ripped flesh and broke bone as it moved up her body and shattered through her rib-cage. Moraphen shoved his hand over her mouth and nose as she began to cough up blood. Red soil bathed the forest floor.

"I hear tale that if an elf dies a most gruesome death, that the spirit will come back from the dead, a vile thing. I will return one day to see if this is true." He wrenched the dagger with an unnatural strength and dragged it up through her body until it rested in her neck. Mossa gave a few last twitches and fell limp in his hands. Her clothes once green, were now stained red with her life blood.

Moraphen pressed on the dagger and shoved it through the back of her neck, clear into the tree behind her. He then walked away from the body without a word as it hung pinned to upon the dagger. His eyes scanned the ground for traces of his prey. His cold eyes found a trial. He slowly walked off into the direction of the elder's village.

∞∞∞∞

Foran burst into the sky chamber. People scattered at the sight of him. He ran to the sky chamber and burst through the doors. "She is dead, someone has killed my sister!" Foran wore in his usual battle armor, but his skin had taken on a wooded appearance. His hair had turned into grass and his nails into long thorns. His voice came out choppy and ragged. Foran's throat could not form the words. His whole body looked partially formed of Nature.

Selkroth stood and shouted, "He needs help, he has drank too much of the *Melthanna* and his soul is in peril! He needs help at once!"

"No father, listen to me." Foran grabbed at his father's robes. "Mossa has been slain. She is now a Sask'a'roht."

Selkroth's eye wide with shock. "What how? This can not be. She was here hours ago."

"No, father, she is dead." Tears streamed and beaded in a thick amber color around his slightly brown eyes. "She was horribly destroyed. I gave her back to Nature then came to warn you. The killer is still in the forest!"

Selkroth begun to cry as he hugged his son to his chest. He waved off the others that had come to his aid. They stood in a useless circle around him. It was too late for his son. He will be part of Nature soon. A noise and scream broke him from his grief. Foran tired to speak but his face had gone stiff in an expression of grief.

One of the elves burst into the sky chamber. "Elder, a man in black has stolen a horse and *Melthanna*. He rides from us as we speak. My lord he stinks of elven blood!"

Selkroth stood and tore his son's fingers from his robes. "Tend to my son and make him comfortable. I will see this murderer dead." He stormed out of the sky chamber and skipped lightly from the branches to the ground. He barely caught a glimpse of the killer as his horse made it to the village's edge. The horse reared by the tree as the murderer looked back one last time. Selkroth gasped. "It cannot be, but he is dead and lost! Now he is evil?"

Moraphen took a drink and then shoved the liquid into the horse's mouth and forced it down the throat. An arrow struck the saddlebags on the horse as Moraphen kicked it into a burst of speed. As soon as the horse's feet touched the forest, both horse and rider blinked in and out of sight as there bodies materialized by each tree along their path. The horse and rider shot out of sight within seconds.

"Elder what will we do? We will not catch him now. He has destroyed the reserve *Melthanna* except what we carry."

Selkroth spoke with coiled rage. "Do not worry child, he will not go far." Selkroth reached into the ground with his hand and closed his eyes. In hurried tones he spoke to the earth. "Rise woods of green, new and born, feel my hand. Bring the growth, cut the path, feed the land." A rumble shook throughout the forest. Selkroth opened his eyes. "Rally the guard; hunt him down."

Moraphen watch as the forest suddenly closed in around him into a wooden path. The horse flew down the path as he spurred it in the ribs with his legs. The sounds of screams fell behind him in seconds. He had traced the prints to the village. He knew they had departed *Terwise*. The target was well in hand. As Moraphen rode, a noise came from everywhere. A deep rumbled rose from the earth as the trees raced away from each other. Instead of each tree tightly packed by each other like a wall of wood, the trees were at times twenty even sometimes fifty meters apart. Moraphen could not understand; he hurried the horse even faster, but no matter how fast the horse went he could not gain enough ground. This never happened with the elven tree drink before.

He spotted it. Tree sprouts emerged out of the ground all around him, hundreds of them. The new sprouts made the *Melthanna* weakness in the dense tree sprouts. Moraphen stopped the horse and got off. Now the trees were back to their normal distance, but he had to hurry, He could already hear the sounds of pursuit had caught him up. He had lost too much time from the elven trick.

Selkroth was with his men as the raced through the forest on their horses as fast as they dare. He advised none of the men to drink any *Melthanna*. He could see Moraphen in the distance. They had passed the horse farther back and now had only minutes before they would catch and kill his daughter's murder. "Be wary men, if this is the man I knew once, than he is as dangerous as Blackus. Remember he was once the master of shields. If you can, do not attack him, try to capture him or lead him into one of our game snares. If you must, kill him, but remember, we must try to keep him alive for Mossa. She is a Sask'a'roht and needs her vengeance to be free." The men all nodded or gave a brief answer. All of them knew what was at stake. Selkroth knew if they did not catch him soon he would hit the edge of the forest and hide in unfamiliar territory. He spoke in the same magical words, but had to concentrate much harder since he was on horseback with his had within the natural soil. All the new sprouts that were made died and withered before their eyes. Selkroth orders everyone to drink the *Melthanna*. The trees became a tunnel of wood. Now it was time to make the murder pay.

Moraphen stepped gracefully to the edge of the forest when arrows flew all around him. He pulled out his sword and batted them easily away. He heard two people scream in pain. One voice went silent.

"Moraphen is that you? What have you done to be this way?" A rich voiced yelled from the woods.

Moraphen spotted Selkroth in a nearby tree, an arrow shaft vibrated in the tree limb at his feet. Moraphen stood calmly in place, he looked into the enraged face of his old friend. "I do not have time for this. Tell me where I can find Delex and you will live another day in your green cage."

"Never." Selkroth bellowed.

"Then die." Moraphen shrugged.

Arrows streamed out of the forest all around him. He batted them away like pesky flies. Another elf fell to the ground, an arrow stuck out of his throat.

"Stop! Do not attack him. Do not let him entice you to fire!" Selkroth jumped to the ground by the tree he was in and walked to Moraphen. "I know you and I know your abilities. You cannot harm me if I do not attack you. I know this."

Moraphen gave Selkroth a dirty glare. "Do you now? What do you want?"

Selkroth glared. "I want your head. You made my daughter a vile thing of revenge. I will see her have revenge, so she may rest."

Moraphen grinned slowly, "Ah so it is true. Give her my regards and thanks."

Selkroth's face went from slight green to red, "You flaming, ashen son of Nulx. You motherless scum, I will have your head for your words!" Selkroth almost lunged at Moraphen but caught himself at the last minute, but to his surprise, Moraphen lunged at him and sliced his robes. A thin line a red opened on Selkroth's chest.

Selkroth jumped back in surprise just as a vine net fell over Moraphen. Moraphen quickly cut his way out and dodged a new volley of arrows. Two more elves fell dead and three more cried out in pain. No more arrows came at him. He raced to the edge of the forest and saw Selkroth merge from behind another tree. "Damn you and your magics elf!"

"You will not leave this wood." Selkroth growled. He held his chest as his blood leaking out over his fingers and down his robe.

Moraphen growled. "Your archers are dead or wounded and you have not the strength to harm me, nor the means. Stand aside and live or fight me and die."

Selkroth glared deeply into Moraphen's eyes and slowly backed away. "I may not have the means but some might still."

Moraphen laughed and shoved Selkroth as he went by. He heard the old man's mournful cries echo from the forest. Moraphen felt good as he ran with an extra spring in his step. Tears started to form at his eyes. Why was he crying?

Selkroth was still on the edge of the forest when some of his men found him. He looked up through a tear stained face. "Bring me back to the village. We must find a carrier bird to warn Mercadio. He must know of this new threat."

It was nearly midnight when Moraphen heard the noise of tired wings. He looked up and saw a small shadow beat over him. He took up a bow and one of the arrows he stole from the village and took careful aim. The bow hummed softly as the arrow shot from its cradle and flew towards the shadowy dot in the sky. Moraphen heard the cry of the bird and knew he found his mark. It took nearly half an hour to find the messenger dove in the tall grass, but when he did he smiled. He started a small fire, with dry grass and flint across a dagger. Later, he rested on a blanket and cut grass pulled over him. The dove cooked up well with his meager seasonings.

∞∞∞

"What is that?" Delex sat in his saddle struck with a sense of awe. In the early morning light the lake he looked at glimmered a dull grey color. Right by the lake's edge stood a town almost as big as the lake itself. At least 50,000 people must live in the sprawl of buildings, parks, museums, and other points of interest and entertainments. That was only in the city proper. Around the town for kilometers were large and small farms that no doubt supported the city's hungry. He could see caravans leave and enter the city gates in unbroken lines. They looked like lines of ants leave and enter the hive on daily business to support their queen, the city. Delex sighed with relief to see a spark of civilization. He worried that the whole planet was a backwater mess of farms and rundown inns.

Mercadio smiled. "That, my boy, is the grand city of Homgad. Once, a long time ago, they called it Home Guard. That was a long time ago, but time has a way of changing memories and names."

"Why call it Home Guard?" Delex asked.

"Because of that, the heart of Homgad." As Mercadio spoke, out of the mist came a sight that dwarfed the previous vision of human ingenuity. The mist cleared as the day broke over the lake to reveal a castle of outstanding proportions. Sat on top of a mountain plateau within the lake and mist, was a fortress of stone beautiful as it was large. Towers reached into the sky like delicate fingers. Stonewalls curved around the plateau so perfectly they seemed to merge with the mountain at their base. Colored windows refracted the light into a dazzling array of rainbows. The stone shone like whitest ivory in the sun. Lush ivy grew over the entire structure in artistic spiral patterns. The vision seem almost ghost-like as it shimmered as the mist dissipated in the sun. Delex wondered how the castle had survived without overgrowth or as a rundown ruin.

"Home Guard is a castle." Delex grinned. Mercadio nodded, and pointed back to it again. Delex turned to look and nearly fell of his horse from surprise. What Delex took as a mountain plateau before was in-fact and island suspended above the lake's surface. The entire structure rested on a slab of rock shaped roughly like an upside down pyramid. The entire castle isle slowly rotated counter-clockwise. It was truly a castle out of a fairy tale. "Mercadio, that's magnificent, but who lives there, is that the tower of magic you were talking about?" Delex looked at the delicate towers of the castle shimmer like torches.

Mercadio gave a small laugh, "No dear boy, that's your humble little home." Delex looked at Mercadio. If he could feel anymore shocked he would have, but he was already at his peak. "The towers of magic are nothing compared to this." Mercadio waved his hand over the lake. "You see Delex, your parents lived there as did many sorcerers they welcomed. Your parents built it and remained after the sorcerers left. Home Guard was actually what it says. The town was at first an outpost, the first defense to protect their home. As the guards took on wives and such, it grew and grew. Those that retired, stayed to help the new young men that took their place, and some became farmers. About 50 percent of the town's current inhabitants, and that of the farmers around the town, are descendants of those fine men that protected your home while your parents still lived. This is your legacy, your parent's gift to you. Perhaps the town itself."

Delex felt overwhelmed. "I don't know what to say Mercadio."

Soas placed a hand on Delex's shoulder. "That's good enough for us." Mercadio nodded to Soas, and they both smiled to each other. "Now lets get into town. If we are fortunate, we will get to town in another six hours."

As they moved along, Delex was a fountain of questions. When did they live there, why did they leave? Who lived there now? Mercadio only would only smile and say, "We have time for all of that after settling in town." Delex only stopped his deluge of questions after Soas got off his horse and threw a clump of dirt at Delex.

"Stop pestering the old geezer. You will know in a little while. It is unsafe to talk about such things in the open. Besides, you are clogging my ears with your constant blabbering. Even my dear brother is getting annoyed. Look he even has his hand of his sword." Soas pointed.

Delex brushed the dirt out his hair and retorted "Well he always has his hand on his sword."

Soas retorted. "True of word, but he doesn't normally have it partially drawn like he does now." Delex looked back and noticed that Blackus did have enough of his sword out of the scabbard to tap one of his long fingers on the blade. Blackus did not look at either of them when they started to talk about him. He merely continued to tap his blade with a slightly annoyed look on his face.

"Fine," Delex relented, "but when we get our rooms, you both better tell me what I want to know. And Soas, I am going to get you back for throwing dirt at my head."

Soas laughed artfully, "I would not expect anything less."

When they finally made it to the city gates, Delex's rear end was as sore as ever. Not only did it take them about seven hours to get to the city, but they had to wait in line for almost another hour as the city guards search everyone that came in and out of the city. The military background of the city shown in the guards' attitude and performance. Posted signs forbid weapons in the city, other than by the guards or special permission attained by the Major, the town's mayor. When they finally got to the guards, Blackus came to the front and spoke to the group. "I will handle this."

One of the guards approached the group and started his usual speech. "Welcome to Homgad. No weapons, poisoned or illegal natures allowed within the city. You cannot enter without the mandatory search. You must declare any weapons, poisons, illegal natures or items that may cause concern now. If you do not, if our search finds these items, the items are forfeit to Homgad in support of Homgad, the guard and tax relief of the residency. Now tether your horses in search area three, we will begin the search."

"No." Blackus said.

"What?" the guard said a bit taken back.

"I said No. Apparently you are as deaf as you are ugly." Blackus retorted in a toneless voice, which made the insult even worse. Delex, Soas and Mercadio remained rendered speechless as they all looked to Blackus' outburst.

"Why you burning blaster!" The guard blew on a loud whistle. Within ten seconds, the entire gate guard of more than thirty had surrounded the group and cleared out immediate area of travelers. "Now, you will come with use to our containment area where we will take everything you own for inspection and perhaps confiscation". The guard said with confidence. As he talked, more guards filtered in from the city in groups of five. Whistles echoed across the area as far as Delex could hear.

Blackus glared at the guard and lean over so his nose was face to face. "Out of my way, else I cut myself a path." The guard gulped and gave out two more shrill whistles. Archers appeared over the city gates. Delex counted at least fifty. He could even more crossbow bolts sticking out of murder holes from the sides of the long tunnel that led through the gate. By now the waiting travelers had cleared the area except for the guards and the traveling group. Everyone else was either lead away from the area or had fled in terror. Farmers and merchants did not want to have anything to do with this group and showed it by their ability to disappear.

Just as Blackus was going to draw his sword a foppish looking official came bursting through the ring of guards and spoke in quick tones to the guard with the whistle. The guard's face got as white as snow and beads of sweat started to form on his forehead. The guard fumbled the whistle into his mouth and gave out a series of shrill notes. All the guards left immediately in hurried steps, leaving only the original gate guards. The guard came closer to Blackus. He began to apologize to Blackus. Blackus cut him short with a backhand that took the guard to the ground. His metal sleeve rang momentarily from the blow. "I thought I trained you better. You should recognize the line of command. If you did, you would have remembered the challenge phrases for confirmation."

The sweaty official stepped over the fallen guard and came closer to Blackus, but still out of reach. "I would like to apologize for this inconvenience Commander Blackus. I did not think-" Blackus raised hand for silence. The official cut his apology short. The city official looked like a frog that had swallowed a spoon.

"Get that man a steak for his eye and one extra silver Barl this month for his incompetent diligence." The official stumbled and babbled words of agreement. "Also tell him next time, he better study the face roster and pass phrases. They are critical to his work."

All this time the party was taunt with nervous energy. Soas' hand was inside a saddle bag. Mercadio has loosened his staff and held it tight. Delex sat dumbfounded on his horse while confusion and awe, played on his face. Delex had thought they were good as dead, but the masterful way Blackus lead them in the gates and the foppish city official at the gates gave him new-found respect for Blackus.

"Wait, dude, your pass phrase is about cutting a path through people?" Delex asked Blackus.

"What is a dude? I might use that." Blackus replied. His stolid face gave no emotion to his inner thoughts. Was that a joke, or was it sincere? Delex wondered if Blackus played poker. He wondered if anyone here played poker.

Blackus leaned over to Delex and placed his face near his ear. "We use phrasing that would be natural for you to say. With complicated cadences that changes based on the day of the year."

Soas interjected. "So your natural speak is to threaten dismemberment, death, and destruction?"

Blackus continued to look into Delex's eyes without a blink. There was a strength and madness in those eyes. He answered in a cool rich voice. "Isn't everyone's?" Delex felt a chill creep up his spine and goosebumps form on his arms, leg, and the top of his head.

Blackus spoke again as he sheathed his sword back into his side. No one saw or heard him draw a blade that was at least as long as his leg. "Yes, I threaten." He straightened in his saddle and faced forward as the guards parted for the party. "And then I would kill them." Blackus said with a straight face.

The silence was almost tangible. The guards had heard every word and were noticeably shaken. As they rode away, Soas pipped up. "Wait, was that a joke? Blackus did you joke? My world has been upturned!" Soas laughed and mocked.

Blackus failed to react to anything. Soas' face lost its smile. "Blackus? Was that a joke? Blackus!" Soas continued but failed to get a single word from his estranged brother.

The goosebumps took a while to go away. He thought that Blackus was all too capable of his words. Mercadio was silent the whole time but his face was a cracked mask of mirth as he watched Soas' and Delex's discomfort.

Delex shook his head as he thought about being surrounded by his best friends. He had a wizard of great power and knowledge only equaled by his morbid streak. A thief, *oh I mean merchant-of-lost-goods*, clever by half and filled with odd secrets all wrapped around a core of annoyance, jokes and mockery. Then, there is Blackus, the most secretive of them all. His dangerous and indomitable attitude was a tangible terror. Delex sighed to himself. He was a mere passenger in a carnival of the mad.

The city official led the party from the entrance to Nature's Gate, the most elegant inn within all of Homgad. The city official had paid for their first week of stay as an apology and left them, as he muttered nervously to the air. All four walked into a large, and comfortable common room. A few doors inside the room led to various facilities, like the bedroom, a spacious closet, and balcony the overlooked the lake and the floating castle.

Soas laughed with delight and threw his saddlebag through the open door into the bedroom. "Well I am all put away."

Mercadio turned to Delex and handed him his saddlebags. "Delex just put this on a bed, I must be off to the library to converse with my fellow casters." Delex smiled and took the bags without complaint. His eyes looked over everything. The whole room looked as if it was tailored for royalty, and perhaps it was, he mused.

Soas turned to his brother "You would think that you were a king with that treatment you abused upon them." Blackus continued to remove items from his saddlebag without a reply. Soas shrugged and turned to Delex next. "Well, Delex, how about you and I go down stairs and I will show you the wonderful art of gambling."

Mercadio stopped dead in his tracks with his hand on the door to their apartments. He turned slowly and gave Soas a glare that could have made flowers jump out of the ground and run off. "Soas, if I hear of any wrong doings while we are in the city, I will personally notify the guards of your presence, and my personal theories of your merchant business you have."

Soas smiled and put his hands in the air. "Not a problem Mercadio. If I do anything here, we should be long gone before discovery." Mercadio glared harder at Soas. "Besides," Soas waved the glare off, "I just want to show Delex around the city. This is business not pleasure."

Mercadio grabbed his hat and replaced it on his head as he muttered out the door, "I would rather see that rat enjoying pleasure then applying his business."

Soas looked at Delex, "Okay, before we go down I need to tell you about the game called Dragon Moons."

"Is that a card game?" Delex asked. He packed all his stuff in the dresser beside his bed. There were six beds in this room, but they only need four.

Soas shook his head, "No, it is a game of dice."

Delex nodded, "go on."

Soas nodded, "Well there are three different dice, a square die of six sides, a long cigar shaped die with 10 sides, and a round die with twenty sides. The three dice number one through four, now-"

Delex interrupted Soas. "How can that be, there are a lot more sides than there are numbers Soas."

Soas nodded "Well there are symbols as well. One is a dragon face, and the other is a quarter moon, thus the name." Delex nodded. "Well the six sided die has one of each, the 10 sided has two sets of numbers with one of each symbol, and the 20 sided has three sets of numbers and four of each symbol."

Delex asked "That doesn't make it all even though. Why is that?"

"Different chances on each die. Now lets go down stairs and I will show you the rest." Soas jiggle a small bag of coins in his hand.

Delex smiled as they both went to leave but Blackus spoke up. "Soas, leave your dice here." Soas muttered to himself but removed three dice out of his bag and threw them on the floor. "All three sets." Soas started to curse, but removed a second set out of his hair, and the third from some well-hidden pockets around his collar.

Soas and Delex left their apartments and hurried down the stairs before Blackus could make any more demands. Soas smiled and leaned over to Delex as they hit the landing to the bar, music parlor, dinning area and gambling hall. "I have a forth pair now." Soas removed a small attachment to his scabbard at the tip that usually held his sword. Out fell three dice, which he pocketed away. He closed the concealed cup on the scabbard and gave Delex a wink. They both laughed and made their way into the gambling hall.

Delex noticed that the entire inn had a forest like quality to it. The walls looked like carved trees with scenes of deer, dancing elves or other scenery carved between each tree like shape. The ceiling looked carved and painted to resemble different times of day in the forest. It looked so real that the fire from the wall lanterns made the leaves flutter as in a light breeze. The tables of either stone or wood, are placed in artistic spots to make the room look like a forest glen. All the doors had panels carved to look like loosely woven ivy. The thin and long panels all fit together to make hang by each other on strings. It was almost like you pushed through ivy, but unwieldy and made of wood panels. Delex lost himself to the sight as they ordered food from a lovely elven women and made their way to eat in the gambling hall. Soas explained that he liked to watch the competition before the risk of gold. Delex thought this was well, since he starved for a good hot meal. Soas cracked his knuckles and smiled like a cat in a room full of mice.

Chapter 7: Force to Fly

Moraphen looked over the city as it gleamed in the noonday sun. He sneered at it, but for some reason he loved it. *No, that was a memory from another man, a dead man that was killed a long time ago,* he thought. This new man did not care for towns and people nor anything else, except his master's wishes. He yanked hard on the horse as it tried to take the bit in its mouth. The horse snorted and rolled its eyes in fear. It pawed the ground restlessly. The beast made it clear it wanted to get this rider to his destination and off its back. Moraphen smiled. *This horse knew what I was, knew it the moment that it saw me. To bad the previous owner did not.* Moraphen could not get all the blood out of the saddle. He shifted the saddlebags and his new cloak over the more noticeable blood smears.

"I will never hide all of this," he grumbled. Moraphen attention wavered as he thought about what to do. The horse jerked the reins and bucked to dislodge the rider. Moraphen regained the reins and punched the horse in the ear with his fist. He was almost a master level rider. This beast was nothing. A horse like this would toss and trampled a lesser rider.

The though hit him like the moon had crashed its heaven bound weight on him. He chuckled to himself as he pulled out a dagger. The horse danced nervously as it saw the blade. Moraphen cuffed the horse on the ear again. He took the dagger and cut a good sized wound in his hairline and let it bleed down the side of his face, cloak and over the bloody spots from before. "Look what you did." He said to his mount. "It looks as if I fell off you on a sortie into the fields and cut myself open on a rock. Naughty horse, I better go to the city at once to find a healer and sell you for meat." The horse nickered wildly as Moraphen yanked hard on the reins and set the horse at a full gallop towards the distance gates. The guards usually let the wounded to the front of the lines and seldom checked them as thoroughly.

∞∞∞∞

"Ah Mercadio the black, I thought I felt you in the city."

Mercadio smiled to a plump old man close to a heart with a brilliant fire. Piles and stacks of book scattered around the floor, the table and in his lap. His horn-rimmed glasses made him look like a big bug caught under a pile of books. "Narsis the green, good to see you. I see you have not set the library on fire yet." Mercadio kicked a few books back from the fireplace that looked in danger of a stray sparks.

The old man shrugged. "What brings you to Homgad?"

Mercadio frowned for a second. "A great many things. First off the dark one has risen in power. His minions pursued me through a *tempra*."

Narsis cringed. "Fowl weather news, but not unexpected. That can not be what troubles you my friend."

Mercadio took a pile of books off a chair and slide next to Narsis. He leaned closer and lowered his voice. "Indeed it is not. His shadow attacked us in the woods. We barely escaped. Blackus is in the city and his half-wit brother Soas." Narsis took in a deep breath; Mercadio wondered which of the three scared the old man more. "Do not fear Narsis, his shadow can not follow us here yet. Blackus, though fearsome, is honorable. I have bought his contract for a year."

"That in itself in an act of courage Mercadio, and an act of poverty as well, I should imagine. What of the thief?"

"He is being lead around by the nose by his brother." Mercadio smiled, also amused at the imagery. Narsis nodded approvingly. Mercadio looked deeply into Narsis eyes. "But this is not a social visit. I need you to get word to the towers that I am coming. If possible, we must warn them of these attacks. I have spoken with Blackus, and he is aware of a massing of evil in small pockets. Can you do this for me?"

Narsis placed a friendly hand on Mercado's shoulder. "I will my friend. But you have not told me everything."

Mercadio took on a slightly abash look. "No, you are right I did not, but for the time being, I fear I can not. I do not think I am out of danger just yet."

Narsis nodded. "Well and well, I know your wisdom is greater at things like this."

Mercadio stood to leave. "Thank you my friend, but I must be off as soon as possible. I wish I had time to sit with you longer."

"I understand Mercadio. Take care." Narsis turned back to his books and pulled a lite pipe from his robes.

Mercadio shook his head at the pipe. He never could figure out how he did that. *Well, each wizard has his own secrets*, he mused. He said a few more good-byes and promised to return sometime. He left the library quickly and hurried back towards the inn, but when he arrived the street had filled. Guards tried to keep order to the mass of people that blocked the streets.

Mercadio pushed his way through the crowed towards a guard. "What has happened here?"

"Go soak your head old man, this is city guard business and none of yours." The guard shoved him roughly back into the crowd. Mercadio got his footing and stood in front of the guard again. Before the guard could speak again Mercadio spoke roughly and took one slender finger and waved it in front of the guards eyes.

"Now listen to me young whelp. I am Mercadio the black, leader of the darker arts of the towers, and high council member of wizardry. You push me one more time and you will have to find new armor to fit the breasts that I will give you, not to mention the rest that comes with it." The guard's eyes bulged with fury as he went for his sword. Mercadio was faster. His prepared spell snapped out like a whip. He pointed to the guard's boots. Light flared briefly as the guard's boots turned into women's slippers. From the look of the guards face, was he scared and in pain. More than likely the shoes were a few sizes to small.

The guard screamed out in terror and scurried back from Mercadio. The whole crowed had gone silent and slowly moved back from Mercadio's baleful glare. He faced the crowd and spoke in an irritated voice pitched loud enough for all to hear. "All of you leave, else I test my imagination further on one and all." The crowd was in motion before he finished his sentence.

Mercadio smiled grimly at the guard and walked past him as he huddled in terror. His fingers groped under his leg armor to get the painful shoes off his feet.

Mercadio burst into the inn and found the whole place a commotion of guards. Cooks brandished butcher knives, scared costumers scurried for the exits, and one worried looking inn keeper dripped beads of sweat into his plush velvet shirt.

Mercadio headed for the loudest part of the chaos. That seemed to be from the gambling and food hall. Mercadio gave a deep sigh as his eyes caught Soas and Delex surrounded by guards. A third man dressed in fine silks and leathers sat in the corner. Several more guards surrounded him. A bloody rag was on the top of his head. It held back a flow of endless blood.

Mercadio shoved his way into the ring of guards and frowned down at Soas and Delex. "Care to explain or do I have to guess?"

Delex spoke first. "Well Soas caught that guy over there cheating. Well, when-"

"Hold, are to speak truly, Soas caught a criminal?" Mercadio asked with a puzzled look on his face.

Soas grinned at Mercadio, "that's right, I saw that man cheating at Dragon Moons and when he was found out, he pulled a knife and went for Delex and I."

"Yeah So Soas slapped the dagger out of his hand and it ended up flipping into the air and landing on the guys head." Delex mimed the dagger's spin with a whirl of his finger and ended with a poke on the top of his head.

Soas nodded to Delex, "Luckily for him it was a palm dagger or else he would be using his eyes from the other side of life right now."

Mercadio just glared at the both, "Well I am glad you are both having a gay time of this. Yet, do not think enticing a riot in the best inn in town is the proper way to make friends?" Soas and Delex both looked a bit abash. "Soas I will have words with you alone. As for you Delex, go find Blackus and tell him to collect our belongings. We are leaving at once."

Both Soas and Delex started to protest. The room darkened as every flame in the room started to stutter. The menacing look from Mercadio spoke worlds of threats. Delex hurried to out while Soas walked over to a corner with the angry wizard. It was uncommon practice to upset wizards. Although, when wizard tempers flare, it was common practice to hide. Soas looked like a scare rabbit. "All right Soas now tell me the true teeth of the story."

Soas looked up at Mercadio and spoke quietly. "His name is Bashor. He was a thief with a price on his head for stealing from the guild-bonded thieves. I knew this and so did he. I forced him to act. So, I got him caught by the guards. He will probably not make it to his trial. The guilds were looking heavily for him. The reward will probably get me yet another year of free practice."

Mercadio nodded, "Well thank you for being so blunt for once, but next time you decide to go on a bounty hunting party, try to leave the future savior of magic out of it."

Soas nodded with a look of shame. He looked up and scanned the room. A puzzled look came on his face. "Mercadio, where is Delex?"

"I sent him to find Blackus, remember." Mercadio replied.

Soas looked at Mercado "I saw Blackus go upstairs a moment ago." Mercadio nodded to Soas and motioned to head for their rooms. When they reached it, they found Blackus huddled over the center of the room near the floor. He didn't look up from his examination. The ransacked apartments lay in disarray. All of their belongings lay sprawled across the floor in disarray. Mercadio rushed to the bedroom as Soas went to check the adjoining rooms.

Soas came back into the main room, "It looks like everything has been gone through but its all still here."

"Not precisely." Mercadio said in an empty voice. "It seems Delex's items are missing entirely."

Blackus looked up to both of them. "One man, light on his feet. There was a struggle but it was short. Delex fell over there." Blackus pointed to an upturn table. "The man took him through the window and down the wall. He must be of great skill." Mercadio rushed over to the open window and peered out.

Soas looked to his brother. His usual smile changed to the same wax look of rage played on his brother's face. "This only happen minutes ago. We may still catch them at the walls." Both brothers nodded and went for the door. Mercadio was right behind them. Mercadio pushed his way to the front of the pack. Darkness seeped from the shadows he pulled the cloak up around his face. The black mage was is full rage.

By the time they got to the street, the crowd had cleared and only peddlers and merchants still milled around for a few stranglers to pawn their good on. They scurried into the alleys as they saw the trio come down the streets. Blackus spoke briefly to another guard. The guard gave a series of whistle and received the whistle up farther ahead.

"I have sealed the gates." Blackus said.

Mercadio was beside himself with rage and feelings of failure. How could the dark one have found them so soon? How could he have failed so miserably? Surprisingly Soas was the most irritable of all. As they passed by people about their business or in their way, he screamed and barked out a series of curses that would have made a statue blush. Blackus did not say a word. He gave a sublet look at a guard and nodded to have him follow in silent step.

By the time they reached the city walls there were over a hundred guards around the gate. Blackus came up to the captain of the guard. "Report."

The guard made a well-polished salute with his fist to his chest. "Commander we have not found the culprit. We are doing everything we can to keep the throng of people from leaving or entering."

"Double the wall and bring up the scouts. I want scopes up on the walls right now. Have all guards on and off duty report to the exits of the city. Cover the sewers, and make the recruits pull the normal duties and house-by-house searches. No house is exempt."

"By the moon commander." The captain bowed and barked out a series of commands. Shouts echoed towards the wall as men and pushed and shoved. In moments, the confusion turned into the gears of discipline and order.

Mercadio looked at Blackus "Isn't this a bit extreme?"

"No." Blackus replied as his stride turned toward the wall. Mercadio and Soas followed in tow. Blackus grabbed three scopes from a corporal and passed them to the others.

The search was only a few minutes in when a women's scream turned all three from the walls to peer down to the gate. Commotion broke under the gate as men's shouts and screams echoed off the city's walls and buildings. Mercadio and the others had taken only a few steps down the stairs off wall when grind of twisted metal shook the ground underneath them. The final crash of metal echoed like a bell above the women and men the screamed in terror.

Blackus and Soas growled as they headed back up the wall. Mercadio beat them both. As all three peered over the wall, dust rose from the gate. They already knew what had happened. The kidnapper broke through the line of guards and had cut the ties to the portcullis. It crashed to the earth and more than likely trapped several people under its immobile weight.

Blackus was the first to spot a lone rider shoot out of the dust. He spurred his horse at a full gallop. Mercadio pointed to a second rider tied to the horse that flopped like a sack of flour over the kidnapper's saddle. Blackus raised a hand and a cloud of arrows flew from the walls for the rider. Most of them missed, but the rider easily deflected the ones that hit. Some of those even flew back towards the walls; only one flew high enough to stick in the thigh of and archer, a few paces from Soas. The rider pulled his horse up short and spun it around. The horse reared under a master's hand. His eyes locked on Blackus. He raised his sword skyward and slowly lowered it to point at the three.

Blackus muttered a single word filled with acid and hate, true emotion finally played across his face as he said "Moraphen." Mercadio and Soas gasped.

"This cannot not be, he is long dead." Mercadio protested.

"No, he is alive; the rumors are true. We will not catch him from here." Blackus turned his back from the walls but Soas grabbed his arm and pointed back at the rider.

The rider took something out of his hand threw it to the ground. Mercadio gave a sharp curse as a black oval opened in the air. The *tempra* nearly finished when the second rider stuck his hand out towards it. A bright glow shot at the *tempra* before Moraphen knocked him unconscious with the hilt of his sword. It was already too late. Delex had scored a critical hit. The *tempra* wavered and became unstable. A claw started to emerge out of the twisting portal. The claw was three times the size of the horse and rider. Three large black talons led off the paw of black leathery purple skin etched with red and blue tendons. The horse reared in fright and shot away from the portal.

The *tempra* snapped closed severing fingers and black juices all over the high grass.

Mercadio laughed in delight. Soas looked at him wide-eyed. "What in the armpit of Fire are you laughing at Mercadio? They are getting way."

Mercadio grinned at Soas, "Did you see that. Delex is learning ever so fast. He tried to counter the spell of the *tempra*. He did not do it well, but it was enough to make it unstable. That was an artifact of power he countered! An artifact! He rendered it useless!"

"Is that what he threw on the ground?" Soas asked.

Mercadio nodded "Yes. Most likely a relic from the last war and extremely rare, perhaps the last." Mercadio got a studied look. "Though I have never heard a case of anything ever being able to leave the *tempra*. They are bound within and cannot cross the boundary. What did Delex do? Not once, Soas, not a single account. Creatures of the *tempra* cannot come out. It is beyond the laws of magic." Mercadio's brows closed together in fearful thought.

"Look Mercadio." A small hiss called from below. All three looked down to see Mercadio's cat Daylow outside the wall. The cat's attention was where the *tempra* had closed. Something small darted over the three severed fingers of the *tempra-beast*. It purred a high-pitched delight and grabbed a man-sized finger despite its small size.

Mercadio shot a bolt of blackness at the creature but it dodged the beam and faded from sight. "Soas that is not good. That was a demon imp. I shudder to think what he will do with that finger."

"Well no time now to contemplate Mercadio. We must get out of this city." Soas said with a nod and started down the stairs. Blackus was already at the gates near the destruction.

∞∞∞

Delex opened the room to the apartments and saw a cloaked figure there. At first, he thought it was Blackus but as the man turned to reveal his face he knew this was trouble. The man dropped a bundle to the ground. It was Delex's bag. "Hey that is mine you thief!" Delex picked up a paperweight and threw it at the man. Before he could blink, he was hit so hard in the face that spots formed in his vision.

"I assume you are Delex, the wonder whelp." The man sneered. "I am Moraphen, I have come to collect you for my master. Play along and I will hurt you less." Moraphen took a step closer. Delex got up and swung at Moraphen, but he twisted the punch sending Delex to the ground again. "Ha boy! Obviously, no one has told you about me. Not unexpected, I guess. Moraphen at your service, master of the shield. Attack me if you wish, but I will counter anything."

"Counter this!" Delex's hand stretched toward Moraphen. A gust of wind picked up suddenly in the room and sent Moraphen backward against a wall. Delex got to his feet. He used the wind to send a vase through the air. Moraphen recovered too quickly. He grabbed the vase in mid-flight, spun in place, and sent it back at Delex. The vase connected and shattered into pieces as it hit Delex's chest. Delex collapsed into a table. His lungs tried to recover the air that the vase punched out of them.

Moraphen chuckled. "Good little whelp. I see you found a chink in my armor, but then you fowled it up yet again. Typical. Your father was the same." Delex wanted to respond. A boot to the mouth sent his wits out of him. Blackness soon followed.

Moraphen slung the pack over his shoulder and popped his back. The little bastard damn near knocked the sense out of him with the wind trick. He picked up Delex and went to the window of a two-story drop. He dropped the pack and slung Delex over his shoulders. It took a bit of work to maneuver, but he managed to get down the wall and onto a new horse. It was easy to find Delex. He followed the gossip that floated about after Blackus' little stunt. His fist tightened on the reins as he tied his prisoner and saddlebags on the horse. He thought to himself, *Blackus will pay. He will pay for not dying with the rest. My pupil will pay. Everyone will pay for leaving me to die. They will know what real terror is, when they face my master.*

"Come in Vex," Valash waved a hand towards the door and the little imp fluttered with a finger the size of a full-grown man. Valash's interest peaked at the sight. "What do you have there my little one?" Vex sputtered out a series of squawks meows and half words until Valash waved to him to be quiet.

He stood up and paced the floor around the finger. "This cannot be Vex. No, it cannot be. Nothing leaves the *tempra* that did not enter it." He spun around and pointed with a glare at the finger on the ground. "So how it is possible, That, that boy could have done this!" Valash stuttered in fury. Spit flew from his mouth. Vex scurried to a corner to mewl quietly. "How is it that a brat, an ignorant sorcerer like him, could do what is impossible! Nothing created with in *tempra* fake time can leave!" Valash's voice echoed from the walls. He was more jealous than he was confused. "I will have him and his secrets!"

Vex mewled and cooed to calm his master. Valash still breathed heavily, but his temper cooled. "Good Vex, tell Moraphen to hurry and do not fail more than he has. Also tell him to begin the testing." He turned to the finger. "As for this, I think I will experiment. Might as well put it to good use. Come back to me after you give him the message." Vex scurried out of the chamber even quickly when he saw his master start to smile. Vex faded from sight. Imps where one of the few creatures that could do that. They made good messengers. They could transport large items but nothing living. Valash contemplated this as he eyed the finger.

$$\infty \infty \infty$$

Delex woke with a sputter and a round of coughs as Moraphen emptied a canteen of water over his head. Delex glared in return. Moraphen bent down close to Delex and took out a knife and placed it under Delex's chin. "I do not know how to kill a sorcerer but I do know how to kill a boy. Mind you, do not do any more tricks or I might deliver you a little less alive. You still know nothing of magic." Moraphen stood up and threw the knife between Delex legs. Delex skid backward from the knife. A dead rabbit flopped at his feet next to the knife. Moraphen took another out of bloody bag. "Clean it."

Delex obeyed but with ire. It took him a bit of practice. Supermarkets did not make customers skin and clean their food. Moraphen walked him through how to clean the kill. The man was harsh with his words, but he taught like a practiced at leadership. Night had fallen by the time he was finished. Moraphen had started a cooking fire.

Delex had not spoken a word to Moraphen, but he decided to take a chance. "Who is your master?"

Moraphen just finished with the first rabbit. It now cooked on a stick over the fire. "I think you know that well enough by now."

Delex redirected. "Who are you?"

Moraphen did not look up from the fire. "I was a man of great respect, but he is dead now."

"Did you know my father?" Delex asked.

Moraphen chuckled. "I knew of him, but that was a long

time ago and before my time." Moraphen finished with the other rabbit and pulled out some bread. He brought over a small pot and tore the bread into little pieces and added them into the pot. Next he added a good amount of water and spices. He looked back up at Delex "Look kid. I will not harm you as long as you follow orders. But the moment you disobey you will feel pain, memorable pain, understand?"

Delex nodded, "If you are, I mean was a good man, what changed your mind?"

Moraphen took out some green beans to cut over the pot. "I died, I told you."

"I still do not understand." Delex said confused. He still tried to figure this guy out and hopefully an escape.

Moraphen stabbed the knife into the dirt. "Look if it will shut you up I will tell you the whole story. A long time ago about 50 years, there was a war against my master. I led the army called the Spinning Moon Army. We were a mighty army, never defeated, not once in any way. I lead them with glory. We fought for all nations, for peace. We thought we could take the dark one, my master, and kill him once and for all. Our army was glorious in battle and had the army of Valash on the run. It was a trap, cleverly made by Valash himself."

Delex nodded as Moraphen spoke. Moraphen went into detail of battles and traps. As he told it, the war did not favor either side for a long time. Delex notice something odd too. As Moraphen spoke more and more, his attitude became less frosty and short. At first, he called Valash 'my master.' As he spoke he started to call him other names, like 'the dark one.' Delex took a mental note in hope he could use it later. Something Moraphen said caught his attention. "Did you say Blackus?"

Moraphen's eyes flashed with hate. "Yes I did boy. The traitor with you is Blackus, my old pupil."

Delex gave Moraphen a shrewd look. "That seems far-fetched. He would be very old or dead by now."

Moraphen glared ice. "Indeed, but him and his brother Soas

seemed to be blessed with a long life that none can figure out. Soas can do magic of sorts so that might be a reason. Blackus can not cast a spell any better than a cat could romance a dog." The fire reflected the hate in his eyes. "He is the reason I died. I lead the men into a trap yet again, but he took most of the men and betrayed me. He did not follow my order and I died in that trap with my men. We lost, soundly defeated, that day. Ever since, the army calls itself the Broken Moon Army." Moraphen took the rabbits off the sticks and begun to cut the meat and toss it into the pot.

"Blackus lived, but the bastard of evil found my body and raised me back from the dead to be his slave and assassin." Moraphen finished the meat and put the pot on the fire. Moraphen looked up at the stars. "I have no power over it. I do not care anymore. The only thing I care about is having the chance to kill Blackus for his failure."

Delex looked at Moraphen "I do not think it is failure to want to live and use good sense."

Moraphen lashed out like lightning. Before Delex could react, the knife Moraphen had in his hand flew through the fire and stabbed into Delex's right leg. The knife sliced in and skidded off the bone of his thigh. Delex stared at the knife in shock. He did not immediately feel pain, but when it came he screamed and writhed.

Moraphen stood and towered over Delex. "Never say that again. Remember you have to be alive for my master. He said nothing about being in one piece."

Delex barely heard the words. He pulled out the knife and with Moraphen's help, and a few threats, bandaged the wound. By the time they were done, the stew was ready. Delex did not want to eat, but Moraphen's glare made him down the stew. He was hungry and still felt ready to vomit. Delex figured it was the pain.

Moraphen tossed him a bedroll. "Go to sleep. While you were bawling like a little girl with no date for the barn dance, I received word from Valash. You will begin testing tomorrow.

I think the first task I will test you on how to heal." He threw a bedroll on the other side of the fire. "Mercadio does not know spells from his ass. Valash told me how to teach you and what to say. I do not do magic but it will have to do until Valash can show you himself."

Delex shuddered from the cold, or was it from the loss of blood. He slept on the bedroll and took a blanket out of his pack. It took a while to get to sleep, but exhaustion finally stepped in. Before he knew it, his eyes closed into a dreamless sleep.

Delex woke in the middle of the night to pain and fear. Moraphen was already up and had half the camp packed. A plate of cold sausages was on the ground by Delex. He quickly ate them and packed his gear up.

Moraphen threw Delex a saddle. "You'll ride, I can keep up. If you try to run or can not keep rein of the horse, I will make sure you regret it."

"What about my leg?" Delex asked while he hobbled over to the horse.

Moraphen waved him away. "You figure it out."

Delex did not argue. He was not confident in his skill, but what he lacked in skill he made up in imagination. They settled in, Delex on the horse and Moraphen on foot. Moraphen took charge of the horse. They walked the horse for the first few kilometers, a canter the next few. Then, came a trot, and finally a gallop that ate up kilometers until they slowed and repeated the process. Moraphen said they had to make good distance and this way the horse would not die or become hurt.

Delex was never taught how to heal. Moraphen only had the most basic instructions he read from a message. After a few hours of riding with the constant jolt of the saddle, he was would try anything to heal the pain. He decided to remember everything that the wizard Mercadio had said during the ride to Homgad. The wizard takes from his surroundings, whereas the sorcerer is part of his surroundings. Wizards pull from without, sorcerers pull from within. What do you do when it is yourself though? *How do you pull from within to fix your-self from outside to inside?* This became a little complication. Delex had to try something. He pictured his body as it was. He imagined the pain in his leg as a fire that would not go out. *No, that's not right.* He will never get his pain to leave if he thought of it that way. He pictured the pain as a dirty spot upon his clean skin. This was harder on horseback as his rear and legs moved all over the place.

Delex moved his hand down to the wound and imagined himself wipe off the pain as if it was dirt. Delex felt an odd tingle as the pain flared briefly but went away.

Delex heard someone scream. "What in the endless track of Void did you just do?"

Delex gave Moraphen a confused look as the horse pulled to a stop. They had traveled several kilometers, but Moraphen did not appear to have built up a sweat.

"What do you mean, I healed myself didn't I?" Delex chided.

Moraphen pulled Delex from the horse and lifted him by the shirt. He glared at him eye to eye. "That was not the sorcerer's way, who taught you that?"

Delex was confused. "I... I did it, no one taught me. I just imagined that I was wiping the pain away."

Moraphen let go of Delex. Delex fell to the ground in a heap. He looked down at Him. "Listen closely. Valash says there are only two ways to heal. A sorcerer pulls from his own body to replenish what he needs but it leaves him weak. A wizard pulls from the surroundings and places it in them. It does not leave them weak but has side effects that make him ill, so both ways can be deadly. The best way to do it, which can be only used by a sorcerer, is a little of both. Heal from the outside and inside. This way you can do it more often and with fewer side effects What you did has never been seen, nor even possible. You just made the wound become nothing as if it was never there. How do you feel? Do you feel weak, or do you feel sick?" Moraphen was nervous. He did not want blame for the boy's mistakes.

"Well, neither. I just let the magic do it. I am hungry now

though, starving actually." Moraphen's face had gone a slight lighter color. Delex did not think this man could fear anything, but the look that he gave Delex was like a deer in the headlights of a bus. Delex knew Moraphen would not understand that metaphor.

"I do not understand magic, but I can teach it to a degree. I do not know how you feed your body pure magic to do that stunt, but I do not want to see it again. You fused magic directly to the wound. You will learn the proper way of the sorcerer. I do not have time to stab you and make you do it again." Moraphen threw Delex the reins. "We have ground to cover." Moraphen gave the horse something to drink. The horse nickered and laid its ears back.

"What the hell was that?" Delex asked. He could barely keep on the horse as it begun to buck in place.

Moraphen shouldered his pack before he responded. "Your friends are in pursuit. I did not want to give the horse this, but we must." He looked to Delex. "You will next learn barriers."

"When can I learn attack spells like fireballs and stuff?" Delex's teeth rattled from his hold on the horse.

Moraphen almost chuckled, "Fireballs? Never heard of it. You will never learn combat magic." Moraphen jumped on the horse with Delex and took the reins. The horse shot forward like it was insane.

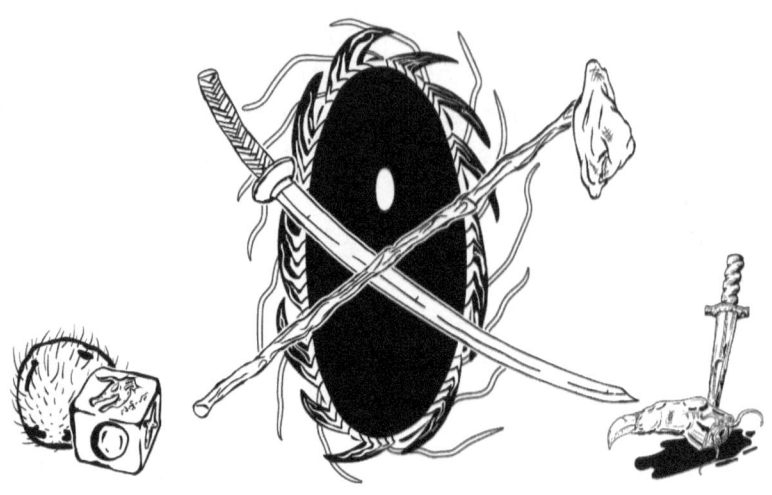

Chapter 8: Tactics

Moraphen and Delex speed over the countryside like lightning. Whatever was given to the horse made the beast feral and wicked but it also made it fast as death. Moraphen said they would not to stop until the horse did. Moraphen had to ride the horse just to keep up. When the sun crested and shown its light over the plains, they continued to ride. The horse never stopped.

Moraphen yelled over the horse. "We'll ride Moonwise until we get Avanside to place called Dreadwik. I would take the faster route Moonset, behind us, but I am in no mood to deal with the dwarven nations and their tempers. Then we head Terward to Poht were we will board a ship. You try anything stupid, I'll leave you to learn to swim."

"I know how to swim." Delex growled.

Moraphen gave him a wicked smile. "You know how to swim for hours at a time bragged by a rope?"

Delex did not say another word to him. Lately he had been rude and snappish. He probably would not throw him over board but; than again, Delex did not want to take the chance. He looked down at the hole in his pants where the knife had torn through.

His practice with barriers had started to pay off, even if it was against his will. At first, they would waiver and collapse on themselves. Sometimes Moraphen would make him do different barriers of Earth or Fire and Wind. The fire was dangerous and had to be made on rock or sand. If a fire got loose here, even the unnatural speed of the horse would not be fast enough to escape the heat.

Lately his barriers have stayed until he could not see them in the distance. He could almost swear he could still feel them and know when they were tampered with. He told this to Moraphen. Moraphen merely nodded and said that his skill was impressive. That was the only compliment he had for days. Delex tried to use some barriers to trap Moraphen one time when they stopped to relieve themselves. He smiled at Delex and took a small ornate knife out of his boot and cut through the barrier like butter. Delex's confidence popped like a bubble. Valash supplied a bag of tricks, and the knife was yet another tool Moraphen used to thwart Delex. The ancient sorcerer had thought of everything. That night, Delex looked into the night sky and thought about all the people he had met. He was amazed, but the night quickly soured and turned bitter when he rolled over and saw Moraphen. He closed his eyes to sleep with a lonely rock in his heart.

In the morning, Delex knew the horse they rode had signs of wear. Moraphen said it had been almost nine days since it took that horrible drink. It could have been weeks as far as Delex cared. His mood turned from lonely to utter misery. The horse did not look like the free spirit it had before. Now it looked like a dilapidated plow horse. Yet, it still ran at the same speed, day after day. It was like the horse burnt off its own body as fuel. Delex saw it eat every night. It never slept. The horse ate and ate and then ate some more. It was creepy. Delex could hear the 'clop-clop' of its teeth in constant rhythm as they chew and rip all night. His sleep had to contend with the constant 'rip, rip' of the grass, 'clop, clop' of the teeth and guttural noises of the throat and mouth. Then it started all over again. Each morning Moraphen would feed a little more liquid to the horse and it was off to the races.

Delex was snapped out of his thoughts when Moraphen suddenly turned directions headlong for a small village nestled closely to a huge orchard of apples. "We need a new horse this one is about to die." Moraphen gave Delex a hard look as if to challenge his word.

Delex said nothing; his face still held bruises from the last time he spoke up. *Best if I just sit and wait for an opening. I need to think of a plan of attack and look for weaknesses.* Delex had a few ideas in mind, but no opportunity presented itself. His mood turned bleak, but hope still burned quietly in the back of his mind.

He knew a few facts of Moraphen. He went through the list in his mind. Moraphen relied on artifacts and magical items for all spells. He did not have a speck of magic in him. His style of testing was mostly to boss Delex around until he got it right and quote from a list of messages Valash had supplied.

The other weakness was that Moraphen was a great fighter and could deflect most attacks, but what he could not deflect magic and natural forces. Delex remembered when he slammed the jerk into the wall inside the inn. Delex still smiled about that. What he should not have done, was blow that vase at Moraphen. He should have kept him pinned to the wall with the wind pressure or made him fly out the window. *Too bad there are no walls here,* he thought.

Moraphen had a bag of items. Delex tried to nullify Moraphen's bag of tricks but every time he tried to cast at the backpack that held them, it prevented him. The spell would slide over the surface of the backpack like rain over a duck. Valash must had made wards to protect the backpack and items. Or was it the backpack? He added that though to the list.

Delex wish he had trained with Blackus more. Right now any kind of fight he tried would end up in yet another broken leg. Delex still rubbed his leg from time to time. He earned it when he tried to nullify Moraphen's bag of goodies. Delex was weak for a whole day after he was forced to heal the sorcerer way. He still did not understand what unnerved Moraphen so much about the first way he healed. To him, it felt natural. It had been nine days since he was abducted. He came to this planet, his home, but begun to doubt his reasons. Until now, he had not had time to himself to think. What first felt like an adventure, now was an all too real prison away from everything he grew up around.

Delex came out of his thoughts at the sounds of the villagers. Moraphen had stopped about a kilometer out of town and took everything off the horse. While Delex watched the horse, its eyes rolled into its head and the horse fell over. The once noble muscles of the beast now lay under a shriveled frame of skin and bones. The horse gave on last sigh of relief and lay motionless in the noonday sun. Moraphen didn't give the horse a second glance. He shouldered the belongings. "Try anything while we are here boy, and I will slaughter every last thing that can flee." Delex gave a small shiver and quietly followed Moraphen into town.

Inside the town a few people passed by and gave them quizzical looks, but they shed away under the baleful glare of Moraphen. Delex noticed that not everyone was human. They entered the town. He saw a dwarf merchant with metal pots. He glared when anyone approached his stand. An elf was near with herbal medicines. The both talked to each other with a curious civility. Delex also saw a few races and animals he never seen before but when he wanted to stop and look, a quick slap to his head from his kidnapper changed his mind.

∞∞∞∞

Mercadio scanned the remains of the last barrier. "This is odd, yes odd. It seems Moraphen has a great many artifacts at hand." Mercadio stood up and brushes his hands free of dirt.

Soas was by his side. He eagerly awaited Mercadio's assessment, "And that means what, oh great wizard, of the obvious? I could have told you he's been cheating." Soas was back to his usual annoying self, but now with a friend in danger, he was on a whole new level. Blackus had silent since they rode from the gates. It was hard to read how he felt about the whole ordeal. He was motionless on his own private horse with his eyes on the horizon.

Mercadio glared at Soas, "You're one to talk you half-stock. What I mean is Valash must have given Moraphen artifacts to use. This last barrier did not require me to dismantle it. It was not countered. It was destroyed, sliced clean through. I believe it was a magus knife. They are rare and dangerous to use. They tend to melt in your hand. Our records showed all daggers destroyed from use."

Mercadio looked as if he was about to give a big lecture so Soas stepped in again, "lovely story old man, but we have more pressing issues, like preventing the world from being covered in Valash's stench. How does that matter?"

Mercadio glared long and hard at Soas before he answered. Either he was mad or prepared his words in certain terms for Soas. "It means when we catch up to him, we won't win. We can't catch him right now, because he used something on his horse." Mercadio pointed to some horse droppings. They were dark, small, black and hard, but they knew it was fresh. "We have been using the small amount of *Melthanna* we have left and my limited Nature lore. It is not enough."

Soas nodded, "Yeah, because he has this." Soas brought out a small black root with red veins through it. "He has fireheart root, Probably a drink."

Mercadio yelled, "You had this all along and did not tell us. We could have caught up to him already and–"

Soas yelled back, "And been soundly defeated, you said it yourself. We can not win. Besides, if I had given this to the horse it will probably die. This is a poison, its not magical but it is dangerous. It attacks the body and burns all your fat, muscle and whatever else it can get in to. Everything speeds up but it kills you. We merchants use it to help a dying friends live out one more party, or measured amounts will bring a great edge in a horse race."

"And too much will kill the competition I assume." Mercadio said with venom.

Soas shrugged and looked away. He was a real good lair so even his mockery looked real, "But Mercadio, why would someone be so cruel and evil." Soas said with wet eyes. He got serious as he crushed the root in his palm. "I suppose if you slipped it into a tea you could render someone dead after a week of no sleep and constant movement. The heart would literally eat itself to keep the body going. If you give just the right amount and you give the antidote to it as well," Soas pulled out a light blueish leaf that was so thin it blew in the breeze of Soas' breath. "Skydream leaf might counteract it before you die." He crushed that into root the but added five times as much leaf to the mixture.

Blackus nodded, "A good plan." He had already caught on to Soas' plan.

Mercadio ground his teeth at both of them. "Fine but if you kill the horses, the cost of new ones is coming out of both your coin, not mine."

The brothers nodded silently as they crafted the potion and doses. They also gave the horses and themselves the last of the *Melthanna*. Mercadio used his limited Nature magic to produce temporary trees sprouts out of the ground. The horses speed like lightning and nickered badly, but they made a speed that was so swift that any farmer they crossed fled in terror.

"We still need to think of a way to stop Moraphen once we get there." Mercadio yelled through the horrible wind. Daylow, his cat familiar, was hunkered down in his robes. He paid the cat no mind as he growled, but when Daylow started to claw at his back. Mercadio was about to throw the feline into a saddlebag when Daylow hissed and bit Mercadio's ear. "That is it, we are stopping!"

The party ground to a halt and secured the horse with three ropes each. The horses were bitter and angry but they looked healthy. Soas promised the mixture would wear off by dusk. They had made an incredible distance of travel in only a few hours. Blackus had said they had gained several days and were about a day behind.

Mercadio yanked the cat out of his rob and glared at it heatedly. "Look Daylow, I know you hate the ride but If you use me to sharpen your nails one more time I am-"

"Nova," The cat said in a delicate whisper.

Soas took a sharp breath. Even Blackus showed a moment of shock before it was swallowed away again. Mercadio looked at the cat dumbfounded like the world had suddenly exploded under his feet. "You can not be serious. Nova is more unstable than Soas and more deadly than Blackus. We get his attention we might as well send a map to our next of kin, so they can have our belongings."

Daylow looked at his master with those unblinking cat eyes as if he knew he was right. Of course, cats normally were. Mercadio groaned in defeat. Soas swore.

Blackus shook his head his in disagreement. One shake of the head told the party volumes. Soas continued to arguing. He whipped his arms around wildly. "That monster will kill us all! There is a reason the living races are afraid of that thing and I don't want to ever meet one!"

Mercadio looked at Soas with a very curious expression. "What do you mean again?" Soas didn't answer. Mercadio asked again but louder and more angry. "What do you mean again Soas?"

Soas looked away, "It was another lifetime." The way he spoke was mournful. Mercadio did not have the patient to probe further. Delex was with a madman, and seemed only a mad plan would do. *Although I have never seen Soas so far in reflection, he thought.* It disturbed him.

"Lets find your dox Nova. I will summon him tonight." Soas Growled.

Mercadio nodded and said no more. It was time to summon a powerful ally and hoped above all hope they were not all killed for their trouble. Blackus said nothing. He scanned the horizon and cleaned his clothes from dust. They rode a small distance to find a place to camp for nightfall.

∞∞∞∞

Moraphen had bought two horses for their escape. It was apparent he wanted to keep a low profile in town. The villagers informed him not to leave tonight. A new kingdom of Quatll-kaat stalked the grass plains at night as they set up a new burrow. They have not been able to higher anyone to deal with the threat. Moraphen took their advice and rented a room. He didn't want to face an enemy behind him and a highly intelligent band of lizards ahead of him. He made sure he took a room with only one exit and no windows. After they had dinner, Moraphen forced Delex back to the rented room. Moraphen gave Delex the bed and placed his own gear at the door. There was no escape tonight. He warned Delex again about the horrible bloody fate of the village if he decided to call out to anyone.

Delex nodded his understanding. This was his fight, his responsibility. He saw no reason to get villagers into his mess. He was pretty sure the villagers would feel the same. They have retired early in the evening but Moraphen wanted to talk to Delex.

Moraphen looked to Delex, "You have done well with the barriers. Valash is pleased with the information. It seems he likes what your body can do. He has given you the time to recover during our stay in this town. I fear your friends are about a week behind." Moraphen smiled smugly.

Delex nodded, saying nothing. *The dude is lying!* He felt they were much closer. For one thing his barriers did not fade as before. Someone took down the latest ones, possibly Mercadio.

It was a much shorter time. Delex pondered. *Nothing had been taken down for several hours, maybe he was right.* Delex just didn't know.

"Also," Moraphen continued, "The magic ability is like a muscle. You need to rest it so it can become stronger or testing will falter." Moraphen raised a knife at Delex. "Do not use magic in this town. I will know if you do." Moraphen glared at Delex for a little longer then curled up by the door. Tonight there was no escape from his captor.

As the candle danced upon the last dregs of the wick, Delex thought about his power. He was angry that it was locked away for so long. If he only had time to train, this kidnapping probably would never had happened. He thought about his father Jim back on Earth. He longed for home. Delex travel to a new place, a new world! This world held a wonder he had yet to explore, but back home had its own mysterious. When would he be able to return, when would it be safe? The light gave a final burst and fell dead.

In the darkness, Delex cried silent tears of longing. His body quivered with emotions unbroken for many years. In the dark night, the only relief he had been the shadows as he silently poured his heart out. He cried until sleep took him. In his dreams he was over a vast landscape of black. It was not scary, as he thought it would be. It felt familiar and safe. This didn't feel like a normal dream to him. It had been many days of travel, but he had not felt safe until now. As he stood in the darkness, sensations came to him. He could feel his body out there somewhere. He could here himself breath and feel the beat of his heart. Delex studied this odd sensation. Delex dreamed but was also awake. He was within his own mind, but it all was dark. He wanted light, and by magic, sources of light illuminate the darkness of his mindscape.

As on request, the darkness sparkled with light. As Delex focused on the lights, they silently expanded into a sky of stars. Delex pictured every light as a part of his mind, and those lights connect to his body and the world around. Everywhere he looked there were points of light. He was in a galaxy of stars. It took his breath away. He felt his body take a long breath and saw a relaxed ripple mirror across the mental starscape.

The stars burst with a momentary light. He felt a force wash over him and send goosebumps through his body. It was raw and powerful. Was it his magic? *No, from another source.* He felt another burst closer but not nearly as strong. As he focused on this, a violent shaking woke him from his dreams. His starscape shattered as his eyes opened to Moraphen. "What have you done!" He screamed.

Delex looked around confused. Outside the sounds of screams could be heard. Moraphen had everything packed and threw Delex his boots. He quickly put them on and followed Moraphen outside.

"I said no casting you whelp! Now look what happened!" Moraphen pointed to the town as he screamed. For a brief second he seemed honestly saddened. Fires burned everywhere. Townsfolk threw water on burning buildings. Others hauled the dead away in tears. It looked to Delex like several bombs had gone off in town.

"But I was asleep, I didn't cast magic!" Delex's mind huddled away from the screams of the children and the moans of the wounded.

Moraphen glared at Delex with death in his eyes, "Someone did boy, and it was not me. I set magic charges over the town that would glow if any magic took place." Moraphen grimaced, "It was a large magic force, too much for the wards. Instead of glowing, they all exploded." Another explosion emphasized his point.

"What can we do?" Delex shouted over the inferno. *Did I do this? In his dream, did I kill all these people?* "I might have done this Moraphen, I was in a dream and-."

Moraphen spun around and backhanded Delex to the ground. A few villagers slowed down to intervene, but another explosion ripped through a home. The townsfolk quickly forgot about the two and hurried to calm the fires. "It is not you fool. Whoever did this, they are still doing it! The wards are still exploding! Now get to the horses and follow me out of town or be delivered burned and scarred!"

Delex followed Moraphen to the horses. Moraphen took a small cube from the rafters and hurled it away across the street. He gave Delex a look as he tossed the small cube. Moments later, the alley exploded into flame and loose debris. Some debris hit Delex and Moraphen. A curse came from Moraphen. In his hands was the broken remains of the potion he gave the horses. "By Nature's ashen breast!" Moraphen cursed and hurled the pieces away. There would be no quick escape. Delex would have smiled if it were not for the horrific sounds from the village, burning people, and explosions.

Moraphen yanked hard on the reins. The horses reared and shot from the stables into a frightful gallop. Delex followed suit but looked back as they got out of town. Orange mist covered the town from hot steam and fire. Delex felt sorrow for the town, but he couldn't do anything about it. The night swallowed the two riders as the screams of the town faded behind them.

They had decided not to give the horses more of mixture. They needed the horses fresh and healthy. It was late in the night. The lights of the nearby town shown into the darkness. Vast fields of crops sprawled out around the sleepy town. Beyond was a grassland full of wild flowers and packs of grass-wolves. Soas called a halt. "This will be far enough, we can not get closer to the town or else they will all panic."

Mercadio gave a nod, "So how are we to summon him?" He asked with a small amount of awe. Blackus shrugged as he rummaged in his saddlebags.

It was Soas that spoke again, this time in a whisper. "We

summon him in the old ways."

Blackus spoke from behind Mercadio in a cold whisper. "We sacrifice one of our numbers and feed his blood into the spell."

Mercadio started to laugh at the absurdity. His hat tumbled off his head as someone pressed a black hood over his head and tightened it around his neck, cutting off his mirth. Mercadio gave a loud cry and tried to pry the strong hands from his face. As he held a spell on his lips, the hood came off.

He was face to face with Blackus. "Just kidding," he said with an emotionless stare.

Across the way, Soas was struck with a look of amazement. He couldn't decide if he was more surprised at the cruel joke or Blackus being so mischievous. Mercadio was a mixture of horrified and angry. His mouth opened and closed without words as he tried to work thoughts at his mercenary guardian. His hands squeezed in tight fists until the white of his knuckles were visible in the dark night.

It was Blackus that spoke again. He offered Mercadio the black hood. "This is private, you can not watch."

Mercadio glared at the brothers. Soas cleared his throat. "He is correct wizard. This is a secret you can not see. You must wear the hood, or we can not summon Nova."

Mercadio kicked his hat on the ground then picked it up. He pointed at them both. He broke out of his shock with a flood of profanities. His eyes were livid with anger. "You dox, ashen, hedgerotten, lightmind, zephwilled, soakfaced, graveleye, nullards! Blackus I never had thought you could be so cruel! You... you! And you Soas, I-" Mercadio couldn't go on.

Soas looked mildly shocked that a great wizard knew such insults. He smiled, "Amazing Mercadio, you hit all eight gods in one filthy sentence." Blackus nodded and handed Mercadio the black hood. Mercadio glared as he placed the hood over his head.

Soas nodded to Blackus and stepped a bit further away. Daylow emerged from the grass as Mercadio placed the hood on his head and watched Soas silently. Mercadio, the ever clever wizard spoke a ritual under his breath and summoned arcanic sight. Though he could not see what Soas did, he would be able to see the magic as a smear of colors like wet paint over the black background of his mind. Arcanic sight did not require the eyes to see and actually worked better when one could not. Soas, nor his brother noticed the spell.

Silently, Soas breathed in the night air. It was cool and sweet. The stars were a brilliant splash of light across the night. They twinkled like diamond sand thrown across the heavens. Soas stripped to his waist and pulled out his hair. The long silver locks floated like spider silk in the night breeze. He lifted his hands in front of him and held them parallel to the ground. The air begun to hum with energy. Soas felt the surge begin to build and gave a sigh. It had been a very long time since he has done anything like this. How many years? Decades? How many cursed lifetimes?

Mercadio watched within his arcanic sight. Everywhere around him he saw silver light with his inner sight. A vague shape of a man outlined the blackness. A sudden burst of prismatic light almost blinded Mercadio's arcanic sight. Two large silver wings blast forth around the vague shape of Soas. Mercadio cried out from the sudden light and held his head, but the arcanic sight penetrated all. Mercadio turned away and banished the sight. It was Chaos magic, pure Chaos magic! It was stronger than he had ever seen on any human, what was Soas! What was he really? *Was he an Aspect! Oh, gods! I hope not, not a Thorn! I hope that was just rumor!* This was one of the numerous reasons Soas has always been a thorn in the wizards' sides, and a curiosity that would never burn out. *Thorn aspects never live long. What was he?* Mercadio did not dare remove the hood.

Soas shown no signs of wings. The air writhed with energy. Soas' hair dance in the magic breeze. The grass begun to emit an emerald light within the blades. Small droplets of water formed in the air. The earth sifted like a nest of snakes and the air shimmered with heat. Soas' hair gave off a silver. Minute black lightning played out around him inside an ethereal fog that hovered around his feet. Soas closed his eyes and whispered silent words. Though there was no sound, his voice staggered the air. It shattered silently like slow cracks across a mirror. Soas' body lifted from the ground.

Blackus was on high alert. His swords were in his hands. He gripped them loosely as he watched for signs of trouble. His eyes could see into any darkness, his heart beat slow as a winter river. In the distance Blackus saw the town nearby erupt with fire. His arcane sight told him this was unnatural. The fire and distant explosions seem to pulse in strength as Soas' ritual gained power. Blackus made a decision. He walked over to Mercadio and yanked the hood off.

Mercadio was startled to see Blackus but his faced dropped when he saw Soas. "Amazing!" He knew Soas was a wizard or something akin to it, but he nor any other wizard knew to what extent. *Maybe he is a Thorn?* Only old records from long dead mages had spoke of men named Soas before him, yet even those records seems to be more opinion than fact. To witness this firsthand was more than he could bare. All around Soas signs of the eight magics spun about him. It crawled and writhed and flew and splashed. Mercadio could not pull his eyes away. Blackus brought him out of his revelry with a quick slap to the back of the head and pointed to the town with his sword.

"Mercadio, you are hereby sworn to secrecy. If you violate it, I will know. I will feel your words, your writings, your thoughts slip from across any distance. You will vow eternal silence to what you witness." Blackus voice rang with commanded. "Swear by it now, your right to disagree is a challenge of combat."

Mercadio looked into Blackus' eyes. "I swear by the moon." Mercadio didn't know why he swore that ancient phrase. It felt correct.

Blackus raised an eyebrow. Apparently he didn't expect the wizard to say that either. He nodded and thrust a sword towards the town. "I have need of your knowledge and no time to wait for the ritual to end." Blackus' words did not have the quiet whisper of threat. It held the strong command of the leader of the Broken Moon Army. It almost made Mercadio shiver. Mercadio nodded as his eyes ran down the length of the sword toward the town. In the distance Mercadio could see the sleepy town erupt in panic as fires burst forth like liquid fury.

"Blackus, is this what happens when Soas uses magic?"

Blackus shook his head while he sheathed his sword. "No, this does not occur but it looks linked."

Mercadio pondered the town for a while, it was still half a day's ride. None of them could make it in time. He had to figure the answer out before he could help the town. Then, like a bolt of lightning, it struck him. He turned to Blackus and grabbed at his clothes excitedly. His grip was weak on the heavy metal clothes. "Blackus, Moraphen must be there! I dare say he warded the city, but the magic Soas performs overfilled the wards. Those are arcane explosions from arcane objected called tinder-cubes. They alight or ignite when it detects magic nearby. This it is too much. They are exploding. Moraphen is there!"

Blackus nodded but remained calm as usual, "He will wait, we need Soas to finish." He eyes were stone as he looked upon the town. He knew they needed to over power Moraphen. If they charged after him now, it would only mean disaster. Mercadio ground his teeth in despair for Delex but nodded. They stayed with Soas as his body burned with power. Mercadio wept silently. He did what he could to dampen the power as it extend towards the town. He turned away. Even his morbid streak could bear no more.

Soas was oblivious to his surroundings. For him all there was in the world was the raw Chaos that flowed through his body. He needed this much to contact and summon Nova. The air sparkled with silver dust as Soas poured even more energy into to search for Nova. Finally, he felt an alien mind in his void of Chaos.

"Hark! Who hast death so imprinted on thy soul that they disturb mine to rub thy existence clear of thy world!" A voice roared.

Soas growled with anger. It was Nova all right, arrogant as always, and that stupid archaic speech. "Hey Nova. It is Soas. Nova, I-."

"Soas!" Nova interrupted, "You! King Scoundrel in mind if not flesh. I want mine book back!"

"Oh come on, I found that book fair and square." Soas retorted.

The voice grew with anger. Soas could feel it boom and reverberate in his bones. He was dealing with a strong and powerful personality. Outside, none could see the battle of wills that took place. "Foolery naive! Mine form was fast sleep upon thy tome!"

If Soas could smirk in his mind, he would have. "Would you knock it off! I have something more significant to tell you."

"Speech spewed upon thy lips air rot akin to manure and tis beholden to less worth." Nova responded. It was about to start into another tirade when Soas blurted out.

"The heir has been found! He walks among us but has been captured by Moraphen." Soas screamed in his mind. He had to get Nova to help. He would not lose Delex or the world. Soas started form a close friendship with Delex. Delex had liked Soas almost instantly. He was not afraid, like all the others of this world were. He had finally found a friend, and he would not lose him now! Some of his emotions bleed through the link. Soas was embarrassed. The last thing he wanted was Nova to know how invested he was.

There was a long silence in his mind. "Verily? Moraphen hast spirited Doran's blood from hidden coasts? We parley and more anon Soas. Mine speed, it comes for you, Soas. It comes." The chill of his words penetrated his mind. The contact closed like a slammed door. Soas thought, *Did he mean he comes, for me; or comes for me? Uh oh.* In the real world the power and all the magic faded in a moment. Soas woke to the world with a scream and fell to the ground. He quickly placed his clothes back across his chest and tied his hair back up. Mercadio and Blackus had their gaze towards town. It was fully embraced by hungry flames. By morning there would be nothing left to salvage.

Blackus turned to Soas like a wolf that cornered a wounded sheep. "We ride." He words spokes volumes as he pointed. Soas spotted two long shadows stretching out over the plains. It had to be two riders from the city. Soas knew that Delex was on one of those horses.

Like death unleashed, Blackus shot towards his horse and took the lead while his companions mounted and rode behind him. All three faces wore grim masks in the fire light.

Mercadio spoke, "Did you find Nova, will he help?"

Soas' face softened for a moment. "I hope so, for all our sake I hope so. Either way, Nova comes."

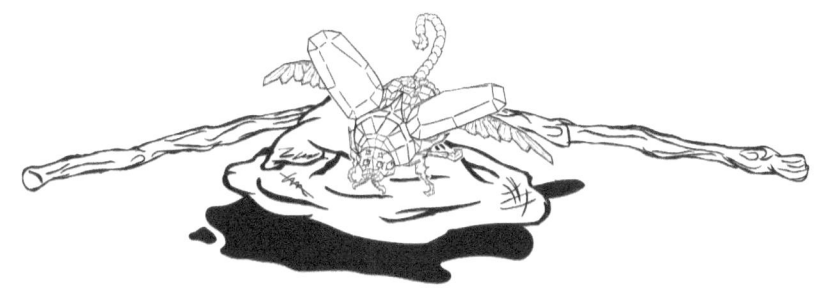

Chapter 9: Tooth, Claw and Magic

Moraphen streaked out of town with Delex in tow. He stole second a horse from the stables and planned to give both horses the speed potion. That would not happen. His gloves still dripped from the ruined potion and he had no supplies to make more. The horses would be under normal power. Whatever set off the tinder-boxes was close. He had to assume it was Delex's band of fools. He cursed under his breath and spurred his horse faster. Moraphen gripped a rope to the other horse tightly. It was dangerous at these speed, but he had no choice. The sounds of the fires quickly dwindled into a wash of mumbled screams and shouts.

Delex was close at hand. He looked back to the whelp just to make sure he was still there. He was surprisingly quiet. *This is a fool's errand ordered from a fool. I do not know how Valash, but I will find revenge for what you made me, who you made me. I will find a way to end you once and for all.* Moraphen thought to himself. He was once the leader of Spinning Moon Army, the most feared and honored protectors of the lands. He formed his army from the collaboration of all the races and kingdoms that governed land. The Spinning Moon Army had formed to help police and maintain order against any threat deemed a kingdom sized threat or higher. Their power went across borders and had jurisdiction above any king. He held that power with honor and respect.

No king was beneath his scrutiny. He was like a king when it came to justice and protection. That all changed the day over 80 years ago when they discovered Valash's armies. It was the one failure in his whole life he wished he could have changed. He tried to use a *tempra*. It didn't work. Valash, or some of his cronies, placed a *tempra-lock* during the war. That is what his army-wizards said anyways. It just didn't work unless you could break the lock. The Spinning Moon army employed only a few casters. Moraphen ground his teeth at the thought of magic, he despised it. He looked back to Delex and gave him a hard stare. *Valash, I do not know what you plan with this child-man but I hope to find a way to ruin it.*

He could kill him, the last living sorcerer on the planet. Kill and remove the taint of that magic from the world and then try to go against Valash again. Pain erupted from his head. He slowed then stopped the horses. Valash still had him under his spell. He may not ever recover or break free. What if he did? Would he die, Without revenge, without justice? So he killed and slaughtered; and lost a piece of himself with each horrific act. *Why do I even try? Not for hope. Hope deserted me a long time ago. Why do I try?*

Once again he pondered the question that has plagued him for so many years after his death. Did he die? He still bleeds. Was he brought back from the brink or did he cross over? He was so wrapped up in his own thought that he almost did not hear the gallop of horses. Sometimes at night the plains could echo sound for many kilometers. No one knew exactly how, but if you were in certain areas the sound seemed to travel and spring up from the ground. This was one of those times and places. This time the sound of horses echoed around him. Moraphen quickly scanned the plains and spotted them.

"By Ter's testicles!" Moraphen cursed. Delex looked back

and spotted the pursuit as well. He gave a stupid grin of hope. Moraphen yanked hard on the rope, and nearly spilled the young heir to the ground. He spurred the horses again and dug into his bag Valash had given him. He hoped something was in there that would help.

∞∞∞∞

"Dox! He spotted us!" Mercadio exclaimed. The fireheart root gave the horses great stamina, and the skyleaf removed most of the harmful effects, so they gained ground on Moraphen. Mercadio decided not to employ more of his magic. He had been doing it for days, but it had worn and sicken him more than he would like to admit. Mercadio wanted rest, and time to recover. He wished to reserve his remaining magical strength for whatever could happen next. Mercadio still held power, but he needed it to handle Moraphen and possibly Nova. That beast was too unpredictable to rely on for long.

"We need to do something caddy-cat!" Soas yelled above the drum of the horses.

"Caddy-cat?" Mercadio shouted back. A plan started to form in his head it shattered over Soas' obnoxious timing.

"Yeah! This is your nickname. Mercadio is Caddy, and Daylow is cat. Caddy-cat!" Soas piped up. He had recovered from the strain of his communication with Nova and was in an oddly cheerful mood. In any case he gave Mercadio a smart-mouthed smile.

Perhaps it was his friend and goal in the near distance. *Perhaps it could have been the honey-wine he downed after his talk to Nova.* Mercadio smirked. Mercadio rolled his eyes. "You wind-whipped fool! I do not have time for your childish rantings. I had something. Blast, its lost!" His shot a withering glare at Soas. He focused again to the pursuit. Moraphen had spurred his horse faster. *He was probably beating them to death. If only I could slow them, with-* Mercadio sighed. The thought was back again. It was risky, dangerously risky, but it would work, it must.

"Mercadio, what are you doing?" Daylow asked from the folds of Mercadio's cloak. The cat remained unanswered. "Mercadio do not cast that. It is forbidden magic." Daylow hissed at his master. Mercadio lined up his staff and aimed at the distant figures on horseback. "Soas, Blackus, stop Mercadio, I think he attempts a *Terrica Lance*." Daylow may have been a cat, but he was the cat of a wizard and in that relationship he has gained life and knowledge. No one knew how he spoke, he just spoke. Matter of fact, he spoke several languages. Mercadio assumed it was because of the sorcerer power Daylow was around. Daylow knew it was because he was a cat. Cats just do, cats just are.

"Mercadio, think about this! No one wizard has made that spell work! Not a one. It took a team. It has been forbidden for the knowledge as much as it for its ability to kill the caster!" Soas yelled.

Mercadio yelled at them. "Don't you think I know this! We are not catching up fast enough. He is slower but our horses suffer. Dox-in-pox! Only Chaos knows what trick he has next. We need to make him fight in our battlefield, not his! You aim this spell by sight. You look, it strikes. Only Moraphen will be hit."

"I hope so," Soas said without conviction. Blackus remained silent. No one could actually stop the wizard.

Mercadio could feel the forces of Spirit, Void, Fire and Earth powers combine. They twisted and pulled away from each other, but he added some Chaos into the mix. He could feel the inside of his body warm. If he added too much of any power, he would literally cook himself to cast this spell. He had never tried it, never in his long life. Soas was wrong, secret tower books told of wizards in the war. Some have survived, at least long enough to describe how they died. Survival was on average, four percent. Mercadio figured he had better odds. Wizards had invented this spell. Sorcerers did not use it for the spell could not work within their bodies. They knew the name of the spell like children knew nightmares. The *Terrica Lance* was the great equalizer.

Blackus handed him a fist full of the skydream leaf. Mercadio stared in confusion. "Eat it, it may help." Mercadio nodded and ate the leaf. Immediately his body felt cooled. The magical energy coiled together more smoothly, but he could feel his mind slow as well. He had to act quickly before the Skydream leaf destroyed his concentration. Mercadio pointed his staff at the lead horse. The spell cracked the air with a bar of raw light. It shimmered silver on the edge as it burned the air. Half way to the target something went wrong. The finger thin beam of energy suddenly shattered into a kaleidoscope of colored beams. The beams refracted in numerous directions. They sliced clouds and trees in half and dug furrows into the earth down to unknown depths. This spell could cut through almost any barrier, yet it had hit something solid.

"It was no barrier." Blackus said with the same line of thought. A few seconds passed when they all heard a noise above the sound of the horses. A crystalline buzz hummed in the air.

Mercadio felt a cold chill rip down his spine far colder than any skydream leaf could make. In all his ancient texts he remembered one description of noise he feared without hesitation. One noise described from with clear terrific detail in all those magical creations. Mercadio yanked hard on his horse. He forced the horse to stop so sudden, that he almost topple himself and Daylow over its head. Blackus and Soas looked back to see Mercadio turn his horse around and gallop directly away from the pursuit. The crystal buzz got stronger as it got closer.

Soas gave a shrug, "I'll get the old man."

"No. Penance is faster than your mare. I will get him and catch up, stay with Delex." Blackus shouted above the new sound. He turned his horse and raced at a full tilt toward Mercadio.

Soas sat for a moment undecided and turned his horse back

to Delex. Just as he located them again a swarm of bugs zipped past him and knocked him from his horse. "What on Ter'Avan was that?" He shouted to no one as he got up. He heard the buzz from his clothes. There, upon his leathers was a palm size beetle made of pure crystal. It looked like glass and shimmered in the near darkness like a prism. In the shadows, it was almost invisible. It wiggled and danced on the skin of his clothes in an almost comical fashion. Soas reached down to grab it, but received a shock as he touched it. The paralytic feeling traveled up his arm and to his head. He toppled over stunned and landed on the beetle. He felt it shatter under him. Soas tried to cry out in pain but his muscles would not work. He tried to cast one of the few spells that he knew but the magic just was not there. He laid prone as his horse nickered and tried to remove the reins from Soas' clenched fist.

Blackus raced towards Mercadio as the small swarm of crystal beetles caught up to him. He quickly counted nine flying objects. His sword came out and cracked eight of them out of the sky in quick succession. The last was out of his reach and zipped towards Mercadio. He did not know what they were, but he safely assumed it was from Moraphen.

Mercadio saw the last beetle and screamed in horror "Bittle-Beetle! I knew it! Oh, gods! No! No!" At that same moment the beetle caught up and crawled up his arm. Mercadio screamed and fell as he grasped for the horse. Saddlebags, packs, Daylow and wizard tumbled like thrown dice across the grass. Mercadio tumbled over and over in the grass and hoped the beetle would be crushed. He did not care if he broke bones in the process. Mercadio rolled to a stop, but still felt a sting of a bite rip through his body like a brush fire. The Bittle-Beetle had found its mark.

Blackus caught up to Mercadio as the wizard twisted and screamed on the ground. Foam and spittle leaked from his mouth and nose. Blood seeped from his eyes and ears. The Beetle burrowed halfway into the skin of his chest and continued to move deeper. Blackus did not stop to think. Thought and action, two sides of the same coin. Action. He thrust his sword into Mercadio and heard a crack of glass. He had struck the bug thing under Mercadio's skin. The bug thing dissolved into smoke and left behind a ragged bloody wound.

Mercadio felt nothing. This was far worse than when Delex ripped his spell apart. It was worse than being set on fire. It was worse than death. He could as easily compare the pain of falling into a bed verses falling down an entire mountain, twice. The measurement failed him. Bittle-Beetles were ancient war-time weapons of a singular gnome wizard. They were created as a toy for young sorcerers. Yet as gnomes do, they succeed with failure. Bittle-Beetles injure and corrupt the spell casting ability of sorcerers. He had only stumbled on them from ancient texts within the Homgad castle while Doran was alive. He knew one thing though. Wizards were back in ancient times as well. It could weaken sorcerers to near death, but it killed wizards if left unchecked. To this day 'Bittle' was still uses as a highly vulgar curse word, even if only a select few knew the origins. All this and other thoughts raced in his mind as he felt his own body tear itself apart. It attacked the mind, it made the mind use magical power unchecked and uncontrolled. Raw energies poured into him and had no release. He would continue to draw magics in until he popped, magically. It was a bug of Chaos made from Chaos and meant to bring chaos. He was going to die. Mercadio knew no remedy. He was dying. He felt the bug shattered. Mercadio had a momentary second of hope. That second lapped as the circuit of energy weakened but continued to draw magic in. *This is how I expire. This is how my book ends?* Mercadio started to feel his mind shutdown as magic broke down his mental defenses.

Blackus watched Mercadio run both hands through his wire of hair and grip it tightly. Blood formed on his mouth as he chewed his lips repeatably. He did not think the wizard was aware of his actions. Something still attack him. Black checked the wizard's body and found no other bug thing. Mercadio still held his head. *A mental adversary, Interesting.*

Blackus removed the rest of the skydream leaf from his pack. He jammed the wizards jaw open with the pommel of one of his hidden daggers and shoved leaves into the wizard's mouth. He took his water-skin and rammed it in and squeezed. Blackus wondered if it would help. He had heard tale of people that overdosed on skydream and slipped into death as the mind collapsed. Yet, this seemed like the opposite reaction. Mercadio's mind looked locked into a full gallop. If this did not work, he may have just killed the wizard and finished his contract early. *No other viable attack.* "Skill and will, Mercadio." Blackus pulled out the pommel and stood back as Mercadio swallowed.

Mercadio shuddered and went limp. Blackus kicked the corpse a few times. Blackus than checked for a pulse and breath but could not find any. The smell of urine told him that Mercadio had released his bowls. Blackus gave the body one last kick could and turned to his horse Penance. Daylow came from out of the grass and shadows and sat on the wizard's chest. He looked to Blackus and back to Mercadio. Daylow narrowed his eyes and stuck his furred out from all directions. His soft fur suddenly rattled like crystal and sparked with specks of electricity. He hissed so loudly and hatefully that Blackus spun in place and drew a sword. Mercadio gave a shuddered breath and went still once again. Blackus barely held his composure.

"Bittle-Beetle," Daylow summarized. "I think he may still live, We must take him to rest." Blackus recovered quickly. He threw Mercadio's belongings and limp body over his horse Penance and hurried back into pursuit. He caught up to Soas and helped him to his horse. Blackus almost felt bad for kicking the wizard so many times.

"Blackus what was that?" Soas coughed as he wobbled in the saddle. Blackus shrugged. Soas shook his head and got his horse into a run. They only thing that kept him in his saddle was pure determination to save his friend.

∞∞∞∞

"No!" Delex shouted, "No more!" Moraphen urged Delex to lay down some deadly barriers, but it was too much. If Moraphen could have reached back and hurt Delex he would have. He was more worried about escape.

"Do it boy! Do it or I will kill all of them!" He shouted above the horses.

"No! I will not hurt them!" Delex shouted back venomously.

Moraphen was silent as he dug into his bag. "You leave me no choice." Moraphen emptied a bag of crystal-like bugs as he rode. "I do not know what those are, but Valash told me to use them as a last resort." He gave Delex a grim look. "I hope you know what that means."

Moraphen was going to say more but a beam of intense light shot forth from over the plain from the pursuit and exploded into a rainbow of deadly rays. His eyes burned with afterimages. His horse collapsed from under him then turn above him. The horse flesh slammed into as he twisted from the saddle and knocked the air from his lungs.

Moraphen stumbled to his feet. He blinked his eyes but all he could see was a slurry of afterimages. He stumbled in a circle has he struggled to get air back into his lungs. A hand grabbed at his ankle, but he kicked out of its grasp. Air was all he thought about. He needed to breath! Sounds became muddled as his mouth opened and closed like a fish on dry land. Snot and tears washed his face. He collapsed to his knees as the afterimages washed from his sight. Delex lay prone. He had almost freed his trapped leg from under his horse. Moraphen tired to focus on him, but his sight started to become a black tunnel with Delex in the far distance.

Then, the world went black. Moraphen collapsed to the ground. His eyes reflected the distance cold starlight then started to glaze over. His chest gave one last surge but it only gurgled up flecks of blood over his mouth then fell silent.

Delex stood over Moraphen in a daze. He never seen someone die before. Sure, he saw it on the movies, but this was different. You could see the light leave from his eyes. Actors faked death on TV. This man turned from a living thing into an inanimate object. Delex felt sick to his stomach. He turned away from Moraphen and looked across the plain. Two riders could be seen in the starlight. The moon was a much smaller speck in the sky.

He wanted to wave, to be cheerful, but it was all too much. He looked for his bags. One horse was dead, and the other horse moaned on its side. Delex went back to the living horse as it moaned. The horse suffered from two shattered legs, a third leg could not be found. Only a burnt stub remained. Jagged lines crisscrossed the ground and carved into the grass, dirt and rock into untold depths. He stumbled from the weight of his bag as he pulled it free. A sudden vice-like grip latched around his leg. Delex looked in horror as the corpse of Moraphen rose and yanked Delex off his feet. Moraphen started to breath again but the dead look had not left his eyes. His eyes were bloodshot and unfocused. With supernatural speed his hands latched around Delex's throat and begin to squeeze.

Moraphen did not seem aware. A wicked magic blocked him from death but it also poisoned his mind. All he wanted was hurt everyone and anything around him. Delex tried to cast a spell, any spell to get Moraphen off him but Moraphen wrapped his head on the ground several times and shattered his concentration. He could hear yells in the distance. His friends were close but would they make it in time. He tried to grip the hands around his throat but could only get a small amount of air.

Moraphen looked up and leaped out of the way as two horses almost struck him. His eyes locked on Blackus. Blackus stood regal in the saddle and looked down at Moraphen. "Moraphen, give back the heir and I will kill you swiftly."

A feral growl ripped from Moraphen's throat as his face filled with fresh hate. "Blackus." Was all he could say. He stood up and stretched as he released the grip on Delex. Delex crumpled to the ground. A round of pops and crack sounds emerged from his chest and spine. "It has been a long time coming, but today, I will end your reign, and your life."

"Greater men have tried." Blackus said and swiftly stepped down from his horse. Penance immediately darted away from the area. Mercadio still hung from the saddle only slightly aware of his surroundings. Blackus walked away from the horses and lead the enraged Moraphen with him. Soas jumped from his horse and checked on Delex when Moraphen screamed and launched himself at Blackus.

As they clashed, Moraphen struck first. He ran to Blackus and thrust a hidden blade at Blackus' face. Blackus stepped coolly to the side but the blade still grazed his cheek. Blackus spun his blade at Moraphen's outstretched wrist. Moraphen caught the blade on the dagger as he pulled back his arm. Blackus followed swiftly. He drew his other blade in a reverse grip and thrust the handle at Moraphen's ribs.

Moraphen twisted and caught the handle with the dagger and whipped it down the length. Blackus quickly dropped the sword and pulled back his hand to save his fingers. "Still quick." Moraphen said. His body became smooth and fluid as he yanked his mind back from the edge of insanity.

Blackus did not respond. He stepped forward with a series of thrusts and slices, but Moraphen continued to counter each attack with his dagger. He still had yet to draw his own sword. Moraphen laughed as he countered each attack. Blackus remained silent.

"You should have died with us all Blackus! You should have followed orders." Moraphen stepped towards a thrust to the face of Blackus single edged sword and spun in place. He dropped to the ground and whipped his blade at Blackus' legs. Blackus stepped back, but the blade still caught on his clothes. A shower of sparks splashed out of Blackus' dark clothing but left a dull red glow along the slash. A small fire started in the grass at their feet. It illuminated their fight as Moraphen stepped back to recover. Blackus and Moraphen ignored the flames.

Moraphen had a surprised look as he circled with Blackus. "So it is true. You got your hands on spell-weave metals, and you made a dress."

Blackus gave a quick nod as he spoke. "It is called a Samurai Kimono, traditional. Crafted from diagrams found by ancient *tempra* wizards that traveled to other lands." Blackus spoke again, but with sing-song voice of emotion. "Cultured elegance, beyond your understanding, too strong for the weak."

Moraphen spit on the ground and shrugged. "No matter. You have never beat me in a single fight Blackus. We both know this." He pulled another dagger out and spread his hands wide. "We both know how this will end. Just accept defeat." He pointed a dagger at Blackus. "I am the master of shields! My defense is my offense! My defense is unbreakable." Moraphen screamed at Blackus. "What are you!"

"A samurai kimono." Blackus replied in a dangerous voice. They both heard Soas snort from the witty retort.

As Moraphen glared from the remark, Blackus kicked a small fire at Moraphen. Moraphen tried to deflect it all but pieces hit his shirt and lit it on fire. The deflected fire splashed around him and ate like hungry beasts into surrounding the grass. Moraphen screamed in hate and ripped his shirt from his body. His chest was a series of scared with a huge rend over his heart.

Blackus looked momentarily at Soas and shook his head. Soas had been on the sidelines ready to throw daggers. Delex was with Mercadio as the wizard tried to regain his footing. Moraphen took advantage of the distraction and flipped a dagger at Blackus. Blackus caught the dagger with his sword but it shattered on impact and sent wicked sharp fragments into his face. He dropped to his knees as he tried to clean off the bits and blood from his eyes. "I made that personally for you, very fragile. Shatters on impact." Moraphen laughed. He launched himself at Blackus and whipped his blade downward. Blackus spun his sleeve up to deflect the slash. He rolled backwards and sliced his sword in the air. Moraphen didn't move as the sword swept by him harmlessly. He kicked Blackus in the chest hard enough to send him to his back. Blackus still could not see. The blood had pooled into his eyes. "Time to end this and your precious Delex. Good bye old friend. Tell the gods to pucker their collective lips upon my-"

Blackus performed a mighty kick with a leg and let the momentum roll him backwards. As he kicked, he tucked in his torso and pushed off the ground and straighten his body. Moraphen jumped back from the kick in surprise. Blackus' net result was to kick at Moraphen and perform a backward flip from the ground and land on his feet facing his nemesis, with his eyes shut. As he landed, his foot stomped down on the tip of his second sword he dropped earlier. The sword tilted the handle into the air. The handle whipped upwards as Blackus knelt down in the same motion, parallel to the sword. He shot his empty arm underneath the blade like a pivot. He struck the handle with his other sword as his moved his foot off the blade. The sword rapidly whipped away from him with a buzz as it flew at Moraphen. Moraphen easily slapped the blade to the ground. The entire length rang as it slammed into the ground and bounced. At the same time Blackus rolled and thrust his other sword at Moraphen. Moraphen deflected the sword upwards but felt a stabbing pain. He reached down to grab Blackus' hand as it slid the other sword further into his side. Blackus' other sword now rested a good hand span inside Moraphen's torso. The blade had hit the ground and rebounded upward. Blackus had thrust with one sword and grabbed the handle of the other out of the air and shoved it inside Moraphen. Moraphen may had scored first blood, but Blackus had scored the first meaningful blow. All this time Blackus was still blinded by his own blood.

Moraphen staggered back in shock. Blackus got to his feet with both swords. The fire now raged around them. Soas and

Delex had moved the remaining horses and the dazed Mercadio from the fight. Blackus finally opened silver eyes as he smeared a handful of dirt over his face. An inner fire in his eyes reflected with the flames. "No defense is unbreakable." Blackus' face had lost its cold mask. Dark red dirt clogged his wounds. He opened his eyes wide with determination and righteous anger. "Valash taught that lesson once before. This time I will carve the memory into your hide, weak willed traitor to life." This only made him look colder. Moraphen felt the hairs on his arms raise.

Soas breathed in a quick breath. "Holy crapping Chaos. Blackus will kill him Delex. I have seen that look before. It was right before Blackus went through a thousand man bandit camp after they had raped and looted a small town. They killed everyone but started with the children first and forced the adults to watch." Soas looked back to Delex. "Blackus went before dawn. By dusk, he had hunted down and killed every last one." Soas turned back and looked with awe at his brother. He spoke quietly. "The bards claim they could not find any corpse in less than three pieces."

Delex swallowed. He held Mercadio's head in his lap. Mercadio looked dumbly at the sky in a stupor. It was still unclear if he would live the night. Daylow lay in his lap, his yellow cat his filled with tears.

Moraphen lost all bonds on sanity. He stepped backward off the blade and flung his dagger away and drew his sword. "Now the real battle begins." Moraphen sliced his sword savagely. The blows forced Blackus backward as he countered with a series of thrusts and jabs. Moraphen returned each attack with an additional countered as he continued to press Blackus.

Blackus continued to attacked with a grimace on his face. His swords flashed in the fire light but Moraphen caught each stroke and countered. Each counter to Blackus' attach scored yet another hit inside Blackus' defense. Each strike left lines that glowed hot upon the metal cloth across Blackus' chest and arms. If it was not for his woven spell-weave armor,

Blackus knew he would have been horribly wounded. "Just die Blackus, we all do it. It is not as bad as you think!" Moraphen screamed. He launched his sword at Blackus' face once again.

Blackus stepped back, deflected, then attack with a precision cut at Moraphen's vitals. Moraphen countered, but the attacks rang loudly across Blackus' swords. Delex thought Blackus had finally gained an advantage in the fight, but the ring in the swords increased. In fact, it was only one sword that rang louder until it was a hum. Blackus had not been able to score as single hit since he pushed the sword into Moraphen's side.

Blackus made a sudden feint with the sword in his right hand. The sword hummed from the blows punishing blows Moraphen inflicted upon it. It vibrated terribly but Blackus held it with an iron grip. Soas reassured Delex that Blackus would not drop it. A Knowledge whispered a thought from the back of Delex's mind. *Resonance.* Delex was about to cry out the warning, but it was too late.

Moraphen brought his sword down across the humming blade. Blackus' Blade snapped cleanly away from the hilt. In the same motion, Moraphen grabbed at Blackus' metal weave clothing and punched the tip of his blade through the heated clothes. The spell-weave did not break, but the heat forced the threads around the blade. Blackus stepped quickly back, but not fast enough. A pool of blood appeared at Blackus feet. The hit was not fatal but it had been a good score. Both combats labored as they circled each other again.

Blackus' hand shook from the blow. The ring of his sword and the sudden shattering had left his arm numbed to his elbow. "One more hit Blackus, this is all I need. You quiver within a shell of compromised armor with a broken sword. You are not looking too strong after all." Moraphen sneered as they circled. "This ends tonight my dear pupil. Tonight I will teach you one last lesson. The final lesson." Moraphen's eye glittered black, ringed with blood in the growing fire. The scar above his heart glowed red like an infection on his pale skin.

Blackus went to one knee as the blood continued leak from him. He had left a line of red grass and wet dirt as they circled. He hung his head down as he slowed his breathing. "I am going to kill you Blackus. Then, I will hunt down your men and do them the same service."

Blackus looked up into Moraphen's eyes. "You will not touch my men. I protect them."

"Not after tonight." Moraphen grinned. "Tonight the Master of Weapons will fail under the Master of Shields."

Blackus stood and sheathed his sword on his right side and stepped backward several more paces and rested into a ready stance. He did not take his eyes off Moraphen as he gripped the handle with his left hand. His right hand still was numb and a cold sensation was spreading through his body. "While you have been dead, I have been learning. I will show you one last attack."

Moraphen nodded to his opponent and readied his weapon across his chest. "Good bye Blackus, after this attack I will make your end swift."

Blackus stared into the face of the man he knew better and longer than any man. His teacher, his mentor, his once friend and ally. Now a burnt out shell of hate, and madness. His face became the same emotionless mask.

Soas and Delex held there breath. The plains seemed to have gone quiet. Even the flames seem to weaken and darken a little. In a blink, a mere momentary flutter no slower than a bat of a butterfly's wing, Blackus made his move. In one swift move he whipped out his sword and sheathed it all at the same time. He turned from Moraphen and said in his cold whisper. "Return to silence."

Moraphen stood dumbfounded for a second as a sudden boom ricocheted like a thunderclap across the plain. Moraphen's sword shattered outward down its length in ragged fragments into Moraphen's chest. His gloved hand on the sword tore away. His clothes and skin peeled away to expose innumerable cuts clear to the bone. Moraphen lost large patches of hair across his face and skull. A deep gash opened slowly across Moraphen's chest and arms. A cascade of blood poured out as Moraphen sunk slowly to his knees. Blackus walked slowly to Moraphen and looked down at him with cold emotionless eyes. "My Windcutter. I created after you died. You surprised me, you could block most of the attack with your blade. Unfortunate. You will now suffer much longer."

Moraphen tried to respond. His mouth worked but no words came out. He toppled with a confused and shocked expression on his face.

"Dude! So, this must be how he faced a thousand men." Soas whispered. Delex looked at Soas. Dude? H*e used the word correctly.* Before he could ponder more. Soas jabbed him in the side with his elbow. "We better go help him." Soas didn't wait for a response. He worked his way across the fires to Blackus.

Delex stayed with Mercadio. Mercadio sat upright with a cloth wrap over the wound in his chest. Daylow sat on his lap and slept contently. "Delex, I am fine now. Weak but fine. Has Blackus dispatched Moraphen?"

Delex grinned, "Yeah, it was craze-balls."

"What?" Mercadio looked at Delex confused. "Son, I do not understand Earthen phrases." He got to his feet slowly with the help of Delex. "I assume it was a spectacular display of combat and expertise."

Delex chuckled. "Yeah, that is what I said."

Delex and Mercadio smiled to each other as a large winged black mass of tentacles and claws popped from nowhere, into the middle of the combat zone. "Daaa daaaaa," It spoke it a cute little impish voice. It was Vex, the daemon imp, but now grown and mutated to the size of a two-story house. Before anyone could react it swept a single massively muscular claw into the ground that sent a wave of grass and dirt in a semicircle towards the party. The blast of debris swept away everyone and everything and flatten them to the ground. The horses screamed in terror while Delex, his friends, and most of the animals flew off their feet.

It deafened them with a roar. "DAAA DAAAAA!" Vex stooped down and picked Valash's bag of tricks from the ground. In a single crunch, it smashed contents into pieces within its horrific maw. It slowly circled in place. The dead horses and Moraphen were crushed into the ground under its clawed limbs.

"Dear gods." Mercadio whispered as he coughed and spit dirt. Most of the fires engulfed in dirt. He had a hard in the starlight, but still recognized the monstrosity as the small imp from Homgad. "What has Valash done to it? It looks like part *tempra-beast* now." He remembered the finger it has stolen. "Dear gods Valash, what have you unleashed on this world?"

Vex eyed the weary travelers with great red eyes. It grinned and purred happily as its eyes locked on Delex.

Chapter 10: Relations

Delex was too stunned to speak as the light dimmed from the dust and debris that churned into the air. Two red dots glowed with inner fire within the gloom and dust. Vex swished his stubbed tail happily as the guttural purr vibrated in Delex's bones.

You must move. Get up, and move. Holy crap snacks… DELEX MOVE! Delex blinked but did not move. The fires in the plains dimmed and went out. Only the starlight above illuminated through the clearing dust. Mercadio lifted his arms and sent black lightning into the monstrosity. The spell carved into the monster flesh, and left great rends.

Vex swung his head slowly towards Mercadio. Its great maw grinned merrily. It slowly and deliberately lifted one paw forward, then the next, and inched towards the stricken wizard. Delex looked for the others but could only spot Soas. Soas used his dagger to chip away at mounds of dirt that buried the thief. Only his head and his right arm was free. All the horses were dead or had retreated before the battle. The contents of rent saddlebags and packs lay about like fallen leaves. Delex focused his thoughts, it was no time to look at the devastation. He had to help Mercadio.

"Run boy," Mercadio whispered, "Whilst I have this beast's ire." Mercadio said as he sent a splash of black lighting into the teeth of Vex's face. The wound from Mercadio's spell begin to knit together. The monster's shattered teeth fell out as sharp new teeth pushed from the gums.

"Daaa daaaaa," It croaked in a loud childish whisper. The sides of its lips begin to tear along a line of flesh between its jaws. As it split, the grin widen and exposed even more teeth. The mouth opened wide to expose a mass of twisted tentacles with barbed hooks. It was almost too much for Delex to see. Horrible memories of his trip through a *tempra* made his heart race.

Mercadio screamed to Delex, "I am not sure but I believe that small imp creature has been infected by a *tempra-beast*." He took several steps back as Vex's clawed arm came down while it slowly advanced. "Perhaps it contains their weakness as well. Run boy, while I hold it off."

"Mercadio you can't!" Screamed Soas. "If it is still an imp, it can phase anywhere it wants." He had dug out most of his upper body and now was wiggled in place to remove his legs. "Don't you wizard types have wards you can make?"

Mercadio shot another bolt at the creature as the head swung towards Soas. "Over here you vomitous beast! Soas, stop talking! We have the skill to ward from simple imps, but I do not have the time to-" Vex moved his head back towards Mercadio and begun its slow steps as it toyed with their fear. Vex suddenly rushed forward and startled the wizard so badly, Mercadio fell backwards to the ground as a reflex. Mercadio screamed and looked up in horror to see teeth inches from his face. Just as quickly Vex scooted back to where it was and made childish giggle sounds. Mercadio scrambled to his feet and glared angrily at the beast.

Delex thought to himself. *Is it feeding on terror, it likes it? It plays like a big cat toying with a meal. What can I do?* If he moved, he was afraid he would draw its attention. The red eyes were just a dim glow now in the starlight. He noticed how bright they glowed when they gazed at him. He ran through his thoughts as something clicked. "Mercadio I trained with barriers. Are they similar to wards?"

Vex turned back to Delex. The red eyes glowed brightly. It started to pad swiftly towards Delex. "Daaa daaaaa!"

"No!" Mercadio screamed. A white light flashed brightly in front of Vex and Blinded Delex. "Be quiet boy, it wants you!" Delex stumbled to his knees. "I knew it. I blinded it, like a *tempra-beast*. Hide you fools!"

Delex blinked and scurried for a mound of dirt and grass. Vex roared in annoyance. "Only I will speak fools!" Mercadio yelled and shot a black bolt at Vex. "Imps are easy to distract. They are great tools to send messages, but are easy to over-stimulate!" Mercadio snapped a finger. Bluish flames erupted on Vex's face, but Vex appeared to be unaffected.

"This is no imp Mary!" Soas yelled and ducked behind more debris. Vex swung his head towards the sound and lifted a claw towards the noise.

"Don't you dare call me Mary so-ash!" Mercadio yelled in retort. Vex's head swung back to Mercadio and placed his claw down. "You are the one with looks like a silver fairy!"

"You bearded coat rack!" Vex's head swung again.

"You silver stump!" Vex switched again.

"Why you! Keep my size out of it you homeless fortune speaker!" Soas retorted! Vex swung his head again.

"Fortune… Bah! Baaah! Dox fool!" Mercadio barked.

"No! You are!" Soas chortled.

"You are!" Mercadio replied.

"You are!" Soas yelled back. Vex's head swung back and forth between the two as they bickered. Delex watched the display in stunned horror. He jumped as a paw touched his face.

"Be still!" Daylow's whispered voice spoke in his ear. "Mercadio had me get you. He said to make a barrier around the creature while Soas and Mercadio distracts it."

Delex looked back to the scene and nodded. He thought the

same thing but did not know how. "What type?"

"How would I know? I am a cat, I have no need of silly things like that." Daylow said and licked his paws. "Imps appear and disappear, stop that part!"

Delex rolled his eyes. *The cat could talk. That figures I guess.* He concentrated and cobbled some energies together. Without a plan or any good working knowledge, he could only try. When Moraphen trained him, he was not allowed to draw on the energies like a sorcerer would. Instead, Moraphen forced him to learn how wizards cast magic. He sighed, it left him sicken. It would have to be enough. He worried about that last time with the storm. He just did not have enough practice with his sorcery. As he concentrated, Vex roared in disapproval and swept the area with its claw again. Dirt and dust interrupted all thought as it rained down without mercy.

"Concentrate!" Daylow whispered. "Something is happening, you are doing it!" There was a shimmer of light in the air then a flash. Vex suddenly stopped all movement. Delex took this moment to dig himself out as the other Soas and Mercadio emerged from the earth.

"Where in all of Ter's backside is Blackus!" Soas yelled. Delex looked around and spotted a lump of silver hair poking from the dirt. He motioned to Soas and they both dug out Blackus. He had been hit on the head by flying rocks. A large cut bleed from his head. As Soas worked on his brother, Delex stumbled to Mercadio.

"Fine work boy." He nodded, "and you Daylow." The cat ignored the compliment and padded into the dark. Vex's eyes shown brightly as they swiveled towards Delex.

"I didn't know what to do, so I just encased him." Vex's body twitched against invisible bonds. "I have no idea how long it will last."

Mercadio shook his head, "Nor I lad. We are dealing with a new born threat, if I could only take some of his tissue-"

"Look!" Blackus growled. He had regained consciousness and stood with his sword drawn. Blackus looked worn and unsteady but his will to fight burned bright as ever. He lifted his sword point towards the darkness.

All heads turned to see a figure emerge from the darkness with an unresponsive Daylow in a loose grip. Valash snapped his fingers. A purple flame appeared above Vex. It hung in place and illuminated area in needed light. He tossed the cat at Mercadio's feet. Daylow flopped with two bounces but did not move. Small puffs of dust proved he still breathed. Mercadio lifted his head from the cat and glared murder at Valash.

Valash smiled warmly. "Did I come at a bad time?"

Nova sat on a mountain cliff that overlooked the vast plain. A singular bright orange light flickered in the distance. A sigh transitioned into a frown of displeasure. *That Soas, that little thief.* The transgression nearly forgotten so many years ago. *That rogue has the nerve to come and ask for help.* Nova looked down to the armored fist and punched the ground. The ground shuddered from the impact.

"Ashes!" The word echoed from the cliff. *What if I refuse to go?* "Tis a vexing. Mine word on it, to travel hence. Word is water, clear and true." Another deep sigh finished the sentence. *Yet, Who cares if the heir was home. Was it his home? Could he even remember having a home? The whelp has been gone for centuries.* Nova calmed down with a deep breath of cool mountain air. *At least it would be a distraction from everyday life, a solitary life. Life without words, without speaking, with only thoughts. How long has it been since I spoke to someone?*

Purple eyes looked up to the stars as they twinkled in the night sky. Minutes passed by as thoughts of loneliness passed by on gossamer threads. *When did the years stop counting?* Nova looked down at the armored hands as they tightened into fists. It was the only hands those eyes would ever see. Nova tried to picture the fingers underneath before the sealed armor. The picture would not form.

"Mayhap, mine hermitage tis grown a mighty tooth." Nova pondered. The fire in the plain intensified. Time for contemplation was in short supply. The choice had to be soon. *I am not beholden to Soas, or the crazy wizard and his cat, or even the rumor of the heir. I like Blackus.* Of all of them Blackus was easiest to talk to. "Most like, for he doth speak the least." Nova said with a smile. It had been over fifteen years since the last conversation.

Nova sighed. "Alas. Tis a riddle to rattle thought and form. I see, doth the path break from thought to word then action?" Nova asked the night sky. "Dox! Soas! Nothing but speck and dust to me, yet still a troubled weight betwixt my shoulders. I swear Chaos himself would steer body and soul clear of thee." He looked back to hands encased in armor. "But heir true, in form and less than thought. Mayhap, he shares of mind, tears that rust across mine armor?" Nova's chest suddenly hurt and tightened. *Was it loneliness? Was it need?* "A true heir." Nova whispered to armored hands. "Benign of heart?" The tightness faded, and filled with the rush of blood.

A surge of excited quickened with each heartbeat. "An heir! Ere anon, in mine sight!" It was all too much. "Tis this excitement? By gods, tis a feeling far lost, thus found and clear touched! Touched, as face to sun!" Nova stretched, popped joints, and flexed muscles under weighty armor. "By the by, I whilst reclaim tome and Soas under thumb; both in turn!" Nova coiled muscle and tendons and rushed towards the ledge. With a might jump the entire armored form catapulted outwards to career over the ledge towards the scree and boulders. Dirt and rock scattered into the air as nearby trees swayed from Nova's surge. No animals were nearby to be swept away from the sudden wind and pulse of energy. None were stupid enough to stay in the area Nova used for solitude.

The air whistled around Nova's armor as the ground rushed up like a greedy lover. Nova felt none of it. The armor held special magic to protect any within it. It could give you a full tactile response to the touch of a feather, or shelter from the deepest cold and hottest fires. Nova's heartbeat drown all of this out. Blood pulsed and strained against skin and armor. "I ride. I come, you dox fools!" Nova screamed into the night. The ground would not have Nova today.

∞∞∞

Valash crossed the stone floors to his viewing room. The cool damp air was thick with the pungent smell of mildew and mushrooms. Sickly green and purple light reflected off the slick stone floors. He closed the door behind him and approached a large floor to ceiling mirror set into the stone wall. He gestured to the mirror. The silver surface slowly churned. Valash waited as he concentrated on the mirror. He extended his influence into it. The silver surface begin to glow and light the room. As the light expanded, it spewed out like a gas to reflect on the surfaces of the chamber. Silver-blue images appeared around Valash as the mirror emitted magic. The images cleared, became more defined and solid, yet still ethereal and ghostly.

The silver-blue scene placed him near where Vex called. He was in tall grass near the scene of horrendous damage. Vex, now mutated into something akin to a *tempra-beast*, was befuddled by the comedic act of two buffoons while Delex lay exposed, but safe. Vex suddenly stopped its attacks. Valash glared. He had come at the perfect moment. As the company of fools mooed like cattle to one and another, Valash approached. The wizard's cat came towards him. No doubt it had felt his magical presence and would warn the others. He moved quickly and quietly. His hand struck like a viper, to size the image of the cat a vice grip. The image was solid to his touch. He could feel the texture of the fur, the muscle squirm, the claws dig without purchase.

Before the cat could cry out, he brought the elbow of his

other arm against the ghostly image. The cat image went limp in his hand. He slammed it into the ground several more times and approached the clear once more. The imaginary scenery of light moved behind him and melded into the wall to become a projected image. The images in front of him, near the wall of the mirror, emerged from the wall and became three-dimensional. Valash did not move forward in the room. The light scenery shifted underneath him and kept his feet buoyant above the stone floor.

The hired mercenary pointed towards him. The ghostly people turned there heads in his direction. He tossed the image of the cat towards the group.

Valash snapped his fingers sending his magic into the mirror and to the destination of the group. A purple hue filtered through the ghost images. "Did I come at a bad time?" Valash chirped and smiled. The ghostly image of Blackus pushed away from the rest and grabbed his sword. Valash motioned for the sword and it spun into the night. "Ah not this time. No surprises please." He laughed and made his way delicately over the ruined terrain. "Oh! It seems Vex enjoyed himself, yes?" Vex tried to respond but could only turn its eyes in his direction.

Blast and fire. Who did this? Valash felt a sudden moment on insecurity as he studied the weave of elements that made the spell that held his pet. He smiled cheerfully and laughed. "I see you caught him in a pitiful spell. Let's keep him inside that for a time while I talk, yes?" Valash frantically and quietly went through a series of counter-spells to find a key spell that could shatter the protective barrier.

"I see the night has brought out the worst kind of animals." Mercadio's image cursed at him. The sounds echoed slightly as if it was across a great distance.

Valash stepped forward as the images backed away fearfully. He kicked at the cat image. "Perhaps one less, yes?"

Mercadio's images lunged towards him but was quickly stopped by Soas and Delex. Valash still had not found a good counter-spell to break the barrier. He looked at each face to discern who could have crafted it. If he was there he could have read the signature, but through the mirror, it was impossible. He tried to discover the location of the group, but he could only home into the bag he had given Moraphen and Vex's mental awareness. They could be many numerous places.

"It seems I struck a nerve yes? Oh, do not worry Mercadio, familiars or made of stronger stuff. I am sure he will survive, if the wizard still lives the night." He grinned as the silent threat sunk in.

Soas went back to stand by Blackus. The brothers spoke in whispers to each other, no doubt to plan an attack that would shatter the magic of his spell. He had taken more precautions this time. A strong magical barrier now protected his image and would take several attempts to break. It would give him enough time to curb any feeble attack. The mirror diminished any magic across the contact, even his, but he kept up a strong smile. He still groped to find a key spell that could break the barrier around Vex. He decided to throw everything at it all at once. The barrier did not flinch, but he noticed fissures in the magic weave from the inside. Vex would break free on its side if given enough time.

Impossible! They must have their hands on ancient knowledge, Mercadio, it was him no doubt. Perhaps an artifact from the World Greed War made that barrier? He decided to keep the fools distracted until Vex could break free. He had run out of choices. Vex could be ordered directly and have Valash's commands obeyed without distractions. Every silent spell he had still could do nothing to break the barrier. *Each time I think I found a spell it shifts. This barrier feels like it is actively fighting against me!* This scared him above all else. Valash kept up a smiling facade as he launched all his counter spells. *This is only working because the barrier suffers our attacks from both sides,* Valash thought. It made him want to shudder.

Mercadio noticed Valash's gaze and turned to the monster.

"You created this didn't you?" He pointed with anger at Vex. "Even you should have known to never tamper with Nature like this Valash! You have created a beast like nothing ever witnessed on this planet or any other world."

Valash shrugged. The wizard had not noticed. He smiled. "Not my problem, yes." All the fools glared. "I love praise on my work, but I come on business."

"No!" Mercadio yelled. He stepped forward. He pointed and jabbed his finger forward. "You could have doomed us all. You tamper, and tamper and in doing so you whilst dame even yourself!"

Valash sent a bolt of energy into the wizard and picked him up of his feet. He fell backwards where he stood and coughed and cringed from the pain.

"It seems you are still in pain. Still hurting from the Bittle-Beetles, yes?" Delex stepped forward and Valash held up a warning hand. "Easy now young one. Us men are talking."

"You monster." Delex growled.

Valash held a finger to his chin. "Yes, I suppose." He crossed closer the Delex. Delex circled around him and eyed him down. *Hmm, no fear in him. He must have a strong will.* Valash gave himself a small smile. Blackus and Soas was nowhere in sight. Mercadio had sat up and was slowly placed his cat into the folds of his rob. "But sometimes it is the monster that is needed to fix things, and not the weak sheep of the world."

"What would you know about fixing the world?" Delex flexed his arms as he paced. "You call killing and pain fixing the world? I have known people like you in my world and it never worked out well for them."

Aha! He is trying to distract me. Let's play along. "In your world Delex? This is your world. You think your time in that barbaric magic barren world means anything here? This is where you were born. This is where your blood calls. I knew your mother and father, I can tell-"

"Do not speak of them!" Delex roared. The silver-blue images wavered for a moment from the power of the young man's cry. "I warn you Valash, I will rip you apart if you speak of them again!"

Valash shrugged and cross his arms behind him as he rocked childishly side to side. He mocked Delex, but, behind him, his hands clutched each other in a tight grip. Was it from anger, excitement, fear? A thought started to churn half formed in his mind. He batted it away but hung like a spider in the shadows of his mind. "You can threaten all you like, but I hear as much the same as the mewling cries of a baby in the crib." Valash grinned as Delex glared.

Sudden movement came from two sides as Blackus and Soas shot from concealment, both with a dagger in each hand. Valash did not have time to react before the ghostly images stabbed into his form. Even though the ghost forms were solid to him, they could not cause any damage or pain. The ghost images recoiled from the spell he had prepared earlier. A flash of light and a small pop exploded around him and sent both brothers backwards in pain and confusion. "Someone prepared, yes?"

Delex shot a blast of black lightning from his hand. It was weak and ill formed. It died almost immediately as it formed, but it gave Valash a chill through his body that did not leave. Valash's face twisted into a bowl of hate. He did not like the taste of fear and this little ash of a boy had grown too strong and too fast for his own good. Black lightning was a highly advanced spell and even though it failed, it made him worry what the boy could do if he had more training and time. He reached out his hand sent his own bolt at the child. It struck him in the chest and put Delex to his knees.

"You seem to try my patience. YES!" He shot another bolt and Delex cried out in pain and went to both knees. He looked to all the ghost images around him. "You all try my patience!" He made a sweep around him with both hands and send thick twisted bolts of black to the others. Each person collapsed to the ground as he continued the assault. The black bolts shot from his body towards the walls of the stone room. The ghost images swallowed the bolts up and then reeled in pain. He released Delex's ghost image and stood over him. Delex breathed heavily and looked up to him with a dazed look.

"I honestly struggle with you Delex. I keep wondering should I let you live, or kill you. Live or kill you." He mimed a tilt motion back and forth with his hands. "I find you could be useful to enslave, to mold into a powerful sorcerer." Valash reached down to the image and cupped Delex's chin is his hand and lifted him from the ground. He sent Void energy into the ghost form and felt it shudder. "I wanted your body for myself, but I figure I can manage with just the fundamentals."

Delex moaned but could not respond more. Valash stood up and held his hands above the form. Real red droplets of blood started to drip upwards from Delex and pool into a ball floating in the middle of Valash's hands. Delex screamed and begin a series of painful moans. Valash stepped away from Delex, but Delex remained suspended barely above the ground.

"I can make do with your blood." The moans intensified. The others tried to get up to help but the black cords of energy tied them to the ground with pain. "Have you heard of Geotelology?" Valash purred. "Few have. Mind, it is a lost art of the sorcerers. We could send objects across vast distances, much like an imp. Or pull them close." Valash paced around Delex as he drew more blood. It was a slow process, but he had time. It was fun to tease and belittle his prey.

"Only the greatest of sorcerers could send themselves much like an imp to-"

"Teleportation." Delex coughed. Valash looked down in undisguised anger. "Teleportation. Earth, Star-Trek. Charles Fort first coined the phrase in 1931, but it dated back as far as 1878." Valash concentration wavered for a moment to stare in befuddlement at Delex. The complex mix of spells stuttered to a halt as Delex talked through the pain. "Telegraphed-transportation is a more precise term, teleport for short." Delex looked up at Valash in defiance. "Teleport. Much easier to say and sounds less stupid than Geotelology." Snickers and laughter erupted around him as Soas, and Mercadio defied him with their mocking noises. Blackus image remained quiet. His eyes never left Valash.

"Sounds like he got the best of your monologue. Let us listen to Valash trying to sound superior and educated." Soas mocked. "Tell me Val-ash, Can you geotelograph? Why are you not here? Perhaps it is as hard to cast as it is to say." Snickers erupted from Delex. Valash breathed in his budding rage.

"Tis the donkey the brays loudest when it has the least to say." Mercadio chortled. A small gasp came from Valash. His eyes opened wide. It seemed as if all noise ripped from the stone walls and fled the room. His blood thumped loudly in his ear. All eyes looked to Mercadio.

"Heehaw," Blackus brayed quietly. Soas gasped and looked to his brother as if he looked at a stranger. "My apologies," Blackus whispered in his silken voice, "I wished to mock the jester as well."

Rolls of laughter broke out from the ghost images. Valash's aged face somehow drained of less color as he rapidly blinked, then quickly reddened. A numb cold went through his body. He gestured at Delex. Delex slammed to the ground. The laughter changed to angry curses. He heard none of it. The laughter still echoed in his mind. His hands started to shake noticeably as he extended them back over Delex. He released a torrent of energy into the boy.

The Delex scream overpowered any other yells as Valash forced Delex's blood to squeeze from every pore of his body. The ball of blood hovered over the boy's head as it quickly gain in size. Delex's face twisted in pain. He whole body started to lose the red tint. His hands and face turned noticeable shades of white and blue. Delex crumpled to the ground. Valash looked to the others. "Hither now, is this not a jest, yes?"

Valash extended a hand towards the ground of his chamber. A stone urn and pedestal rose from the stone of the floor. The blood ball floated into the urn and continued to pour from

Delex. "In a matter of minutes you will be dead. Your friends can spend the rest of the time in relative peace watching the last heir die before them." He looked to the stricken faces of the ghost images. "I only wish I could be there to listen to the lamentations and the gnashing of your teeth as you bury the husk that I leave! YES!"

Valash stopped picking at the barrier that held Vex. He had not forgotten about Vex or the ancient spelled barrier. *Blast and fire that Mercadio!* It was weak enough now that Vex should break out by itself. Valash refocused his attention to the cup. Valash grinned. The blood slowly formed. It appeared as an image. In small flash it became red as he summoned it across the distance. He was lucky to have the bag he gave Moraphen as a temporal anchor. Without the anchor, Valash would have need to know the exact location first.

The blood slowly drain into the cup. As he prepared the next remarks to mock and torture them, a brilliant burst of energy lite up the stone room. A beam of energy erupted from the sky and bathed him with a solid blast. The energy should not have damaged him, yet the brilliant strike picked him up off his feet and slammed him into the far wall. The light in the room flashed and went out. Smoke and char was heavy in the air. Falling ash covered everything. Valash's body lay upon the floor, burnt and broken. It took Valash an uncomfortable amount of minutes to regenerate and bleed the residue of the attack from his body.

When he recovered enough to stand, he looked around the room. The mirror did not shatter. It was utterly destroyed. Only the black and cracked frame of stone and blacken hole remained. Valash looked around the rest of the room. Long black cracks ran through every surface and rendered the chamber further ruined. They extended outward from scorched hole of the mirror frame. He questioned what could destroy his chamber through a shadowed spell, but a more urgent thought obliterated all concern. He quickly approached the urn filled with Delex's blood. "No! No, no, no, no, no!" He screamed. The urn was a black mess of crusted over remains. Valash continued to dig his fingers in the urn and made a triumphant sigh as his finger pulled out slick with a red drip of blood.

"Not much, oh not much, but I will work with this. I will take much longer." Valash grimaced. He pondered what could have struck past his spell and through the barrier of the mirror. *Too many questions. Too many to care.* His rage forgotten, he pondered his next steps. He would have to use all his power, all his resources to hurry this blood spell. Delex would have to wait. He had what he needed, and he was a sorcerer. Valash lived beyond the touch of time. He could let his minions dispose of the trash.

The light overpowered all senses. A roar followed like hundreds of thunderclaps that vibrated against the heavens. Delex tried to cover his eyes from the light but even with eyes pinched shut, and his hands over his face, the light remained. The light snapped off. The world seemed quieter than it should. Delex cautiously lowered his hands and peered out. The world swarmed with ash like a plague of flies. Delex stood and tried to breath, but the ash and blood loss doubled him over in a bout of coughs.

He could hear people call out but the sounds were far away and vibrated with echos and distortion. Delex felt a pain all over, but especially in his chest. Delex recovered just enough to see Vex's face. He could have reached out and touched the monster. He felt the last bits of his barrier shatter. The monster breathed out over him and grinned.

"Daaa daaaaa," It purred. As Vex spoke each word, it bit off tendrils that fell and squirmed on the ground. Vex's body seemed to distend as it looked deeply into Delex's horrified face. It raised a paw to swipe at Delex.

A growl emitted from the smoke and ash. An armored claw reached out and gripped Vex about the neck. Vex twisted his head to peer into the dark. A gust of wind blasted around them as a pair of wings beat away the smoke and ash. The creature emerged covered from head to tail in armored scales. They glisten and shimmered shades of blue and silver against what little star light emerged. Its eyes shown with a white light and the mouth opened to sharp black teeth. Luminous steam rose from its mouth it trails of silver. A great muscled body with legs and a tail came into view.

Delex heart pounded. There was only description; it was a dragon. A real-life dragon was there. This scaled monster was twice the size of Vex. Small spikes adorned the face in elegant rows. Around the eyes was a bone ridge much like a crocodile. The spine had a series of scales that protruded outward almost like spikes. The tail ended in three long spikes that moved and clicked like scissors. A dragon, there was no doubt; Delex was face to face with a dragon.

Vex growled as it placed its paws on the ground. Its body begin to ripple and split. The dragon looked down at Delex and spoke in a surprisingly gentle deep voice. "Heir, I gladden to see thee. Tis an honor to be held." Its gripped tightened on Vex but it squirmed and shifted its form in the hold. The Dragon peered into the dark ash. "Soas! Thy spineless milkmaid! Get thy dusty backside out and upon mine sight!"

Soas emerged from behind a pile of dirt and walked up to Delex. He sighed and sat on the ground with his legs pulled up to him. He motioned to Delex and the dragon.

"Delex, meet Nova. Nova, Delex." Delex took a step back as Vex's body writhed and ripped open like rotten fruit. Long tendrils squirmed out of the rends in its flesh. "Tell me Nova, you still talk to yourself? I find it adorable, but others may think you do not get enough air while flying. I just can't stop thinking about if-"

Nova roared in anger, "Tis not thy time, mouse of man!" It looked down at Vex, "what in all thy realms tis this mockery of life?" He turned back to Soas. "And where is mine tome Soas?" Dragon voice roared with terror and venom. "Where is mine book!"

"Not the time Nova!" He pointed to Vex as the lumps of flesh slipped from Nova's grasp.

The pile of flesh pulled together to become a mass of tendrils, hooks, teeth and slime.

Mercadio and Blackus stepped close to Soas and both fell to the ground. "Dust and breath, it is a *tempra-beast* fulling formed, loose upon the real world." Mercadio spoke in a horrified whisper. Delex shivered as he tried to make sense of what he saw.

If Delex's terror peeked before, he would have lost his mind as he looked into the nightmare of flesh and terrible noises. Its hooked tendrils oriented on Delex and spoke from hidden mouths. "Daaa daaaaa."

Chapter 11: Churned Earth

The *tempra-beast* screamed in rage as it yelled again. Delex couldn't move. So much had happened. His body quivered with exhaustion. He looked to his friends for help, but they looked just as bad. He had been through endless days on a horse. Mercadio had survived death from the Bittle-Beetle. Blackus staggered from his fight with Moraphen. Vex trashed everyone and everything around him. Valash took his blood for some messed up reason. *Did I mention all the riding?* He thought. Delex took one long shuddered breath. *I am so tired, so very tired.* He tried to muster the magic within, to pull anything he could, but it felt as if he clutched at sand. The magic continued to slip from his grasp.

He looked up to see once again the horror of mouths, tentacles, hooks, eyes, and tendons. Behind the nightmarish monster was a pair of enormous eyes that glowed white-hot in the smoke. It was Nova the dragon. It looked down to Delex and gave a slow nod and returned a glare to the monster. Delex's heart soared for just a moment. His body was ready to collapse, but his mind still wanted to believe there was hope.

The monster became aware of Nova and whipped its massive body around. Nova stepped back gracefully and whipped a claw down the front of the monster. Tendons and limbs sliced through easily but the monster did not seem phased by the attack. The cut limbs immediately begun to regrow. Several claws and hooks shot out from the monster too quick to dodge. The hooks and claws bounced harmlessly of the dragon's skin. Nova roared a challenge and slammed into the creature. Both gigantic beasts rolled past Delex and the others into the night. Novas body begin to glow with a slight, silver light. Lines of light appears from under the plated dragon scales. The claws shimmered with blue smoke as it reared and clawed at the combatant. Yet no matter how many pieces where torn from the *tempra-beast*, it still ragged on as it slammed itself into the dragon.

The beast pulled back from the dragon. Many mouths worked in unison as it spoke. The words tumbled like rocks from too many voices. "Give it to us, we want it, we must feed from it."

Delex and the others had formed up in a group around him. They shuffled back to the small amount of cover they could find. Soas whispered in horror. "Dear gods, the beast is getting smarter." He looked to Mercadio. "Can they do that?"

Mercadio looked at the thing with open-mouth awe. "I do not know. None have ever come close to explaining the *tempra-kin*." He shook his head and visibly shivered. "My nightmares could not dream of such as this, and my knowledge even less."

The *tempra-beast* had now grown to the size of the dragon and seemed to be much quicker on its limbs. Nova looked surprised. Nova spoke in a dusky roar. "It speaks. It thinks." It raised a claw that glowed with energy. "Hark? Does it cry?" Nova launched itself in a fury at the creature. The creature roared back and intercepted the charge with a hail of slices and bites. It screamed in pain as the dragon's magic tore anew into the thing. The limbs still exploded from the dragon's clawed but it took more effort to rend them. Every limb fell away grew back stronger and the flesh harder. Nova hissed in angered.

The creature roared again. "Give us the child. We must feed on the magic." It grabbed at Nova's wing and hauled hard. There was a rending noise as the skin between the flight bones torn open. Nova screamed in a rage that made Delex's teeth vibrate.

"Fascinating!" Mercadio exclaimed. "This is the first look into the reasoning of these beasts. To think that they try to feed upon magic. Well I guess it stands to reason that if one can summon a *tempra* that one would-"

"Mercadio! Not the time you rattle-hat!" Soas pointed to the dragon. "Look at the dragon! It hurt Nova, it actually hurt a dragon!"

The group looked to the dragon. The once beautiful blue and silver skin of the wing was now a tattered mess. Brilliant silver blood dripped and glowed upon the ground. Everywhere it dripped, the ground writhed with multicolored fire. The blood ate at the ground and burned everything it touched. Nova's eyes shimmered with red. The dragon looked enraged. Mercadio gasped. "Oh Soas, that is not good. A dragon's blood is pure magic. Do not let any of it touch you, it will burn until gone, and nothing will be able to smother the flame. Curiously the very blood that-"

"By all the Gods toes and teeth! Mercadio, shut up the lecture! What can we do to help Nova?" Soas yelled again.

Mercadio quietly looked at each face and sighed. He held his chest in pain. "We can't. Well, I. I cannot save us."

Blackus silently placed a hand upon the wizard's shoulder. Mercadio looked at the silent protector and gave the briefest of smiles. The party looked back to the dragon and the twisted beast and prayed to any gods out there that this nightmare would finally end.

Nova was a completely new creature. The dragon slashed, bit and clawed with renewed fury. The monster reeled from the attacks. They both twisted and turned and spun around each other as they seek an advantage. Slowly the *tempra-beast* lost ground, but the dragon looked in bad shape. The dragon had fresh new scratches that dripped the poisonous blood to the ground. Despite the fury of wounds, both combatants had not slowed in the fight. They both appeared to attack with quicker more desperate moves. The beast still screamed to feed upon Delex, but Nova ignored the cries. The dragon focused upon its attacks to rip the beast to shreds. Each calculated strike hit with a force that vibrated through the ground. The dragon timed each feint and dodge to reduce damage to itself and deal maximum punishment.

As Nova and the beast fought, dragon blood peppered the ground like scattered raindrops. Everywhere it touched the ground burned. The dragon remained the better combatant. The beast slowed as it lost mass. Shreds of *tempra-beast* in tatters around the combatants. Most of the pieces lay inert, but Delex noticed several of tendrils wiggle like worms towards and on the dragon.

"Nova! Look out! Those pieces are all over you!" Delex screamed.

"Tis not moment's tarry for conversation!" The dragon growled out between attacks.

"Give me the boy, I crave it. I want the power. I want your power!" the *tempra-beast* cried out. Tentacles shot out and latched to the dragon. Nova roared in defiance and clawed and bit at the beast.

The pieces of the tentacle monster suddenly tighten and constricted Nova. Deices of the monster covered the dragon from head to tail. Nova struggled against the monster and blew forth dragon-fire. The pure white blast of energy shimmered with rainbow light as it easily cut a swath into the monster. Nova bathed itself in dragon-fire. The fire had no effect on the dragon. In seconds, it was free.

Delex and the others scrambled even further away from the fight. The dragon-fire produced an intensive heat. Clouds of black and white smoked mixed into a caustic fog. The *tempra-*

beast smoldered in bits of muscle and sinew. What was left quickly formed back together. Nova took a deep breath for one final blast of dragon-fire, but a deep crack sounded from the dragon's chest. A large breast plate of dragon scale shattered and broken away. Several pieces of the *tempra-beast* body poured from out of the wound and burst into flame. Dragon blood oozed out of the exposed wound in an intense radiant light. Nova roared in pain and clutched at the wound.

Nova looked down to check the wound and momentarily forgot all about the fight. The dragon tried to put the chest plate back together, but it clattered like a broken vase and fell away. Nova had a look of intense concern with an edge of panic. "Dear gods, no, no, and no again!"

It only took that one second lapse in defense for the beast to strike. The *tempra-beast* shrunk in on itself and lunged at the dragon. The body twisted into a spear and stabbed like with razor speed into the wound. Nova's breath caught as it reeled in shock. The dragon shook out of the daze and clutched at the monster as the thing dug deeper into the wound.

Delex didn't understand what just happened. The attack did not look like a wound, but an icy cold crawled up his spine. Nova screamed. Nova screamed like Delex had never heard a creature scream. It was feral, intense, lonely and angry. It was full of fear and nightmares. The scream sent goosebumps down Delex's arms and up his neck and face. He felt the power behind that scream slam into him and slap him to the ground. The scream blasted through friends and each in turn collapsed towards the ground. Mercadio went unconscious immediately. Daylow flopped out from his hood into the ground. Delex didn't see when the cat had been picked up, but his heart gladden for a brief a moment.

Soas gritted his teeth as he tried to stay on his feet, but he and Blackus were soon overwhelmed by the dragon roar. Soas slowly tipped to the side and went limp. Blackus went to his knees and remained that way as he went unconscious. Only Delex seemed to be able to stand the roar's mighty percussion. Nova trashed and clawed at the ground as it tried to angle its formidable claws into the wound and retrieve the parasite from the chest wound. The *tempra-beast's* tender flesh burnt way as the blood touched its body, but it became harder and more dense as it pulled in on itself. It dodged the claws and begun to withstand the fire. Delex watched in muted horror as the last of the monster slipped inside the wound. Nova went limp with exhaustion. The dragon blood continued to pour from beneath the scales. It burnt a pool of blood into the ground. Everything it touched burned with white-hot fire. The blood chewed away at the ground as the fire burned deeper into the earth.

Nova turned to Delex and pleaded with him, "Dear heir, save mine form. Tis crawling inside, upon mine, inside mine. Tearing within, chewing, feeling, tis trying to open fatal wounds." Nova winched in horrible pain. "To succeed means the end, a doom to all thy friends. Mine scales protect less without, verily, from trifle harms." Nova winced in pain. "Nay, Tis armor to trap and contain power imbued within mine blood, bone and flesh. Mine immense magics of mine core self radiate presence that mine armor protects from eruption most violent."

"I don't know if I- wait, eruption most violent? Explode, you mean explode!" Delex stammered. Nova gave a small painful nod. Delex hands flew to his head. "I never, I am, I don't know how. I am new to all of this." Delex gestured with his hands. "I am just a boy. I don't know how to DEFUSE A DRAGON!" Delex screamed as panic seized him.

Nova's great eyes dimmed. The pale blue light faded from its orbs to reveal a muted purple eye that glowed a human iris, not a reptile. "Thy self tis much more than eyes hath seen in thousands of years. Reach within mine breast and wish away this abomination that so makes home within. I may heal anon, if thy deed-" Nova cried out in pain. "If thy deed is fast complete." Delex looked at his hands and back to the dragon. "You are kin to mine race, mine flames will not harm thee." Nova winched as the great body shuddered. Delex felt the danger leap up his back like raw lightning. "Hurry. Trust. If thee tarry, mine form will explode in radiant magics, and all perish upon them. Quicken! Now before it passes all the deeper in mine flesh." Nova rolled to the side and clawed open the wound. Blood drained in a steady pour from the ragged wound.

Delex took a step back from the heat. "Nova it's hot." He looked to his hands and back to the dragon. "Are you sure? It is burning the ground. No, its literally melting the ground." Delex breathed heavily as he thought of what he must undertake. *Radiant explosions!? Wonderful! Dragons are flying nuclear reactors? What the what man!?* He looked once more to his friends by they were all still unconscious.

Nova stayed calm and smiled to the would-be-heir. "I trust in thee, this life of mine, last dragon that walks upon these lands. I trust in thee this heart of mine, last of the ancients akin of blood. I trust in thee Delex, because thy eyes tell me so." Nova closed its mighty eyes and went still. It lifted the claw with the wound once more. A silver tear ran down the face but still held a smile. It was a smile of trust.

Something inside Delex sung to him like a mighty blow of a drum. Goosebumps flushed down his whole body. *I trust in thee Delex, because thy eyes tell me so.* Something deep within repeated those words like an echo in his mind. A coil of power rose from his chest. The drum of power pounded deeper with each heartbeat. Time seemed to slow, each pound of the drum poke to him. The magic was there, it pleaded for Delex's trust. Delex calmed his nerves with a breath and approached the dragon. With each step Delex took a step towards Nova, the heat intensified. The heat from the blood and fire seemed to double with each step, but Delex did not burn. A silver shimmer energy begun surrounded him. It poured through him and washed away the heat as it cleared his mind. His fears and concerns evaporated like smoke on the wind. In the corner of mind, he sensed his friends. The had roused from the dragon roar. They sat or stood in silence. Mercadio held Daylow in his arms. The cat was awake, bruised and indignant, but safe. Soas and Blackus held each other upright. None spoke as Delex made his way across the uneven ground.

Nova panted shallow breaths as the great dragon eyes tracked Delex progress. It winched and moaned but dared not move. The blood continued to pour but had slowed to a trickle. Nova closed those great eyes as Delex neared and touched a claw to steady himself. A sigh rippled through the dragon. Delex's resolved intensified. This mighty dragon held true trust that Delex knew how to save them.

"Look at him Mercadio," Soas whispered. "He will do it! I would eat my own hat to know what he was thinking." Soas spoke and went silent. The pain of talking was too much to bare. Mercadio did not respond. He was witness to something new, something never seen. Yet deep down he too wondered what went through Delex's mind. He would surely cook up his dearly loved hat to know those brave thoughts.

Holy crap a dragon, a freakin' dragon talking like bad poetry! Shakespeare would stab out his own ears! What the crap am I going to do! Holy crap, holy crap, holy triple crap. Waiter, another holy with a side of crap, hold the salt! What am I doing! Magic surgery? Bomb disposal? I am going to do magic bomb surgery disposal? I can't even stuff a turkey correctly. Tolkien never prepared me for this. Delex thought as he took his final position. His face remained a mask of calm as his left hand touched the dragon's skin. He heard music well up within him. It was an orchestra of crystal. It poured out of him and into Nova.

"I hear music," Nova sighed. "It is-" Nova could not speak. Silver tears poured freely from both eyes. "-words fail, words fail."

Delex was lost to the music. His other hand reached beneath the scale. The gush of blood stopped as his hand went inside the wound. Even with the shimmer of magic around him, the heat from the wound begun to hurt. He gritted his teeth and pushed his hand deeper. He closed his eyes from the light and let his touch guide him. Delex could feel a wrongness in the meat of the dragon. His hand pushed towards the source. He could hear the dragon scream, but it was far away. A scream echoed from down upon the tops of mountains yet it felt weak and without power behind it. He refocused on the slippery taint. It touched his skin and the magic recoiled from it, but he pushed more. His forearm fully inside the dragon. Something grazed his fingers. It was hard and sharp. He could feel it wiggle and burrow. He grabbed at it. It reacted to his touch and wrapped itself around his hand. It spoke with a singular voice.

I have you now. I will eat your magic, and then feast on the dragon. Your friends will be consumed as a snack. I will prey upon this world from the beginning to the end of time. Delex heard the voice intruded into his thought. The dragon's thoughts leaked into his mind. He saw a world covered in black. No, not covered, it was the creature. A world of one creature, a hateful creature with many eyes that looked into the sky full of stars, the meat of the universe, and became hungry.

Delex and the dragon growled with anger. His magic responded and wrapped around the creature. It suddenly understood the trap it was in. It wiggled and writhed and clawed and chewed as it tried to escape the grasp. Delex gripped it tight as it forced his arm deeper inside the dragon. Something powerful was nearby. It beat over and over as it kept the dragon alive. *Dragon heart, dragon heart! First mine, then you! I will become We. I will feed on you all!* The *tempra-beast*, now like a living dagger clawed towards it. Delex roared with anger and held it back. The creature tried to scream at Delex and send insanity into his mind. Delex was too enraged to listen. He sent a mental slap to the beast shut it up. His magic surged and the *tempra-beast* burst from existence.

Nova shuddered for a moment and went limp. The crystalline like music faded away. Delex panicked for a moment and focused on the dragon. It was about to die, he could feel it. He could feel the magic within the dragon start to boil over. In the last moments, the *tempra-beast* scored into the dragon and pierced past its flesh. He could fill a scratch on the heart. The magic pushed from some other dimension to surge against cut.

Instinctively, Delex felt what happened. *Oh crap, Nova is about to go critical? Like a nuke! Funny its name is Nova, cause it's going to- Focus dude! No time for this!* Delex thought to himself. Somewhere, a world away, his friends cowered from the intensity. He knew he had to do something or everyone would die.

Delex reached deeper into the wound past the flesh and touched the core of the dragon, the magic within the magnificent beast. He could feel the heart of the dragon send vibrations into his hand. The heart was not the true core, but a gateway. It was the force that kept the flow of intense magic from binding in one spot. The music returned and intensified with his touch. He strained against the intensity. The magic felt like it wanted to burn into him, to make him part of it. It was an odd feeling. He could feel his heart start to beat to the beat of the dragon. His breath started to breath shallow and quickly. Nova moaned. Nova did not wake from any of this. The dragon was on the verge of death, *then explosion,* he thought. Delex resisted the urge to sleep as the dragon slept. He realized this was the true challenge. He had to overpower the foreign magic and heal the dragon, but he did not know how.

As he struggled to breath, he felt his body get weaker. His legs lost the struggle. Delex leaned on the dragon only because his arm hung him there. He would soon fall and his hand would slip from the dragon. He concentrated on his lungs. As he deliberately broke from the rhythm of the dragon, his lungs became his to command. A rush of strength came back to him as his lungs filled with air. His confidence returned. He concentrated on his heart and broke it from the beat of the dragon. In his mind he grasped the foreign magic of the dragon. Delex became the temporary owner of dragon magic. He tried to heal the dragon the special way he would heal himself but realized he could not. He could not just wipe away the wound. His hand would remain inside the dragon. If he did, his wrist would be trapped, sealed within. He slapped the mental image away before it formed. *Gross!* He tried to focus on his left hand that remained on the outside but the dragon immediately shuddered in pain.

No, that isn't it. Dang it. Delex's thought shuddered in frustration. He tired to think of a way when Nova's words came back to him. *You are kin to my race... of the ancient race akin of blood.* Delex understood now the cryptic words of Nova. He pulled on the dragon core and brought it towards him. As he did, he healed the core as a sorcerer would heal himself by drawing magic from within to repair in another spot. This time he would draw on his own reserves, and not the dragon. *Great! I am doing magic transplant surgery, defusing a bomb, and jump-starting a dragon like a car battery!* He pushed the magics inside. His senses failed him. All he could feel was the core of magic, of Nova, as he shaped it in the image that formed in his mind. His thoughts shaped the dragon whole and healthy, but the image would not stick. Nova's magic fought the image like a cornered cat. Time was running out. Nova's magic started to cascade in power, there was no more time. Instinct took over. His magic took over. As he concentrated on keeping Nova's magical self from explosion, an image slapped into place. He didn't have a chance to reflect on it before his world filled with silver light.

Eons passed, time took but a second, time never existed. The silver light cleared away over a million years and a blink of an eye. Delex felt himself on his back. The air felt cool and absent of terrible fires. The sun would soon crest the plains and the ray begun to cut beautiful orange and gold across the storm clouds. Delex opened his eyes with a soft warmth across his chest. A woman lay in his embrace. He left hand was on the small of her back and his right lay pinned under him upon her breast.

She woke and looked into his eyes. Vibrant purple almond shaped eyes looked back to Delex. Her hair was black as a night sky and shimmered blue in the light. Her skin shone bronze in the new day sun. She was shapely and tone. He felt her moved smoothly over him as she sat up. Delex's hands slipped away from her as he blushed. She was completely nude.

The rain broke. A small trickle of rain from a scattered cloud sprinkled down on them. The dragon disappeared completely. Only shreds of dragon skin and scales lay about Delex and the naked woman. All the fires were out with only a wisp of smoke. The broken ground lay turned and rolled, tilled by angry gods. They saw rocks and roots scattered everywhere. Large boulders that had never seen the light of day in billions of years, rest churned and tossed about like forgotten toys. Delex friends stood in a circle around him, but he noticed none of them.

His eyes locked upon the beautiful woman sat spread legged upon his hips. Her skin was flawless and hairless except for the long black trails of straight hair that grew from her head to her hips. He blushed deeper. She noticed his eyes and looked at her self and gasped. She moved her hands over her skin as if she was as amazed as he. Her hands ran to all parts of her body, and Delex's eyes numbly flowed every motion. She laughed as the rain dripped down on her in small rivulets that set off a wave of wet goose bumps and aroused her body. She looked into the sky and spread her hands wide, unconcerned for those eyes around her.

Meanwhile, Delex lay in mute shock and without a clue on how to proceed. He tried to roll her off him but this only brought back her intense purples eyed gaze. She squeezed her legs and bent over towards him. Her hands went to each side of his head. She looked into his eyes as she slowly lowered her face to his. He was about to apologize when the kiss took his breath away.

This was not an ordinary kiss; it filled them both with magic. Delex felt it roll through him. The crystalline music played quietly in the background. A heat rose from him as both bodies became completely aware of each other. The kiss seemed to last for eons. His lungs ached for air but his lips refused to part with her.

He tried to reach for her but as he did, the kiss slipped away. Her purple eyes had filled with tears. Her sad, joyful look poured into his soul, "I Thank thee, dear heir." She whispered in a rich sultry smoke that sent goose bumps down his back. Just as quick, she toppled over unconscious with a small smile framed upon her face. Delex scrambled to his feet and looked down at the naked young woman. All eyes lay on her. Even Daylow looked at her with intense curiosity. The cat sat near her and lightly pawed her hair. No one said a word. They looked at each other in confusion.

"Wait, are you telling me Nova was a girl sorcerer?" Soas said with a slow whistle. All eyes looked to him in confusion. He looked back questioningly. "What? You didn't know? Dragons were once sorcerers. It is in the book after all."

Mercadio looked to the thief in wonder. "The book of dragons? You mean? Her? They?" The wizard stammered. His hair matted to his head in ugly patches of dirt and mud and his skin was pale like moonlight. He looked like death warmed in room temperature tears. He mustered up a grimace of rage. "That book is in an ancient language that none can read. Stop playing the jester with this nonsense and-" Mercadio brandished a clod of dirt like a weapon.

Blackus laid a hand on Mercadio's shoulder. "Not now." Blackus spun the wizard around suddenly, this produced an immediate outrage from the wizard. Blackus stripped the cloak off the wizard's robes and laid it over the girl.

Mercadio smoothed his robes. "Well, yes. We should look after her. Besides, we do not know if this is Nova or if some other magic moved her here."

"Delex called it a teleport." Soas chirped. The wizard rolled his eyes. Soas turned to Delex. "Hey lover boy, Shouldn't we get away from here and make camp?"

Delex looked to Soas. "Why are you asking me?"

Blackus looked into his eyes. "You lead." He had recovered his sword and scabbard and ran he fingers over that damage to his spell-weave armor. He looked like a mop that lost a fight, but somehow still seemed regal. Delex looked to Mercadio. Mercadio gave a small nod.

Soas smiled. "Yep, you are going to have to face it. You are a sorcerer and despite all the trouble, you saved our hides back there." Soas picked a dagger from out of the dirt. "You showed courage."

Delex waved his hands. "Courage! I was so scared I could feel my anus climbing into my neck."

"A curious remark." Blackus said. He walked to Delex and jabbed him in the chest. "You are leading. Go lead."

Mercadio leaned over to the young man and whispered as Delex rubbed his chest. "Dear boy, oh I mean dear young man, we were all scared." He looked at Blackus as the mercenary leader kicked at the dirt in search of supplies. "Well, any normal person. What makes you the leader was your ability to look past fear, and make a change, to take actions we required." He nodded to the girl. "And I dare say performed a scale of magic I have only heard your father speak of in their own legends."

"So, you think that she is really Nova?" Delex asked in wonder. "I just felt something. I am not sure what I did. I let my magic take over."

Mercadio shrugged. "I doubt it can be anyone else, but we should wait until she rests more before we ask her." Mercadio walked Delex over to the girl. He lifted the cloak slightly. Delex immediately turned away. "No Delex, you need to look at this."

"I saw it all Mercadio, I know what a woman looks like." Delex answered the wizard a little annoyed. The images of her, the taste of her lips, they were not yet memories, they were still fresh in his mind. His heartbeat had not settled from the experience.

"Not that son, just look. I noticed as Blackus lay my cloak upon her." Delex sighed and turned back. Mercadio lifted the cloak to reveal her collar bone and upper breast. Upon her left breast was a raw wound barely healed enough to remain closed. A soft silver glow emitted from beneath the smooth wound tissue.

"Wow, I did not see that." Delex reached toward the wound to touch it.

Mercadio quickly slapped the young mans fingers away. "Now son, a little modesty will do." Mercadio patted Delex's shoulder as the young man stammered an apology. "I dare say your attention focused upon other," Mercadio emitted a soft cough, "Biology."

Blackus came over and nodded to Mercadio. He looked to Delex. "Soas has gone to find transport." Delex nodded. Blackus nodded back and walked across the broken battle field for open grass. Mercadio and Delex followed behind.

Delex sighed and walked toward Blackus, "Blackus." Blackus turned without a word and looked with his deadly stare at the young man. Delex swallowed. "We should go about a mile and make camp. We need to tend to our wounds and assets what provisions we could recover."

Blackus stared at Delex without moving a muscle. His eyes locked on Delex with his common stare of death and fearlessness. Delex was about to change his mind when Blackus gave a brief smile. "A good plan." He turned back and started to search the patchwork ground. "Tell me when we reach a whatever a mile is."

Mercadio came over to Delex with a tired smile. "It is okay. Even though he seems like, or is, a murderous killing monster, he has a good heart." Mercadio slung a half ripped bag over his shoulder. "He just has a hard time following orders unless you have paid him a small fortune."

Delex growled. "Well, it was his idea." Delex found a saddle bag that seemed in good repair with various items in it. He walked with the wizard. Daylow that cat, now without a cloak to hide in, padded softly at the wizard's side. He found a small bag of water and dragged it through the mud until the wizard picked him and the bag up.

"That does not mean he must like it. I usually refer to his

direction, but for some reason he insists you take the lead." Mercadio shook his head. "I am not sure what he is up to, but that little to change his attitude." Mercadio reached into the ground and slowly pulled. The ground shifted and flowed towards his hand. He lifted his hand from the ground as an unwieldy dirt staff came with it. He gave one quick tap and the staff became light wood. "You know the saying, You can't teach a rock to roll uphill."

"Actually, I have never heard that before." Delex replied.

"Ah yes. Well, I have never heard the word 'Wha-ah-ow' Before."

"It is wow," Delex shook his head. "It means with wonder or something like that. I'm not an English major."

"They have armies for languages?" Mercadio said with a small shock.

Delex's eyebrows knitted together, "What!?"

"A major in the English army. I know of the ranks of most of the countries Earth world has, but I did not know of armies for language." He looked to Delex, "your old world is a backwards place."

Delex was about to correct him when he thought otherwise. It seemed the only person that understood his Earth speech was Soas, and that made no sense. Delex rolled his eyes. "Just drop it Mercadio."

Mercadio looked to the water bag he held and let it fall to the ground. It hit the ground with at his feet with a squish.

"No dude!" Delex sighed. He handed Mercadio back the water. "Come on, just catch up with Blackus." Blackus had left the scorched earth with a few more items and was once again walked for open grass. He made a series of whistles and a great black steed charged up to him. It was the only horse that survived the attack, Penance, his personal mount.

Mercadio nodded and shook his head. "Curiously backwards," he said to himself. "While we are speaking, what is a mile?"

Delex put his hand over his face and pinched at his eyes. It was barely morning, but he knew this was going to be a long day.

Chapter 12: Parting Introductions

J im sat at his kitchen table with his eyes locked on the golden cube. It was small and could fit in the palm of his hand. All sides were a smooth gold except on the top. A single black circle covered the golden side. Mercadio had used his unimaginable powers to erase Delex from all paper, electronics and other forms of recordings. Each recording had touched lives and those lives had found memories gone, or altered. It was Jim's job to weed out the few places that had not been connected or where the memories were deeper rooted or missed by the magic. He had to travel from place to place, mostly nearby, guided by the golden cube. Colored lights had scattered the surface and around the edges. As he neared a source of light it would travel to the center of the black circle and become brighter. Jim thought it worked like magical radar. When he found the target person or writing he would simply place his finger upon the dot and reality would shift.

Jim knew fairly little about physics and the laws of the universe, but he knew this was by the far most perplex and disturbed thing he had to see over and over. Each press of the button made his body shake and brought tears to his eyes. It was like he slowly killed his son one memory at a time. He witnessed every moment as it faded from existence. Jim believed in god and firmly believed his actions in life were not against Him or Her. He believed that if god had made science, he had surly had made magic. Yet each touch of the black little button tested his faith as he saw the light of knowledge fade from faces, and watch his son's name fade or get replaced by another and pour into his mind. He didn't truly change reality, that was beyond the wizard's ability. Jim was a stout man of god. Yet, he knew magic too. He knew this could erase knowledge or replace it, and it would stitch together reasonable alternatives.

He didn't want to see his son get replaced or removed. Yet, this was what was required to keep this world safe from harm. If evil from the other planet came here with the power of magic, who knows how it would upset the balance or what wars would come of it. Mercadio said wizards used this device when they visited Earth long ago, or was it when they will visit in the future? Each visit could disrupt the order, history and even religions of entire cultures. This device helped prevent those ripples. Jim shook his head. *Those time tunnels make for tricky business.*

Jim reflected on a past conversation he had with the wizard, since magic no longer block his memory. He was given the device many years ago, and taught how to use it. It could either lock a memory, or remove it. Today, Jim destroyed them all. Only a wizard could unlock those memories. Jim chuckled to himself as he remembered the old man tell him the true history of Merlin. *Who would have thought...* Jim shook his head again. Mercadio was so full of emotion. Merlana, '*tempra* traveling trouble maker,' or that is what Mercadio called him. *Or, did Mercadio say 'her'?* Jim thought.

"I will forget that too." Jim frowned, as grabbed the cube and spun it a few times on the table. "I am stalling."

It did not take too long to remove Delex from each source, but each touch of the button was a test of resolve. Jim sat at his kitchen table with his hands drawing warmth from a cup of hot tea. He eyed the silent companion across from him, the cube. The cube offered no support for his pain, but placed no demands upon him either. Its golden surface did not judge him, it did not coax him, nor share even a cold comfort. Yet it spoke to him with a single white speck that glowed in the black circle. It blinked in a slow rhythm. It blinked at Jim. He moved to the side and the light moved in the circle. Jim leaned away from the table, and the white speck moved in the same tiny proportion. The world held no memory of his son. Jim held lifetimes of wonder and memories in his heart.

Jim stood and walked over to the kitchen counter. He rummaged through a drawer until he found the sturdy plain candle he kept for an emergency. He carried the golden cube and candle to the fireplace. Jim lit the candle with a long matchstick he kept in a case on the mantle. He felt a kinship to the candle. One candle to light his way when it all went dark. The thought tore at his heart.

He wished he could cry, but it escaped him. Jim captured each memory, stole it away. He saw each one at it was plucked from existence. *Crafty wizards,* he mused. He knew first hand, Delex grew into a fine young man. His influence on the world was a blessing. Jim, stole each one, to protect the world, to protect them all, to protect his son.

Jim looked to the cube in his hand. A single touch of the black dot, and it would be over. Yet, as his stood in his parlor he could not come to terms with his emotions. He placed the golden cube upon the mantle of his fireplace and watched it blink. The rhythmic tick-tock of his spring driven grandfather clock bore a silent witness to Jim's turmoil. Without a word Jim walked into the kitchen and held to his cherished thoughts of his son.

Jim placed the burning candle in the kitchen window. "I am the last burning light."

∞∞∞

Selkroth, Ruler of the elves that live in his forest, sat upon his wooden throne in the sky chamber. The once glorious golden beauty that shimmered in the wood and light now was muted in deep blues and purples. The woods echoed his heart. He had lost two children in a matter of days, one to the villainous Moraphen and the other to an overdose of the elven drink *Melthanna*. Spiders crawled upon the wood of the chambers and turned the light into webbed shadows. He looked at them a knew he should use some minor magic to drive them away, but his heart found no purchase.

It was close to midnight and the light of the moon glowed in the sky chamber. Yet, tonight a thick fog had crept into the woods. It was an unnatural fog. Selkroth had wished this time would not come, that his daughter would be buried and at rest, but this was the wishes of a father, not the knowledge of a ruler. He knew this fog, he knew the time was at hand.

The other elves had hurried to their houses in the trees at the first sign of fog. They had heard of what happen to Mossa and Foran. They did not want any part of what was to happen next. The wail was the first sounds that had emitted from the forest for the last few hours. It screeched and raged in the darkness. Elves huddled deeper into there homes as they touched and whispered for protection within the trees. An invisible specter swept past them all.

Selkroth had gladly let it into his home. He wanted to see his daughter one last time. The wood of the proud center of his elven glen remained dulled to the fear. There was no magic here, just spiders and moonlight. Though she was silent as death, he felt her approach, like a shiver that rose from the toes to the neck. He turned his head toward the door just as the shade of Mossa entered the sky chamber. Her feet touched the wood as soft as the moonlight that settled in the room.

Everywhere she touched the wood resonated with power. It began to sparkle with stars of light, but they glimmered with distant cold and shed no comfort. The power of the sky chamber shudder to her demand. The silken strings of unkempt webs scattered the moonlight into every corner of the room. Selkroth looked upon the image of his daughter.

Mossa was always one of the most beautiful elven women of his village, but the magical moonlight that played in the sky chamber made his breath stand in his lungs. She was without mark, blemish or injury. Mossa's image shimmered of pale blues and s. Her once green tints were nothing but a memory. Yet, she still was one of the most beautiful creatures Selkroth has ever seen. He wished his wife, her mother, was still part of this world. Selkroth wished she could see the woman she had grown to be, even now. The ruined image held a perfect frown that gave no warmth, and a black emptiness that lived where her eyes should have been. *Yes, ruined and incomplete,* he thought.

Tears freely fell from his eyes, and he took a step toward her. He had to hold her one last time, to comfort her in her misery. The shade of Mossa stepped back and brought up hand to warn him from his touch. She could not talk, for any words that formed would be turned into terrible screams and moans. Her soul was at peace for the moment, but this was a small reprieve. She had come here for a purpose that only Selkroth could offer. Rumors often said, the dead had infinite patience for they had infinite time from the worries and wants that still bound them to a world of life. This was not the case for a *Sask'a'roht.* They burned with revenge, with desire, and the longer they lay without fulfillment, the stronger they grew. That rage drew more upon the world of life.

Selkroth did not speak, for it was dangerous to speak to the dead. It connected you to their world, and gave them power to draw upon you. She gave her father a nod, and he returned the gesture. It was time for ritual. What could have been said, could have been wished for his daughter held no weight in the world of the dead.

Selkroth stepped back and held his hand high. By his silent will the top of the sky chamber opened. Vine pulled leaves and webs back of the chamber to fill the middle with soft moonlight. She had come to him to draw power for her desire of revenge. What energy that would have taken years to gather she could have in a single night. She could draw upon the moon and forest in a ritual only Selkroth could perform. Most *Sask'a'roht* did not perform this ritual. Mossa, had knowledge that most elves did not. Mossa and Foran were trained in knowledge past down from generations of elves.

Selkroth stepped to the back of the shaft of moonlight to give room for Mossa. His desire for revenge echoed hers, and muted his inner misery. Selkroth's hands clenched to his sides out of anger and fear. Mossa silently entered the moonlight. Selkroth quickly closed his eyes and shuddered. Where once Mossa stood in shadowed light, she had her beauty and had it amplified. As she entered the direct light, her features turned ruined and torn. Here image started to reflect the damage that killed her. The great rend of flesh, that cut up her naval to her throat and exposed her inner workings. Black smears of blood coated her body in a patchwork of remembered pain. Light played through the wound. Her body lay in the ground. The image reflected the rot the image shared now. Black veins and rotten meat crossed her flesh, while whole pieces of her appeared to been chewed away by animals. Foran had not found her before the scavengers.

Mossa tilted her head back and whispered invisible words into the moonlight. Selkroth begun to chant with her. The moonlight flowed into him and out again towards Mossa. Mossa stretched and lifted off the ground. Her head tilted back as her body begin to glow. It took almost all the energy Mossa had to form and travel to her father, it was a risk that could have set her back decades. The risk had paid off. Her father, still struck low with grief, would grant her the blessings of the sky chamber and sustain her form.

Forbidden magic does not exist to the elves. If you had the power to use a craft, you could, but with guidance and understanding. In years past this has caused trouble, but the elvers have always taken responsibility. Through the study of magic, caution has been introduced. They have adopted the philosophy that through acts of wisdom and caution, an elf can prove themselves safe for dangerous knowledge. If an elf seeks knowledge of the power they have but to ask. They are never told no. Yet, the unwise are never openly directed or enlighten to greater works. As Selkroth once said, '*you do not spend time teaching a fish to shoot a bow. Yet, if the fish asks to learn, you give them a bow to understand they cannot shoot it.*'

Selkroth was one of the few elves that knew all the magics. He had studied them and keep the records safe. He craved the knowledge and felt a duty. Yet, as he filled his dead daughter with the energy that would allow her to walk among the living and kill anything and anyone that tried to prevent her revenge, he felt a pain of guilt in his heart. Did he do the right thing? What horrible consequences would be his to bear.

The clouds shifted and the moonlight faded away. Selkroth opened his eyes and looked at Mossa. Mossa was once again an otherworldly beauty that glowed with eternal moonlight. He mustered the courage to speak to her. "By ancient right of sun and moon, of sky and dirt by life and death." Selkroth swallowed and took a step back. He could feel her magic bleed towards him. His heart almost faltered. "I grant the blessing of our race, of our ancestors. Seek those that have harmed us and bring the justice that you deem. Carry now, carry and may your journey end in peace."

Mossa knelt to her father. She had a look of longing as she looked up to him. She bowed her head and faded from view. A rush of cold wind blew suddenly from the corners of the room. The wind scattered the cobwebs out windows and cut through the fog. The fog rushed from the village towards the plains.

Selkroth fell to the floor exhausted. A rim of frost covered his hands and feet. Blood ran freely down his eyes and nose. To be so close to a creature of revenge had its own perils, and to speak to it made it worse. Yet, it was worth the injury. His daughter now had enough magic and energy to travel and hunt down Moraphen. He knew he was still alive, because Mossa left to seek revenge. She would fade once Moraphen met the revenge she desired. He only hoped his daughter will be satisfied.

Selkroth left the sky chamber and ventured into the woods where the elves buried there dead. He was not surprised to see his daughter's grave blown open. Dirt and grass made an outward bloom on the ground, like it could not stomach her touch as it spewed her forth. He wished to find some remains, but it was futile. Mossa had feed off her own remains to gain the more power.

He walked away from the graves and went to the last place he desired. He went into his own personal gardens. The gardens were full of flowers, fruits and vegetables. Dried meats of animals smoked in a nearby hut. The night played dark purples and blues over the night. It was a rare night of beauty, but he saw none of it. His stomach rolled as he approached the newly planted tree.

His son, Foran was planted in his garden. He had swallowed too much *Melthanna* and suffered the results. Now his son has fully formed into wood, bark and leaves. He rested his hand on the tree and stood with eyes towards the canopy. Foran did not resemble any of the bright man he once was, except his face. Bark and wood etched deep groove on his face in his silent rest. Selkroth had used magic to set his face. Selkroth sunk to the ground and rested his back upon the tree. He lay with his face in the stars until sleep mercifully took him.

Hours later Wilor came for Selkroth. The young elf friend of Foran woke his beloved ruler and lead him back into his home. He too had lost so much, and like Selkroth, words could not be spoken of the loss. Wilor stepped back into the forest trees. The branches of the trees seem to reach out and touch him as he went by. The forest felt sympathy for the elves. Yet the elves could not hear them. They were still children after all.

∞∞∞∞

Another quiet knock came from the door. The elderly men behind the desk looked up momentarily and went back to his work. A few minutes later the knock came again. The knock came and went for over an hour. He was too busy to worry about that now. The cranky old man was curious if it was the same person or if they took turns. He scoffed. Students, it had to be students. They come to ask for favors, or curry them, plead for mercy or ask revenge of a teacher. Hundreds of reasons. He has heard them all. To be Headstaff, you here them all.

Maltort was almost finished with the intricate scroll when a series of laborious pounds slammed into the door. He startled his ink pen through the thick parchment and spilled ink over the document. Maltort Manycolor was his full name. His wizard order gave him the Honorname 'Manycolor.' It was the wizard version of the *royalic.* He sighed and brushed the parchment into the trash. He was way too old and tired to be angry. Maltort would need to start his six-hour infusion later. He motioned to the door with a flick. A metallic churn came from with int the wood.

Narsis the green pushed open the door in a huff and motioned the student behind him to leave. The student bowed and quickly scuttled back down the corridor. "I sent a runner ahead to get your attention. I make it here to see you still waffled about with things." He motioned to the desk covered in papers and books. Narsis usual flow of speech and calm ways failed him as he blustered with annoyance.

Maltort sat up higher in his desk, "It has been only a few hours Narsis, this could have waited for lunch?" Maltort noticed large travel stains and cuts all over Narsis. His curiosity peaked.

Narsis plodded up to the desk and rapped Maltort over the head with a knuckle. "It has been three days brother." He dropped into a cushioned chair on the other side of the desk. His face looked red, and it was not from travel.

Maltort rubbed his head for a second. Though Maltort was Headstaff of the Tower of Practice, and Narsis was but a Ledger-seeker, Maltort was the younger brother and still after all these many years the roles never faded. He was one hundred and fifty-three years, Narsis ten years older, yet he was the one who looked ancient. "Well that would explain the smell. I should go bathe. We can speak of this after." Maltort stood and gathered his robes.

Narsis growled. "Sit down Malty. We have problems. I did not fly here as a bird, to see you bath. I even used a *tempra*! A *tempra* Malty. You know how bad I am with them!" Maltort sat down with a curious look. "Valash is on the rise, and he has been pestering Mercadio. It seems he even had to hire Blackus to guard his rear." He shook his head. "A trouble, a triple."

Maltort sighed. "It was bound to happen. Less and less come to the towers, and more of us are hunted." Maltort busied his hands with his desk. "This is news, but not unexpected." Narsis nodded his agreement. Maltort looked up from the desk, "Blackus, can be trouble. If he is angered, or his army, it could destabilize agreements between lords and make kingdoms question each other." He waived his hand in the air for effect. "Fires and ash! Just him walking around can cause more rumors than we could stamp out in a year."

Narsis had settled comfortably and his mood changed as much as his speech. "You cannot teach a rock to roll up hill." He chuckled. "Blackus is not the problem. A few days ago I felt an *Envenus Ritual* coming from the forest." Narsis saw the shock raise on his brother's face and felt the hairs on his arms rise. "Yes, the elves have empowered something or someone."

Maltort growled with a slam of his fist. "That is forbidden magics. When will the elves stop tampering with Chaos?"

Narsis shook his head. "The elves do not believe any magic requires forbiddance, but they do not encourage or help the fools. So many of our young arcane go to them to learn. A leaf still falls, in frost or plucked." Narsis sighed, "Yet, that is not the new which troubles me. Mercadio's words and posture troubled me. There was an attack at the gates of Homgad. Rumor says they saw Moraphen." Narsis held up a hand of restraint at Maltort. "I did not see it, but I investigated the tavern in which they stayed. Mercadio had someone else in their party. I could not get a description. From the attacks and rumors," Narsis leaned towards Maltort, "I believe the Heir has returned and Valash is hunting him for unknown purposes."

Maltort looked pale. "Crack of the gods! How sure are you?" Narsis shrugged. Maltort ran his hands over his head. "We will have to investigate. Grabs some twelfth year staffs from around Homgad, and look for him or her." Maltort pointed a finger at Narsis. "And find Mercadio. Get him back here. Drag him by the hat if you must. He will probably be with the Heir."

Narsis looked skeptical. "Twelfth year staffs? Are you over doing it a bit?" Maltort's face redden and an outburst was ready on his lips. Narsis held his hands defensively. "Settle your hat. I hope we will not need them. The wizards from the Tower of Practice can be a bit zealous in application."

"And the wizards from the Tower if Records can be a bit boring." Maltort smiled. He stood and rounded the desk to hug his brother. "Be safe Nerry Berry. I hope we are all wrong. If not, the mystics are going to be a bit smug before they all start weeping."

Narsis nodded. "I'll be cautious." He took a few steps back and rubbed his hands down his clothes. They became clean again without a single stain. "I best remain only for lunch. Take care Molty Malty." He gave his brother an affectionate wink and left. Maltort smiled for a bit and got back to work. The parchment could wait. If these rumors were true, he had to prepare the towers for a prisoner. "Dear gods, what terrific power will this Heir be?"

∞∞∞∞

Delex woke up as vomit rose and emptied beside him. It was cool and dark. No clouds were in the sky and a light breeze brushed across the tall grass. A campfire burned brightly in the middle of the beaten grass on the campground. In the distance the remains of the battle still smoldered in the night. Delex puked again. Soas jumped back. "Blackus, Mercadio, he is awake!" Soas quickly restrained Delex's chest with a hand on his chest. "Don't sit up Delex. You will be fine. Just lay back down for a second."

Mercadio approached with a wet cloth and placed it on Delex's head. The cool cloth slowed the hammer inside his head. Delex sighed loudly. "Now steady, now steady boy. You have slept for four days. We made camp when you collapse near the girl." Mercadio touched Delex's head and the pain subsided a fraction. "Sorry, son, my abilities to heal others is not on par with the most minor wizard. This is the most I can help."

Delex choked back the urge to vomit again. "What happened?"

"You fell over." Blackus tossed Delex a bag of water and walked away.

Soas rolled his eyes at his brother. "We made camp, and you just looked at us, and mumbled, then–" Soas whistled while he slowly slapped his hand to the ground. "You made a nice thud sound."

Delex grimace. "What is that smell?" He felt better but his guts still felt like they tied themselves in a knot while he slept. The strong smell of sewage did not help.

Mercadio lifted a finger and looked ready to lecture when Soas butted in with a grim smile on his face. "Oh yeah, they don't talk about that part in the bardic stories, do they? Well Delex, when you are asleep your body keeps working." Soas looked to Delex and waited for the recognition to set in. He laughed at Delex, "Yep, you crapped yourself. A few times. We don't have any other clothes, but she cleaned you up as much as she could." Soas pointed to the young woman near the fire. Her eyes were still a vibrant purple as she looked right through Delex.

Delex's eyebrows tried to climb into his hair while his face turned a deep red. His heart skipped a beat every time he looked at her. Yet, at this moment, it just wanted to die. He could feel the shame on his face. She noticed his eyes on her. She smiled and touched her lips with her fingers as she studied him. That unguarded look she gave him suddenly batted away his inner turmoil. Her ways mesmerized and forced away his embarrassment. Her tan skin shimmered golden in the firelight. Thankfully, Mercadio's outer cloak wrapped around her and sheltered the memories of their first encounter. She stood and walked over to him. He watched every step of her foot. She barely touched the ground. She had a grace and sway to her step that shut out everything else from the world.

"Delex, dear Heir." She said. Her voice still held the music he once heard. "I bathed thee as I could and beg thy apology. I hast become familiar with thy contours." Delex tried to speak, but she took the fingers she had touched to her lips and rested them on his lips. "Speak not. Hearken to mine words. I hast been brief of word to thy men of valor. I wouldst hold my tongue until thy waking." She helped Delex sit up. She sat back. "Mine name is Nova. Dragon and lady, one of same. I am, or hast been thy sorcerion in blood."

"We thought as much, but we don't understand. How can this be?" Mercadio asked. Soas was about to retort with a smirk on his lips when Blackus smacked him on the top of his head with his fist.

"Mine Book of Dragons holds thy truths." She glared daggers at Soas. "Tis true we were once sorcerers, like heroic Delex. We build of things, and lived of life. Hark, we craved extension of knowledge, and lives anon our gift." She smiled. "We built of wonders great, and among them a cubic. Tis later decried thus thy Dragonical. Thy human wizards hath known as thy Dragon Box. Tis a magic solidity that crossed our souls. Tis a cup filled to overflow and poured deepen within." Her smile faded, "But this alas, put an oddity upon us."

"Dragons." Delex said. She nodded to him. Somehow he felt the truth within him. He continued the story for her. "You sorcerers turned into dragons and built skin to contain the magic within you." She nodded, but he saw a tear in her eye. He understood. "You couldn't change back could you?"

Nova shook her head. "Blessed flesh, timeless touched. Mine magics drew deep, raw and limited mine nature. Our mastery of self birthed unmeasured year." She looked into the fire. "We hast weakness, upon weakness our brethren feared. Thy other sorcerion, in acts of love, struck our knowledge from history, and abandoned us." Nova eyed the ground.

Mercadio placed a hand on her shoulder. "That is enough dear, I can finish from here I think." Mercadio cleared his throat. Both Blackus and Soas mirrored the others' curiosity. "The sorcerers removed all knowledge on hoe to become a dragon. I only know they are related because of Doran. AS for the rest of the world, they thought of dragons as beasts and hunted as such. They suddenly appeared, thousands of them." Mercadio spoke under his breath gestured with his hands. Pieces of the campfire flames broke off and flew to Mercadio's hand. He raised his hand above his head and placed the fire in the air. It shimmered and expanded and changed into multiple colors. It turned in a series of pictures as he spoke. The pictures looked like colored ink illustrations from ancient books.

"It was one of the few times all the kingdoms came together and let fear rule them. Without the knowledge the sorcerers could have shared, The world hunted them down, almost to extinction."

Nova reached her hand towards the magical flames. Her touched made the flames shimmer as the pictures moved with a lifelike appearance. Mercadio gasped at her magical talent as Nova spoke. "Truth. Many thousands ashed to hundreds. Tis a butchery that ravens would salivate from taste of memory." The pictures showed knights clad in bright armor as they slammed into many types of dragons. The dragons in turn would unleash horrible energy from their mouths. Many knights would melt under the energy and explode into various effects. "Tis horror. Dragon form explodes anon death." The pictures changed again to show a dozen knights as the hacked into a fallen red and black dragon. As a knight stabbed deeply into the heart, the scene burst in a flash of intense red and black light. Delex thought it looked light a nuclear explosion painted from nightmares. The light faded, into blackened landscape void of vegetation and trees. Twelve oddly melted slagged of metal lay scattered about the clean white bones of the dragon.

"Alas, Time removes fools but leaves thy scars. Wizard minds, tooled of craft, make works to twist thee death-blossom and meld thy energy skyward into barlight." Nova cried freely. The pictures showed four knights with lances that flashed with lightning. As they slammed their weapons into the fallen green colored dragon, they held up shields with both hands. The green death-blossom energy rebounded and shot skyward in a concentrated beam of pure green. Around them trees sprouted from the ground. A small bit of green energy escaped and slashed through a knight. A bloody branch punched through a knight's chest armor as a tree grew out of him. *Barlight? That is a laser! They funneled the energy into a magic laser. So that is what they call it, barlight.* Delex thought as he watched the horrid scene.

Nova sat back. The pictures turned back into illustrations. "Tis a, tis a-" Nova could not finish the sentence. She moved to Delex and buried her face into his shoulder.

Mercadio coughed. "Well that is enough. I think we all agree you are who you say you are. I have no doubts." He looked into the sky. It still shimmered darkly with stars. "Delex, you need to rest. You should be recovered enough to travel in the morning. The others and I have had time, now must you. Come now Nova." Mercadio took Nova by the arm, but she shrugged it off and gripped Delex tighter. Mercadio sighed. "Well and well young lady." He stood and walked away.

Soas nodded to Delex. "Yeah, we have a lot to discuss tomorrow morning." He stood and nodded. He and Mercadio stepped away and talked in a whispered conversation. Delex laid back down. Nova still lay huddled to his chest. She was already asleep. Delex lay for a time with the sound of her soft breath in his ear. Then he too, fell back to sleep.

In the morning Delex woke and left Nova to sleep. Soas guided him to a stream that was about a ten-minute walk from camp. He took time to fully bathe himself and clean his cloths. The stream was cold enough spur a rush of goosebumps down his skin. Soas sat on the other side of a tree and talked about stories of his escapades while Delex's clothes dried in the sun. It made Delex smile, but his mind remained on last night's brief conversation and the smokey beauty that lay in the middle of it. He looked down to his hands. Delex still wondered what magic he performed to change her back to a sorceress. Human, Delex still thought of himself as human. Sorcerer was more like a race of human to him. The inhabitants of this world, his world, seem to view it as completely different. Perhaps in time he could change that.

Delex and Soas arrived back in time for lunch. They were on the edge of the plains. Rolling hills and light speckled the countryside to his north, if that was north on this planet. It was a beautiful day. Behind them to the west, Moonset on this planet, the white smoke of the battle fizzle to weak ribbons.

"Ah, boys, you're back, good, good. We have a lot to discuss." Mercadio said happily. He handed both a bowl of steamed oats and grass. "Sorry lad, it is the best we could cook without proper supplies. If we track back the way we came and head to the hill towards the Terwise. They are speckled with villages. We should be able to barter for greater provisions."

The familiar Daylow scurried out from Mercadio's robs in a flurry of motion and claws without any regard to the safety of his pet wizard. He sat with his face in the bowl and ignored the verbal tirade from his pet human.

Soas laughed. "Sometimes I love my brother. He sure knows how to make a joke." Soas grabbed the map from Mercadio before he beat the cat with it and looked it over.

He looked to Delex and shrugged. "It seems the old dust clod thinks its best we split up." Delex stopped with a spoon of the gruel halfway to his face. Soas nodded and Soas pointed his spoon at Delex. "I agree, its time we part ways soon. You're just too much trouble."

Chapter 13: Across the Distance

Delex looked at Soas as emotions rose like a thunderstorm in the distance. So many questions rattled around in his head. Why do they need to split up. What happen to make them push him away. *Why do they all want... Hey wait.* His confusion threaten to overpower him. Delex's eyelids pinched together slightly as his skepticism took over. Soas immediately smiled and laughed. Delex punched him in the arm. "You're a real jerk, you know that right?"

Soas laughed even harder, "the look on your face!" He chuckled more. "No bid could purchase it!"

Delex rolled his eyes, "You mean priceless?"

Soas' laugh died on his lips, and he pondered for a moment. "Hmm, yes, priceless. I like that." He gestured with a finger. His face became serious. "But I was only joking a little. We honestly must get rid of you."

Before Delex could question him further Blackus walked over and slapped Soas on the back of the head hard enough to tilt him forward. "Stop teasing him." Soas growled and pulled out a knife. Blackus effortlessly slapped it away into the high grass. "Stop playing with toys."

Before the two brothers could get into a larger fight, Mercadio and the delicate woman Nova approached the others and spoke. "Now, now boys, not in front of the stronger sex." He smiled to Nova. She tilted her head in kind then looked to Delex.

Delex barely heard his words. Nova and Delex made eye contact. The world seem to dim. Delex could feel the pulse of his blood beat in his neck. Those purple eyes seemed to expand and take over his world. Time didn't seem to matter. A small pain snapped him out of the spell. "Ouch! Daylow!" The cat had bitten him on the leg, and quick as a thought, darted into the high grass.

"Sorry about that son, Daylow gets a little frisky when he can't hide and lay about." He smiled and looked at the two. "Seems we have some things to talk about, and we need everyone's attention, so please bare with me." Soas sighed and rested back on his elbows. Blackus stood, solid as ever and took a moment to scan the area. "Blackus and I have spoken at some length. We have devised that Valash has somehow been tracking us since we came into the world from the original *tempra*." He paced a little as he talked. The staff of his thudded quietly on the packed grass.

"Now, we are not sure of the magics he used to devise our location and track us, perhaps it was a meta-clairvo spell, or perhaps a reverse tracer, not like it would work, yet it could be an absence sense spell," Mercadio waved his staff in the air, "but on a planetary scale that would-"

"Focus." Blackus said. Mercadio coughed and stopped his ramble. Blackus gave him a pinched look of annoyance.

"Yes well, no matter what he used, we have been able to determine that the tracking has been lost. Perhaps from the recent battle and enormous forces that took place. The sheer power of Nova's breath alone-" Mercadio realized his words drifted to ramble again. He looked to Blackus. Blackus' eye bore directly through him. Mercadio shivered a little.

"The morning is still a bit brisk." Mercadio commented. Soas snickered as Mercadio went on. "Delex, son," Mercadio sighed and a looked forlorn sadden washed over his face. "We need to take this opportunity to split up and take alternative routes. Soas, alone, Blackus and I, and you and Nova."

Soas immediately shot to his feet. "Are you addled like a baby rattle!" Soas growled. "We have barely managed to keep ahead of this fight together. You suggest splitting us thrice? What if Valash or his minions find us in the open like this again?"

Mercadio lifted a hand of silence. "I know young rogue, but we, Blackus and I that is, believe that we are easier to track because of our proximity to each other. If we split in three, this will separate our presence and scatter whatever spell Valash weaved."

"But, I thought you said the battle ruined the spell." Delex shifted a little as Nova sat down beside him. His thoughts scattered momentarily. She smelled like fresh flowers and dew. He shook his head and heard her giggle silently. "So why do we still need to separate?"

Mercadio nodded at Nova to speak. She smiled towards the wizard and begun in her rich voice. It was light like silver bells, but had a smokey rumble like a dragon. "I query this hath much ado with magic convergence. Tis something even wizards known not." she blinked innocently at Mercadio. "As known, wizards carry gift of second sight. Tis thy poor guarded secret attunement to magic betwixt sight and mind. Tis a poorly shadow of sorcerers, useful in thy lesser form." She smiled anew as she tried to spare Mercadio's feelings. Mercadio seemed enchanted with the young women as much as Delex was. His return smiled was proof enough he felt no sting to her words. Delex felt a slight pain in his heart but brushed it aside. He too was enchanted by Nova's crazy way of speaking.

"A sorcerer tis trained of grand making. Tis a mere spattering anon few hundred years." She waved her hand nonchalantly. "I ponder Valash has seen potential magics. Mayhap he doth undertaken much to scry liken to a ferret." She shifted her legs to keep the robe closed around her.

Delex became aware once more that she still had nothing but the cloak to hide her skin. Nova seemed to sense his thoughts and gave him a pert frown. It was as if she said *Now is not the time, focus you clod.* A slight smile said she was appreciative of the attention. Delex's face colored a little. "So you are saying Valash can use magic sonar?" Everyone looked at him with a puzzled face, even Soas. "Um, sonar, sensing things hidden."

Nova rolled her eyes. "Mine words spoke, dear heir." She raised her arms as Daylow came back out of the grass and settled on her lap. She began to absently stroke the cat. "I think not. Valash doth not carry mastery. Yet, thy magic potentials bleed one as beacon. To scry Delex would be a trifling and hearken thy quickening of eyes."

Mercadio nods, "That does explain the farg he was riding his first appearance." Nova nodded.

Soas interrupted, "With all the magic unleashed, we have blinded him." Blackus padded his brother's head like a dog that performed a trick correctly. Soas slapped his hand away.

Delex had a thought click in his mind. The answer seemed to leap up at him. "So you are going to split us up, make false magic trails and force Valash to hunt them all down to pin point us?"

Mercadio looked genuinely impressed. "Exact answer Delex! How did you know?"

Delex shrugged. "I play lot of video games." He saw confusion in their eyes. "I play visual games that use sight and sound. Hmm, like the fire last night." They all seemed to understand him more. "In the game we used a smoke that disrupts sight and um, artifacts, that track us. We run in different directions and make noise to make the enemy chase us while the main player sneaks into their base under the distraction."

Blackus had a grin on his face. "We are going to talk about this visual-game at another time Delex. I am curious." It was one of the few times Blackus didn't look bored to death, or show his teeth. Delex thought the smile and eagerness of Blackus' face would haunt his in his dreams.

Delex tried to chuckle, "Sure Blackus. If we ever get back to Earth, I will introduce you to Call of Duty."

"I already have a call to duty." Blackus replied.

Delex was about to correct him when he thought back to his time trying to explain to Mercadio. "Yeah, well, anyways. Mercadio, a fair amount of us give off magic potential. Sooner or later Valash will pick up on that."

Mercadio motioned back to Nova. "I can teach obfuscation of thy presence. Thy crafty fox sorcerer, dear Delex. Til anon, I shall play mistress to both mine on yours. Tis burden and toil. Practiced, I am far from kin." Nova blushed.

Soas snapped his fingers and pointed to Nova. "Ah, that is why I could never find his, I mean her location!" Soas shook his head and smiled. "So we set up false trails, hide the real ones, and slip away like a thief in the shadows."

Mercadio raised an eyebrow. "True amazement it took you this long to think this through, given your profession."

"What does a merchant have to do with it, you magical skeleton!" Soas retorted.

Blackus slapped them both on the back of the head before they started another famous argument. "Not now children."

Nova burst into laughter. Daylow growled on her lap and snuggled in more. Delex clapped a hand over his mouth and choked over a few laughs. Mercadio cleared his throat and waited for Nova to settle into quiet giggles. "Well then, Delex, this is our plan, but we needed to get your thoughts."

Delex shrugged, "Why, that seems as good as plan as any."

Blackus spoke again. "You are leading. You make the final choice. You have proven courage, swiftness of choice and even superior tactical knowledge from your visual-games." Blackus pulled his sword out of the beaten scabbard a finger width and dropped it back in. It was a curious move he often did when something was on his mind. "You will need this training and I trust you with it."

Delex shrugged and smiled. Oddly enough, today felt different. He stood and brushed the grass from his legs. "Well, I guess I am stuck with it." He smiled. The pressure of leadership didn't seem such a lodestone today. "I say it is a good plan, and we should do it." Delex held his stomach, "But, if you do not mind, can we eat first?"

Soas chuckled and offered to get him some food. Nova smiled and said little at breakfast. He wanted to spend some time alone with her, but could not get the chance. He wanted to talk to her about what had happened, what he had felt. Delex didn't understand what he performed, and frankly, she did not either. He wanted to ask her what she had felt, or what she thought, but deep down he just wanted to spend time with her. She seemed eager as well, but under the circumstances they could not find the time.

The evening quietly slipped into a night sky full of stars so thick it casts a gauze of starlight over the world. Delex lay awake with his eyes cast into an alien sky. He reflected again back to how he came to Ter'Avan. His fears and worries melted away beneath the milk of starlight as a purple and red galaxy rose over the mountains.

"Dragon's Eye. Tis a given name common upon tongue and text. Mine memory whispers ancient words, Soul of Stars." Nova approached Delex and lay on the grass near him as she pointed to the galaxy that lifted into view. Delex remained quiet. He was still unsure of himself with her. His blood rushed when he was near. She rested on her back and looked into the stars. "Tis say, a tradition. Cast eye upon thy star jewel, whence new year births. Grant thee a single wish. True to wish, thus a sign granted. Thy Dragon's Eye, grants but one wish in a night's breath."

Delex looked over to Nova. She looked at him as well. "Nova, I'm sorry." Nova gave him a puzzled look. "For changing you, I don't know what I did."

Nova laughed a silver melody. "Change me? Vex thy mind

naught. Thy hand quicken mine true self from seed to breath. Thy works purchased chance twice over." She leaned on her side and touched his hand with hers. "Dear heir. Our race endeavors gave work from word, spell from thought. Our eyes cast one beam through blinded path. Thee lite mine path. Fore, dragon be but chattel and hunted with gay revel. Dire hunt forced mine race doth flee thy ground for skyward thus." Nova spoke quietly as she pointed to the tiny moon in the sky. Tears formed in her eyes. "I knew not thy hope birthed in mine breast."

"So you are not angry?" Delex absolutely refused to look down from her eyes. *She had to say breast! Dude, she is still wearing just a cloak. That is like a blanket with arm holes. If it slipped open she- NO!* Delex wanted to change the mood and thoughts. He didn't want to see her cry and get the image from his mind. He was not sure what magic she had over him, or if it was magic at all. Delex just did not want to see her so heartbroken. The next moment reassured him, he did not know woman or their feelings well, or at all.

"Oh, but thy eyes shine liken to a puppy!" She squeezed his nose and laughed. "Thy speech is queer and crisp. It makes merry mine soul." Nova laughed again. Delex's face was a wave of emotions. "Yet, fears protest. Mine speech is dust. Tis ancient as much thy tongue so alien." She smiled and looked down to her body still covered in the single cloak. "I do query. Why thy chosen form? Tis a grander frame than once possessed." She ran her hands over the curves of her body once again and hefted her ample bosom under her cloak. She was noticeably happy with it. "Queenly framework." She took his hand again.

"I did not choose anything." Delex shrugged. He looked into the sky. His hand felt clammy in hers. *Oh, please someone, something save me! I got this hot girl eating up my every word and I can't think! What am I doing!* His abdomen muscles down to his pelvis twisted with a sharp pain. He suddenly knew he wanted her for more than just the physically attraction. Something bloomed inside him. He hid it all under a mask as his pulse rapidly beat in his ears. "It seemed right. I don't even understand it myself. I guess, I focused on repairing the inner you." Delex looked back to her. The stars and galaxy reflected in her eyes. "Maybe it is how you saw yourself?"

Nova smiled and nodded. For once, she did not have the words to speak. She rested on her back again and moved closer to Delex. They lay without a word as they gazed into the stars. "Delex. Wish this night. Wish upon thy Dragon's Eye together. Tis a time since I had need to gaze upon it." Nova Whispered.

"Sure, that sounds good." Delex whispered back.

"Upon thy strike of three, shutter thy eye, open thy heart. Wish thy desire."

Delex nodded. They both closed there eyes as Nova counted to three. Delex was not sure if it would work, but in a short time his whole world changed, literal and figurative. He had seen and made wonders that he never knew existed. *What does it hurt?* He thought to himself. Delex reflected on the new friends he made and the ones he left behind. He thought about his father Jim, and the mother and father he had almost no memories. Many of these choices in his life were choices he had no power over. Choices that bound him to a higher purpose also bound him to a fate that didn't say he would succeed. It was almost like a story book on Earth, but this story did not have a prophecy or special item that would guarantee he would win. Nothing promised he would survive, or grow with wisdom, or survive without permanently scar and injured. What of his friend's lives? Would they return from this? Who knew how many Moraphen had killed just to capture and hold him. Here he was, half dead, half starved, and in a marathon for his life just to face the one that tried to kill him life some magic teleporting vampire. It made little sense.

All his thought tumbled loosely in his brain as he struggled his wish. Nova's hand suddenly tightened on his. *She must be making her wish.* He hurried and grasped the first solid thought that came to mind. *I wish I can protect this world for as long as possible with an honest heart.* Delex sighed. *I sound lame. Pretty sure anime characters yelled better oaths in their sleep.*

As he finished his wish, a bright light made him open his eyes. A shooting star made a fiery path across the night sky. "Is that the sign you asked for Nova?"

Nova shrugged, "may hap a rock falling. Mine arm hath hurled many a rock at what doth displease mine eye. Nary a wish would grant from it." Nova giggled.

Delex raised an eyebrow. He would have thought a world that seemed so backwards from the technological world of Earth would have little concept of what a meteor was. He grinned with pleasure for some reason he could not grasp.

The shooting star made it across the Dragon's Eye then exploded in the sky. A shower of rainbow waves and energy erupted from the explosion. It was so high in the sky and no sound reached them, but Delex could feel magic in it. He was about to ask Nova about it when one, then another shooting star made the same track across the sky and exploded close to where the first had detonated. The second and third shooting stars erupted in the same rainbow of magic.

"What about that Nova?" Delex asked a bit bemused.

Nova had a serious expression and she contemplated the sight. "Tis naught set witness to mine eyes or memory." She looked to Delex. "Tis new in mine sight." She smiled. "May it be thy sign required, but for which wish?" She smiled anew at Delex and rested her head on his chest. "Now off to sleep. I require it now." Delex thought she was joking with him. She wiggled further into him and closed her eyes. *Oh, she well. She plans to sleep right by me.*

Delex couldn't help but smile as he looked at her face. A rustle of noise drew his attention down her neck and the cloak which had slipped open down her length. It heaved opened and closed at her chest with each breath. He thought once again of their meeting. He cut the thought from his mind with a mental slash. Delex didn't try to look at her breasts, but something still drew his eye towards her chest. The scar over her heart glowed with a slight inner light. He had no idea what it meant, but he was certain the answer would crop up later. He could only hope it was a good omen.

"Art thy eyes lewd upon mine form?" Nova said without opening her eyes.

Delex almost jumped from her voice. "Um no! I saw the scar, it still glows. I didn't look any lower, or anywhere else, I swear."

Nova shifted the cloak closed. "Drop a tear, pick a pity. Thy chance lost, for mine new skin chills in thy eve air." Nova said with devilish mirth. She wrapped the cloak warmly around her and buried her hips chest and face deeper into his side. Then she pulled one slender arm out and ran in over his chest and cupped his face. "Sleep thee sound."

Several words popped into mind, none he wished to repeat openly or in his thoughts. It took him a better part of an hour for his sense of her to dull enough to finally rest. He could have sworn at one point, she giggled in her sleep.

In the morning the travelers took stock of the supplies that they had left. It was apparent, without more, they would all be in trouble soon. Delex suggested they scout for a town or village. Soas told him about a little village just over the hills. They all decided to head in that direction. It would take them a few hours to arrive. In the meantime Mercadio decided to once again instruct Delex on the local histories and wildlife. Delex sighed noticeably. Blackus and Nova conversed quietly in that time. Delex felt a small pang of jealously. Delex tried to come to terms with the idea that everyone found Nova of interest in one way or another. Everyone except Soas. Soas avoided Nova like a plague, and Nova, for her part, found every reason to approach Soas and pester him openly with threats about returning her book. She toyed with him with vague threats to down right graphic enough to make Blackus smirk and Daylow's hair rise. Sadly, everyone agreed she could somehow make any of them possible.

"With tarry a thought, twist, twist. What tis inner, tis outwards and practice akin to an aqueduct." Soas left camp to vomit. Nova came over and gave Delex a chaste peck on the cheek as she happily skipped through the camp.

Delex mouthed a silent '*Help me.*'to Blackus.

Blackus countered with a flat. '*No,*' and a shake of the head. Mercadio was oblivious to it all.

Delex knew she was teasing, but he also understood she was once a dragon. None of them, including Nova, knew what she was or her new strength. Mercadio was interested in the histories of magic and dragons and had little fear of her. Blackus actually kept a conversation with Nova for a whole twenty minutes about battle knowledge. Even Daylow spent time in her lap and gave Delex catty smiles.

After an hour of what Soas described as 'relentless education' as Nova picked at everything Mercadio said, the wizard switched subjects and asked Delex about what he had learned while under Moraphen's care.

"Well, he had me stabbed a few times, or broke my bones. Then he made me heal them all." Delex's face reflected the pain of the memories. "He became enraged when I did it wrong the first time."

"Oh?" Mercadio lifted an eyebrow. "Was it a wizard sickness or a waning of strength?"

"No, I just wiped it away." Delex shrugged. "It felt good." Delex gave them all brief description on the events that lead up to the injury, what he imagined, and how he had removed the pain from his leg. Nova Listened calmly, but her eyes were wide with shock by the time he finished.

"Curious, very curious. No magical friction? Not one person has ever survived-" Mercadio nodded as his sentence died on his lips. Mercadio seemed calm, but a trickle of sweat rolled down the side of his head. Blackus was only interested when Delex told them what Moraphen did to his leg. Soas made a snore noise until Blackus glared at him. Nova looked afraid. Nova had not had a human body for a long time. Delex noticed she held many emotions on her face. He figured she just was out of practice of holding back her emotions in a humanoid form. She shook her head and spoke up.

"Delex, tis not natural. Thy words speak impossible wonder."

Delex nodded his head. "Yeah, apparently Moraphen was really peed off."

Nova's eyes opened wide. "That naive urinated upon thee!" She was a mixture of mortified and shocked.

"What? No! I mean, he was super angry!" He looked at Nova a little perturbed.

"Speak thy meaning. Doth not banter with Earthen play words." Nova was a mask of emotionless femininity, except for two red dots a color on her cheeks. Delex thought *it looks like she is getting a crash course on hiding her emotions.* Delex sighed. *Fricken woman. Seems they are alike on any planet.* Nova gave him a quick glare. *Did she read my mind?* Delex thought. Nova smiled for a moment and went back to her glare before she turned away and picked up Daylow and smothered him with affection.

Soas chuckled, "She is not reading your mind buddy." Soas poked Delex in the arm. "She just knows all guys are the same on any planet."

Delex grinned and looked back to Mercadio. "So what do you think?"

"Oh what, yes?" Mercadio waved him away. "I will think on it. Go carry out your meaningless socializing." Mercadio walked away in deep thought. Soas and Delex looked at each other and shrugged.

The rest of the morning lapsed in peaceful thought. The sky was an open blue with a few light clouds. A slight breeze blew thick with the sweet smell of flowers, yet Delex could not find the source. It made him smile. He needed smiles. There was not much he could smile about. His body grew bruised like a vegetable garden, and his skin felt like a taiko drum from all the beatings. Only by the grace of his friends has he survived the attacks from Valash. Delex's mind drifted in thought when

Soas approached again. His usual thievish smile held a grim look that reflected in his eyes.

"You don't look like you have good news." Delex bumped his shoulder to Soas. Maybe *he is just melancholy.* It was a wishful thought. Soas gave a brief smile.

"Blackus and I have been going over the battle." Soas looked at Delex. "We did not find any sign of Moraphen."

"How? Nova and that thing trampled him as they fought, like several times." Soas shook his head as Delex talked. "Soas, the dude was fifty shades of dead. I would call him roadkill, but that would offend roadkill."

Soas barely managed a smile as he looked into the distance. "I wish I could say how. Moraphen is not human anymore. He can't be. If we had more time to find tracks, we would have found him. I know this; he was not there when the fight ended." He held up his hands. "His corpse is more than likely crushed underground. We cannot do anything about it, other than watch and be ready if he appears." He nodded to Delex. "On the sunny side of news. It is close to noon and a town where we can resupply is over the last hill."

Delex sighed. "Well, that is good. I guess every cloud has a silver lining." Delex smiled. It was a problem he would have to face in the future. At this moment, he could not do anything about it.

Soas gave him a troubled look. "Silver smile, and don't say that. Bad luck."

The pain was more than he could have ever imagined. His world lived in a daydream. He would pass out for long stretches of time only to come back awake. He did not know where he traveled, or how far. His eyes sagged like crushed fruit in his skull. His would see only darkness. Skin hung off him like tattered cloth. Large chunks of meat and muscles were missing. At one point he had felt birds peck and chew on his back. He was certain a rodent had taken residence in his leg.

Moraphen still crawled on. He should be dead. He had never felt this before in all the time Valash had him enslaved. Moraphen never knew the magic that infused his body and captured his mind rooted so deeply inside him. Whatever magic had Moraphen in Valash's power, was literally beaten out of him. He should be dead. His mind begin to clear and with each new second, his memories boiled to the surface.

He tried to cry but his eyes didn't work. He could feel the grass under his hands and hear his lungs wail. The things he had done, the faces etched on his soul, the cries from the wounded and maimed harassed him as he crawled. Where did he travel? He did not know. He just wanted to survive, so he crawled. Moraphen knew he had to get away from Blackus. *I am laid low by my student.* His disgrace, revisited upon him once again.

The sound of a rhythmic thuds interrupted his thoughts. He knew it was a horse. It approached and halted. Moraphen stopped his crawl and waited. He had no weapons and doubted he could move his muscles to defend himself. Perhaps this was his final-end. He hoped whatever came to him could help or end his suffer.

The sun on his back cooled. He knew it was cast by a shadow of whoever held his fate. Then a voice spoke over the sounds of screams in his mind.

"By all dear gods, what happen to you friend? No, do not speak." He felt hands turn him over and gasp. Quick steps shuffled away from him. "Gods, gods, gods, gods! How are you alive?" Moraphen was vaguely aware of what he looked like. He has felt pieces of him fall off or drag underneath him as he crawled. Folds of skin and viscera trailed in strings underneath him, like a jellyfish dragged across the grass. His burned and rotten spots speckled his entire body. The wind blew on the patches of hair that still clung to his shredded scalp.

Moraphen tried to speak but the few strings of flesh the held his tongue within his mouth snapped and made it slip to one side. The man approached slower and mumbled protective curses under his breath.

Inside Moraphen, something stirred. It was a mild discomfort at first but begin to grow into a rabid itchy desire. Moraphen tired to move, to remove the itch, but it only grew stronger. The stranger hovered near him. A light touch was enough to hold Moraphen to the ground while he tried to sooth the injured man with kind words. The itch was now a fire in his bones. It shook him and radiated from his hands and feet in twinges and tingles.

The stranger screamed something at him, but Moraphen had a hard time with the words. The drum in his ears overpowered everything. He felt the long grass bend straight as the stranger straighten and walked back to his horse. The booming and itch calmed, but only to flare as the man approached again. Moraphen felt a desire scratch through his brain. He needed the man, needed to get close. He felt hungry.

Moraphen's body sprang at the man. It twisted and trashed like a puppeteer in a ground quake. He heard a scream of surprise as he overpowered the man and the screams intensified as Moraphen took his first bite. Both men thrashed for dominance, but Moraphen's body was more powerful than either of them. Moraphen screamed as well with the man. His screams of terror only made the man scream more. Moraphen's teeth gnashed like a savage animal as his throat worked the man's warm meat down his throat. He felt his body slide back into place and pieces regrow.

His eyes burst with light. Moraphen looked at the stranger in horror. It was a middle-aged man, stout, with a beard with the first signs of grey. A brown horse nickered and pulled at the roped tied to a lone tree. Its eyes rolled in its sockets as froth formed on the shiny hide.

Moraphen looked back down to gaze into the eyes of the poor man. The man's hands and lower jaw ended in gnawed stubs. Chew marks gouged out large sections of the man's chest. Moraphen could feel the man's tongue in his mouth. He absently swallowed it like a chunk of wet fish. He tried to vomit it back up, but his muscles wouldn't respond. The worst part, the poor traveler was still alive. His breath pumped erratically, but his eyes shown bright with fear. He wanted to scream, but Moraphen saw his hand held his throat like a claw. Moraphen couldn't look away. Tears ran down both of their faces. With a whisper, the man's breath shuddered and stopped. His eyes lost the light. The body twitched and laid still. Moraphen closed his eyes as his body bent down for more meat. He tried to scream between the mouthfuls, but he could not take the smallest control away from the hunger.

Moraphen slowed down as his hungry begun to ebb. His stomach was full of raw meat. A coat of drool covered the poor victim and himself. The smell of salt hung heavy in the air. It was his tears. Of all the things he had ever done under the yoke of Valash, this was beyond all atrocities. This, was a fresh nightmare.

A small female chuckle whispered in his ear. "Do you not hear me Moraphen?" The giggle repeated itself. "Do you not know you are mine? You cannot die before we meet again. This is not Valash's command, but mine."

Moraphen stood quickly. His body felt completely healed. His body felt light and strong, repaired, more now than before his defeat by Valash. Every scar and ache vanished. Some wicked magic repaired him to his prime. He looked at the horse for the source of the sound. The horse tied to the tree had passed out from fear. He spun in place. "Show yourself! Who are you?" He had no weapons to guard himself. He felt strangely vulnerable and frightened.

The giggle turned into a soothing shush. "Hush, hush, dear Moraphen, my Moraphen." The voice emphasized the word 'my' viciously. "You do not hear and recognize? I am coming for you. You will not perish until I can touch you."

"Who are you!" Moraphen screamed. He rushed to the horse

and searched the bags for a weapon. He found a small dagger and gripped it in his hand. "Show yourself!"

"I am not near sweet Moraphen, but I will be. I will always be coming, and looking, and searching. Until we meet again upon leaf and wood."

Moraphen felt a deep chill hit his body like icy brine on his heart. "Mossa?" He looked all over his surroundings. "*Sask'a'roht*?"

An explosion of laughter erupted from all around him. Moraphen dropped to the ground and covered his ears. He curled into a ball as the laughter pounded into him. The laughter fade quickly into silence but Moraphen whined in a high pitch moan almost too feral to be human. Moraphen cowered as fear shook him. Several minutes passed before he could stop his quiet screams and moans. The cold faded with the shakes. The horse next to him was still on the ground, but changed. There was no more brown healthy horse flesh. The horse's skin was a pale, bleached yellow. The horse was cold, and drained of all life.

Moraphen let out a deep sigh of relief. *I survived.*

"Until we meet, my love," whispered in his ear. Moraphen felt a pain erupt from his hand. He looked down to see his hand chilled blue. Frostbite and ice rimmed a perfectly etched image of a kiss on the back of his hand. It took him several minutes to stop his screams of terror.

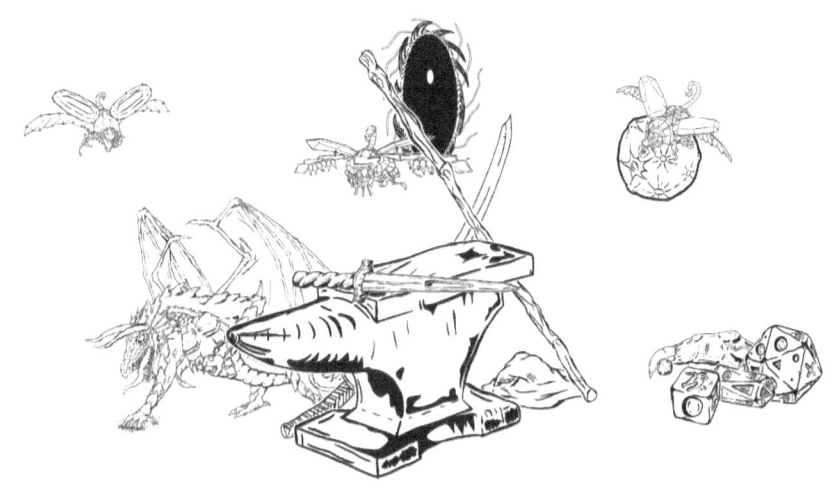

Chapter 14: Farms and Fanfare

True to word, Delex and the party arrived near the village at noon. As they crested the last hill that overlooked the village, they could hear a commotion from the village. The village was a collection of thatched homes with a wide muddy road and old stones between them all. Kids, chickens and dogs passed through the feet of eager faced villagers as they saw the first of the group come over the rise.

Blackus had them halt at the top of the low hill as a roar of applause and cheer echoed into the woods and farmland. There could not be more than a few hundred people in the village. Yet, it was an impressive fanfare. The group looked at each other in surprise. Mercadio gripped his beard in fear. Blackus eyed the crowd with suspicion but held his had from his sword. Even Soas had a faint look of worry on his face.

Delex lean to Soas as he held a forced smile. "Does this happen a lot as you enter a village?" He waved to the crowd. A few of the women cheered and bounced up and down. One overly zealous man danced and shook on his feet until he promptly passed out. "This is bizarre." He looked to Nova for help.

She gave him a look of *'don't ask me'* and pulled the flimsy magician's robe closer to her body. "Never mine memory, tis common course."

As they pondered, the village erupted from the mere uncommon display of love. Several more villagers passed out, become overwhelmed with emotion, or took deep breaths filled with tears. Soas openly shook his head and had a dagger pulled mostly out until Mercadio bated his hand with a whip of his staff. They both exchanged a series of face gestures and glares until Soas relented and slipped the dagger back into its sheath.

"Such a curious display. I wonder if magic inflicts them or a lasting curse?" Mercadio pondered. The cheers and jumble of words begun to boil into a chant above the crowd. "Perhaps this warrants a study?"

Soas slapped the hat off Mercadio's head. Daylow gave him a small feline growl. "Stone's teeth man! They are frothing down there and you want to ponder?" He pointed to the crowd. "Delex, do something?"

The group looked to Delex as one. He took a step back in confusion. "What do I know that you don't?" he shrugged. He pointed to the crowd. "Hey you?" Delex noticed a boy stood apart from the others. He watched the crowd with a smile. He was a red haired youth about the age of eight and held the rope of a hawk on a gloved arm. The boy jumped happily and ran towards them.

Blackus nodded to Delex and gave him a small smile. "Good." Blackus had relaxed noticeably and went back to his routine scan of the surroundings.

The boy ran and bounced up the hill to the group and skidded to a stop. He danced about on his bare feet as he looked to them all with eager purpose.

"Um, Hello, kid." Delex said awkwardly.

"By the gods you are here! We wanted you here, then you took a long time, but you are finally here, and my pa said you would be but, my ma said you weren't and you came!" the kid took a breath and eyed them. "Oh you have chanters and miss-

chanters and kitties!" He went to reach for Daylow but Daylow made such a hissed that the hawk on his arm flapped in warning. The kid released the hawk into the sky and bounced up and down. "Now my pa is a' smart as reap hoe and I told that dumb Bilden that his pa has the brains of a grass snake in a horse's rear, but Bilden punched me head, and it came to a red mark between us all up and down on my arm and bum and legs, but it doesn't mat-" The kid jumped up and down in excitement as he rattled on in a single breath.

"Hey!" Soas yelled. The kid looked to Soas with a grin. "Can you kindly get the person in charge and bring them over?" Soas said with a sweet voice. He waved the kid away with his hands.

"Right as tight I can!" The kid spun in place and looked like he was about to run back down the hill. Soas turned to the others and smiled in victory. The kid lifted his hands to the side of his mouth and shouted much louder than his little body seem to produce. "HEY! THE CHANTERS WANT THE HEAD LUMP UP THE HILL!"

Soas' eyes pinched tight, as his smile faded. He sighed and dropped his shoulders. He looked to his friends, "and this is why I do not breed."

"Blessed tis fortune hath the world many times untold." Nova said quietly. Mercadio nearly lost his composure as he stifled his laughter. He looked to Nova with merry eyes. Nova winked. Blackus smirked.

Delex distracted Soas from the gentle teasing before Soas angered. "Soas, thanks for getting the kid to stop talking." Delex smiled to Soas.

Soas grinned back. "Little brat has some lungs." He pointed to a lone figure that came out of the crowd. "Seems it worked though."

A decidedly female voice roared toward the hill. "Augges! Get back to your mother before I tan your backside three ways till morning!"

Augges, the kid, jumped and skittered back down the hill as fast as his legs could take him. The hawk spun down to his arm as they both disappeared into the crowd. The woman turned to the crowd, She said something as she squared her shoulders. They all became quieter but did not leave. Even the words of the village leader could not scare them away.

The woman in charge walked slowly and purposely up the hill with a large grin on her face. She was in a green, lose dress which showed off a modest amount of cleavage and her bare arms. A white apron adorned her waist. She wore a wide black leather belt about her waist that had an assortment of tools the clattered and swung from loops and pockets. Sturdy boots helped her take easy strides up the hill. Her long brown braid of hair swished back and forth with her gait. Her skin had a rough baked tanned from many days in front of fires and under the sun. She approached with a large smile and easy, open demeanor As she got closer, her smile begin to fade. Her hands gripped the skirts of her dress as she took the final steps to the group.

She eyed them all for a long moment and spoke softly with a smooth voice. "You are not the group we await for. Who is in charge?" Her hand went to a large hammer at her hip. Delex noticed that her arms were muscular and tone. Patches of skin seems worn rough, scared and blacked, especially around her hands.

"I am ma'am." Delex spoke up. "I honestly don't know why you are all cheering but I think you have the wrong people."

The woman grunted. "Truth to words." She mumbled as she looked over the group. She looked closely at Nova. Her stern expression soften immediately. "Dear child! You have no clothes and look like worn iron. What happened to you!" She looked to each person again. "What happen to you all?"

Surprisingly, it was actually Blackus was who spoke for the party. "An attack out in the plains, Quatll-kaat. We lost our supplies." He gave a look to the woman that flayed her from foot to head. His eyes pierced through as he measured her up.

The woman stared back into his eyes, unruffled by his stare. "Yes, I saw smoke on the horizon, even heard some sound." She removed her hand from her hammer. She took Nova by the hand and started down the hill. "I think it is best we get you all looked at, then you can tell me more. My name is N'Mora." She pulled Nova away. With in seconds they both whispered and giggled as they made steady progress down the hill into town.

Delex shrugged toward the others and motioned down the hill. They had no other choice but to followed Nova and N'Mora into the village. By the time they got to the crowd, N'Mora had explained briefly that they were merely travelers. The excitement vanished like fog on a hot day. N'Mora led everyone except Nova to the middle of the village to a building next door to a modestly sized inn. She stepped inside and waved them all in. The building was a single story building with a vaulted ceiling. A large open space with benches and a single desk covered most of the room. Two doors led behind the desk to other compartments.

"This is the mayor's house, the main hall. We only use it when we need to, else I would be at my home hammering metal." N'Mora took her tool belt off and tossed it on the floor near the desk. The belt made a huge thump on the wood floor that startled Delex. She went behind the desk and sat with her feet on the desk. She made sure she took time to adjust her dress for modesty. "Start talking."

Soas gave her a smirk. "Every cloud has a silver smile, and we got a full bite."

N'Mora gave him a small chuckle. "That you did. I intend to stay here until someone gives me an explanation or enough of village gets nervous and comes looking for me. You can be assured, they are well armed." N'Mora smiled politely to them.

Delex nodded to Mercadio. "I am Mercadio the black, leader of the darker arts of the towers, and high council member of wizardry." He motioned to the others. "This is my bodyguard Blackus, my guide Soas." Mercadio almost choked on the word, "My apprentice Delex, and Nova a maid we rescued in the fight."

N'Mora kicked her feet off the desk and stood up. "Well, I

believe most of that, but none the matter. All I care for is the safety of my village Hilltan." N'Mora motioned around her. "I apologize for the welcome. We have been seeking aid for the village for three full years. We thought you were the wizards we had requested from the towers of magic. Our crops have supported us for now, but they are slowly dying. This may be the last year we can feed ourselves."

"Perhaps we can help. I know many magical types of knowledge, but not about crops." Mercadio said. He pointed to Delex, "But I think my pupil has a talent that we can use here."

N'Mora finally smiled. "If it as you say, we will offer you bed, food, clothes and anything you need if you are still on a journey."

"That we are." Mercadio confirmed. "May we discuss this more tonight?" There was a knock on the door. They all turned to see some villagers enter with fresh clothes.

"I spoke and given measure of need." Nova said with a smile. She had returned in a simple blouse. She looked to Delex briefly in a way that made them both blush.

"Truth to word, I was going to provide you with enough for you to survive to the next village, but if you say truth, we will offer much more. Like my father said in his time, don't argue with a rock's shadow, when you should be stepping to the side." N'Mora smiled. "Until then, get some rest. We can discuss more tomorrow." She pointed the group towards the two doors inside the mayor house. One led to a small kitchen while the other led to a changing room and bathroom.

This was the only house for the tonight. Once the inn keeper found out they were not requested wizards, he refused to allow them rooms at his small inn. The only option that night was the floor of the mayor house. This was fine with the party. It was a vast improvement to how they slept the previous nights. The guests rested comfortably with offers of food, drink and thick blankets.

In the morning N'Mora arrived with breakfast and sat with them while they ate. Mercadio once again explained in more detail of who they are and where they plan to travel. He left out as much of the story as he could, especially Delex. To the mayor, he was a simple apprentice with great potential. They were on a journey to the towers of magic to test him for acceptance. N'Mora accepted this explanation enough to not question it. Her main goal was to discuss what the party could do for the village of Hilltan.

"Well, I imagine we can help here. I have some ability in the magic you desire, but I dare say our young Delex would have a better ability." Mercadio said as he stroked his chin.

Delex gave him a withered smile. Soas clapped him on the back. "I have no doubts Delex. Like the storm remember, just with a lot less chance of death!" Soas chuckled.

N'Mora frowned at Soas. She, like the others, have come to realize how much he like to annoy others. "I do not care how you do it, as long as everyone is safe. I hope you will do it soon and leave." She leaned forward as her voice became serious. "I know you are not telling me everything. I know, there are dangers that follow you. Yet, I am a woman of my word. You will have your help to get to the sea if you help us here." She leaned back and finished her ale. "Just do it quick."

"We will attempt it tomorrow night. I will speak with my apprentice and prepare him the best I can." Mercadio nodded. Delex and the others nodded in agreement. Delex was still a bit wary of his abilities, but he figured if he never tried he would not get strong enough to face Valash. As he thought of Valash, his hands tightened into fists. *Yes, this will be good. I'll kick your rotten hide Valash!* Delex thought to himself. He looked to Nova. Her eyes were on him. She had a smile and a determined look in her eye. He felt a tingle down his back.

"Mercadio is right. If we can help, he should help N'Mora." Delex said as he stood. N'Mora smiled. "We will not fail."

N'Mora stood. Her face was full of hope as she clasped hands with Delex. She looked to Mercadio. "He's special isn't he?" She looked back to Delex and looked into his eyes. "I don't know how, but you fill me with hope young man."

Delex couldn't help but to grin, and try to get his hand back before it was crushed in her grip. That look of hope in her eye filled him with confidence. Nova stood behind N'Mora with a smile as well, but her arms crossed before her and the smile didn't quiet reach her eyes. Delex chuckled. "Well, I guess Mercadio and I will talk." He looked to Nova, "Perhaps you can help too Nova?"

Nova smiled more and slide past N'Mora, but her movements force the mayor to break her hand shake with Delex. "As wished. Mine hand lent and given freely." Her smile reached her eyes, but now it seemed like a cat that caught a bird. She looked hungry. She looked to N'Mora with an almost hidden look of victory.

N'Mora ignored the looks. She pointed with her chin to Blackus. "Blackus is it?" Blackus nodded to her. "I have some things to discuss with you. I am not highly skilled but I think I have a sword rusting up my shop I can modify to your needs." She turned for the door. She looked back to him. "Come to my smithy, and we can discuss some payment."

Blackus nodded and left with N'Mora. Soas looked at the both with a raised eyebrow. "Well that was an odd look." He smiled wickedly to the others. "I guess I'll go and get a list of supplies." He skittered quickly to the door before Mercadio could warn him not to steal anything. The sound of Soas' laughter echoed from the street.

∞ ∞ ∞

The judge sat like a regal bird of prey as he looked down at the man covered in chains. The sounds of fire and commotion still echoed from outside the courthouse. Smoke and ash hung lightly within the room, as officers stuffed wet rags into any opening they could find. The judge looked down upon a single man.

"The accused will hear the accusations, and have pronouncement thereafter." A mumble came from the man below. The chains held tight as the man continued to mumble. The judge motioned to an officer to remove the gag.

"I swear Jaxcel, if you make one more remark about my weight, hair, intellect or wife, I will have that gag affixed permanently to your tongue."

The man, Jaxcel, worked his jaw for a moment. "You got it judge, no more jokes about that." He gave the judge a sideways look. "You don't happen to have any children? Ah! Okay, okay, okay!" He yelped as and officer started to approach him with the gag. "Just kidding. So why all the Dwarven jewelry?" Jaxcel said as he wiggled the chains draped over him.

The judge growled, "Have you not listened to a word at all, nor the shouts, nor the witnesses?!" He motioned to the smoke billow past the window outside. "You are lucky this building has spells against fire. Or else it would cook us like prized a roast." He pointed his gable at Jaxcel. "Jaxcel of Rin, Here by lies accused of willfully and with purpose unknown, fail Rin and the kings," He waved his hands dramatically, "and caused fire to the peoples of Rinward, and ruined much of the city."

"A dream and a horse." Jaxcel replied.

The judge looked to him in confusion. "Pardon me?"

Jaxcel shrugged. "I can't. I am not a judge, plus I don't think you did anything wrong. You can pardon me though." Jaxcel wiggled his eyebrows in anticipation.

The judge seemed to age on the spot. "Jaxcel, you ash-headed dullard. Ever the kings' most annoying of knights. What do you mean by 'a dream and a horse'?" He glared at Jaxcel. "And this better not be a punchline to another vulgar joke. The court has heard enough of those today."

Jaxcel shook his head. "No, but that does remind me of a joke about a nurse and a donkey. Any of ways. I had a dream last night, I was, chosen or some foolery, gave some power, or unlocked?" Jaxcel shrugged and looked to the ceiling in thought. "Well, long short of it, I have ma-a-a-gic!" Jaxcel wiggled in his chains with mock intimidation.

The judge rolled his eyes. "That is more than apparent." The judge sniffed the air. "Without a mistake, the fire has reached the royal bakery."

Jaxcel sniffed the air. "Oh good, I thought I was the only one smelling overcooked bread. I was told by healers, that is a bad sign. Now, if we only had a large vat of butter-" Jaxcel noticed the glare of the judge and continued on. "Okay, so I was swishing and swashing the sword like an ashen god today. Didn't think twice about the dream, when the horse sorta exploded on fire."

The judge read from a report. "Witnesses say you looked at the horse and yelled, I quote, 'Boom-a-looma', unquote. Wherein the horse's mane and tail exploded in fire."

Jaxcel shook his head. "Total accident. I was day dreaming of being a wizard and blasting Fire."

"Then you laughed." The judge said in a dead pan voice as he pointed to the paper.

"From surpri-i-i-se." Jaxcel rolled his eyes and exaggerated the word as if this should have been obvious.

"Then cheered." The judge added with a dead look.

"Because the dream was real." Jaxcel retorted.

"Then slapped the horse on its hindquarters, which enraged the beast and spurred it to break down the gate and run screaming into the city." The judge growled as he crumpled the paper.

Jaxcel sighed. "Okay, that one is on my deed." Jaxcel tried to point at the judge but the chained held his hands down. He had forgotten about those. "To be fair, I did not know it was a trained war horse, a royal horse, nor how freakishly fast it was." Jaxcel looked to the officers and chuckled. "Am I right guys, like super fast, and way more flammable than advertised." The officers ignored him.

The judge pounded his gable on the desk. "Enough. We have heard enough! Jaxcel I see you have no remorse and I doubt you have any understanding of the problems this new-found magic has wroth. I would dearly love to just sentence you to death, but you have, and are, one of the kings' favorites. That unfortunately still holds weight in the court."

The judge motioned the gag placed back in as Jaxcel was about to make another snide remark. "Furthermore we cannot imprison you for fear that this new magic is not fully understand, not only from us, but especially from you. The danger is too great."

The judge sighed and ran his head through his wispy hair. "Thus the court here by exiles you from town, from kingdoms, from rank, and title. We give you last pay and gear we could salvage before the fire burnt down your home," the judge turned red in the face, "And mine, and many others."

Jaxcel tried to protest and shook mightily in his chains, only to be rewarded with a boot to his back. He glared at the officers, but only received smirks.

"We must concluded this, so we can help save the rest of the city. Good bye Jaxcel and good riddance." The judge tossed down a backpack, a bag full of gear, food stuffs, and a slightly burnt sleeping bag. The judge addressed the officers. "Take this beggar to the edge of the farmland around the city and wait for the army." He looked to Jaxcel. "Do not remove the chains until you hand him over at the destination. Jaxcel, your escort will take you from the city wherein the army will remove you from our lands." The judge leaned over the desk slightly as a small smile rested on his face.

"Any last words for the court Jaxcel, perhaps you can have a dream less dangerous and more exciting?" The officer had dragged Jaxcel to a wood cart in the corner of the courtroom, They deposited him and his gear with a thud.

Jaxcel worked his jaw as the gag came lose. "Yeah, but if I dream like that again, your wife won't stop blushing for a week."

"GET HIM OUT!" The judge screamed.

∞∞∞∞

The party spent the next day gathering supplies. N'Mora and the people of Hilltan gave freely, and had no doubts they would finish the contract. It was N'Mora that convinced everyone the night she met Delex. Since then, she had been locked away with Blackus hammering away within her workshop.

The night settled softly. Fluffy pink clouds melted into purples and blued until even they lost color as the sun went down. The breeze moved across the land like silk and whispered secret comforts. Laughter and excitement echoed like raindrops across the little town. Everyone had come in from the farms to attend what might hail as one of the most exciting moments in the little village. Word passed along the village this could be dangerous, so everyone returned from the fields while casters performed their works.

Mercadio explained to Delex that this was one of the many services the wizards do for the kingdoms. They do it all for free, not only to train and test the wizards. It also helps keep the towers of magic self-sovereign. "These services brings in many young hopefuls to the towers. All in all, it was a mutually beneficial for everyone." Mercadio explained.

"That is great and all, but I am not a wizard Mercadio." Delex shrugged on his new boots. The village supplied the travelers with new cloths and a few traveling supplies, with promise of much more if all worked out tonight. Delex was in comfortable dark green wool pants and shirt, with a brown leather vest and soft leather boots. A dark leather belt wrapped around his waist and over his shoulder to support a sword N'Mora had given him.

Mercadio had recovered his outer cloak from Nova and somehow had repaired his robes himself. He had found a new staff again, or grown it from the something. Delex was not sure. His grey hat remained as battered and shapeless as ever. "This is true son. You have a knack for it but in as much as an infant has a knack for learning to dance."

Delex rolled his eyes, "Well thanks professor with those self-esteem issues."

Mercadio smiled. "It was no slight. It takes a group of about six wizards to perform what you are going to try. I am merely going to contain, and anchor the impressive amounts of magic you are going to perform." Mercadio gave Delex a series look. "What you perform tonight is no simple task. Take comfort in that. We could not ask for any better cover for mask. The residue from the plant growth will grow and further confound any tracking our mutual problem will try. Do you understand why we must try?" Mercadio did not want to say his name where outsiders could hear it.

Delex nodded and sighed. Without another word Mercadio and Delex left the major's common house and walked to the center of the town. An immediate cheer rose from the village. Soas joined them from outside and happily waved and blew kisses to the crowd. Delex couldn't help but smile at his new friend. He had a natural charm that many fell for. It showed now as smiles and waves increased.

In the middle of the town was a raised platform. On the platform N'Mora quietly talked to Blackus. Blackus and N'Mora spent all day within her home and workshop. They only appeared within the last half hour. N'Mora had a look of pure exhaustion. A smile still played on her face as she talked to Blackus and made idle conversation with a few town folk. Blackus unconsciously lifted and dropped a new sword in his scabbard.

None of that registered for Delex. All he saw was a lone figure on the platform. She stood regal in a brilliant blue sleeveless dress which shifted and swung in the air. A broad black belt held it to her waist. Her skin glowed in the torch light. She noticed him and smiled. She hooked her long hair behind her ear and turned back to talk with N'Mora. They both looked up to him and smiled. He couldn't help but smile back.

He approached the platform and everyone cheered. N'Mora settled them down with a quick raised hand. "I know you all are eager to see these wizards perform this great service for us." She paused and gave Mercadio a sidelong glance. "They are eager to help, but we must show these wizards the respect they deserve. This means we must stay quiet. A distracted caster is a hot iron tossed into a crowd." There were mutual agreements and nods. N'Mora raised her hand in welcome. "But that does not mean we cannot eat and drink and be merry as we watch them perform." A cheer erupted from the crowd then settled into a cheerful murmur.

Blackus stepped off the platform with N'Mora and Soas. Mercadio turned to the other two. "This is our plan. Delex will concentration on the soil and summon up Nature magic and improve the ground." He pointed to Nova. "You young lady will channel as a bridge. I will use some of that magic to perform the smoke screen, as Delex put it, to cover our magic. We will escape and split up while the spell works to confuse any sensory ability Valash has." Delex and Nova nodded.

"Well, I guess we should get this party started." Delex shrugged.

Nova laughed. "Oh thy merriment has last since dusk-set." She kissed Delex on the cheek. "You speak in riddles. Tis not the time for thy weird speech."

Delex grumbled under his breath. "You're one to talk. We need to fix that soon." He spoke to the others. "Yeah, well I guess I just sit down and get comfortable?" Mercadio nodded. Delex sat down in the middle of the platform and closed his eyes.

Delex recently had more time to practice concentration and meditation. You had few hobbies on a world without TV, radio, manga or anything else. Plus he had plenty of time to withdraw within himself during his happily little time with a kidnapping psychopath. Delex took a depth breath. The fell of the world slipped away quickly and left him suspended in a void. He reached out with his senses. Around him the world focused into a brownish fog. This represented the farmland and village around him. Within the fog there were ribbons of green smoke that hung near his feet. This, he though, was the healthy nutrients set deeply into the earth. He also noticed a bit of black as that hung almost unnoticed in the air. This felt wrong to him. It was unnatural. He tried to trace the source but it would slip away from him. Delex tried several more times unsuccessfully but it only wasted more time and increase his frustration. *I have a job to finish and this is not it! It is like I am trying to catch smoke.* He thought grumpily.

He set his mind back to task. He reached out towards the green smoke and tried to encourage its growth upward. The green tendrils grew slightly. He could feel Nova outside as she channeled some magic he preformed towards Mercadio. He had no idea how she did it, but it amazed him. She told him it was a simple magical transference. To him, it was like a fish speaking to a bird.

He hoped the plan to confuse Valash would work. He could not worry about any of that right now except the job Mercadio dropped in his lap. The tendrils of green suddenly retracted. Delex grumbled with confusion. It should have worked. He focused his thoughts and noticed some green smoke dissipated when it touched the black ash. The brown fog swirled in lazy currents of air. It remained unchanged by anything Delex tried.

Delex tried again but with the same results. Every time he made progress the ash would get in the way. He focused on the ash again but it slipped away. It felt odd, like he tried to look at the tip of his nose to focus on a distant point. He knew it was in front of him, but when he focused on the ash, it was to his left or right. Delex redoubled his efforts and bored down with all concentration on the green smoke. He ignored the ask and bent all his will into it the green tendrils of smoke. Several of the of green tendrils suddenly burst with power shot upwards like tree trunks through the ash and brown fog. Delex cheered in his mind. *Well, that finally worked. I better keep going.* He thought.

Soas tried to shake Delex awake. Screams of unrest and worry framed his face. N'Mora shouted to the crowd to settle down and all was fine. All was far from fine. Nova held Delex in her lap. Nothing they tried would wake him. Mercadio had successfully tied his confusion spell into the magics an hour ago. The misdirection used would spread an invisible magical sensory cloud over a hundred kilometers in every direction. Not even his wizard sight could penetrate it. Nova made sure he fine-tuned the spell to befuddle even a sorcerer. It would last for several weeks and even longer if he had time to maintain it. There was even more power than predicted. Delex was a font of energy. With this much, he could send out dozens of fake trials.

Yet, none of that mattered. Delex would not wake. He had successfully improved the soil of the ground. His magics had pulled deeply rooted nutrients and Nature magic close to the surface. It would sustain the region for decades.

Yet, Delex continued his work and nothing they tried could stop him. Plants sprouted everywhere, even the old dead wood of the houses. The fields were ripe with food. Villagers scrambled to collect the bountiful harvest. At first, it had lead to massive celebration. As the vegetation started to grow wild and crawl over every surface, people begun to panic as they beat back the creeping horde of delicious plants.

Everywhere, the ground bloomed with edible vegetation. Every house had vines or stalks that crawled skyward. Mercadio looked to the others and shouted. "If we cannot wake him soon we need to ride from this place."

Soas shouted back. "What about the reward? We need those supplies to get across the sea."

Blackus spoke in his quiet voice, but it still was heard over the confusion. "No need, reach out and take your fill."

Soas snorted. "Not that, we need much more. Money, spare horses, blankets, and, well more!"

Nova gave him a glare. "From mouth to word. Thy needs be nary a trifle for thy fingers, naive." She glared at them all. "Speak not, whisper less. Mine inner thought shalt quest him."

Nova closed her eyes and bent her will to connect to her hero. Her heart pounded with worry. Everything went black as the world fell away. In the outside world the ground suddenly shuddered and lurched everyone from their feet.

Chapter 15: Triggers and Trials

Nova wandered in the darkness with arms stretched out before her. It was full of colored smoke and ash. She never seen another sorcerer's 'mind's eye'. Every sorcerer has a signature way they view magic. It was private, and to view someone was akin to a peek into their soul. It was almost intimate. What she needed, made her blush. Yet, she must find him. Delex was powerful. It scared her, and she just begun to know him. He was like a child at times when it came to magic. At other times he performed magic that would take adept sorcerers decades to master. This was one of those things. He had mastered magic in his own mind's eye. Amazing.

This technique involved seeing the magic itself around you and extend your influence outward. It took a tiny portion of a sorcerer's own inner magic to manipulate the world. Wizards had a different way to manipulate the outside magic. It took extreme effort and skill. They had to draw it in before they could influence the magic and world around them. Wizards found ways to decrease this effort in practiced spells, memorization and other structured rituals. Wizards could not see natural magics like this.

Nova suspected they found a way to see magic after crafting into a spell. Wizards could use natural forces if they sequenced them in a specific order to play off each other through a spell. They can be at times extremely powerful, but also tedious to cast. Nothing a wizard cast could compare to a sorcerer's speed and direct control. Yet, humans had more versatility in manipulative techniques. Delex showed something far beyond being versatile. His focus barred all distractions. They could not wake him with mundane or magical means. That unnerved her to the point she decided to invoke her final idea. Nova had to commit a sorcerion taboo and violate his mind to save him. The thought of what she would do left a terrible guilt in the pit of her soul. Yet, as she looked at helpless face of the only other living sorcerer, she couldn't leave him to die, forever lost in his mind. A single tear rolled down her cheek as she closed her eyes and concentrated.

Nova tried to refocus the environment around her and see the natural magic paths as her mind's eye would. The magic fog and smoke around her briefly shifted into bands of colored light but a force overwhelmed her like she was a child. The light snapped them back into place. Smoke, fog and ash hung around her in shifting curtains. Nova's eyes opened wide in shock. The only time she had ever felt this kind of resistance is when she visited the other dragons on the moon. They spend hours in Mind's Eye cultivating the moon's magic into a livable spot to live. They were masters beyond any degree. Sorcerers view the magical essence as they personally imagine it. This would not hamper the way other sorcerers viewed it. Yet in here, Nova faced an untrained mind no less powerful than she felt from her kin on the moon. Furthermore, her vision shaped to Delex's vision, not her own. Nova shuddered from the revelation. This was an impossibility. If Mercadio only knew the extent of Delex's power, he would strongly consider physical imprisonment or worse. She shook the thought out of her head and composed herself. She refused to let her mind wander down those dark paths.

As she searched, she begun to feel a pull in a single direction. She followed her instincts and walked in that direction. She didn't truly walk, yet her mind wandered as one's thought would wander. Her body remained where it was, yet her mind could travel great distances across the planet. Since her and Delex was part of the spell that blanketed this area in magical confusion, it did not block them. If Valash tried to the same right now, he would hit a tangle of magic that would nearly blind his Mind's Eye. Even still, if she had her dragon form right now, it would be no trouble to locate Delex in this mind realm. She still had the power, she could feel it, but it was out of reach. Her new body that Delex created was part of her, but at the same time, alien. It would take time for her to master the magical pathways and regain her magic. She smiled in her thoughts. She already referred to herself as she. It settled her nerves to the new life, yet she still felt that-.

"Nova?" A voice echoed from the darkness interrupted her mind as it distracted her from the task. "Nova is that you? What are you doing here?" Delex emerged from the darkness and stepped up to her. "And why are you naked?"

Nova's eyes widen momentarily as she looked down. She was nude, her skin glistened smooth and shapely like when they first met. She used her will to make a purple dress flow around her body and cover up her arousal and embarrassment. "Most gracious apologies." She turned away to hide the red that slowly made its way into her skin.

"Am I dreaming you?" Delex grinned. "If I am, then the dress is the last thing I want to see." He chuckled. The dress flickered out of existence.

Nova turned back and slapped him soundly on his face as she willed the dress back on. "Tis not feverish malady cad of man!" Nova's face turned red, but not with embarrassment. "Tis meditative slumber and sorcerion skill betwixt thy lay."

Delex's face drained of blood as understanding sunk in. "Oh crap! Nova I am so sorry. I thought it was a dream. I didn't

246

mean to, to, uh-"

Nova signed and placed her hand on his shoulder. "Pay no toll. Mine mind ask nay a cost but silence. May hap anon this comedy play upon action anew when upon we meet skin and skin." She gave him a wink. Delex took a moment to understand her. She held back how perturbed she was at that. Her beautiful ancient flowing speech, like water upon a river, reduced to cobbled stones down a landslide. She would have to learn and adapt. Luckily, she was very good at languages. Sadly, she was not very good at focusing to a task. She mentally sighed and shook her head, and released to late, she sighed and shook her head. You had to be very careful in here. You inner monologue, could easily become normal monologue. In the past, it had caused many a sorcerer grievance when- oh yes, Delex. Nova looked to him. "Now, to thy troubles. Pray thee speak true, why doth thee not returned?"

Delex took a moment to brush off his confusion. *I will never understand women! He cleared his throat.* "Okay first off, Nova, your speech, it absolute murder. In my world, I mean Earth world, you sound like you are play-acting at bad Shakespeare. It honestly sounds like a third-rate drama student."

Nova gave a small understanding pout, but her clenched fist spoke otherwise. "Tis mine normal mode of soliloquy."

Delex comforted her with a hand on her face. Nova almost gasped from the touch. "I know, I know, but I only bring it up because it is so hard to understand you. I want to get to know you and be able to communicate with you."

Nova gave a small nod. "Verily, truth to word. Mine thoughts rest within thy words when thine but moment born. We practice anon. Yet purpose pursued we act on now?"

Delex nodded. *Is she getting worse? That last sentence sounded like Yoda murdering iambic pentameter.* He folded his arms while he tapped his lips with his left hand. "And second, I want to repair the ground but this ash is everywhere and I cannot get it to go away. It is unnatural." He gestured all around him as he paced. "I keep trying to trace it, to get it out of the way, but it eludes me, then comes back."

"Tis thy Mind's Eye. Thy sorcerion brethren meditate to see magic. Thy thoughts shaped thy perversion of sight." Nova said as she studied the ash.

"So you say I am seeing the magic of the world, or this place?" Delex asked. Nova nodded. "So I just need to see it another way?" Delex questioned himself.

Nova was about to tell him that the way sorcerers view the magic is unique as it was unchangeable. As she opened her mouth, the world shifted and nearly took her to her knees. The smoke and fog slapped to the ground into small tiles. Underfoot, green and brown square tiles stretched in every direction. Now and then a black tile appeared within the mosaic. Nova startled and fell to the ground, or at least the surface it represented. She was speechless. *No Sorcerer can match this. No Dragon does this!*

"No. Better, but not right. The ash stopped moving, but it is still random tiles. How about-" The world shifted again. Green and brown threads of magic ran in all directions and positions. Far about blue and white threads laced through each other. Several threads of black stretched in one single direction. Delex turned back to Nova with an innocent smile of achievement. "There we go!" He pointed. "Come on Nova, lets figure this out."

Delex touched a string of black. The mental world around him started to shudder. Delex fell to his knees with the string still held in his hand. A third figure materialized from the darkness. The threads shuddered violently around him.

The smokey darkness revealed a tall dark figure. It loomed over them in silent disdain. Delex looked in horror as his eyes locked on Valash. Delex cried out and looked to Nova to shout a warning, but when he turned back, the image had disappeared. "What was that?"

Nova shook her head. "Me thinks memory twists within thy cursed thread?" Nova's head hung in a curtain of soft black hair. Vertigo held power over her as she slowly recovered her sense of self.

Delex shrugged and waved his free hand through the spot where the image appeared. "Not sure. I think it came from this." He motioned with a nod to his hand that still held to the black thread. "Maybe if I follow it to the source."

Nova placed a hand on his shoulder. "Unwise eight ways from straight. Thy forms wilt by distance spent. Mine mind has not thy power to follow."

Delex nodded. "I'll be fine. I need to figure how to get this taint out." Nova grimaced but said no more. Her look was enough to tell Delex how foolish he sounded. Delex colored a bit in his face. "Just watch over me."

Nova nodded as her image vanished. Delex figured she had left to report back to his friends what happened. He turned his attention back to the thread and concentrated. He slowly slipped down the thread. There was no real feel of movement in this world within his mind, except he knew moved within the magic of the world. He felt a pull towards his body, like a stretching of taffy, the further it went the more the pull resisted, and weaker he felt. He was vaguely aware of his location but since he was relatively new to this world. Nothing made sense to him. The world felt like it curved downward and upward. The thread kept going on this curve towards a glowing river of red threads.

His movement slowed as Delex thought about going back. *If I stop now, I fail this town.* He shook his head. Delex gave a quick smile as he thought about shaking his head. He only imagined he shook his head in this world of the mind. Somewhere in the back of his mind he could feel his body and his friends desperately try to rouse him. They worried, but he had to keep going. He forced all his concentration on the source of the black thread. The ghostly world of colored threads flashed by him. He found himself in the center of what he could describe as a massive net of crisscross lines of color. He couldn't count them all. There had to be billions of these lines of power. His one little thread felt like a drop in an ocean.

He thought about the ocean. The threads started to turn into liquid. Delex quickly concentrated, and the liquid turned back to threads. There was many colored of threads, and even black or grey ones, but they did not have the same oily, barbed, feel as the one held in his hand. They felt natural. This thread was still wrong. He concentrated and moved through the threads. Delex felt a small amount of liquid on his lip. He touched his lip and looked down to his fingers. A small bit of blood touched each finger. He knew this must be a reflection of the real world. He couldn't change anything about the bleeding here. Delex couldn't heal himself here. His body was too far away. He could only protect his mind. Delex shrugged and moved deeper.

"We have to stop him Mercadio!" Soas yelled. Soas held Delex's head in his lap. Blackus and Nova held down his arms and legs as his body writhed and shook. Soas soaked up blood that poured out of his nose.

"I wish we could, but his mind is not here. I am unfamiliar with this." He looked to Nova for help.

She shook her head. "Tis skill drenched of magic. Nary few counted as masters. Mine Delex wades harked magics liken shallow waters."

Mercadio sighed. "As I feared. He performs some of the most complicated magic easily, yet has trouble with the simple things. It may eventually kill him." Nova's face immediately cringed with worry. "Oh, no, not now dear." He patted her shoulder. "He will be fine, not now, I am sure of it."

The villagers hurried away from the scene a few hours ago and a guard posted to keep the onlookers at bay. The growth had stopped and now reversed. Brown started to appear throughout the vegetation. Mercadio worried that the magic would leave the village in worse shape than when they started. He worried about the people, and the animals not only here, but other places. If what Nova said was correct, there was a much bigger problem that was hidden in underground. None of this mattered as much as Delex.

Mercadio returned his concentration to Delex but was not proficient at healing magic. Indeed, he was terrible at it. He could not apply the advanced techniques he learned with Delex's father. He resorted to pouring greater amounts of pure wizard magic to increase his chances. Mercadio begun to speak with a sing-song quality in his voice. His hands moved in intricate patterns as he summoned magics around him. He produced bits of powder and salts to increase the magic. Mathematics and patterned learned over decades of study flowed from his mind. Underneath him, Delex's body settled to fluttered twitches. His nose slowed to a trickle of blood.

Mercadio collapse to the ground. He changed so little, and suffered a heavy dose of magical poisoning. "That is all I could help. The rest lies with him."

Delex was caught in a web of strings with no end. Yet in this maze he had finally come to the end of the black thread. A spike core of black punched into the center of all the multi-colored strings. It feed on them. The strings looked slightly weaker from its touch. Something drew power from the core of the planet. As he watched, one string bleed corruption and turned the unnatural black. This was the source. Delex moved his blackened string off the dark spike. It immediately turned green. He hoped that would repair the problem of Hilltan.

Delex was about to go back, but his curiosity overwhelmed him. What was the black spike? Why was it there. He wished he had more time to find out, but he had to leave. Delex sighed, took a mental note, and made his way back to his body. He woke to his body racked with pain. He felt weaker than he had ever felt. Delex knew he overworked his magic and made his body suffer. Without a word his friends helped him up and led him back to the common house of the mayor. New growth covered the ground and house The villagers didn't seem to mind. They cheered and celebrated around him. The growth had finally settled into a healthy compromise. Some people ran naked with hands full of vegetables and fruits. This was quickly subdued by the village guards, but they all had smiles on their faces. About why the villagers celebrated naked, no one dared to ask, especially the guards.

N'Mora walked them back to the building. "Well that was probably the sloppiest bit of magic I have ever seen, but in the end it all worked out." She shook her head. "It was bad for a minute, but suddenly everything just came together." She gripped Delex's hand in a fierce shake. "Rest well master wizard." She turned and motioned with a nod. Without a word Blackus followed her into the night.

Soas lifted an eyebrow. "So That's what he is in to." Soas turned to Delex. "Are you okay? You had us all worried. Nova explained a little."

Delex sighed and tried to explain what he saw. Mercadio was extremely interested in what he saw and how he saw it. He had Delex repeat himself several times as he listened. Mercadio was eventually forced to stop his inquires when Delex started to fall asleep as he sat. He was exhausted. Nova offered to stay with him and watch him through the night. Delex shuddered asleep in her arms and drifted peacefully into a dreamless rest.

Nova worried over him. She looked into his face as he slept. She tried to absorb what she saw last night. Delex was strong, she had no doubt about it. He remained untrained. He knew almost nothing of the simple ways of magic and just used his power like a brute to force his will against reality. The scary part was, it worked. He performed things that would take masters decades to learn or was commonly agreed, impossible.

She let a silent tear fall from her face. His body was not ready for such power. She should have seen it sooner. They all should have seen it. His power was too subtle. If Delex continued to push his way through the impossible, it was bound to push back. His body held no resistances to the forces that course through him. It was the danger of the sorcerer. Wizards had magic go through them that poisoned them sickness. This was recovered very quickly, getting past the sick feeling after you vomit. Sorcerers feel the magic to the core of their being and weakness as they expel their own magic until exhaustion, and possibly death.

Nova held Delex closer and cried into the night. She knew the first moment she saw him, he would change her world. She felt drawn to him but could not explain why. *Am I in love? This is too soon.* She felt trapped in a flat spin she could not recover. She loved it. When he touched her she felt sharp pains in her stomach and hips. It was a sharp hurt, but also felt pleasantly sweet. It was all so foolish. She ran her fingers through his hair and Delex sighed. She sighed with him. Nova slowly drifted to sleep with Delex's head in her lap. Tomorrow they would get more answers, but tonight, it was time to rest.

The morning came too quickly for the group. A large celebration started up yet again. The town leader, N'Mora, was in no condition to slow the revelry. Her eyes were blood shot and her hair was a mess. Soas noticed right away and had asked her if she had worried about them all night. N'Mora blushed red from head to foot and told him to keep his thoughts on his own business. Soas shrugged and wandered off to find ways to amuse himself. Mercadio had a few last things to check He wanted to make sure his conceal magic and the miracle Delex performed last night were secure. Blackus had still not appeared. This left Delex and Nova with N'Mora to finish the details on departure.

"So, you two," N'Mora gave them both a knowledgeable smile. "Sleep well? I heard you both didn't come out of the gathering hall until morning."

Nova gave her a small glare, "pray, forgive mine darken deed.

Hark, Mine eyes bare nay sight nor word spoke of Blackus. Mayhap thy mind or crafty eye may speak his passing. For mine eye doth last scry thy warrior gather with thy chambered hall? Alas, he yet is smoke unseen."

N'Mora coughed into her hand, "Well, it is not my business how you slept. Blackus is probably with your new horses and traveling gear. I should tend to my business." She walked to the fields for a morning inspection.

Nova gave a smile triumphant smile and spoke quietly. "That thee should, that thee should."

N'Mora waived Delex and Nova over. They shrugged and followed her over. N'Mora look at the fields and gave a long happy sigh. All around them the fields were fresh with crop. The plants that grew stunted or weak, now grew in a bloom of perfect health. The town still lay in heavy overgrowth, but the people were as efficient at cleanup as they were with the celebration.

"You've changed everything for us. This is much more than we had ever dreamed or asked for." She looked to Delex. "You are not a normal wizard are you?" Delex tensed for a second but N'Mora quickly put up her hands. "I had plenty of time to hammer at this. I don't want an answer. I want you to know, this village will never forgot you." She cupped Delex's hands in her own. "Thank you, thank you all." N'Mora let his hands go and turned away. She immediately started to bark orders to her people and stopped some more crazy antics.

Delex smiled to Nova and waved go bye to N'Mora. "Well that was cool." Delex smiled.

Nova gave him a queer look. "Tis nary a temped touch. Thy air tis brisk, yea wittily warm."

Delex gave a sharp laugh and walked away with her. "Okay, that is it. Your speech lessons start now. You are driving me crazy." He spun around and started to walk backwards as he smiled to her. "You sound like bad Shakespeare. Like, real bad."

Nova grinned and just agreed while she watched him smile

and be happy. Maybe she was over reacted with her thoughts. He seemed healthy without injury. "Mine words rattle nigh spear in jest or war."

Delex could only shake his head and laugh. "Come on, lets go gather the others. Pretty sure Soas and Blackus have everything ready."

∞∞∞∞

A few hours later, after a large breakfast and roughly a kilometer out of town, Mercadio signaled a halt. "We are getting close to the border where our screening spell is most potent. If we travel more together, Valash will spot us once again." He gave each person a hard stare. "We must split and part ways while under the most cover."

Blackus spoke first. "I will ready my armies." Blackus looked back the way they came and started to turn his horse. Mercadio placed a hand on his shoulder.

"Wait Blackus. I will travel with you until we get back to Homgad, I will search for more information. I still believe we may have been betrayed." Mercadio scratched at his shoulder in his cloak. Nova had given it back after she received new clothes. Daylow was most appreciative. A loud purr rumbled from the folds of the hood.

Soas let out a long exhausted sigh. "Fine, but I hate this idea. Who will watch over the big guy?" Soas twitched a thumb to Delex.

"He is strong. He will live." Blackus whispered with dangerous confidence.

Nova walked her horse close to Delex. "I will be on him over his sides."

Mercadio, Blackus and Soas gave her an odd look.

Delex smiled. "I have been teaching her to speak more modern. I think she meant she will be near me, by my side." He chuckled and pinched his finger and thumb together. "Still needs a bit of work." Nova gave him a punch in the arm and a pout.

Mercadio ignored them all and mumbled to himself. "Yes I think it will be fine." He pointed a finger to Delex and Nova. "But no magic! Either of you could easily tip off Valash to the real trail. We have many dummy trails out there, but remember this. He will send scouts to investigate each one." Mercadio adjusted his robes as he peered at each person. "No heroics. Hide and sneak away. Let them believe they found yet another fake trail."

"They will be pawns, but powerful." Blackus warned.

Soas nodded his agreement. "Yeah, but I doubt he will send out the big guns until he finds the right source." He winked to Delex, "So be sneaky. I will be up ahead with transportation at the ready."

Delex squinted at Soas. *Big guns. As far as Blackus has told me, guns do not exist here. Soas, had to travel to Earth, no doubt.*

"Hold. Anon, anon. Where? What court, we-?" Nova asked but couldn't get the correct modern phrases. She looks to Delex.

"Where do we meet at?" He gave Nova a small smile. She return it with a nod.

Soas glared at Mercadio. Mercadio rolled his eyes in a rare display. "To the towers of magic it seems. We need research and they have it."

Soas grumbled under his breath loudly. "The twig into the fire." He looked to Delex. "It is the only way. They have one of the few libraries on this planet that has information of Valash. We need to know more."

Delex raise on eyebrow. "Why not ask Blackus. He was there. He battled him."

Blackus shrugged. "I had retreated."

Mercadio tipped his head towards Blackus. "But not everyone. The towers have a few witnesses. We must find those documents."

Soas sighed. "A shame we could not have interrogated Moraphen before he was destroyed."

Mercadio growled. "An unfortunate but necessary loss." He looked back to Delex. "Go to the towers and take this letter of introductions. Obtain a student membership."

"We are wasting the day." Blackus glared. The tone of his voice, as usual, left little warmth. He turned his horse and rode slowly away.

Soas checked his straps and gave them all a bow. "I'll meet you towards the sea. Look for the largest port." Soas whipped at the reins and shot away.

Mercadio moved his horse towards Delex. His eyes were full of tears. He gave Delex a large hug and held him by his shoulder. "I never had a son of my own. If I had a son, you would be the image of him to the very bone." He looked to Nova. "Keep him safe."

Nova moved over and gave Mercadio a hug and kiss on the cheek. Mercadio colored slightly pink. "With word unbroken." She looked to Delex and back to Mercadio. "I give you my word?" Delex nodded to her.

Delex thought for a second. "Actually, the way you said that, was beautiful. Not everything of archaic origins is bad. Somethings are worth the beauty." He looked at Nova and gave a small grin. He words carried more meaning than just her speech.

Nova caught the innuendo and gave him a sly fox smile. "Windless water, you are. Else in thy words, very smooth."

Mercadio smiled to them both while he struggled with his goodbyes. The weather had darkened and clouds have gathers to lay a light rain. The rain only emphasized the mood.

Delex felt like he said farewells to a man he hardly knew. Yet, in memory, he had been there since he was born. Delex swallowed several times before he spoke. "Until we meet again Mercadio. Please be safe."

Mercadio turned his horse away and galloped towards Blackus in the distance. Soas had already dissipated like a ghost. "Well, it looks like just you and me. Guess we have time to get to know each other." Delex knew Nova liked him a lot, but he was also concerned. He had saved her life, and changed it in ways even he could not understand. If he was in her shoes, he would be completely infatuated. That was the problem. He wanted a relationship with her. She was beyond beautiful to him. It was clear to him she had skills and intelligence that complemented him. He just needed to be sure this was affection and not affliction. He wanted Nova to see him as a friend, not a savior.

Nova seemed to sense the hesitation in his eyes. She took his hand and gripped it softly then let it go. "Yes. I have love for that."

"I would love that." Delex corrected. Nova stuck her tongue out as they turned the horses towards the sea. The sky stretched over the horizon in overcast clouds. Small bars of light cut through and made pools of light on the ground. In the distance horizon, over the mountains, a line shimmered below the rising curve. This was the sea. Normally, this would be swallowed up by the curve of the planet. This was no ordinary planet. Delex finally understood. The memories had finally returned.

The planet itself was roughly two globes pressed together with a saddle in the middle. Somehow Ter'Avan remained separated or being crushed together. This left the shape much akin to a peanut. It also left navigation extremely easy, if you looked up. Delex still found it odd and it amused him to no end. It left him to giggle about it at odd moments. Delex asked. "Mercadio didn't say how long this would take."

"Several months towards thy sea." Nova responded. Delex was still astonished how quickly she could understand and change her way of speaking. "We will have time of great amounts to know thee and mine alike." She smiled to him, and in that smile it seemed she could part the clouds and bring sunshine in the middle of the night. Delex's heart skipped a beat.

Delex smiled, and felt no need to correct her. It would have spoiled the moment. "Well, lets get going." He clicked his tongue at the horse. The horse turned a confused eye to him. He clicked again and wiggle the reins. The horse rolled into a lazy trot with Nova's horse at his side.

∞∞∞

Three days later, Delex had a dream. It was the same dream he always had. He was on the open plains with majestic purple mountains in the distance. The clouds floated high above. They lazily bumped and shove past each other. Some details where much clearer in this dream. The air had a heady perfume. The sounds of wind rippled over the grass. He looked to his arm and saw goosebumps roll over it. The soft breeze lifted the hair as it went. If he didn't know he was in a dream, he would be certain this was real.

"Hello Delex." An unknown voice said behind him. Delex turned and saw a man with his hands behind his back. He wore an ornate black coat embroidered in blue thread. It hugged his frame and stopped just below the top of black leather, calf-high boots. Underneath was a grey wool shirt and pants. His hair was a mop of ruffled light brown, combed back at the sides. White brushed at his temples lightly and wrinkles made simple lines around his eyes. Yet, this was the only wrinkles on him. His skin shone with youth. His grey eyes brimmed with kindness as they studied Delex. "It is good to see you."

Delex had never seen this man before. He looked at him with obvious bewilderment. He was nervous but he felt no malice. "Do I know you?"

The man gave a wide grin. "I hope so. It has been a long time since I had seen you last. A few hundred years." The stranger walked to Delex and place his hands on Delex's shoulders. "Hello again, son."

"Doran?" Delex eyes opened wide as the knowledge flooded in. "Dad!"

Doran erupted into laughter. Behind him the floating castle of Homgad flashed into existence. Its majestic towers and gleaming walls showed no age. Below the Castle a small fort held vigilance. In a blink of an eye, time expanded the fort, into a castle, then a town, then a city. It kept expanding over a brief few seconds. Finally, it settled into the fortress city of Homgad, with its sprawling farmland and grand walls that mountains on either side of the lake. The floating Castle gleamed light a steady beacon, without change.

"Welcome home Delex." Doran's smile was contagious. Delex laughed out loud as he gave his father a hug that could crush a tree. A sudden wave of memories flooded back to him. He was so young. He saw his dad as a hero, a giant among men. Delex wanted to be just like him, wanted his father be proud of him.

He held his father and wept into his shoulder. It was warm and strong. He remembered those arms as they held him as a child. Even though he was just a small thing those arms still felt just as big, and the shoulder, just as wide. His father smelled of pine, his father's favorite scent. It was all so real. He reluctantly pulled himself away. His face was a mess of tears and moisture. "I thought you were dead?"

His father shrugged. "Technically, I am." Doran turned to walk and Delex followed with him. "Though, I am in your dream, I am still real. I died a long time ago, as time relates to this world. What Mercadio told you is true, we hid you on another planet, Earth."

"Why not just send me away somewhere here?" Delex asked. He could still feel the power of that hug. Here he was, his father, the man that had raised him, but had died. He momentarily felt guilty. Jim was also his father and a real good one.

"Your face looks troubled." Doran asked. His eyes reflected the clouds as they passed by. "You are thinking of Jim?" Delex nodded to Doran. "Perfectly fine son." He smiled to Delex. "I picked Jim for that role."

Doran walked steadily, almost regal with his hands behind

his back. Delex had sudden memories of his father when he paced back and forth in his study, talked to leaders of the world, or even just the kitchen cook. He always had those same measured steps; his hands held loosely behind him. It was the same for everyone. No one was greater or lesser in his father's eyes. He treated everyone with the same respect. Delex had a sudden pain in his heart. Here was his father again. He walked by his side, treated him as an equal, with that same respect. His throat tightened. He cleared his throat. It was hard to speak through all the emotions that washed over him. "Jim? You picked him?"

Doran nodded. "It was your mother's idea and my contingency. We sent Mercadio there to find a suitable replacement if things went all gnomish." he grinned, "and boy did it." Doran frown momentarily.

"This isn't a social visit is it?" Delex said. He felt an unsteadiness in his father's eyes.

Doran closed his eyes and took a deep breath. "It is not son. I am here now with limited power and borrowed time. My connection can become dangerous to you, so I cannot spend much time. This may be the only chance that I get." Doran stopped walk. The wind had picked up around them and the night begun to fall. The world faded into darkness as stars winked into being. "I need to tell you how Valash is still alive and how to kill him once and for all."

Delex shivered involuntarily. A fire erupted nearby and gave Delex a momentary startle. It was a campfire with two log seats positioned around it. They both walked over at sat on opposite sides. Doran's face mixed into light and shadow. It made him look grim. Delex asked his father, "so, what do you mean still alive?"

Doran stared at the flames. His eyes seemed old now. The weight of his wisdom pressed down on his shoulders. "I mean he is still alive, yet he has already died." Doran looked up to Delex. "Just like me. If not destroyed, he will lead the world into permanent death, and rule it thereafter." A ripple of thunder played behind Doran in the far distance. A storm brewed, but it gave off only malicious fear.

Chapter 16: Moving Pieces

Doran waited for Delex to weigh his words before he continued. "Let me explain. Valash, your mother and I were the last sorcerers on the planet. We had lived for hundreds of years, but sorcerers do not last forever. We live for about a century before we begin to feel age. Valash was the oldest of us all and as our senior, he was also our leader."

Delex blinked. "He led you? I thought he was your enemy."

Doran shook his head. "Not at first. He was powerful and wise. More powerful than your mother and me combined. He had lived for 1200 years, and somehow survived. We sorcerers advance to our prime in life like humans, but we retain our youth for centuries." Doran poked at the fire with a stick. It sent a small sparks high into the sky. Delex almost forget he was asleep and in a dream. Doran continued with his steady voice. "Only near the end of our life, our bodies begin to age again. The aging is rapid but can be an emotional crisis for the unprepared. Over a course of about ten years, we age from a look of a human age in our twenties, to like we are in a human age of 90 or more." Doran looked down into the fire. "It can be painful if mismanaged. Once it starts, you know your time will come in a mere decade or two."

Delex looked to his father. He didn't understand why his father told him this. "So, we age fast?"

Doran nodded. "He was so proud he did not show the kiss of time. He felt he was special. My hair started to turn. I knew I was about 300 years the younger and Valash tried to comfort me. Overnight the same year, he woke to white hair, the next day, his beard. Over a course of a year he looked worse than me. I think he blamed me somehow."

"So he attacked you?" Delex asked. He still didn't understand what this all lead to, but when his father spoke, it pulled you in. He must have been a natural diplomat and leader. His voice soothed you.

Doran shook his head silently. "No, it was not like that. We had you, you were not even a year old. We were no threat to him, but there was a tension. Valash was always fascinated with dragons and how they stayed eternal. For a time it begged little interest, but his quickened age drove him. Then he disappeared."

Doran shifted in his seat and stretched his legs towards the fire. "He was gone for three years. When he returned, he had changed. He claimed to have experimented and found a way to remain alive forever. He shared this knowledge with your mother and me in his excitement."

"What's my mom's name?" He had heard it once but forgot. He hoped Doran would say it, but Doran referred to her as 'his mother.'

Doran smiled as his thoughts became distant. He eyes drew on a cherished memory that held her name. "Her name is Zelexi."

"Zelexi, you are named after both of us." Delex repeated the name back to his father. Her name felt warm and comforted him in ways he could not describe.

Doran nodded but his voice was serious. "I am sorry, son. I know this is a lot but this is serious. I need to tell you this knowledge before you wake, I may not have a second chance."

Delex pinched his lips together in annoyance but remained quiet. Doran gave him a rueful smile. "Zelexi made that same face." Doran's smile faded. "Where was I? Ah, yes, he shared the knowledge, but he immediately became suspicious. I think he regretted our involvement."

The storm finally reached them and showered the land in heavy droplets. The stars where hidden under a blanket of grey. None of the rain touched them. It was a dream after all.

"Time is not on our side. So I will have to quicken the story." Doran said as he eyed the weather. Only the light of the campfire shone. "After that, Valash disappeared again. One day the next year, he returned." Doran crushed his hands into fists. "He found it. He came back aged but vibrant again. In that cost, he would kill everyone. Valash had tied his life force to the living. He found a way to siphon the life off others to sustain him. In a way, I have performed the same on you, but my magic only lives in a dream. My way is harmless."

Delex finally started to understand. "So that is how he cannot die, because he sustains himself."

Doran put his hands over his face and wiped them away. "If that was all, it would be a simple matter to kill him. He has found a new corrupted way to survive. The life is without a body, but remains whole. He never shared how he did it because he discovered after I died. My beloved may have known more."

Doran began to fade and appear ghost like. "Dad, you're fading." Delex's eyes filled with concern.

Doran looked down to himself. "Time has left us. I wish I could stay longer but it would hurt you. I only take what will not harm you. The power Valash uses to keep himself alive, or what we call alive, harms everything. If left to continue, the world will not be able to sustain magic, not like we know it. Only Valash will be left, and even he will one day fade away, like this. Unless, he has time to find more ways to grow stronger, perhaps challenge the gods." Doran held his arms out. The light of the fire glowed through his arm. It reflected of the rain and wooden seats. "He will undertake any deed to last as long as possible and if given time, he may find even more dangerous magic to keep him alive even after the death of Ter'Avan." Doran's words became quiet like his voice echoed from a great distance.

"But what do you need of me?" Delex shouted. He felt a great distance, like his father stood on another side of vast chasm in the dark.

"Find the source of his power, but be careful. You will have to defeat Valash first. He will not die if he merely restarts the spell. Sorcerers have magic within them."

So he can jump start himself, great. "But how do I defeat him if the spell keeps him alive and protects him?" Delex yelled.

"That is the puzzle I have yet to figure out. Know this my son. It is a spell. All spells can be undone, but sorcerers are not spells. Our magic is us. You cannot unravel that. Halt the process, not the magic." Delex could barely hear him now. "Son, know this, I have always been with you, as does your mother. Look to her knowledge. She has always been the better sorcerer of her and I. Just, don't tell her I said that." Doran winked as and faded away.

Around Delex the world became completely dark. He stood in the darkness of his mind for a long time. His thoughts went over everything his father had told him. He concentrated on his fathers words, so he could remember when he woke. He knew there was something in them that was a major clue to the answers he needed. His concentration failed him. *I have always been with you, as does your mother.* This one sentence seem to encompass all others. Delex faded back into his subconscious and fell into a dreamless sleep.

Delex woke to Nova's smile. Most of the dream had faded. It had been five days since they left Hilltan and the oddly grateful village. There were no signs of pursuit. Delex and Nova found themselves in a small valley. A small creek wove its way down the center into a little lake. Delex smiled up to her. "How long have you been sitting there?"

Nova smiled but said nothing. She wore a long dress. It was a dark purple wool that traveled well. She had switched from a light airy cotton to this. Delex thought it was too warm, but it didn't seem to bother Nova. He figured she wanted to protect her new skin. She moved away from him and served up a hot breakfast of eggs, cheese, and golden-burned bread. "I made breakfast. I hope you like it."

Delex took a bit of his egg. His stomach growled in response. They both laughed, "Guess that was a yes." Delex happily ate more. "It is, almost like my breakfast from home." Delex suddenly missed Earth. "I mean from Earth. I didn't mean to-"

Nova placed her hand on his. "I understand. You have two homes now. Try thy ruined bread. I placed butter upon it as mentioned." Over the past three days Nova made significant progress with her speech. He amazed her is so many ways.

Delex nodded while he ate. "Dude! That is good." Delex dipped his toast into the egg yolk and moaned with delight. He quickly finished the meal and helped Nova clean up. With in an hour, they were back on the horses. Two supply horses followed on ropes behind them.

The day wore on as beautiful sounds of the forest echoed around them. "The forest is almost like I am in a national park at home." He pointed to the trees. "They sound like birds from Earth but just a little different."

Nova smiled. "Yes, we stole many of thy species from Earth. Did not Mercadio tell thee?"

Delex shrugged. "A little."

Nova nodded. "When thy God of Chaos placed thy Tower of Chaos, thy world went to war over it. Many races died, but thy wildlife was most devastated." Nova gestured to the trees. "Tis when dragons gave knowledge to thy wizards of Earth. After thy war, wizards used *tempri* to scry for other worlds like our own." Nova pointed to Delex and herself. "We filled with shock. We found another world, which had not only human-oid life, but close as kindred. Wizards theorized that some unknown means had placed humans on thy planet or ours. We believed thy connection once existed."

Delex pondered openly. "So you say humans came from Ter'Avan?"

Nova shrugged, "Or from thy Earth by way of Gods and magic. The Book of Dragons, crafted by thy first dragon scholars. I was deciphering the lost language when it was stolen thus. Within may be thy secret of thy worlds."

"Stolen by Soas?" Delex asked. He didn't want to open a can of worms, but, he figured it would not hurt. Soas was not around for her to murder.

Nova Chuckled. "Well, yes and no. This Soas is too young. The rouge's soul likes to come back and cause trouble. No, it was an older Soas. Blackus is his brother, but he has never been seen before. This is thy first Blackus and mystery. Soas has come back many times through history. He is-" Nova paused in search for the right word. "-Odd, a vexation beyond tale. You both seem to like each other, but I would advise caution." Nova looked to Delex seriously. "He is no friend to dragons. Blackus is cold though."

Delex raised an eyebrow. "I think you mean Blackus is cool though. On the bright side, you are not a dragon anymore."

Nova, looked away and ran her hands down her arms, "no, it seems not." Nova became quiet. "When thy world Ter'Avan, suffered and broken from war, needed succor; thy dragon kindred helped wizards rediscover Earth. Thus, we took needfully to repair Ter'Avan."

"Were you there for the war?" Delex asked.

Nova's eyes glowed purple. Her golden-brown skin became flush. "Mine flesh tis not an ancient husk!" She slipped back into her ancient tongue. She took a breath. "Did not thy mother teach thee never to speak to woman of age?" Nova gasped. She spoke before realized what she said.

It was too late. Delex looked away from her. "Well, no. I only had Jim." The conversation went cold. An awkward silence spread like dirt slowly falling into a grave.

Nova pressed her lips together. "I am sorry Delex. We

dragons do not age. We can go through a Shedding. Tis complicated matters. I was not born that long ago, and yet I was. Thy World Greed War tis birthed ten thousand and one years into thy past. It took many thousands of years to recover from thy apocalypse wroth by Chaos."

Delex whistled. Some birds responded from the trees. "That must have been a bad-" Delex looked at Nova. She seemed highly agitated and tense.

"Press thy airy whistle anon." Nova whispered. A bead of sweat started to form on her forehead. Her speech slipped further back as she grew agitated.

Delex gave her a puzzled look and whistled again. The birds responded from the trees. Nova grew more agitated. "Pray thee, whistle thus, steady and constant." Delex gave her the same puzzled look. "Please." Delex nodded and kept whistling. Nova listened for the responses from the trees. "Mimis," she nodded.

Delex was curious but kept up his whistle to the birds. It didn't feel like it was a good time to question. Nova packed up there gear with an odd slow gait that was betrayer by her fearful face. All around the birds responded to Delex's whistle from the trees. They both got on the horses. Nova led them away, but slowly. She never went closer to the sounds in the trees. After what seemed like hours of whistles, Nova stopped and looked back to Delex. "Mayhap, we are safe now."

"What was that about?" Delex questioned. He was curious and still a bit unnerved.

"Mimi Birds." She looked to Delex for recognition. "Didn't Mercadio tell thee anything?" Delex shrugged. "Mimi are hunter-scavengers, meat eaters. They mimic the mating calls of many types of animals to lure them into ambush. They quickly strip thy prey's meat from bones while they struggle. Mimis are one of thy more dangerous life forms upon Ter'Avan."

Delex made a rude sound, "Great, flying tree piranha." Nova looked at him oddly. Delex continued, "Nova, Why didn't we just speed up the horses and run?"

Nova shook her head. "They become highly aggressive if they spot prey that flee. They attack so warnings will remain unheard. We walked thy horses. They fear we are fools and to stunted of intellect."

Delex chuckled. "So since we didn't respond and come close, we are dumb?"

Nova gave a small smile. "Something like that. They will not leave thy ambush unless it becomes compromised. They do not attack dumb mating animals. Mimis fear illness. These birds are highly susceptible to disease. Tis their greatest weakness."

Delex blushed. "So they assumed I was whistling for a mate?" Nova nodded to him while she hid a smile. "And, by continuing, they thought I was too stupid to understand them?" She nodded to Delex again as she held back a snicker. "Well that is truly insulting." Delex exclaimed dramatically.

Nova laughed out loud. They continued to walk the horses through a section of the trees far away from the nest of mimi birds. The tension eased when the found a small trail that started to climb out the other side of the valley. The day grew long. They had a cold lunch on horseback and allowed the horses to graze happily and drink from streams they found along the way. Delex and Nova had a peaceful conversation. They mostly talked about Earth. Nova had many curious questions and Delex was happy to answer her. It took them some time to traverse the valley, but there was no more encounters with dangerous creatures. Three days after the mimi birds, they settled camp on the other side of the valley. The day faded into night. Stars twinkled brightly as the moon started to rise over the horizon. The darkness turned into a light cold white.

Nova fell asleep curled up near Delex. The last few days they had become closer, but at a slower pace. This was okay to Delex. Delex never had much luck with women and wanted to take things slow. He saved her life and gave her back a piece she had though lost for all time. He didn't want that to be the only attraction. Delex smiled. Jim would be proud. He had drilled Delex the ways of a gentleman. Oh, he had past romances, that would have made Jim angry, but this was not one of them. He lay awake for a time and thought about his other friends. Were they okay? He couldn't shake the feeling of unease, even as he stroked the hair of Nova as she slept. Something nagged him. He hoped it was just the fear of the unknown, on an unknown world, as he walked into unknown danger. He finally went to sleep still with the wonder if his friends were safe.

Down in the valley the mimi birds had picked up the sounds of new prey. It was close to the nest. They remained silent to not startle the meat. There was no need to lure it. It would be an easy kill. It was almost to the kill point, a small clearing in the heart of the nest. Mimi birds did not have the best night vision. Yet, they easily spotted a dark medium-sized creature on four legs enter the clearing. All they waited for now, was the leader of the nest to give the kill command, and they would feast.

The small dark creature made a high-pitched cough. Immediately two more entered the clearing. The mimi birds tensed. The leader silently glided closer and landed on a nearby tree. Three black figures looked up to the mimi bird. The mimi bird did not recognize what they were, but immediately felt danger. The leader sprang from the tree and gave a shrill cry to warn the nest. He was already too late. The first dog creature jumped to the trunk of the tree, sprang off it, then snatched the leader from the sky.

The rest of the mimi birds took flight and abandoned the nest without a glance back. They left any young fledglings that could not fly without hesitation. They hoped the ones left behind would give them enough time to escape. Even now they could hear cries from the slow or young. There voices winked into silenced one by one. Mimis were smart, dangerous, and organized. They also knew you did not need to be smart, to be dangerous. Tonight the survivors would search for a new ambush, and new nest, far away from this valley. It would be many generations of mimi birds before any would consider this valley as a nest and venture back.

∞∞∞

N'Mora closed the door to her house from a long day of blacksmith work and crop collection. A full week, nine days of harvest, had yielded a years worth of crops, but the harvest would finish soon. The next day, the village would pack much of harvest into cold cellar storage. The rest would go to market, and replanting would commence.

She walked to a chair and slowly slipped off her boots. She sighed and wiggled her toes to get a bit more circulation back. It was late at night and the clouds had rolled in over the moon. The entire house held its breath in patches of black shadows. Only a single candle at the table shed light, but it was enough to make her way to her bed. She was hungry but it could not compare to the exhaustion she felt. N'Mora sat on her bed ready to remove her work clothes.

She suddenly felt silky threads brush past her face. She was about to brush them away when a sound came from behind. It sounded like someone snapped a blanket taunt. N'Mora tipped forward to the ground. She tried to brace her fall, but her face hit the ground with a sound thump. Pain erupted in her eyes, but it was dull and faded quickly. She tried to yell out in pain, but her voice would not come. Her head hit the table and tipped the candle over. The candle rolled back and forth and shed more light as the flame burst forth from the exposed wick. She blinked in terror as he head as her eyes came to rest as on the monster.

Suspended above her bed was the black smooth body of the largest spider she had ever seen. Its body was the size of a full-grown woman, completely hairless with a carapace that shimmered and glistened. Eight spindly thin legs pinned it to the dark corners. Two legs held the rest of N'Mora's headless body in place while the four hooked appendages on its face sucked and chewed at her open neck hole with greedy delight. She had never seen anything like it. Then, the realization hit her. That was her body, her headless body! She looked at her own death. Shock, confusion, terror and grief swept through her in a matter of moments.

The light faded from the room rapidly, but the candle still burned. Her face felt cold. She was light-headed and felt like her head expanded as her skin went numb. The sound started to echo from the world like from the end of a vast tunnel. Her vision flashed with specks of light. Her mind started to flip through memories faster and faster as she fought to remain conscious. The horrific scene took only a matter of moments, but to N'Mora it could have been a lifetime. No sight, no sound, no senses at all were left. Her feelings as thoughts blended into mosaic of rudimentary basic forms. Each thought condensed into a shape, a color, even the heat of hot iron and the remembered sound of the blacksmith's hammer. Then, even those thoughts faded away. N'Mora's mind drifted into darkness as one final confused though bubbled out of the nothingness. *I need pulled out of the water.*

It had been two weeks, eighteen days since Blackus and Mercadio left Hilltan for Homgad. Mercadio was fast asleep at an inn. He woke suddenly to an immediate terrible feeling. At that same moment a small pain erupted from behind his right ear and just as quickly vanished. Mercadio slapped at the bite but felt something furry there instead. He first thought was Daylow. His familiar liked to pester him with bites. He could hear Daylow breath, but he was on his left side. The bite came from the right. Mercadio sat up with sudden concern. Daylow hissed and shot past him. Mercadio reached to light a lamp but a sudden burst of light came from the door as it exploded inward. Blackus stood in the doorway weapon ready. Mercadio felt some strands of spiderweb brush his face.

Blackus barked out a command. "Cower!" and threw his sword at Mercadio's face. Mercadio ducked his head as the sound of cloth snapped behind him as Blackus' sword connected with something above him. Mercadio looked up to see a massive slick-bodied spider pinned by the head to the wall. Wizard reflexes moved him out of the way as the spider's legs gave way and the head tore away from the blade. The massive monster dropped to the bed with a loud thud that nearly toppled the wizard to the ground.

Mercadio was about to breath a size of relief and confusion when Daylow burst out from under the bed with a red ball of fur. Mercadio screamed and pointed to the drethcon. Blackus quickly shut the door. Darkness abruptly swallowed the room. Mercadio quickly cast a spell that made the walls and floor glow with bright blue light. Daylow was on all fours near the door. His fur stuck out in all and directions like protective armor. In fact, his fur clinked against each other like crystalline pins. He hissed at a ball in the middle of the floor that quivered as blood poured forth from it into a large puddle.

Mercadio already started to feel weaker. He knew it had got to him. The drethcon had tried to escape, but failed, so it desperately tried to transform into a stronger form. "Kill it, Quickly!" Mercadio shouted and shot a bolt of black lightning at the bloody ball.

Blackus pulled his second sword in one fluid motion and brought it down a split-second after the spell blasted it. The ball of fur crumbled to grey powder in a matter of moments. Seconds later a timid tap came from outside the door. Mercadio guess it was the innkeeper or someone sent by him.

Blackus opened the door with a glare. "We are safe, leave." Which, sent a maid immediately away.

Mercadio took a moment to survey the scene. A drethcon had sneaked into his room and bite him to take his body.

Drethcons could not use wizard or sorcerer powers. This was an execution. He was to be drained and copied. He looked to the huge spider. Mercadio had never seen or heard of this creature before. He was not sure how it killed, but he could safely assume it feed on anything it wanted. It had a terribly strong look to arms. Its fangs looked built to chew, perhaps more. He quickly retrieved his belongings a donned his hat. "Blackus, have you seen this before?"

"No." Blackus said, as he retrieved his other sword from the body. He stabbed the creature twice more with a twist. He wiped the blade clean on the bed and returned it to his sheath. "I have never heard of it."

Mercadio sighed as he looked over Daylow for any wounds. The cat was still angry and unhinged, but he did not bite Mercadio. Daylow still swore under its breath as his fur reverted to soft hair. Mercadio would have thought it was humorous to see a cat swear like a drunkard, but the problem overshadowed novelty. "Two assassins. Someone sent two creatures to kill me. One to take my form, the other to remove the original."

"I killed the one in my room," He pointed to the dead remains of the drethcon. "There was no spider."

Mercadio rubbed at the wound behind his neck. He decided to check the rest of his body. Blackus helped search, then they both looked over Daylow. Blackus had never removed his armor. "Still, we have both been marked for death. Daylow stop swearing!" Mercadio stomped his foot down. Daylow stopped but gave Mercadio a look of pure spite. He sat on the ground and cleaned his fur, but the look of feral rage did not leave his cat eyes.

"Two assassins; this does not make sense." Mercadio Had no doubt Valash sent the drethcon. He also knew a drethcon could only regenerate if the host was alive. If he died, it would weaken the creature significantly. So why send a second murderer? "We need to find out more, what that creature is." Mercadio pointed to the massive dead spider. "Maybe it will lead to more answers."

It had been two Ter'Avan weeks, since he had left Delex alone. That was a total of eighteen days. They were back in Homgad to rest from a long ride and look for more answers. They had found a discreet inn to lie low, but it seems it was not discreet enough. Mercadio and Blackus came down the stairs of the inn. They had decided to look for other lodgings. It would be hard to find one so late in the night, but he hoped an innkeeper would take them in.

As they left the inn, they heard commotion in the streets. Screams of terror and whistles from guards echoed off the stone buildings. A few small fires flickered down walls and alleys. Blackus took a whistle from under his spell-weave armor and blew a series of notes. Within moments the street filled with a squad of guards. "Report," Blackus snapped in his detached monotone.

The highest ranked guard stepped forward. He did not salute or signal to his leader Blackus. Blackus and the guard had performed some subtle clue that Mercadio had not guessed. It times of war or attack, the command was to retain respect, efficiency, and secrecy. "Lord Blackus, the city lays overrun by red balls of fur and daemon soldiers. They seem to bite people and transform into, into-" The guard stumbled with the thought.

As the guard tired to find words to explain, another guard turned the corner and stepped into formation. Blackus ignored the first guard and approached the new arrival. He slipped his sword from the sheath. The other guards stepped out of the way. Blackus quickly rushed the guard and cut with his sword.

Mercadio gasped in shock but did not have time to react. "Blackus! What have you done?"

Blackus ignored him and wiped the blood off his sword and quickly placed it back in his scabbard. He turned away from the guard. Behind him the guard toppled into two pieces cut crosswise at the chest. "These creatures create bodies that will be hard to kill. Aim for the heart, that is the weakness." Blackus instructed. The body finished falling to the ground. The cut had separated the heart in half exposing a red ball. He looked to Mercadio.

Mercadio recovered quickly. "Yes, drethcon. I know you may have heard of them. You must hit the heart. Better to remove the ball at the heart and strike it dead. They have tricks that fools the mind." Mercadio pointed to the body. It did not look like a normal guard anymore. The skin was blood-red, the eyes glazed white. The guards only took a fraction to recover from shock. They are solders of Blackus' army and were trained to expect worse at any moment.

Blackus clapped his hands. The guards turned to him and snapped to a rigid stance. "You must find and eliminate them. Look for blind eyes. They can hide the red skin, but not the eyes."

The lead body guard spoke up. "Lord commander, but they look like us."

Mercadio pointed a finger to the sky. "I can help with that." He turned to Blackus, we will need to gather the guards in groups. Blackus nodded to him.

Over the next hour, guards gathered in groups around Blackus and Mercadio. Mercadio touched each on the head. The guards would be able to spot the doppelgangers created by the drethcons on sight. In front of the inn lay several more human shaped drethcon corpses. They had killed each one and reduced the hearts to grey powder. The spell would only last for a few days, but Blackus made it clear no drethcon would leave these walls. Scouts rushed to the countryside as others guards, tasked with bows, watched the skies. More covered all exits and took even space along the walls. The rest of the solder and guards took the duty to cleanse the city.

Mercadio was still worried. "Blackus. These unprecedented behaviors trouble me. This was not an assassination. This was an army. Valash had made a move."

"War." Blackus replied.

Mercadio agreed. "We still have no answers that we need." An explosion flashed green across the sky. It was still a few hours before morning. Out of the flash, a tree stood in its place. Mercadio pointed to the light and tree. "Just the man I needed to find. He will be there." Mercadio ran down the streets while Blackus trailed close by.

It did not take them long to find Narsis the green, the wizard Mercadio spoke with the last time he was here. He stood near a tree that had erupted from the flagstones. In the branches, nearly a hundred drethcon bodies hung impaled by branches. Each drethcon had red skin, white eyes, and through the body. They all wiggled in various levels of pain and anger as the unsuccessfully tried to dislodge themselves.

"I see you have been busy Narsis." Mercadio said impressed. He approached the wizard with his hands outstretched.

Narsis turned to him alarmed. "Who goes there! Wait, Mercadio?" He grinned wildly. He noticed another person approach. "Blackus!" Narsis' smile snapped away.

Mercadio rolled his eyes. "He is harmless."

Narsis glowered. "He took my toes."

Blackus shrugged, "They grew back." Mercadio poked a low corpse with a finger. "You are a wizard of renowned healing."

Narsis grabbed a staff propped on the tree. "A fact, Blackus, you were unaware, at the time!" Narsis looked bedraggled. His smashed hair jutted out from under a leather cap. The frazzled white hair shot out at all ends. He looked like he had spent the entire night in battle.

Blackus took a meaningful step forward. "And you did not know your place." Blackus' hand rested on his sword.

Narsis leaned on his staff and shook his fist. "I should have my Staffs in the city come here to teach you a lesson Blackus!"

Blackus took another step forward. The air seemed to become thick. "I would be happy to break them like tinder and lay them at your feet."

Narsis retorted, "The Staffs are people."

"I know." Blackus responded as he slipped a sword slightly

out of his scabbard.

Mercadio quickly stepped in, "Now, now, Narsis. It is the past, the past!" He pointed to the tree. "We came to find out about this." Narsis paced angrily. He had developed a limp as he walked, as if his foot remembered past wounds. Narsis quickly calmed as he educated Mercadio on the disarray.

"Yes, the tree." Narsis stepped to it. "They swarmed me. Flaming drethcon from all sides. Ashen creatures hounded me, So I slaughter them myself." Blackus gave Narsis a solid nod of approval. Narsis noticed and visibly calmed. He returned a small nod. Narsis waved a hand at his surroundings. "By Chaos' luck they were as slow as uphill gravel. I have been pegging them with branches like a macabre children's game all night."

Mercadio laughed heartily. "My apologies, it is funny." Narsis shook his head in mild shock. Blackus looked at him without a word or emotion. Mercadio recovered quickly from his morbid titter. "Why yet and now? We have seen but a handful. Why attack you so dramatically and not Blackus and I?"

Narsis pointed a thumb over his shoulder, "because of this." Behind him was the library Mercadio had found Narsis in weeks ago. It was a normal library but it was large enough to also collect a fair amount of magical text. Past combat splashed across the steps. Most of the path lay adorned with a large pile of drethcon. Vines, thorns and the like, punched through the bodies or had torn them to pieces.

"Ah, knowledge." Mercadio said. Narsis nodded. Blackus seemed unmoved. "Valash had made his move, and it seems he has targeted the books. He is trying to eliminate a weapon, or perhaps a weakness. By why just this library?"

Blackus spoke up, "Who claims this library is the only target for knowledge." He looked to Narsis and Mercadio to see if they had come to the same conclusion. "Think wizards."

With cold realization the two wizards both came to the same thought. Narsis was struck dumb, his voice would not come. His imagination of the true problem was far worse than what happen tonight. This was Narsis' true fear. Mercadio spoke that fear out loud. "The Towers of Magic. Valash has struck the towers."

Upon Mercadio's fearful words Narsis' eyes rolled up into his head as he tipped backwards to the ground with a solid smack.

Blackus pointed to Narsis with an almost imperceptible smile. "Now, that is funny."

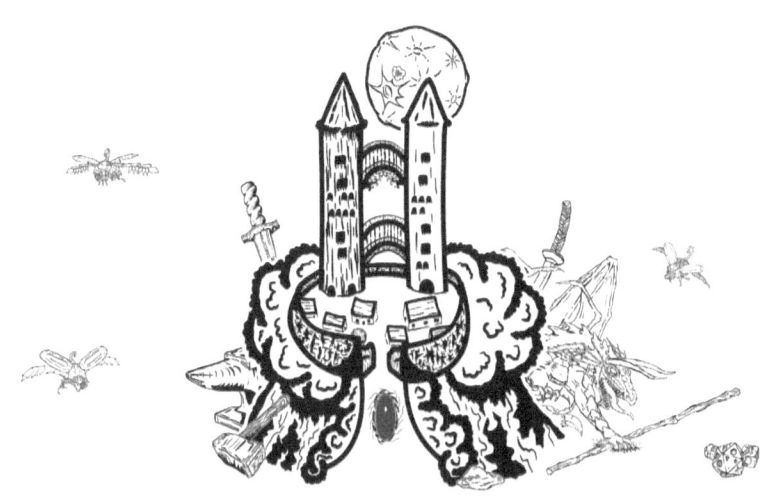

Chapter 17: Runaway Questions

Maltort woke from his desk to rhythmic pound on the door. He had fallen asleep again. "Yes come in!" His head throbbed like the owner of the monstrous fist. He waved his hand and suspended the lock magic on the door.

One of his many assistants came into the room. He couldn't place the name, but he remembered the young man's fist. He was the son of a fisherman that pulled nets to fish. Maltort suddenly had an overwhelming hatred of fishing nets and hands. "Master Manycolor, I am so relieved!"

Maltort rolled his eyes. "A nap, ah, young?" He snapped his fingers at the young wizard.

"Bartlon, master." The wizard replied.

"Ah yes Bartlon. I was taking a nap." Maltort responded and started shuffling his papers.

"It has been two days, master." Bartlon rubbed his hands together in worry. "That has been happening a lot."

Maltort dismissed his worries with a flick of his hand. "The length of my naps are not up for discussion. Now, was there something else?" The tone of Maltort suggested the assistant should leave or face his wrath. Maltort looked over his papers in confusion. Some of them were not where he had left them, and others he did not recognize. *I am overworking myself.* He thought.

Bartlon, to his credit, stood his ground. "Yes master. It seems there has been high numbers of missing students. This is beyond attendance issues. They cannot be found." He took a worried step forward.

Maltort growled, "Send a finder squad and drag them back to the towers."

Bartlon retorted, "We have, and they have also gone missing." He took another step forward. "I found a path in the puzzle. None of the reported missing wizards had left the tower."

Maltort growled and blew into his beard. "I will authorize a scrying spell inside the tower." Maltort grabbed the appropriate parchment and quickly inked the permission. "Bartlon, correct?" The assistant nodded. Maltort continued. "I knew your father, good man, good fisher. I give you the lead on this Bartlon." The assistant grinned. Maltort glared at him. "Don't fail this. Find out where they are, and don't overstep your power. Take whomever you need to conduct a ritual, not just a casting."

Bartlon eyes widen when he heard what Maltort just commanded. He quickly nodded and hurried to the desk. Maltort flicked the parchment at the assistant. Bartlon caught it from the air and quickly scurried to the door. "I will do everything I can."

Maltort waved his fingers sarcastically, "Yes, yes, praises and parades all around. Remember to scry the Tower of Records too. If the Headstaff, Mirimas Quickcast over there gets her parchment in a wad, you tell her to come to me."

Bartlon mumbled some agreement under his breath. Maltort sighed and rested back in his chair. It was not the first time wizards disappeared. There was many secret passages that riddled the towers, even some he had not found. The scrying spell would pinpoint an area, possibly some tunnels or rooms and flush them out. Maltort remembered a few times he had used the tunnels for forbidden projects or just to be alone with a date. *They better not be starting another cult.* He thought to himself. Every few years some foolish young wizard would 'discover' his own way of spell forms, usually while drunk with bravery. Then the young wizard would tie that discovery to an imagery being, or worst, the influence of the more dangerous sentient books and make a mess of things.

Maltort turned back to his desk. So many papers, so many requests, reviews, and 'blah-blah-blah' on paper. He wished he had more time to cast. This was the Tower of Practice after all. Right now, Maltort wished he was Narsis. Though his brother was a ledger-seeker, he got to travel and have fun. Yes, he confessed to himself, he was a bit envious.

Mercadio eased Narsis into his favorite chair in the library. The old wizard had woken back up but remained quiet and remorse. The spent the next three huddled in the library. They harvested and protected every book of magic the library had to offer. The battle outside seemed more sedate since the guards started Blackus' orders and strategies. The fight took one day to win, and two days to clean and search for hidden dangers.

Blackus dragged the corpse of the gigantic spider into the library for study. "I brought the insect for you weak wizards." Blackus' attitude and gone from cold to rude over the last three days.

Narsis snapped out of his morose as soon as he saw the corpse. "Where did you get that?" He jumped out of his chair in a panic.

Mercadio slowly blinked. "I thought you would recognize it." He pointed to it with his staff. "It attacked me in my bedroom before the attack of the drethcon."

Narsis snorted. "I doubt that. The Garrote Spider has been extinct since-" Narsis stopped for a moment to think, "since the Chaos tower was on Ter'Avan. Plus you should be dead, they sneak up on the prey as silent as a thought and remove your head."

Blackus lifted an eyebrow. "Impressive."

"You do not know the half of it." Narsis scoffed. "Then it sucks up your blood while it eats your insides in quick order." Narsis made rude slurping and chewing noises. "Lastly it uses your body by filling your leftover skin with eggs and webbing."

Mercadio pointed to the spider. "Interesting history lesson, but we need to focus. Drethcon in the city, and garrote spiders, Valash had made his move."

Narsis shook his head. "No, Valash has found a way to influence drethcon. Garrote spiders, I doubt this is one of them. They are all officially dead, completely extinct for hundreds of years." He seems less sure. "They lived deep underground where they hibernated. Wizards used spells long ago to find each one and destroyed them as they slept."

Mercadio looked at Narsis. "Well it is obvious they are not anymore. I believe Valash had somehow brought them back or found an undiscovered lore. Also, I have never seen but a few drethcon since this day. I think Valash had breed an army."

Narsis became worried again. "The towers of magic! Mercadio, we need to go there at once." Narsis almost tripped over the books that encircled the room. "I was studying a way to travel, without use a *tempra,* like imps travel." Narsis pointed spread his arms towards the books that surrounded him like an army of paper towers. "I was close, Mercadio."

Mercadio looked skeptical. "Lost magics." He looked Narsis directly into his eyes. "Dangerous magic."

Narsis took a deep breath. "And worth it. A *tempra* is too unstable. You know I am not good at them, but I used one to go to the tower and talk to my brother." He lifted the hem of his rob to show a fresh scar that traced cuts all around his leg like tree limbs. "I almost lost my leg. The *tempri* seem more dangerous. Something spurred the creatures into a frenzy of the likes I have never seen before."

Mercadio agreed. "I can imagine." The fight with the *tempra* monster came back from his memories.

Blackus paced the room while the two wizards clucked like chickens. He would stop by a book and pluck it from the shelves or from the piles. He would glance at it and tip it onto the floor. Narsis would glare at him with each book.

Mercadio sighed. "Blackus would you wait outside." Blackus shrugged and dragged the corpse of the spider with him. Both wizards paused in the conversation as they watched him leave and slowly tip over stacks of books and end tables in his wake.

"I feel his restlessness. Your play toy is dangerous."

Mercadio looked back to Narsis. "You play with powers best left to the dead." He pointed to a small black and red book in Narsis' lap.

"I agree black wizard. It was just a passing hobby. Sorcerer script is hard to understand and easy to mistake." Narsis pulled his robs back over the fresh healed scar. "Yet the need is great, and we need to travel fast. The *tempra* will kill us. Even with your mastery of them."

The door to the library opened and slammed and nearly startled to the wizards out of their seats as Blackus departed. Mercadio sighed. "I need to find something for that man to do."

Narsis looked at Mercadio over his horn-rimmed glasses. "For your enlightenment, I am ordered to drag you back to the towers. I have eight twelfth-year staffs on hand to help me. Rumor is, you have the Heir."

Mercadio replied smoothly, "Well my, eight staffs would be hard to resist. No Narsis, the Heir is not with me. It is just Blackus and I. We escaped the melding of Soas." Mercadio panicked inside his head, but tried to remain calm.

Narsis shrugged, "Well and well. The day holds some good news." he saw Mercadio sighed with relief. *He said the Heir was not with him, but he did not deny the Heir was on Ter'Avan.* Narsis thought to himself. Narsis let the thought drop. Once Mercadio was at the towers, they would get more answers.

The wizards spent another hour is discussion about the mechanics of the magic. The sun had crested the horizon and mountains by the time they both agreed. They would attempt to use the imps, teleportation, as Delex called it. They both shouldered into the few books of magic the Library of Homgad held. Mercadio wished he had Delex here. Much more tomes of magic rest within the floating castle of Delex's dead parents. What few books that remained here were training and magical theory books the sorcerer's had shared from the castle.

Few knew what Mercadio knew, even those in the towers of magic. Narsis himself, despite his love for knowledge, did not have Doran and Zelexi to teach him, or what they told him in secret. Sorcerers had help found the Towers of Magic, and had been the teachers that had finally given the planet fully trained wizards. Mercadio wanted to share this knowledge several times, but each time, his instincts warned him off. Wizards were not ready.

The one knowledge he shared, was knowledge that a few wizards already knew. Doran had been a good friend, and had taught him how to read sorcerer script. Mercadio deciphered while Narsis wrote in a ready supply of parchments. Narsis was a child in a candy shop. His quill and ink flew from parchment to parchment as he wrote everything word down. Mercadio filled in some blanks in the theories that he remembered from his time with Doran. They hoped they would have an answer soon, and it was the one they wanted.

∞∞∞

Valash opened his eyes and pounded his fists against the stone table. He screamed in rage and scattered parchments and books everywhere. No mater what he tried, he could not pinpoint where Delex and his band of fools went. After they obliterated his mirror, the fools then left a magical residue that lingered across a vast area. Out of the cloud of magical residue, hundreds of trials shot out in all directions. Each trail seemed to move and grow and even pop with small bits of magic. Anyone one of those trails could be the true trail, but most would be false. Valash had to admire the extent they went to hide.

"Moraphen!" Valash screamed. He needed eyes and brains. He realized a moment later, that his faithful slave was not there. In fact, he had lost all connection with him. The rage renewed. Rocks and bits of dust rumbled as his anger echoed off the dark passages.

Valash had sent out a multitude of creatures to scout the trails for him since his mirror melted to magical slag. Dragonfire would burn any magic, and leave it permanently ruined. It would take years to create another. He had to scout each trial. He suspected almost all trails would be false. No doubt, his prey would not dare to use magic. Lucky for him, he had other means. Creatures that could track a shadow in a cave.

With each scout group he also sent out his assassins. He no longer needed Delex alive. He had been able to salvage a tiny portion of blood. Valash let his rage subside as he checked in on his pet project. He crossed the dark passages, slaves, and creatures that skittered back and forth back and made his way to his throne room. The demon arm throne, chiseled from the bed rock, glistened with purple light from the torches. The magical fires where feed by a new batch of magically endowed corpses.

Valash continued to the back of the throne to a freshly dug hole. It was partially filled with dark liquid. Above the hole, a skull had been pressed into the stone of the throne. The skull dripped blood into the hole and made a dark pool that shivered with ripples.

The skull had the drop of Delex's blood, and it slowly produced more with each drip. Valash surveyed the pool. It still was not enough. If he could have taken more of Delex's blood, the project would have been finished by now. Yet, he salvaged the loss. It would take months to completely fill the pool, and then his plans would go to the final step.

Valash dipped his hand into the pool to taste the evil brew. He could feel the magic tingle on his fingers as he savored it in his mouth. He could feel the magic tingle in his fingers. Valash smiled and left the throne room. It would all work out. Valash retired to his bed chamber to rest. The powers that kept him alive had become less stable over the years. His body took vast amounts of magic. If he rested now, he could gather adequate energy for the next step. Valash rested in a stone tub and covered it with another stone slab. He left his commands for his minions and begun his long rest. It was still a pity he could not find his prey, but in the end he suspected he might not need to. He might as well gather his strength and let them expend theirs. It was only a matter of time before he would scatter them all like leafs in the wind.

∞∞∞

Mercadio threw the book in his hand at the wall. "It has been a month! Narsis, we should have figured this out."

Narsis gave Mercadio a shameful look and recovered the book Mercadio threw. "I understand your frustration, but please, do not take it out on my books." Narsis walked the book to a table but accidentally dropped it on the floor. Narsis cupped his hand and sat at the table as he tried to work at his fingers.

Mercadio came over quickly. "I am sorry my friend. Does it still hurt?" Narsis nodded but did not speak.

Mercadio thought back to the last month's research. Mercadio, Narsis and Blackus, with the help of the wizards under Narsis' command, quickly searched the city for a Ter'Avan week for every tome of magic it carried. When those books did not show results, they took every wizard in the area and tried to break into the castle floating above the lake near Homgad. It was an abysmal failure. The castle retaliated with magical wards that were vicious as they were merciless. One wizard died, and several struck dumb for days. Two wizards had all magical abilities shredded and destroyed. This left them unable to concentrate enough to cast the simplest spell.

Blackus took the fallen wizards into his army. He would train them and offer pay to compensate for the striped magical abilities. Blackus also found the kin to the fallen wizard and compensated them for their loss equally to what the Towers of Magic provide. He didn't have to, the wizards were not part of his army. Blackus shrugged and told Mercadio and Narsis it was 'the way of men.' Mercadio didn't argue. The dead wizard's remains would be gathered and his final teachings and thoughts would be made into his book. Mercadio didn't know if the two living wizards would still create any books of magical teachings. Time would cast the final word.

A week after the castle disaster, Narsis came back excited. He had finally created a spell that would transport a cup from one end of the room to another without the need of a *tempra*. The breakthrough amazed them both. It would cement Narsis' name in magical histories for all time. Yet, they looked for more. Another Ter'Avan week of nine days past by. They practiced teleporting objects to greater and greater distance. Finally, Narsis wished to do a live subject. It worked well at small distances, but at larges distances the spell failed. The wizards found small cats, dogs, rabbits and other test animals up trees, fallen from heights, dripping from within walls, or not found at all.

Narsis spent an entire day unconscious after he had mistakenly teleported Daylow, Mercadio's cat and familiar, to the top of the library roof. The cat came back into the room and struck the wizard with one angry paw. The cat's unnatural strength knocked the wizard out in one blow and across the room. Blackus' laughter could be heard echo throughout the library as he dragged Narsis to a bed. Rumors echoed that anyone in the library at that time fled from his laughter. Blackus had a small smile as he stroked Daylow throughout the day. Mercadio had nightmares all night.

When Narsis recovered, Mercadio helped his friend refine the spell, and it finally worked, but it took a mighty toll. It took a ritual of all the wizards in Homgad to help stabilize the spell and send a rabbit several kilometers away. Yet, Narsis did not worry. The rest of another week ended in the creation of amulets that could perform the same job.

The next day, Narsis, Mercadio and Blackus prepared the spell on themselves. Daylow, had decided to swear at them and disappeared into the night. They attempt had mixed results. Narsis was the caster since he was the most skilled with Nature magic, and imps were natural creatures. Mercadio's skills in Nature magic was subpar to Narsis.

The teleportation took them outside the gates of Homgad to a nearby tree. Mercadio landed softly on his feet, but Blackus fell about three meters from above the earth. He slapped the ground soundly and laid their for several seconds before he rose. His face was an unmistakable red of anger, pain and murder.

Narsis did not fair any better. Narsis was found in the tree hung from one of its mighty branches. His left hand had materialized into the wood and suspended him above the ground. It had taken several hours for them to get him down without the need to cut off his hand, a choice he venomously refused to consider. In the end, his hand now was a mixture of flesh and wood. It still functioned as normal, but had a hard time with tiny objects and his hand hurt at odd moments. Narsis refused to try it again until he could figure out what went wrong. Mercadio tapped the library floor with his staff and sat down. "A trouble a triple? Is it your hand?"

Mercadio brought back Narsis from his thoughts. "It is nothing Mercadio, I will have to get use to it." He gathered the books at his feet. "Has there been word from Blackus?"

Mercadio shook his head. "Not since the accident." Mercadio was a bit crossed at his guardian and protector. Blackus had left that night after he dropped to the ground. A note briefly told him that trouble was on the rise and Blackus had to gather his forces. In the note he said he would meet them at the sea if the wizards survived 'playing with deadly toys'. Mercadio secretly thought Blackus left because of anger, and so he would not kill the wizards. At least Daylow had reappeared and helped as much as he could.

Narsis slammed his wooden hand on the table. "Enough! We have to do it." Narsis got a grimace on his face. "We have to catch an imp."

Mercadio wiped his hands down his face. "Are you certain?" Since imps were creatures that could appear anywhere not warded against intrusion, they did not nest or stay in one place for long. "Catching an imp will be equivalent to seducing lightning into a cave."

Narsis shrugged. "I wish it were a lie." Narsis handed Mercadio a jar. "Just a liter."

Mercadio lowered his eyebrows in chagrin. "Of imp urine?" He saw Narsis smile and nod. "Not blood or bone?"

Narsis shook his head, "No, only urine, something extruded and left when an imp, teleports? I love that word Mercadio. Te-le-port." Narsis tried the word out slowly. "Rolls off the tongue. Where ever did you find it?"

"Old sorcerer knowledge," Mercadio lied. Narsis didn't seem to believe him. He looked like he was about to start another attempt to get more information out of him about Delex. Mercadio quickly avoided the attempt. "Well I better try to lure an imp," Mercadio sighed, "and extract the bile."

Narsis waved as he looked back into a book. "Have a pleasant morning hunt."

Mercadio glared and gave Narsis rude gesture Delex taught him as he stormed out of the library. Narsis returned the gesture with a friendly smile. Mercadio told him it was a form of sorcerer greeting he found in translation. *Have that dish and eat well!* Mercadio thought with an uncharacteristic evil flare. *Imps felt* drawn to magical locations, then peed all over them. They harmlessly feed off the residue magics. Wizards would normally train them as pets. The imps would feed themselves as they stayed with the wizard. Mercadio was sure he would spot a few around the castle.

He hated the smell of imp urine ever since his time as a student at the towers. Mercadio had a class project that required him to capture and care for an imp within his personal chambers. It urinated on everything he owned. For several weeks, hallways, classrooms, countless students and one unlucky visiting royal and entourage lived covered in the musky floral rotten meat smell of imp waste. Mercadio not only hated this, he loathed it with a burning passion only young lovers could match. Mercadio returned briefly. Without a word Narsis handed him a dried sea sponge and a stoppered glass jar. Mercadio couldn't muster a single word to convey his thoughts as he stormed back out of the library.

Blackus rode on the open plain back towards the small village of Hilltan that Delex had saved earlier. He had left with orders to his forces to drop all contracts and met at the seaside passage. Blackus has always had an instinct for things, a way that he viewed the world and reacted. Everything within him said he had to move his forces. The drethcon invasion was easy to stop, but he suspected it was merely a test of the defenses of Homgad and other areas of interest. His horse, Penance labored under him without a worry. Penance rested at Homgad when Mercadio and Blackus returned from Hilltan. During that time, Blackus had used other horses under his training. Blackus had breed, raised, and trained the mighty steed himself. Without the presence of others, Blackus took almost no time to sleep and ate upon the saddle. Blackus took care to not risk injury to his steed. Penance was the most intelligent horse Blackus had ever raised. It had a special diet to keep the steed healthy and prevent fatigue. Blackus rested only a few hours a day, and that was mostly for Penance.

Blackus neared Hilltan and glared. It was deadly quiet. Blackus galloped into the village. The village seemed tired and run down. Many of the villagers didn't look up as he rode by. Blackus went directly to the N'Mora's Blacksmith. The shop was silent. The forge fire had died to cold ash.

"She's not there lad." An old man yelled from the shade of a nearby house. Blackus got off his horse and walked to the old man. Penance trotted quietly to a fence and stood there. The horse flicked the reins over the top of the fence.

"Explain." Blackus quietly said.

"Happened weeks ago." He pointed to her house with a stick. "She was killed, only her head was there. Sliced clean off. Cobwebs all over the place." The old man shook his head. "Never seen a sight like that." The old man slowly got to his feet. Blackus offered him a hand. The old man took it with a smile. "Good lad, good lad."

"What else elder?" Blackus asked. They slowly made their way to N'Mora's house and shop. The old man lead Blackus to the door and opened it. A black stain was on the floor and bed. Cobwebs hung in rags from a dark corner. Blackus touched a cobweb. It drew blood from his finger. Blackus carefully gather the webbing to show Mercadio later.

"Well, everyone got all quiet. A lot of remorse going around. Seems none of us can get past our sadness." The old man looked up to Blackus sadly. "She was a fine woman, strong and smart. The village will not be the same." The old man lowered his head. Blackus' eyes immediately noticed a small red puncture mark on his neck.

Blackus knew what had happened immediately. "Has the whole town felt tired and sad?" The old man nodded. Blackus lead him back to where the old man had sat. He left the old man there and scouted the village on Penance. The entire town seemed fatigued and slowed. They suspected it was rapid harvest, storage and sale. It was not. Each villager he saw had a mark on them, a small wound. *Drethcon,* Blackus thought. Even his thoughts reflected the quick deceive nature that defined him. If Blackus was a book, he was open to be read by all, if any survived the reading.

Blackus easily found at least a dozen trails that led from the village. A convergence of trails pointed towards the sea, towards Delex. Blackus kicked Penance into a gallop and shot towards the heir. The trial was a wide swath of land disturbed and torn. The drethcon did not hide any tracks. They looked to be in a hurry. Blackus didn't wast time with the other trails. He couldn't save the village, but he could try to catch up to Delex and Nova. Penance felt the need of his rider and pushed even harder.

They had traveled through the mountains at a slow pace. Neither of them were familiar with this area over the land. They had to a less direct route and stop frequently. There was many small streams and fords they had to cross and this took a toll on the horses. The horses seem nervous since the encounter with the mimi birds. Delex suspected something followed them and crisscrossed there path but did not approach. It either toyed with them, or had a hard time following. After a month and four Ter'Avan weeks, roughly 81 days since they left Hilltan, they were almost out of the mountains. The had finally forded the last major stream and would enjoy a dry camp and rest.

Nova became more withdrawn and quiet over the last few days. Delex couldn't figure it out. Every time he looked at her there seemed to be more sadness in her eyes. It was not a lot, but it was there. Nova started to cover herself every time he was near. Did he do something wrong? Did he offend her? Nova seemed to encourage their relationship the most. Now, she seemed to withdraw from him a little more each day.

They had traveled a long distance with each other. It was a peaceful and happy trip, much different from the harrowed attacks and stress of where he first came to Ter'Avan. He could almost forget the threat that grew from Valash's mysterious plans, except the for mysterious present which followed nearby. He had also tried for several weeks to remember more of the dream he had of his father. Doran looked so proud of him. His fathers easy smile reminded him of himself. He could still picture the face of his father, and the seriousness of the dream, but most of the details where a tangle of emotions and images that would not focus.

Now he had the problem of Nova. He understood her attraction, or to be more precise, his attraction to her. He wanted to take it slow. Maybe, was that it?

Nova came back from her wash in a stream when she entered camp and pulled her cloak around her body. The night was not chilly and the sky bore no rain. He felt ashamed, but of what? Delex decided it was time to get to the bottom of this before it completely ruined their friendship. He walked over to Nova and sat down quietly beside her.

Nova looked up at him and for a moment. She smiled like she had the first few days they had met, then the smile faded away, and she pulled at her cloak.

Delex and Nova sat quietly for a while as their eyes reflected into the campfire. The sweet smell of wood smoke drifted in the air. Dinner eaten, plates cleaned, beds made, the only thing left was rest and sleep. Delex looked to Nova. She looked back anticipation on her face. She knew he wanted to talk. "Nova," Delex started, "I don't know what you are going through. I do not know if I can help, or if I am the problem. If I can do anything to help, I will."

Nova looked at him with tears in her eyes. She hovered there on the verge of speech and fear. Her body shook with emotions. She slowly opened her mouth to speak when they both heard a high-pitched cough come from the woods. Nova tensed, and slowly stood. "Oh thy gods, tis hounds of thy headless craft?" Nova's speech reverted to her archaic origin as her fear terrified Delex so badly his arm hair stood on end. She took a breath to calm herself and take control of her speech. Her words came under her control. "They are all extinct." A second, then third cough came from the forest nearby. Nova quickly cut the horses free and slapped them on their hind quarters to get them to flee the camp.

"Hey! Don't we need them? What is going on?" Delex asked.

"Quickly, climb a tree. Hurry with me." All shyness and sadness in Nova had been replaced with fear. Nova explained as she helped Delex into a nearby oak. "Headless hounds, should be all dead. That is neither story nor tale right now. Just now, they are blind and cannot smell, but they sense movement, from the ground and air. They are much more dangerous than the birds we encountered."

"The mimi birds?" Delex asked as he got comfortable. He wrapped his arm around Nova to help hold her and felt armor under her cloak. Nova immediately shed away but had nowhere to go. She was about to say something more when Delex pointed to the camp below.

Below them a monstrous dog-like creature came into camp. Its slow plod to the center had an air of uncaring laziness. Its body told another story. The creature's skinny body held taunt muscles and bone that constantly rippled and twitched with caged energy. Hairless skin covered long legs and a narrow body. It was slick, but without gloss. Delex studied closer. The skin interlocked in scales that ran down its body. It had a tail the was lizard like and thick with beefy muscle. It had a row of horny scales that ran down both shoulders to connect at the hip. The spikes ended at the of its tail.

"That is a headless hound," Nova said loudly. She hid her face within her cloak as she spoke. Delex gave her a worried stare. "Oh do not fear, they have poor hearing. They know we are here by the feel of our breath and voice, but they only react to movements." Nova looked back down to the dogs. "They are swift as death. They have a throat like protrusion extends from the shoulders. It has several circular rows of serrated teeth that overlap. They saw off appendages and grind the meat."

Delex whispered to her. "How do you know this, can we escape?"

Nova shook her head. "I didn't realize they still existed. I sent the horses into the woods. The headless hounds will not chase them. They hate horse flesh, and moving water. They are weak against drowning." Nova shook her head. Her hair hung around her eyes. "We thought we had destroyed them all."

"The dragons?" Delex asked. Nova nodded her head. Two more hounds approached from the woods. All three barked high pitch coughs as they searched the campsite. All three dogs soon found the tree Nova and Delex climb, and slowly circled it.

"They don't travel in packs unless they are hunting." She pointed to tracks they left around the tree. "They are feeling our steps in the ground." Nova growled, but the sound seemed slightly more feral than a human could produce. "By the first scale, we should have never made them." Nova noticed Delex give her a raised eyebrow. "It was one of our first experiments before we successful made ourselves dragons." She shrugged. "It was not a success. We destroyed there kind." Nova hit the tree in frustration. All three hounds pointed the stubbed, headless bodies upwards. Nova's face showed immediate regret. "Someone has brought them back."

Delex whispered again. "Valash." Novas face said it all, she was thinking the same thing. "We need to fight." Delex worried because he was told not to use magic, but from the size of the creatures and their capabilities, he had no choice. His swordsmanship was still laughable at best, and Nova carried only a small knife.

Nova looked to Delex and gave him a sad smile. "I will never forget our time." She said in a sad whisper. "Remember me in the stars. Try to flee dear Heir." Nova removed her cloak and touched his face softly. Before Delex could respond, Nova jumped from the tree. Before she had reached the ground, the dogs had struck her from the sky. Nova spun from the impact but hit the ground on her feet. Her clothing took the initial attack. The tattered remains would not protect her from another attack. Her sleek womanly figure betrayed the secret she hid from Delex. All over her tan golden skin blue scales bespectacled her body in mosaic patches. Her scar on over her breast had also been replaced by more scales. Scales covered almost all her skin. Nova looked up at Delex in a moment of sadness.

"Tis there not a moment thy eyes see mine naked flesh? Thy gods are jesters and romantic knaves." The headless hounds recovered and struck Nova to the ground.

Chapter 18: Salty Serenade

Delex screamed down to Nova as the headless hounds quickly overpowered her and pushed her to the ground. Each hound was almost as big as her and built for muscle and speed. Before Nova could scream, the hounds had attacked her limbs. Each hound took both arms and a leg within their stubbed protrusions and shoved her limbs into their bodies up to Nova's knees and elbows. Nova screamed in fright as she thrashed with her head and kicked with her one free leg.

Delex started to climb down from the tree. He had no plan to save her, but he couldn't leave her. The look she gave him right before the hounds pushed her to the ground decided it. He had to use magic. Even if he showed Valash and every wizard on the planet where he was, he was not going to leave Nova to die.

As Delex touched the ground and raised his hand for battle, something curious happen. The hounds released her. Nova quickly snapped to her feet and pulled the rags of her dress around her. The hounds looked in obvious pain. One hound coughed out a pile of broken teeth. Nova looked down to her arms to see barely a scratch. Tooth dust and saliva covered the scaled over her arms and leg, but no other damage remained.

"The but break upon mine frame! Tis nothing yet a mark of memory." Nova spoke loudly. The hounds did not seem to notice. In all her excitement, Nova had again reverted to her old speech.

Delex whispered to her. "That's cool and all, but we need to get the blaze out of here." Delex had picked up few curse phrases of Ter'Avan.

Nova walked boldly through the hounds. They circled her and coughed quietly to each other as they organized and planned. "Thy speech need not be a baby breath." Nova flushed. "I mean, stop whispering, it is annoying." She held up her hands to him. "Just do not move. If they cannot bite me, they cannot kill me. You can escape."

Delex refused. "No, I am not leaving you."

Nova retorted, "But look at me! I am a monster. How can you like this." Nova kicked at a dog who easily jumped out of the way. "My scales return, slow and sure. I am reverting!" Nova yelled with her fist. Tears ran down her face fell to the ground. The hounds jumped and twitched as each one hit the forest floor.

He finally understood why she had been increasingly distant. Delex had to get control of the situation. "We can think of something, do something, but we need to get out of here. I think the dogs have figured something out." Delex pointed to the Headless hounds. The hounds had gathered, facing Nova. Their muscles started to tense. They coughed to each other as they prepared.

"They can not harm me. My scales protect me from their bites." Nova smirked. She boldly took a step towards them. The hound like lizard creatures took a step back but did not seem otherwise phased.

Delex had a cold realization. "Nova, What about your head?" Nova's scales did not reach up her neck. Delex raised his hand again. He felt the magic build inside him.

Nova looked back to him with renewed terror. She touched her face. It had remained untouched. She could almost picture the hounds mouths and broken teeth tearing into her. At the same moment one of the three hounds relaxed for a moment and shifted its body towards Delex. The spines down its body quivered in a wave as it tensed its muscles. Nova looked into Delex's eyes. "I am so sorry Delex. As you strike with magic, they will attack. They have greater sense of magic than that of sound. We should have run."

"I know." Delex closed his eyes slowly and opened them to look back to Nova. He smiled to her. "Just to be clear. I care about you, no matter what you look like." Nova's return smile left him without breath. She was beautiful in body, mind and heart, greater than one he had ever meet. She is everything he could want. He didn't care about the scales that slipped over most of her body. It was not her true self. That was only skin deep. His heart grew ever more fond of her, her mind, her personality, the way she smirked as they shared a joke. Her eyes told him that she could be in any form and those eyes would still be Nova. She would always be one of his trusted friends. He wished for more time. He wanted time to see if they could share more.

Delex had no protection. Delex felt the magic inside stir within, his magic felt his urgency. His let the magic use his instincts. The magic inside him prepared for combat. Yet, deep down he knew the hounds will react faster. Someone will to die. He looked at Nova and could see the recognition in her eyes. He saw her face, her hand clenched as her face lost all fear. *No! She will attack and die. I can't let this happen!* Nova got on the toes of her feet. Delex raised his hand again. He made a choice. He would protect her and face the consequences later.

A sudden crash in the forest brought them and the hounds out of the battle. A great black war horse burst through the clearing without a rider and continued into the night. The hounds ignored the horse and the two people. All three remained tense as their faceless necks scanned the woods. Delex thought he had seen the horse before.

A clap of thunder and a blast of air ripped through the clearing. Dust and dirt immediately filled the air like an explosion. Nova and Delex stumbled from their feet. When they recovered, two of the hounds struggled to their feet. The third stood where it was. A thin line in the dirt ran towards and past it. The headless hound slowly toppled to either side of the line, split down its length. The two pieces hit toppled to the ground in wet thuds, and pools of red blood.

Delex and Nova got to their feet as Blackus stepped into the clearing. He spread his feet apart and returned a look of pure murder at the headless hounds. His right hand slowly lowered the singled edged sword Delex knew as a katana. It was the sword N'Mora gifted him. He cocked his right arm around the left side of him and stood with his shoulder to the hounds. One of the hounds immediately realized the threat and back away from him. The other hound jumped at Blackus' face in a blur of motion, but Blackus was just as fast. He whipped the sword forward and let the hound skewer itself down the length. Blackus twisted the blade with both hands then whipped it upwards. The sword freed itself from the hound and sprayed Blackus in a halo of blood. The hound hit the ground dead. Red blood poured from shoulder to tail.

The third hound turned to flee. Blackus spun on his heels and shot a dagger through the clearing. The dagger punched into the last hound so hard sparks flew from the blade. The handle snapped off and whistled into the dark forest. It did not make it to the forest. The hound's body skidded and slammed into a tree as the front legs crumpled underneath it. Blackus slowly walked towards the falling monster. "Gather the horses, we need to move."

Delex and Nova stood dumbfounded as the watched Blackus slowly push his blade into the core of the beast. No emotion registered on his face. He looked down at the headless hound like an angry god. Nova spoke up. Her voice shuddered. "Blackus, what in Void are you?"

Blackus whistled. The large black horse came back into the clearing. Four horses followed behind it. He looked to Nova. "Impatient and unwilling to repeat myself."

Nova shrugged and searched her saddle bags for new clothes. She quickly replaced the torn ones that hung off her with a simple pair of brown pants, tan woolen shirt and a wide black belt. Luckily she had not been wearing her boots or cloak during the attack. "I have known you for a long time Blackus, and you do not seem to be human at all."

Blackus shrugged. "I don't care." He pointed towards the woods. "I scouted a band of twenty human and animal drethcon coming this way." Blackus jumped onto Penance. "We leave, now." Nova gave him a curious glare but let the matter drop.

They quickly left and abandoned anything that was not in the saddlebags. Blackus could probably handle the drethcon without a sweat as he found packs of them. If the drethcon see the heir, the danger could overpower them as the enemies converge and swarmed.

The starlight was bright enough to find there way. They traveled to the nearby stream and pushed through the night until the forest was too dense to see. It was close to morning. Delex and Nova stole a few hours of sleep before Blackus woke them. The group had not gained any distance on the drethcon. They were still about a day behind. They would have to get out of the forest to gain ground.

The next several days left the trio harrowed and worn. The drethcon did not need to sleep or eat and pursued at a steady pace. They could rely on the energies of the victims they continued to drain from the village of Hilltan. Blackus scouted and returned each day. He reported to Delex and Nova the mass of hunting drethcons. The drethcon were not stupid, and a few of them could retain knowledge from the victims they mimic. Blackus was certain the drethcon suspected the heir. If they saw him, it would confirm it and the pursuit would only intensify.

Blackus had been able to attack slower drethcon. Had he killed too many at a time, his presence by itself would only raise suspicion. Yet with every drethcon he eliminated, more appeared. Blackus believed that enemies converged as they confirmed and eliminated false trials. Blackus admired the control Valash had over so many drethcon and other minions at the same time. Delex was decisively not impressed.

Blackus set a terrible pace. They only slept for a few hours before a kick from Blackus' foot broke them from their rest. Eventually, the torturous pace worked. They finally came out of the forest into a light wooden area and took off at top speed. The drethcon were on foot so would not be able to catch them easily. Blackus reported again that night with hopeful news. They had gained several days and could finally relax.

That night they all gathered for the first warm meal they had since the night with the headless hounds. They even opened a bottle of mild wine. Blackus even promised the morning would have a hearty hot meal before they set off again towards the sea. He would still move them quickly and safely as he could.

Delex and Nova sat side by side. The two seemed to come to a fundamental understanding. They sat close. An unspoken conversation passed between them. Nova looked to Blackus with merriment in her eyes. "Blackus, how did you get your name? Tis an oddity." She laughed but did not expect and answer.

Blackus looked up from the fire, quiet and emotionless. His black spell-weave armor reflected the light of the fire in soft patterns. "My mother named me after the cat." Delex and Nova both laughed at Blackus' joke. The smiles soon faded as Blackus continued to stare.

Delex grinned with amazement at Blackus, "Dude, are you joking?"

"No." Blackus said casually. The looks on their faces expressed absolute bewilderment. Blackus sighed. "My mother named me for her cat. She had him for many years. He hated her, but she loved him until he died. As she told me, he was a formidable beast." Blackus toss a stick into the fire. "My mother had twins, I was born first. She told me when I came. I immediately opened my eyes and glare at her like her cat had when it lived. She named me after him."

Nova chuckled. "I never knew." She shook her head in amusement.

"You never asked." Blackus replied.

"What about Soas?" Delex asked.

Nova was the once to answer. "Soas, came right after. His mother felt a compulsion take her tongue. She named him Soas." Nova shrugged, "Or, tis what the legends say."

Blackus nodded. "Correct. The name of Soas always comes to a newborn child after the last Soas dies. Each act like the one before; but I am the first Blackus." Blackus looked to them with a certain amount of pride.

The night wore on in mild conversation. The group rested the remainder of the night. There would be no forced march tomorrow. Blackus said he would let them sleep late into the morning.

Delex smiled to himself. It all fascinated him. Here he was in a world of magic, his world, yet this all was new to him. It was so fanciful. The name Blackus, The most terrifying man on the planet, came from cankerous cat. Delex couldn't help wonder as he thought, *how mean was that cat?*

Soas paced back and forth in the dusty street of Good Harbor. It had been ninety-three days since he parted with Delex and the rest. His nerves felt worn thin with worry. He had bargained, haggled, stolen, then traded to get passage across the sea. Water month had the perfect weather to sail and book passage, but it was also hard to find passage without a reservation. Mercadio and another wizard had shown up two days ago covered head to foot in pig feces. Mercadio wouldn't elaborate. All he would say is the spell worked as intended if not predicted.

Soas thought about this and how he could make fun of Mercadio when he noticed a commotion near the outer gate. A squad of soldier ran to the gate. Two guards broke off to get more help. One shielded the other from attacks that never came. Soas shook his head as he thought to himself. *Blackus has trained those men too well.*

In a minute, three more squads of Broken Moon soldiers went to the gate with those blasted whistles as they tweeted like drunken birds. Soas decided to investigate. As he neared, he saw his older brother Blackus. He pointed towards the hills outside the gate. His men continued with those obnoxious whistles. Men on horse and foot practically poured out of the woodwork. In all the commotion Soas could not get to the gate. He pushed and maneuvered around everyone but it all ended in frustration. *Okay, maybe they are not as well-trained as I thought.* Soas gave an angry huff.

Someone called his name. Soas turned to see who it was but couldn't see anyone. They called again. His eyes finally locked on Delex. A cheer ripped from his throat as his rushed over to Delex. Delex in turn jumped off his horse and practically vaulted into Soas' arms. The both laughed and cheered and rolled in the dirt as they basically frolicked like young stallions in the pasture.

"Delex, you rough pile of dried up pigpen! Ashen good to see you!" Soas laughed.

"Uh, okay Soas." Delex snorted. "I am glad to see you too. Did you make it okay?"

Soas laughed, "I have been here for a week. It was quiet as a dead mouse out there."

"Well you are lucky." Nova said as she gracefully slid off her horse. She gathered all the horses reins as they led themselves to the side. The commotion started to fade as the last of Blackus' men left the town.

"You sound better. No more archaic junk?" Soas joked.

"Only when mine desire to rend limb upon limb from what which disturbs, peeks mine ire." Nova said as her purple eyed gaze bore into Soas.

"Yeah, well, Hey! Let us go meet Mercadio and some random wizard. The best part is they only partially smell like pig waste now!" Soas said with a cheer as he changed the subject. Soas reminisced. "And, oddly of imp. Yes, imp." He shrugged.

Delex and Nova smiled and shook their heads. They followed Soas to a nearby inn set close to the docks. Blackus stayed behind with his soldiers. It seemed he would have to change some of his orders to deal with more drethcon attacks.

The salt air was heavy with moister and heat of the noon day sun. Delex sweat through his clothes by the time the made it to a moderately sized inn called the Whistling Merecat. It featured creature with a cat-like upper half with a fish tail. The sign displayed several musical notes above the merecat. Mercadio and an older fellow in green sat at a table near the fire. They bickered at each other as their hands gestures in exaggerated motions. It was a busy inn, but the tables the wizards were empty. The inn keeper glared at them both from behind the bar. A subtle smell of sweet manure hung lightly in the air.

They both looked up at the group as they entered. Mercadio stamped his staff on the ground and waved. The other man, passed his eyes over each face and stopped at Delex. A certain amount of recognition cross over his face as he stood. He quietly pointed and whispered to Mercadio. Mercadio smiled to him and slapped his fingers down. The man in green slowly lowered himself back to his seat and motions for a barmaid to bring him a fresh drink.

Mercadio hugged Delex in a fierce grip as he approached. "My boy it is so good to see you!"

Delex grimaced. "It is good to see you too?" He questioned as he turned his face from Mercadio. He smelled like crap and pee.

"Oh, I am sorry young man. It was a slight miscalculation on the landing. Narsis and I, oh yes, this is Narsis the green, a wizard of the highest caliber in Nature magic." Mercadio pointed to the man that pulled heavily from his new drink. "Sorry he is a bit overwhelmed. We made a new magic! We are calling it teleporting after your naming of it."

"Oh well, okay." Delex stammered. "Nice to meet you," he said to Narsis.

"Let us collect the details upstairs." Soas said. "They have better windows up their." He walked to the inn keeper and produces some coin. The inn keeper sighed with visible relief when the party left the common room and took the two stinky wizards with them.

The group of friends introduced each other. Nova stayed slightly withdrawn, but Delex stayed by her side and offered her emotional support. They had not been able to figure out how to change her back. Narsis was beside himself. They decided to tell him the truth since Delex's arrival on Ter'Avan. It was obvious the wizard did not have the stomach for adventure. They had to stop several times because had fainted or looked about to vomit.

The story quickly turned to each group's actions up on after they split at Hilltan. Blackus showed Mercadio the webs from N'Mora's house. His face showed no emotion, but his hands dung into the handle of the sword she gave him. Nova showed her arms covered in blue scales. She spoke so quietly, Delex took over and explained their encounter with the headless hounds. Narsis almost puked. Mercadio and Narsis reveled amulets that helped focus the extreme effort of the teleport spell. They went into detail on how they manipulated the required magics and how to use the amulets. Delex followed along with interest. Soas made snoring noises until Nova punched him. Soas had nothing to reveal except he had booked passage to get across the sea and a subtle grin. He left to check on the preparations. It would remain a mystery what trouble he caused when left to himself.

The party talked into the night and enjoyed each other. Soas returned a little uneasy on his feet. It seems the final negotiations for passage was a drinking game. It required an iron stomach and a fortitude to win. The game did not require to keep the contents inside after departing the game with the winnings. Soas involuntary demonstrated this out the second story window. It would have been ignored by the innkeeper if the window did not open above the entrance to the inn. Soas won the bet, but in a way, lost the game. As the party packed and resupplied, Soas spent his time in the outhouse and paying to clean the entrance of the Whistling Merecat.

Soas came back later still rough around the edges, but much improved and lighter in coin. An urgent message arrived from the captain. They had to leave now. There was some trouble with the port authority. Mercadio rolled his eyes. He had expected nothing less. The group hurried to the ship. Blackus had to leave his horse Penance behind but made arrangements to return it back to Homgad.

A group of angry sailors gathered around the dock as the party boarded the ship. The captain cut ropes and the crew made a hasty and messy escape towards the sea. Delex looked back as more sailors pointed and cursed at the ship.

Soas led the party to their rooms with a small grin on his face. He always enjoyed well-timed escapes, even if he was not cause of it. The ship was a cargo ship with a deep wide, long hull, but, the passenger quarters, where small near the outer hull. This made the passengers feel each wave and roll of the ship. Extra quarters bulged with extra food stuffs and cargo. Luckily, The Soas paid extra for the party. They took over the captain's quarters. It was the only room on the ship that could fit the whole party. The captain, they assumed, would bunk with the rest of the crew or one of his officers' rooms. After a full day out to sea, the captain came to visit. A rough knock peppered the door and continued until Mercadio answered.

A man strolled quickly into the room and nearly tipped the wizard backward. He had tanned skin from many years of outside work. A stock of short, wavy blond hair hung to his shoulders. He wore a ready smile as his blue eyes scanned the room quickly. He wore a rough wool shirt, a wide black belt, and pants that went to the calf. On his hip, an expensive bastard sword hung in a leather sheath. "So this is our new cargo. Nice to meet you!"

Delex looked at the man. For a brief second he though the man's eyes were lite with fire. When he blinked, the captain's eyes were back to their normal blues.

Soas stood and looked at the man oddly. "I thought we were going to meet the captain." From the look Soas gave him, he had not seen him before.

"Well, I am the new captain. My name is Jaxcel. I won the ship from the other captain last night." He smiled broadly. The look in the room said no one believed him.

"Is that why we were nearly chased into the sea?" Mercadio glared.

"Oh that." Jaxcel laughed. "That's the old crew. I sorta hired a new crew and didn't tell them. Don't worry, we tossed all there junk overboard, so they could collect whatever floated!" Jaxcel emphasized with open arms.

"And you just happen to win this vessel?" Narsis glared.

"Well, I cheated." Jaxcel laughed. He held out his hands wide. "I mean cheated like a goat herder selling wool, a good proper fleecing." He said with a wink and a hearty laugh. Everyone smiled at the jovial nature of Jaxcel, except Blackus.

Soas laughed with Jaxcel as turned back to the group. "I like him." He turned back to the captain. "So you cheated eh? Want to play a few games of chance. I promise to cheat as the best I can."

Jaxcel laughed. "So, a real game of skill! That would be absolutely wonderful." Jaxcel clapped and bowed. "Well and ways. Now we have introductions out of the way, feel free to visit the ship, and welcome the Filthy Harlot. I renamed her myself."

Nova stopped smiling as soon as she heard the name of

the ship. She immediately lost interest in the conversation. "Buffoonery."

Jaxcel looked to Soas, "So one of your dice, and one of mine?"

Soas grinned widely. He started to walk away with the captain. "So, want to hear the story how I summoned a dragon? It lit a wizard ghost on fire then turned into an annoying woman."

A laugh came from down the hall. "Ah fake stories! I have you beat. I'll tell you a story of my exile from four kingdoms at once! It started with one horse with a flaming red mane and ended with the smell of burnt toast." Raucous laughter echoed into the room.

Nova growled quietly. "I would hear objections now against the purposeful drowning of a thief."

Delex ribbed Nova with a smile. "He bought our passage?" Nova grumbled, but soon giggled as she looked at the silly innocent look Delex gave her.

Mercadio had a serious look on his face. He looked to Narsis. "Did you feel it Narsis?"

Narsis nodded. "I felt it too. He must be an Aspect, a Spark, and a new one."

Mercadio looked to the others. "We will deal about that more later, but suffice to say, we must watch this new captain and be wary of danger."

"You mean like the fire in his eye?" Delex asked.

Both wizards looked at him in shock. Mercadio replied. "You saw fire in his eye?" Delex shrugged.

"I witnessed it as well." Nova said.

"Interesting," Mercadio waved his hand. "Oh but this can wait. We will discuss this later." He pointed his finger at the others. "For now leave him to us, especially you Blackus." Blackus peered out the porthole through the encounter with disinterest. He still did not turn.

"It seems we will have a long trip. Let us make it a happy one." Nova smiled. She held out her hand to Delex. Her hand had started to get a few small blue scales on them. Delex didn't seem to care and took it readily. They both left the cabin.

The sea was a long ocean that spanned the saddle of the peanut shaped planet. The warm waters of the ocean was abundant with life. Only a thin land bridge connected the two major landmasses.

Even with the abilities of fast ships, the waters had frequent storms that made navigation more an art than a skill. It was apparent Jaxcel had little to no experience as a sailor, but the confidence he showed made the crew work harder and more efficient. It would take an entire month, if not more, to span the ocean.

After several Ter'Avan weeks of travel, Jaxcel announced tomorrow they would cross the worse part and everyone not at work on the ship needed to stay in doors. If they had to go above deck, everyone wore a harness with several metal loops. You used the metal loops to tie ropes that lead to long rails with more metal loops. These rails adorned the side of the ships railings, masts, and other points of contact. Without the rope and loop system, the waves had the chance to wash you overboard like a cat would swat a mouse.

The next several days were a turmoil of winds, rain, and waves. Delex had a problem with motion sickness when they started travel on the boat, but now he could not keep anything in his stomach without a good view of his shoes moments later. Nova stayed by his side the entire time. They made it through unscathed, mostly due to the experienced sailors Jaxcel had hired. They were thankful the rough braggart had a good eye for men.

They took some time to know Jaxcel and heard more of his background. Jaxcel recounted exile stole him from his king, land, country and the strange fire and dreams that caused it. He did not hold anything back, nor had a filter for his truth. He even told the previous captain he was going to cheat fiercely for the ship. It was apparent the previous captain had taken it for a joke at the time.

Mercadio and Narsis remained surprisingly silent. The two

wizards spend most of the time near Jaxcel. They shadowed Jaxcel when they thought they were alone, and whispered to each other as they watched the captain. Several times they conferred with Blackus, but he remained silent to what they discussed.

This did not seem to bother Jaxcel or Soas. They spent most of their time together as they cheated each other out of money, clothes, items and outrages dares that usually required them to be naked or wet. It was not the game they played, it was how well they could get away with a cheat, and how well they could spot one played.

Both men spent and entire day naked, wet, and covered in chum when they invited Nova to a single game. She laughed the entire day. Later that day, she gave them back what they had lost, minus the coin and the dignity. She was never invited to play again. Delex spent some time with the two as they attempted to teach him proper cheats. They returned anything he lost. Most of the time he was with Nova. She promised to teach him the best way to cheat if he promised to never use the knowledge like Soas would. He agreed. Thus, Delex's first lesson in dragon lore would be how to cheat at games. One introductory hour opened his eyes to a world of con-artistry. It Blackus was ruthless on the battlefield, Nova was his equal at games of chance.

The rest of the trip became easier when the wind turned to their backs. The navigation time they wasted through the worst of the storms recovered in short order. Delex, who was seasick at the first of the journey, seem to become use to the sway of the ship, especially after the trails of the last few days. The rest of the trip had few problems.

It took forty-eight days to cross the ocean and arrive at another port city called Tower Port. In the distance the Towers of Magic could be seen. Mercadio and Narsis were decidedly happy. Soas gave them both rude looks.

They entire party left the Filthy Harlot the same day. Jaxcel, the captain, was not around to see them off. The crew had not seen him since last night. The first mate thought he had taken a one of the two shore boats to the dock since he only found one strapped to the ship. Soas had paid the captain and crew so there was no need to wait. They had the sailors lower the shore boat and head to the docks. A wagon arrive to haul away the goods that the ship had delivered oversea.

Soas had already got the party rooms for the night, but Mercadio was adamant they left the city at once. So the party found horses and oxen to haul the wagon. They traveled about a kilometer out of town. They still had about another twenty to go before they would reach the Towers of Magic. Mercadio was oddly nervous until everyone ate and settled down for sleep.

Delex had yet another dream. This was not the normal dream he had of plains and mountains. This one was within a room. A room made of soft white marbles and black granite. Tapestries hung down walls and carpets lay sprawled on the floor. Light glistened from the walls in ivy patterns of swirls and leaves. It was the most beautiful room he had every been in. A small pile of steps lead to a dais with two seats. Both seats where made of rough wood cobbled together into thrones. Each had a simple cushion on them, one of blue, and one of red.

Delex walked around the room but discovered nothing more. He decided to push on two large doors that sat on the other side of the room from the thrones. The doors opened easily into a hallway made of light grey granite and hammered iron. The same ivy that grew in the previous room adorned the walls down the hall, shedding soft white light. Delex took in a deep breath. This was a castle. Something felt familiar. Delex took a few steps down the hall, then a few more. Before he knew it, his feet took him into a run. Room after room passed him, each opened and full of invitation. He passed them all as ran forward where the orange light of the sun shown through a window.

Delex ran up to the window with no glass. The wind blew into his face with a cool pressure. Below him a city sprawled.

The streets ran in straight lines in a half circle from a large lake below the castle. The entire scene turned slowly below him. He was at Homgad, on a castle floating above the waters of the lake. He was home.

Two hands encircled him as he felt a kiss on his cheek. "Welcome home." the soft voice said. Delex turned around to see a woman step back from him. She was tall and willowy. Her face held grace and smile while her eyes shown with love. Her vibrant red hair cascaded down to her waist. The woman's skin was smooth and slightly freckled. Dark black eyes reflected deep wisdom.

Delex did not need a moment's glance to know who this was. It was Zelexi. "Mother."

Zelexi nodded. "Yes my love, my son." She walked up to him and rested her elbows in the window seal. "This is your home."

Delex smiled. A flood of memories flooded back to him. He remembered his play of hide-and-seek around the pillars and passage ways, her soft voice songs in the night, and more. Delex and Zelexi spent the entire day together. They shared stories and memories as they paced the castle. The world spun below them. Night came and went, and yet they felt none of it.

They sat at the window again Zelexi leaned out over the city. "My little love, I wish I could stay like this forever, to know the man that you have become. Alas, little one, there is something important for you to finish." Delex did not turn to look at her. He feared what he would see. If he stayed and looked into the city below him, maybe she would move on to other things.

The memories of his talk with Doran, his father, flooded back to him. "You know how to defeat him don't you." Delex asked his mother.

She nodded. "Perhaps. I know what he is made of and how to finish him, if it is possible." She took his hand in hers. "We are all made from the same concept. We take a small portion of energy to be more. You father and I, we take what you give us, your desire to see us, nothing more."

"Valash takes more." Delex said. He pieced together the puzzle that had eluded everyone for so long. He looked at his mother. "The dark spike? The center of the planet?"

Zelexi's smile faded. "Yes, right between the orbs of Ter and Avan." The dream grew cold. "We have no time left. Ter'Avan is dying, it will soon cross the threshold and the cascade will ruin the world."

Chapter 19: Bloodbath

Delex looked at his mother's eyes as the sky darkened around them. The moon slowly turned red and smashed into the saddle of the planet. Ter'Avan shuddered, but the explosion force drained before it could release fire and rock into the sky. The world of the dream grew brown as plants withered. Mountains fell in upon themselves. The atmosphere slowly leaked into the sky in rivets of gas. "So he is killing the planet? A spell is killing it?"

Zelexi pointed to the surroundings. "True to word. Valash died, but somehow separated his inner magic into a spell. Doran almost figured this out before he died. His research lead me to this discovery." She pointed to the scene. "This will happen slowly, over years. The magics of the world will not recover fast enough."

"How am I going to defeat him? If I understand this right, he is dead and if I kill his body, his magic spike attached to the core will remake him." Delex checked off each finger. "If I destroy his magic spike, he just uses his own magic to remake the spike. Plus, the original part of the spell, himself, will not unravel. Should we add he also roughly over a thousand years of sorcerer knowledge, magic combat veteran, and still made of the magic we are trying to defeat." Delex took a sad breath. "We do not know how to break it so the world will die."

Zelexi turned Delex away from the horrid scene of the world as it turned to a dead husk and broke apart to two dead orbs. "My little love, you have something no sorcerer has ever had. Your magics are much stronger than Valash." Zelexi ticked off her fingers as she mimicked her son's gestures. "Your ability to manipulate magic defies normal boundaries. You have knowledge from another world. Plus, I trust you with my heart just like I trusted your father when we met."

He could feel the love from his mother like a radiant warmth. "What do you mean my knowledge?"

Zelexi shrugged. The world grew darker by the moment. The castle walls started to show through Zelexi. "You have something no one else on this planet has, Earth knowledge. Use it. Make your magic your own. You have been trying so hard to do it the Ter'Avan way." She shook her head. "But this is not you. We placed you on Earth to protect you, and to give you more than the little knowledge we have here. Remember, his spell yearns to be whole, thus it duplicated his appearance."

Delex smiled. Her voice filled him with confidence. "Well, I took two years of community college. I was top of my class. We didn't compete. I also spent my time outside of class studying various interests in the library."

Zelexi kiss him on the forehead. He could barely feel the kiss. Her body had become so translucent it looked like a ghost and near impossible to see. "You will be just fine. Now wake. You must go to him tonight, leave your friends in safety. He knows you are close."

Delex sighed. "Where?"

"Where you have been always going. To the Towers of Magic, deep underneath them where he hides from the wizards and cannot leave. This is where his bones lay, and he hooked himself to the planet." Zelexi dissipated completely. The world went black. Her voice echoed in the darkness. "Now wake and remember your father and I are always with you."

Delex climbed lightly out of his dream. He sat up and became face to face with Nova. Her purple eyes looked at his. "You know where he is don't you?" Delex didn't know how to answer her. "You were going alone weren't you?" Nova smiled to him fondly. "Come, before the others wake."

Delex couldn't find any excuse she would except. So they both silently packed a small backpack of goods. Delex sent Nova ahead to watch for any guard to keep the horses quiet. They had to move quickly. He could wake the others. If they took the horses, others would be alerted from the sound. They also could not walk, it would take too long.

Out of the darkness Blackus emerged. Nova and Delex cringed. They had been caught. Blackus walked to them silent as a ghost and placed an object into their hands "Go, finish the mission." He turned away to the stunned pair and disappeared into the shadows.

Delex looked down to see the amulet that Mercadio had used for his teleportation spell. He lifted it to his neck and looked to Nova. She slipped her amulet over her head and offered her hand. He counted it a blessing that he had listened so intently to Narsis and Mercadio's amazing discovery.

Delex closed his eyes and let the magic flow through him. He imagined his destination as well as he could. To his side, Nova concentrated as well. Normally it took a long time to use the amulets. Since the amulets' magic derives from sorcerer knowledge, Delex's instincts showed him how to bypass the specific spell with a massive amount of magical power. He focused this into both the amulets. Nova's knowledge covered the holes in magic he left. Their magics combined and became one focused effort. In a silent blink, they were gone.

The sound of a loud bell rang into the night from the woods and disturbed the sleep of the party camped a kilometer out of town. A few of the party members woke from sleep. It was an oddity, but they agreed it probably came from the city Tower Port. As they turned back to their beds a massive clap of sharp thunder jerked awake Mercadio and rest of the party. That was decidedly not from the city. The sound of it echoed off the mountains. Before they could question the noise, a second identical clap of thunder startled them once again. The sky was clear without any lightning. Everyone scrambled to their feet and scanned for attack. In the distance birds flew in a thick cloud of confusion, but nothing else seemed to disturb the night.

"Delex, where is Delex!" Mercadio panicked. He looked around the camp as he tore at blankets and gear. "Delex!" He screamed.

"He left with Nova." Blackus said. He sat near the remains of the fire. He calmly threw some kindling and a log into the fire to stoke the flames to life. "He went to Valash."

Mercadio stood dumbfounded. He reached under his clothes for the amulet, but it was not there. He sunk to his knees in defeat. "My boy. He left without me."

"He left without all of us." Soas said. He sat on the ground a shoved a dagger through the dirt. "That hurts," he scoffed.

Mercadio turned to Soas. Anger made red splotches on his face. "How can you joke Soas. Have you any human decency?"

Soas jumped to his feet. "He knows what he is doing, trust him!" Soas' shoulders lowered. "You have to trust him now."

Narsis rushed to Mercadio and whispered into his ear as he tried to calm his friend. Another boom echoed into the night. They all jumped, even Blackus. This was much closer to camp. Daylow hissed from inside Mercadio's hood. The boom happen again, but this time the could tell the noise came from within the camp. They all turned toward the stored the supply, wagon, and various gear they acquired in town. A large chest rattled on the wagon as it boomed loudly into the night.

Blackus walked to the wagon and ripped the chest from the rest of the goods. It fell to the ground and popped the locked latch open. The lid of the chest flipped open to reveal the Captain Jaxcel from his ship, the Filthy Harlot. He was bound, gagged, and glared at them all with a reasonable amount of hate.

Narsis looked at the man. "What in the orbs?"

Jaxcel looked at each person as he quickly scanned the situation. His eyes smoldered with power as the restrains on him blackened and smoked. Mercadio point his staff to the man. A flash of light shot from the staff and hit Jaxcel in the head. Jaxcel immediately calmed and fell back to sleep.

"Towers of testicles!" Soas exclaimed.

Narsis turned to Mercadio with a shake of his head. He could not place words to the questions he wanted to ask.

Mercadio lowered his staff. "He's an Aspect dear Narsis, a Spark. As we suspected, I confirmed."

Narsis breathed in deeply and exhaled. "By the gods, not another one." He looked to at Soas. Soas grinned at him. Narsis turned back to Mercadio. "I'll take care of him, you try to catch up to Delex." Mercadio tried to argue but Narsis lifted a hand to forgo discussion. "We both know it is your nature dear Mercadio, not mine. I cannot pursue him into danger, but I can prevent this one."

Blackus rode up with horses already saddled and ready. Soas climbed into the seat and glared at the wizards. Mercadio walked to the horse and mounted without a word.

Daylow jumped out of his hood and sat down by the unconscious Jaxcel. The black cat whispered loudly, "I will watch the Spark."

Narsis sat down by the captain. There was not more to say. Jaxcel would have to wait. The three turned their horses towards the towers, where the first booms came from, and kicked into a gallop.

∞∞∞∞

Delex and Nova snapped into existence and fell a few feet to the ground. Nova rolled gracefully to her feet while Delex slapped the ground face first. He lifted himself off the ground and coughed dirt. "Ouch. Well that worked, almost." The Towers of Magic were a short distance away. They had landed in a grassy courtyard that encircled both towers. The towers rested high on the top of a mountain with the top cut flat. A long incline stretched from the Towers of Magic to Tower Port, the shipping town which docked the Filthy Harlot and the rest of his friends.

Nova looked at him and laughed. The scales that covered her body now fully enveloped her hands and circled her face around her hair line. Her hair pushed out between the scales, but it was apparent the hair thinned as fought with the growing scales. She noticed Delex and pulled her hood up as she turned away.

"Don't worry Nova. After we take care of Valash, we will fix you." Delex said as he held his side and brushed the dirt off himself.

Nova was about to reply when a roar came from the towers. They both looked up to see three streaks of fire arc towards them. The fires slowed and settled in front of them. Two men and a woman stepped out of the flames as they burned away.

The lead man stepped in front of the others. They all wore golden colored robes and white cloaks with ebony staffs. The lead wizard wore a long beard but had a smooth bald head of dark skin. He looked at them both under the gaze of eyes that glowed yellow with inner power. "Halt travelers. We detected strong magics at our barrier. I suspect it was you. Turn back until morning. Or else risk detainment and questions." The other two wizards had there faces covered by their cloaks. They both slowly stepped to either side of the speaker as they gained distance.

"We don't want any trouble, but we need to enter the towers." Delex said.

"At night, without pass, beyond visitation hours, and with sealed gates? The towers will spare no audience to visitors or business. Turn back." The front wizard held his staff towards them. The other two wizards begun to chant under their breath.

Nova grabbed Delex's arm and pulled him back a few steps. "Delex, lets try another approach. I may know a way into the vaults under the tower."

"All paths into the tower have protection, by us." said the main wizard, "Including under the vaults. You will find no passage today." He gave them a dull stare. "We have ears."

Delex didn't have time for this. He softly took Nova's hand off his and glared at the wizard. "Get out of my way or I will chop you in a path." He tired to echoed Blackus' words. He had thought it was cool thing to say; but he was almost certain he messed up the line. The reaction he got was not the one he wanted.

The lead wizard grinned. He slammed his staff down. The other two at the sides finished their incantations. Two dirt and stone monsters pulled out of the earth in front of them. Delex had read enough fantasy books on Earth to know these were golems. They were bulky with a humanoid shape. The lead wizard spoke the same incantation quickly and rapped his staff on the ground. A third golem came out of the ground, but was larger and crafted from pure granite.

The wizards stepped back from their creations. They spoke to them and gave them ready commands to attack. The lead wizard smirked. "Cut away."

Delex turned to Nova, "Okay, not as planned. Any ideas?"

Nova glared at him.

The lead wizard scoffed. "I tell you this. I sense you have magic, so I will be polite. Let us make this amusing. We can have a golem fight. If you win, you may go into the towers. If you lose, we will take you into the tower." The wizard smiled. Delex smiled back. The wizard continued, "As a prisoner." Delex frowned.

Nova cautioned him. "I am unsure. These are tower guardians. They are some of the most powerful of wizards. We can leave."

Delex shook his head. He had no time. He could feel it. Something wrong grew in power under the tower. "Okay, fire with fire. Sure, I will accept."

Delex thought about all the golems he read about in fantasy books. He pictured the massive monster before him made of granite and anger. He thought of how to improve it. A rumbled started at his feet.

"Leadstaff, he is not using incantation." The woman guardian spoke. She took a step back.

"Something is peculiar." The other guardian spoke. "We should end this now."

"Quiet, both of you. I am leadstaff. The challenge has weight, and must have measure. Tower word is tower bond." The leader of the three wizards spoke.

Delex ignored them. He closed his eyes and an image formed. The rumble grew stronger. The earth parted as his golem clawed out of it. His golem surfaced as a massive monster of steel with spikes and blades riddled over its bulky frame. Delex opened his eyes to his creation and grinned. "OH yeah!" The golem turned its roughly chiseled face towards Delex's voice.

"I will confront this one." The woman spoke and lifted back her hood. Her hair was shoulder-length and white. Her skin bore an even tan but also a deep age. The eyes of the wizard remained a clear light brown and full of energy. She looked to her golem. "Push." Her golem nodded and started rhythmic stomp towards Delex.

Nova whispered. "They have limited ability to think. We craft them from elements, so they cannot think for themselves." She poked Delex in the arm. "Think of what you want and order it."

The large spiked golem had not moved. Its rough face looked at Delex as it waited for an order. "Um, golem?" Delex asked. The golem tilted its head. "Defend and attack?" The golem immediately spun around and approached the other golem as it thundered towards them. It swung a massive spiked fist at the other. Delex anticipated a punch that would decimate the wizard's dirt and stone golem.

The other golem stopped in its tracks. Delex's golem attacked, but the fist whistled harmlessly through the air as it swung wide. The other golem pushed on the steel arm. This forced Delex's golem to rotate completely around and face Delex. The wizard's golem cracked slightly on the steel spikes and blades. It gripped the shoulders of the steel golem. The steel golem tried to resist but the wizard's dirt and stone golem gripped with all its might. It shoved down on the metal shoulders with a mighty grind. Delex's metal golem easily sunk into the soft dirt. It tried to move but the steel spikes and blades caught and immobilized it. The magic faded from the golem and it fell apart into lifeless steel.

"Cursed by luck. Rule number one of golemcraft, never make a golem to heavy for its surroundings." The lead wizard smirked. "We have two more golems, perhaps try again?"

Delex growled. Nova tried to caution him, but he already concentrated on a new golem. A new golem burst forth from the ground. It jumped into the air and landed with a light ring. It looked crafted from polished brass and shimmered in the starlight. Its body looked bulky, but it moved gracefully and light. The golem stretched and cracked its metal knuckles in an imitation of life. It crouched towards the wizards and waited for an order. The two lesser wizards looked at each other in caution, but the leadstaff held the same confidant face.

"This challenge in mine." The other backup wizard said. He pulled back his hood to reveal blond cropped hair. A dull white glaze lay over his eyes. The blind wizard turned his face towards his golem. "One punch." The dirt and stone golem nodded.

Delex shouted, "Charge!" His golem moved quickly. It rushed towards the other golem on light feet. The other golem stood its ground. As the brass golem closed the distance, the dirt and stone monster swing its fist into the chest of Delex's golem. Its fist shattered on impact, but the impact made a huge ring like a church bell and kicked up dirt around them all. Delex closed his eyes to the sudden debris and noise. The sound echoed away from them down towards the ocean. There was no doubt the impact would be heard leagues away. When he opened his eyes the dirt and stone golem stood triumphant, minus one hand. The brass golem lay on the ground. The chest completely crumpled, the magic faded away.

"Rule number two of golems. Do not make them hollow. It is impressive you can raise metal, even I cannot." The main wizard laughed. "Enough banter. You have been entertaining, but it is time for imprisonment." The yellow eyed wizard outstretched his hand. His eyes glowed brighter with anticipation.

"No wait. One more try." Delex stumbled, ad wiped blood from his mouth. The leadstaff shook his head in disagreement. "Lets raise the stakes of the challenge. I still have no fought you." This made the leadstaff pause.

The leadstaff lowered his hand and pursed his lips. "If you win, we will lead you to the vaults of the towers. If you loose, we take you to the prison while I ready you to become my retainer for the next five years. You will have a room with food, bed and your woman as payment. Under service, under tower word, tower bond?" The wizard asked.

"Do not do this, we can find a way to escape from the cells." Nova whispered in Delex's ear.

He turned to Nova. "I know, but I do not think we have the time. Can't you feel it?"

Nova's eyes shifted back and forth as she looked into his eyes. The concern melted into resignation. "Can you do it this time?"

Delex grinned. "Yeah, I just remembered something my mother told me." Nova gave him a confused look. Delex laughed. He turned back to the lead wizard. "It is a deal, but to be clear you have to lead us under the towers vaults, and you cannot tell anyone or set any traps."

The lead wizard laughed. "Indeed a curious case. Agreed but, you must face all three golems." Delex nodded. The wizard grinned. "By tower word, tower bond." Delex felt something heavy rest on his shoulders. It was there one moment and gone the next. "The bond of word is complete. Before we start again, I am Chesor. This is Neliea and the blind one is Pont." He looked to Delex for a reply.

"Oh this is Nova. She was a dragon." The wizards smiled at the absurdity. "I am," Delex didn't think he should give him his real name. His Earth last name was Devoy, and he never asked what his parents last names were, so he quickly made up a fake one. "Nicklim, Nicklim Devoy." The wizards' faces immediately lost their smiles.

Nova whispered in his ear, "Fool, only royalty have family names." She saw that he did not understand. "We can talk about this later."

"We cannot attack royalty." Neliea said. Concern was on her face.

"We have no choice, the bond has settled. If we do not-" Pont shuddered.

Chesor growled and stepped far away from his golem. He yelled over the distance. "Raise your golem, because for the next five years I will need my privy glistening clean after each use. I eat rather large meals." His granite monster shifted in anticipation. It seems more aware than the others. "Our golems will attack the moment your has risen."

Delex rolled his eyes and concentration. He struggled to think of a golem that would work. These wizards were obvious masters. He closed his eyes and brainstormed. It had to be metal but would not sink. He disagreed about being solid. If it had an internal structure with hallow and reinforced areas, it would make it light and sturdy. It needed weapons, and armor, not just a metal skin.

He tried to think of something on Earth that he could model it after, like statues that he saw in parks, the Colossus of Rhodes, a cartoon anvil from the sky, an angry bridge? The thoughts got more ridiculous as his mind drifted within the matter of seconds. He thought of one of his favorite movies. It was a similar situation. His destroyer would be what ever he thought of. *The Stay Puff Marshmallow man?* Delex grasped the first image that burst into his head. Smoked exploded around them. All five people coughed and choked as a rumble and the smell of caustic gas filled the air. He recognized the smell. *Is that tear gas and a smoke screen?*

"Delex, what is happening!" Nova yelled and gripped him. Delex heard a familiar sound. The sound of metal on metal lock into place. With terrible realization he grabbed Nova and shoved her to the ground. *That is a gun loading!* A quick barrier slammed around them and pushed away the gases. The golems charged into the smoke.

As the barrier surrounded them, the midnight sounds and smoke cut off. An eerie silence covered them both. "Cover your ears!" Delex screamed. Nova did not hesitate. Right as she covered her ears an explosion ripped through the night. Even with the sound proof barrier, the sound echoed through the ground underneath them. The smoke cleared away enough to see the granite golem shattered into large chunks that scattered all over the ground. Pont and Neliea lay stunned and emotionless on the ground but awake. Chesor stood his ground but looked in obvious pain. His hands covered his ears as he screamed.

The two dirt and stone golems staggered from the blast, but quickly recovered and rushed forward one behind the other. A second explosion rifled through the night. Chesor flew from his feet as the two stone golems bursts into shrapnel. The glow of a yellow object shot through the broken golems and whistled past into the night. The other two wizards sprawled like discarded dolls. Steady snores proved they were not dead, only knocked unconscious. Delex was relieved they were not dead, but he never saw anyone get slapped into deep sleep before. If he was not so shocked, he would have laughed. Chesor moaned on the ground. Luckily Chesor and the other wizards were not near the golems when they were blasted asunder. The smoke finally cleared to reveal Delex's golem. Delex dropped the shield and gawked in wonder.

Delex's golem rolled forward on metal tracks. The sound of its turbine engine growled a hearty challenge and emitted the smell of fuel and burnt oil. Its metal skin formed a layer of sharp flat angles painted in globs of greens, browns, and black. Combat damage, dents and scorch marks adorn its sides like scars. Camouflage netting hung over parts of golem and helped disguise its shape. 120 mm turret whipped back and forth for more challengers. The Turret had a single word stenciled down its length. It said 'FRANK.'

"What craft is thy golem? What did you make your golem from?" Nova whispered as she corrected her speech from her archaic roots. Her voice quivered with fright.

Delex felt the answer click in his head. "That is an Abrams M1A5?" Delex was shocked. He didn't know if that type even existed. *When or where did I pull this tank!* "With CROWS mounted weapons and TUSK reinforcements and extra stuff I don't understand. My golem is-" Delex paused to blink a take a deep breath. He felt goosebumps rise, "-a super tank named Frank, Frank the tank." The turret swiveled towards Delex. The sound of another round of ammo locked into place as the engine quieted. Delex took a step back and raised his hands. Floodlights lite up the area in warning.

Nova hid behind him and lightly slapped him as she spoke. "End the spell, end the spell! Golems obey all commands. Command it to fall apart and disperse or I could knock you out, that will work too!" Nova offered cheerfully to Delex. Her voice quivered with fright.

"Fall apart, your service has ended, um Frank." Delex willed the magic away from the tank.

The flood lights clicked off as the tank rumbled to life and slowly backed away into the trees. Frank the tank kept its main gun aimed at Delex. On the top of the tank, the automated, remote 50 caliber machine gun swiveled about as it looked for additional targets. The sound of broken trees and stone echoed into the night as the tank disappeared from view.

Delex clicked his tongue. "Well, that can wait I guess." Delex walked up to Chesor and dragged him to his feet.

"Who are you!" Chesor yelled. His ears still needed time to recover. The fright in his eyes was almost palatable.

"On a time crunch." Delex snapped angrily. He had been through too many odd encounters over the last several months, Ter'Avan or otherwise. He felt a sickness in his stomach. "Now show us under the vaults!" Nova blinked in surprise. Chesor nodded. Without another word he stumbled towards the tower.

Mercadio, Blackus and Soas galloped towards the towers. The night was quiet since the loud sharp thunder. They would be near the towers soon. He was still angry Delex had stolen from him and left to confront Valash himself, but he also understood his motive. Delex was probably the only creature that could finish off Valash, and tried to protect them if he failed. Still, he wanted to smack Delex's backside with his staff until it glowed like lava.

The horses started to become jittery and restless. Travel at night held unknown dangers. The dirt road lead to the tower was safe, but a rock could easily break a leg. This was not what made the horses jumpy. They sensed something. Mercadio called a halt and pulled the horses to the side to calm them. A rumble came from down the road.

"You see anything?" Soas asked. He struggled with his horse as it tired to bite him. Blackus soothed his horse but he too had partial success.

Mercadio peered into the dark. Something approached as quickly as a horse but rumbled like ten wagons. A sudden glow of intense light bathed over the party. A large tortoise-shell metal wagon roared down the road and slowed as it approached. It rolled on two long extended flatten wheels without horse or oxen. Blood, grey ash and bits of red tissue hung off two rows of metal claws set side by side and attached to the front. It slowly rolled by as it aimed a long breathing tube towards them. Mercadio got the immediate impression of danger. That was not a breathing tube. It more than likely some hole for large arrows from an internal ballista. The horses where frozen with fear. They shivered in place as they watched it roll past. The metal beast turned off the magic torch-light and turned into the trees as it pushed several aside and completely rolled over another. Within moments, it was gone and disappeared into the forest while the cries of shattering timber echo into the night.

"So you think that could be Delex? Why was it covered in blood and ash?" Soas asked as the horses settled.

Mercadio voice his concerned, "I imagine so, but we do not have time to ponder it."

"I like it." Blackus shrugged.

The horses started to get skittish again. In a matter of seconds they kicked and screamed until the three had to get off them and let them run into the woods. Around them creatures and humans started to emerge. They were so distracted by the metal wagon monster that they did not see the ambush settle around them. The creatures were all red with blank white eyes. Hundreds of them poured out of the road. Some of them had fresh marks of combat.

Soas spun his daggers into his hand as his brother Blackus pulled his two long single edges swords. "Ah, blood and ash.

That makes sense now. We are not getting to the tower are we Mercadio?"

Mercadio looked down to the ground in defeat. He took a long breath and held up his staff at the hundreds of drethcon. Some of those faces he recognized from the towers. "It appears, we are not."

Black lightning, blades, and taunts echoed into the night as the three fought to stay alive.

Delex and Nova had left Chesor behind. He had led them through the vaults, then under the catacombs, then into the foundations of the towers. Chesor's knowledge ended at this point. Delex and Nova released him to seek medical attention. They fumbled in the darkness with light from Nova's hand until they finally came across a rough hewed tunnel that bore downward into the bedrock. This was a slough tunnel for excess rain and gutter water. Beyond this nothing was there but a lake of raw waste waters. This had to be it, the start of Valash's lair. From Delex's understanding, Valash's bones anchored him to the spot where he died. Nova said that after the battle fifty years ago, Valash's body remained undiscovered. Nova suspected he was able to make his way below the tower before he finally passed away and rose again stronger than he was before.

Odd noises echoed off the walls. Moans and scuttle noises played into the darkness out of the tunnel. Delex and Nova ventured cautiously downward. The single corridor opened into long tunnels with wooden doors and torchlight. This was no slough tunnel, this was a fully functional lair. Nova could feel dozens of traps and magical triggers hidden all over the tunnel walls, ceiling, and even suspended in air. She quickly dismantled each one, and in a way that they stayed in place, but were rendered useless. She called it Spell-stitching. It was completely beyond Delex's understanding. Without her, he probably would be burnt alive, sliced into bits, or worse several times by now. Dragons had some things to teach him. The traps thinned out and then finally disappeared after several grueling hours of Spell-stitching from Nova. They finally made better time into Valash's lair.

They passed a bank of holding cells filled with people in robes. They were wizards from the tower, caught and weakened. Nova said something drew their upon energy. Delex didn't need to guess, drethcon. Delex wanted to help, but Nova insisted they had to leave them. With great sadness, Delex turned his back to them and traveled deeper into the complex. His eyes shown with unanswered anger.

Delex and Nova hid as several servants roamed by. There did not seem to be any guards or monsters. Either Valash was confidence of his defenses and hidden fortress, or caused havoc above and elsewhere. Delex hoped for the former.

They came to a long stone stair suspended over a deep bottomless crack. They cautiously tested the bridge before Delex took the lead. Delex was halfway across when the air moved. It was not a sudden wind that picked up. The volume of air in the chasm shifted and moved like a river, like a living thing. It was too fast for him to react. They set off one of Valash's traps. It focused on the first person over the bridge. The Air trap punched Delex in the chest. Delex's center of gravity tipped towards the unknown depths of the chasm. He teetered further over the side when Nova stepped forward of Delex on the bridge. She grabbed his hand and spun him up back to the bridge. This in turn spun Nova over the side as she clutched Delex's hand. Nova now stood as the front person on the bridge. The wind changed targets and focus solely on her. She looked at Delex with terror in her eyes.

She mouthed something to him that he could not hear. One moment she was there, the next, his hand was empty. Delex's eyes shifted outward to see Nova, suspend over the chasm. Their eyes locked as their air screamed around them.

Before either of them could raise magic to react or counter the air, the Air trap renewed its effort. The Air trap released all of its magic in one last burst and slammed into Nova with an audible bloody thud. Delex saw a momentary impression of scattered blue scales, spattered blood, and torn out black hair as the trap punched her downward at a frightening speed and the fog swallowed her. The wind died away immediately. Nova's sudden pain filled screamed echoed around him then cut off. Delex yelled over and over for her, but she did not answer. His heart broke upon the rough steps as he crumbled to his knees. *I should have come alone; I should have told her no. Nova!* He wanted to scream her name, but words would only break him.

"Unfortunate. Those steps can be quite slippery, yes?" Valash's voice came from out of the darkness.

Delex glared into the night. His anger neared to rage. He could not formulate the words to replay.

"Come now. I have known you were here since you stepped into my home. Let us finish this visit, so I can focus on significant matters."

Delex roared to life. His magics gathered around him. A deep red crimson glowed from his body and illuminated the steps. "I will end you!"

"Larger armies have tried, yes? Oh, yes. You can try too. Perhaps we can reunite you with family, yes?" Valash's voice whispered in his ear. Laughter erupted all around him.

Delex ran down the end of the bridge. More traps loomed before him, but Delex sensed them now and his blindly wiped at them with his magic. They blew apart from his contact. He sensed them all, every trap, even the ones he left behind. With a scream that echoed around him, he tore at them all. Every trap in Valash's lair blew to pieces. The laughter broke into an angry cry of pain momentarily before it too quickly vanished. Delex stepped off the bridge and took a deep breath. His body shook with fatigue. The magics faded from him as his concentrated on his next move and took time to recover. He had to survive, for Nova, his friends, and the world. *No pressure dude,* his inner monologue morbidly joked.

Several corridors went off in different direction. It continued to mock him from all directions. Delex did not know which one to go down. As he wavered on which to enter, a corridor to his left started to glow with bright white light. Delex ran down that path as it opened into new tunnels. One tunnel had a purple torches, he knew this was the way.

The laughter died away as he entered a room of rock with the most grotesque throne he had ever seen. Two large piles of burned bodies shed white light across the room. Valash sat at the throne with one leg over the other. He kicked his foot in idle amusement. He finally got a good look at Valash. His skin cracked with yellow age and wrinkles. Liver spots adorned it like freckles. His hair was black with grease in some distorted attempt at vanity. Blacked teeth rotten and diseased made his smile into a nightmare. He robes of black, gold and red hung like ancient curtains from a haunted house. It only took Delex a moment to see it at. Overall Valash emphasized the description of 'gross.'

"So nice to see you again. Dinner it yet ready. Care to chat while we wait?" Valash mocked him. Valash sipped from a pewter cup of wine.

"The time for talk is over, if it ever begun." Delex growled. "You are dying tonight."

Valash sighed and poured the remains of his wine on the ground then let the cup fall from his fingers. "Lets begin, yes? I want time to cure your skin for a nice pillow case." He rose from the throne as black energy gathered around him. "Your face will make a nice garment under my codpiece, yes?"

Delex was revolted. He pulled his sword from his hip and braced for the attack. "You are sick, sick to the core."

Valash shrugged and blasted lightning at Delex face. Delex whipped up his sword to defend himself. The lightning grounded out on the sword blade harmlessly. Valash looked closer to the blade. "A barrier? You shielded the blade?" He said with wonder.

Delex smiled. "You have no idea of my capability." Delex charged Valash with his sword held ready for an attack.

Valash swept his hand in front of him. The ground under Delex's feet slipped to the side and caused Delex to trip and fall at Valash's feet. "Better words could not be spoken." Valash grinned as black lightning gathered in his hand.

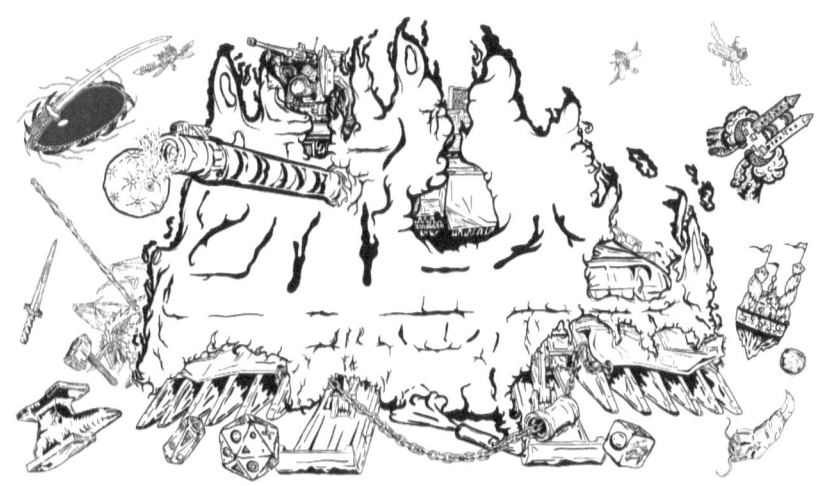

Chapter 20: Thirsty Shadows

Delex's bravado fled as Valash hovered over him. He only had a second before Valash pushed a black ball of lightning at his face. Delex slammed a shield over his face, the same type that he had on his sword. The ball of energy and his shield shattered and dissipated.

Delex rolled to the side and stabbed with his sword. The sword easily pushed into Valash. Valash hissed in pain and turned to the side. The sword snapped in half. Valash grabbed the broken blade and angrily tore it out. Delex took a moment to recover and get back to his feet. Valash didn't care about the wound. It dripped blood for only a few seconds then stopped. Valash held his hand up to show Delex. The deep cut started to seal. "You have much to learn. Sadly, you will not have the time, yes."

Delex didn't respond. This was not a fight to have clever banter. He needed to kill Valash, fast. Valash blasted a ball of lava at Delex. Delex summoned a torrent of water from above, The torrent of water crashed it into the ball. The ball of lava immediately cooled and shattered. Hot steam and fog exploded in all directions. Delex did it on instinct. He looked down at his hands in wonder. Another glob of lava shot out of the fog and slammed into the chamber wall behind Delex. Delex snapped out of his wonderment and sent a line of water outward. It sliced lengthwise across the room. A thud and grunt came from the fog. *Damn, that could have been the end of me. I have to concentrate.* He thought to himself. The image of Nova came back to his eyes. He recalled the look on her face, the sudden terror, the blood and scales as spinning over the chasm as she disappeared.

"An excellent hit Delex, and while I hide in the fog. Well played strategy." The ground under Delex's feet turned to mud for a second then reverted o solid rock. In that brief second, Delex's boots had sunk into the rock. Now he fought to maintain his balance. "But a failed strategy since I can sense you."

Delex fell backward. Delex tried to pull his boots out of the rock. The boot held tightly locked in the stone. He hovered his hand over the rock and willed it soft, but it would not respond. Valash had done something to it. Another ball of fire light built in the fog. Valash crafted something much larger than the lava balls. Cackles of delight echoed in the throne room as the ball of light became bigger of more ominous. *Maybe I should talk, distract him.* Delex thought. He tried to picture what would make Valash stall his attack. "Why are you doing this? You're going to destroy the world."

"Why would I question the dirt where I place my boot nor answer it?" Valash snickered. The ball grew larger, then shot towards him.

Delex yelled and flung out his hand. A wall of bedrock shoot upwards. The rock wall blocked Delex and the throne from the ball of arcane fire. Delex heard a horrid roar and a sudden angry a moment before a detonated rumbled on Valash's side on of the new wall. The massive rock wall muted the explosion on Delex's side. Delex had no doubt Valash took a magnified force. A muffled scream of pain confirmed Delex's wish as the explosion died. Delex pulled out a small knife and started to hack at the soft leather of his boot. The sharp blade ate through the boot quickly. Delex's feet slipped out of the boot covered in blood.

Valash's screamed in pain as his broken body burnt and melted from the magical heat. He had almost forgotten how much magical pain hurt. He fully understood what the corpses felt when he tossed them into the fires to light his throne. Valash almost laughed from the irony. He collected his thoughts and pulled deeply on the thread. Magic swelled up from the center of the planet. His body knitted back together. Ashes swirled around him and settled into a new pair of clothes. When he killed the last sorcerer on the planet, he might as well look presentable. Valash looked at the wall of bedrock. He lifted his hand. The wall resisted. "Oh clever boy, you learn so fast." Valash pushed his magic into the rock. Cracks of light started to spiderweb through the wall.

"Oh great!" Delex groaned. Spiderwebs of light started to run through the wall. Delex sheltered himself near the creepy arm throne. An explosion of rock blasted through the throne room. Hot shrapnel ricocheted in all directions. Delex sheltered himself from most of the assault, but small cuts criss-crossed his face and hands. A loud ring reverberated in his ears. Delex peered around the edge of the throne. Valash lay on his back with a grin on his face. He laughed to himself. He watched as Valash's body and clothes pulled together.

"Mother of-" Delex swore under his breath. *This guy is like a magic terminator! The magicnator? Lame.*

"I have not had this much fun in centuries, and that includes when I slaughtered your parents." Valash said as he stood and brushed himself. "Do you want to hear about it?" Valash peered into the darkness. The battle extinguished the light. Valash created new red and purple light to flare from the piles of corpses. He tried to sense Delex but there was too much magic residue. "Do you want to hear the screams of your parents? I still have it in my memories. It can be the last voices you will ever remember, yes?"

The screams of two people echoed in rage and pain through

the throne room. Valash grinned as he thought. *This would enrage Delex and make him attack in haste and foolishness. Then I will snap the trap.* A bright pinpoint of light shoot out of the darkness and cut through Valash and into the wall behind him. The light swept to the side and through his chest and heart.

"A *Terrica Lance!*" Valash screamed. "Sorcerers magic does not mix with that spell. How child? How did you make wizard barlight?" The *Terrica Lance* surprised him, but Valash created a way to dispel the lance and redirect the energy back at wizards long ago. He tried to goad the boy to fire another. Valash stumbled and faked a mortal wound. A second beam of raw energy shot from out of the smoke, fog and dust. Valash raise his counterspell.

The beam of energy punched through the spell without resistance and through Valash. Before Valash could react to the spell failure several more ripped into him and tore his body to pieces. The wall behind him was a mosaic of melted lines of rock. "Nope, not a lance, A laser. Wizard Barlight, I like that. Let's call it natural Barlight. I used magic to heat and energize specific elements then sent them your way. There was no magic in it at all. Just like this."

Before Valash could put his body together, the air vanished. Every fluid in his body suddenly begun to boil. The line of magic to the core of the planet immediately started repair the damage, it kept his mind intact. His limbs though, had trouble. They did not want to respond. His body twitched and grew puffy as the magic repaired him.

A moment later, Valash collapsed. His body could not hold its own weight. He would have made a squishy noise if there was any air. Valash felt like a bag of leaky water, but everything bubbled and foam out of him. Only his head kept its form. The rest of his body bloated into a formless blob of broken bones. Valash had never felt so much pain in his entire life.

Delex let the assault drop. He started to choke on the dirt in the air. He had shot a laser, now named barlight, put Valash in a vacuum, and instantly powdered his bones. Delex wanted to think of more attacks, but couldn't concentrate. His mother told him to use knowledge that Valash did not have. These attack came directly from Earth knowledge. He hoped they were enough. Delex slid to the floor by the throne. His left-hand splashed in something. Delex summoned a tiny ball of light and looked at his hand. Blood bathed his hand like slick oil. It felt familiar. It felt like him. He looked behind the throne to see a large pool filled with it. It brought him to the edge of vomit.

Before he could investigate further, a huge rumble shook the ground all around. Laughter echoed from the stone walls. The cloud of dirt, smoker and fog slammed to the floor and cleared the air. Valash stepped close and clapped his hands together. "Delex, this has been more than amusing, yes?"

Delex scrambled away and grabbed for his sword only to realize it was not there. He lifted his hand towards Valash. A sound wave of Air hit him in the stomach and sent him into a skid across the floor. He smacked and against the wall on the other side of the chamber, right near his shoes. He could not move, he was held tight.

"Oh, I imagine I picked the correct body." Valash stepped up to the pool. He dipped a foot into it and pulled it back covered in blood. "After you are dead I will-" Valash stumbled. "What are you doing?"

Delex could see it now. A black cord extend out of Valash's back and traveled into the earth. He knew where it went, he could sense it. He reached out with his magic and followed it down as he kept an eye on Valash. In an instant he was there, his magic tear and ripped into the thread that feed from the center of Ter'Avan. He knew this would not kill Valash, but he needed to buy some time.

The thread snapped, but a surge come out of nowhere. It was another thread. It hooked into the core and replaced the old one. Delex snapped that one as well, but in the same instant two more thread took its place and weaved into one.

Every time he snapped one, two more connected. Each thread melted back together into one large spike. Valash twitched with anger as each thread snapped.

"Still trying are you?" Valash mocked. "Still trying to kill me. I am already dead, yes."

"I will not give up!" Delex growled. He slowly worked his way free of the spell that held him to the wall.

"I do not care. You will eventually die. I will keep you there until you starve or sleep." Valash mocked.

Delex screamed and shattered the spell that held him there. Valash ducked around the throne as Delex started another assault. Both sorcerers exchanged lightning, fire, water, and stone. Raw magic poured from them both. Delex snapped up shields in place to protect himself from the attacks. Valash just let the spells hit him. He instantly healed the damage. The earth would shudder with each regeneration. The attacks went on for several minutes, as they turned more complex. It took a toll on Delex. The beginning of sorcerer weakness started to form from his casting. He started to pull the magic directly from the environment. Instead of using a little magic inside him and ordering the surrounding magic to his command, he pulled in inside like wizards. This was less efficient casting. The foreign magics begin to poison him as he used it. Luckily the poison did not further weaken him. It still didn't help him either. He could die from either.

Valash started to form a brilliant ball of lightning in his hand. The electric screamed grew in power. Delex summoned thin metal rods pins and slammed them all around Valash. The energy ball faltered and ground out on Valash, and burnt into his body. Valash shuddered and wiggled then fell over. *Mom was right. His magic body is reacting more, and more like a living body. I basically just tasered him. I can use this, somehow.* Delex knew the electrocution of the lightning would disrupt every cell, but would it disrupt the magic enough.

Delex stretched out his hand and sent a raw bar of Chaos magic into Valash and into the thread that connected him to the planet. Delex say his hand unravel like strings and ribbons and travel up his arm. He almost stopped the spell, but the unraveling reversed. His arm and hand reform as the Chaos magic decided it who it wanted to attack. Luckily, it wanted Valash more. The beams of magic instantly burnt Valash, his thread and the spike to nothingness. Delex dropped to the ground. The light in the throne slowly flickered into nothingness. It was over. Valash had finally been defeated.

Mercadio, Soas, and Blackus stood back-to-back. Blood covered all three as they kept each other alive. The drethcon battled them relentlessly for hours. The sun had started to rise and small patches of sunlight glimmered in the canopy over the road to the towers. They stood there ground on the road, surrounded by blind eyes and red skinned monsters that looked like creatures, friends, and the innocent. Hundreds of defeated drethcon lay dead and turned to ash, but many more surrounded them. Another earthquake shook and toppled them and the drethcon off balance. They could sense their prey fought just to stay alive. The last of the drethcon poured into the road and crowded together. The face of Maltort Many-color grinned back with blood-red skin and blind white eyes. Mercadio stood transfixed, bewildered by the face. A dagger shot out at buried itself into up to the hilt in the face of the monster. The monster growled and grabbed the dagger from its face. It tossed it to the ground as it flexed its fingers.

"Step out of the dream Mercadio! It looks like a rush." Soas said. Mercadio shook his head. Soas continued, "we will not be able to stop them."

Mercadio took a sudden deep breath as labored to collect his mind. His right arm hung loose and broken in his flowing cloak. His staff lay shattered at his feet. He had no time to craft another. Blackus held the side of his neck as he held pressure on wound that threatened to bleed out. Neither of them had time to talk. The drethcon started to scream in unison and rushed.

A blast of brilliant energy poured into the drethcon in a quick circle but left the three in the middle untouched. Dirt exploded into the air. The three companions covered their faces. Something smashed into the ground near them. They opened there eyes cautiously.

A large blue and silver dragon shimmered before them. It eyes crackled with the white-hot glow of energy as it peered down to them. A deep voice resonated with a boom. "Delex fights Valash. I failed him."

"Dear gods, is that you Nova? What happen?" Mercadio moaned. Soas wiped a blade at a drethcon that was still alive. Blackus went around the circle and stabbed the hearts of anything that still moved. Most of the drethcon were already ash.

Nova shook her dragon head. "I do not know. A trap slapped me into a near bottomless crevice. I screamed until I hit water and swept down a subterranean river. I thought I was going to die. My scales must have saved me. When I woke, I was like this. I clawed my way upwards through the ground. I ended up in the woods." She spoke in an oddly quiet deep voice.

"Fated fortune you happened upon us." Soas said. He looked towards the tower. "I guess we better move."

"I do not think we can." Mercadio said. He went to Blackus who had fallen to one knee from his wounds. "It is up to him to finish this, we cannot go further. Nova, are you going to Delex?"

Nova shook her head. "I will not fit in the passages. It would take too long to claw my way through solid rock. I will heal our wounded. We should check the towers. We saw imprisoned wizards."

Mercadio nodded but could nod muster the energy for emotions. The news would shock him any other time. He was too tired. He hoped the towers were not under siege with drethcon.

Maltort woke. He felt more rested than he had in a long time. He smiled and stretched only to feel bodies around him. Maltort recoiled from the touch only to bump into more people. All around him people shifted in various degrees of wakefulness. He was in a cell, in a long row of cell. He scanned the faces of the surrounding people They all seemed familiar, but he was still not awake enough for the thought to finish.

"Welcome back." Said one of his aids. It was Bartlon. "I found the lost wizards." He said sarcastically.

"What happened? Report. Have we been attacked?" Maltort Manycolor, Headstaff of the Tower of Practice growled.

Bartlon shook his head. "More like abducted. From what I can estimate, half the towers are here in cells. I do not know where. Only recently have they started to recover."

Maltort tried to summon his magic, but something blocked him. "Don't bother. Strong suppression magic, sorcerer caliber." Bartlon sighed.

"We must find a way-" Maltort started but a massive earthquake rocked them all to the ground. It was so powerful it rattled the prisoners in the cells.

Delex was thrown to the ground as the largest earthquake yet shook the ground. Laughter howled from around him. Purple light glowed from the ground. Out of nothing, Valash formed and raised his hands above him. He spun in place and tilted Delex an elegant bow. The purple light seeped up from the grown and turned a dull yellow, like puss. It hung like a crown that floated above Valash's head.

"How! I destroyed you. I destroyed your body, spike, the

line and stopped your spell at the same time. How!" Delex screamed.

Valash slowly stopped his maniacal laugh and looked at Delex. "My body, my spell; You fool. Valash has been dead for a long time. I am the spell! I power myself, and I draw on the planet to make me stronger. You cannot stop me! The body is only a convenience." He pointed to Delex, "The same spell that I feel dear father and mother attached to you. I don't need the spike. I draw from everyone."

A cold realization poured into Delex. He had it wrong. He had it all so completely wrong. "How?" *Maybe this guys was a magic terminator. Come with me if you want to non-live? Okay, focus man.* Delex needed to stall for time, but his mind spiraled into despair, and he blindly reached for a solution.

"I made the spell twit! Valash created me from his bones and memory. I am him! You cannot kill me, yes? I have had half a decade to draw and make emergency reserves and pocket them in my own void. You could try for years to kill me and I would draw and make a new thread, and recreate and reattach." Valash stepped closer. "Until you came yes." He knelt down near Delex. "Until I felt your power. I will drink up your blood I have stolen and fully resurrect. Your magic will be mine. I will walk with gods. I will be alive and reborn."

Delex was about to despair when he saw something behind the throne, embedded in the stone. An idea hit him. He had to tread lightly. He had to be strong of heart like Nova and think knowledgeably like Mercadio. Delex had to strike will absolute resolve like Blackus, and attack with brutal efficiency. Delex had to use all his friends, all he loved ones. He had to be more than himself. He had to decide now, his first move. His first move, he had to-. Delex's thoughts cut off and an idea slammed into place.

Delex laughed out loud. "Go soak your face you stage-mage magicnator! You rattle-hat, brainless, drethcon impostor." His first move, he had to be the cleverest one in the room, and insult like Soas!

Valash's face lost all color. His mouth hung open. He blinked in shock. "Repeat? What is a magicnator?"

Delex laughed and stood up. Valash took several quick steps backwards fully alarmed. "You are nothing but a spell. A complex, mindless spell that thinks it has free will." Delex mocked Valash. "Spells can never be gods. Your body is spent like a sailor's coin on shore. You bluff like a cliff. If you had a vast supply of reserves, you would never need to tie into the planet." Delex pointed at Valash and sneered. "That was your desperate emergency plan, a contingency casting," Delex knew in his bones he was right, "and you burnt it up. Face it, you are as real as fart and as easy to disperse." Delex waved his hand near his buttock and laughed at Valash.

"I am not flatulence!" Valash screamed and poured forth a river of black at Delex. He had to react like Blackus. Delex had only a moment to throw up a shield against the liquid Void. Even still, the energy slammed into him into the wall of the throne room. He crumpled, but he held the barrier shield. He coughed up blood as he laughed. "Spells cannot be gods. You are a failure imitating Valash, even more than you are as the spell he cast. You will never live, you never have lived. Valash, you sack of old man's gas, you can bath in as much blood as you want, but it will never be a body." Delex's eyes flickered to the object embedded in the stone. Valash looked for a moment where Delex was cast his eyes. "Your magic is weaker than mine, even if you hold my blood. My blood will resist. My body would resist. So would my parents." Valash glared as Delex spoke. Delex thought he figured out why Valash only took his blood. He had sense Doran and Zelexi tied to his body. Valash didn't want to risk them inside him. Valash didn't want Delex's parents to kill the body, kill Valash. "Face it, you were never stronger than me no matter what you say. You're just an ashen spell."

Valash roared. "I can create a new body if I choose!"

Delex laughed. "Not without your blood. You are a magic, a spell that feeds to keep itself going. You are anchored here, and if you move your bones they become vulnerable to attack. Tell me Valash," He had to attack like Nova. Delex guessed at this, but his instincts told him this was true. "What happens if they become destroyed?" Delex raised a hand. The shield he used sudden reformed. Delex sent it forward as barlight at the bones suspended in the back of the throne. Valash jumped in front of the bolt and took the hit.

Valash was not ready. He didn't have time to create a barrier to negate the energy, he didn't know what the brat made it from. Instead, he used his magic to dispersed in into himself and saved the rock throne from damage. The blast smashed into Valash and blasted the center of him into burnt ash. His fake body recovered quickly. Valash recovered within seconds. The two halves didn't have time to fall. Valash held to the rock behind him as the flesh of the two halves clawed at each other and knitted into one whole body. Valash tore the stone away from around the bones. Inside was a hollow cavity with the skull and a collection of sorcerer bones, the remains of Valash. *Spell reconfiguration? How has this whelp learned such an advanced skill.* Valash was stunned be none of it showed on his face.

Valash growled as his tattered clothing repaired itself. "This is where you are wrong. I have sorcerer blood, all that I need." Valash pointed as he mocked. "I have yours. I will rebuild my body, fuel it with your blood, spelled to supply its own nutrients, oxygen and energy." Valash sneered. "Do not think you are the only one which has seen Earth knowledge. My library has several history books of you Earth wizards. Your battle over the middle of the Earthen realm, and the time when that foolish wizard Merlana traveled to Earthen planet."

Delex looked stunned. Valash visible smiled with pleasure. *Merlana? Merlin? No way! Middle Earth? He thinks J.R.R. Tolkien is a history book? The magic terminator, magicnator just lost all credibility; more like nerdinator.* Delex confidence rose as he spoke to Valash. "What does that matter Valash? You are still going to die. What does reading a few books help you?" Delex had to keep him talking. What does he mean about nutrients and stuff in the blood. Delex felt a plan form in his head, but he needed more. He needed Valash to gloat. He had to have confidence like Mercadio. "I have more knowledge than you."

Valash grinned snapped a finger. Delex slammed up a barrier between them both. Valash gave a small chuckle. "Let me summon them for you. We have time. After all, these are you last moments, lets enjoy them together yes?" The sound of the doors to the throne opened then closed. Out of the darkness fluttered several books. They were all torn or ruin. Most of the books missed large sections, but he had no doubt the books came from Earth. "These books contain adequate knowledges I need to build my body and keep it self-sufficient."

Delex scanned the books quickly. A 1918 edition of Gray's Anatomy of The Human Body by Henry Gray F.R.S.; part of a middle school health class biology book, and the first part of a basic chemistry book. Valash had general Earth knowledge, not as great as Delex, but some. His instincts told him Valash's knowledge was dangerous, but Delex was superior. He had to have faith in himself like his parents had faith in him, faith in his sorcerer heritage. "This is all about humans, we are not one of them."

Valash shrugged, "We operate close enough, yes. I know what I need to live without food, water or the need to breath." Valash shot a sudden attack out at Delex. The magic tore at Delex and tried to rob the water from his body, but the barrier Delex held reacted and blocked the spell. The barrier shattered as it destroyed the spell. "Pity, I wanted to show you first hand." Valash flicked a finger and the books burnt to ash. Delex flinched and brought up another barrier. Valash chuckled. "So timid yes? Cower, you have nothing left yes. As for me, the spell will become my new life force. I will not need the spell anymore. I will live again and become stronger than ever." Valash whispered as he reached back and lightly tipped the bones into the pool of blood.

Delex huddled on the wall. He began to build several powerful barriers around himself in a sphere. Valash scoffed. He turned his back to Delex and concentrated.

He had to be himself. That was the moment Delex smiled.

Delex switched his concentration slightly. He hoped Valash would not be able to sense the change, not with the hot glare of magic which came off the shielding barriers he just built. The stone hummed as their spells built. Valash formed his new body quickly. The lifeless body looked like Valash but young and dashing with well toned skin. Sorcerer symbols flashes on the skin and sank into the body as Valash feed knowledge directly into the bones of the corpse. The blood swirled and stirred as it prepared to be sucked into the lifeless corpse.

Delex continue to build layers of barrier upon layers around himself and created another layer around the throne room ceiling and walls. It muffled the earthquakes and the power they both used. Valash paid in no mind, it helped him as well. The foolish boy did him a favor as he kept the ceiling from collapse. He was quietly impressed. The child put so much effort in his little shields that the invisible barriers made the air ripple near them. It still would not be enough. In his new body, Valash would crack them like a breakfast egg.

Delex felt the tether detach from the spike of magic. The tether whipped back and hooked into the new body. Delex could feel the spike go dormant but knew it would reactivate the instant it felt Valash's destruction. Delex pushed his mind even harder and prepared his next moves. At the same time, he sent a wave of liquid into the blood puddle. It splashed over the stones and mixed into the blood. He could feel his own rush of blood leak from his nose.

Valash looked at the blood and sensed a poison. He quickly removed it with a wave of his hand as the blood drew into the new body. The body flashed purple from the inside. Valash laughed at Delex and flickered and vanished from sight. The putrid crown of light went out.

A voice echoed from the air. "You tried to poison the blood with cyanide. I know of this poison from the books. It would have destroyed this body in minutes, but it would still be to slow."

Delex poured everything he could to shield himself and everything around him as he thickened the barriers. He poured his magic in a sphere around him. The second barrier expanded and moved to become a full sphere large around the room. The throne room remained dark and silent. Delex peered into the darkness as his magic poured out of him. He created so much magic in his shielding, the barriers started to glow lightly with silver light.

A labored breath echoed from the darkness, then another. Each new breath grew in strength and took a deeper draw of air. A thud echoed from the darkness with the breath, then another. It continued, thud after thud. Delex realized what it was. It was Valash's heartbeat. Valash mocked Delex with the sound of Valash's heart as it pounded to life. The real body came to life. Valash had a real sorcerer body once again. Delex wondered if Valash was as powerful as he was in his body crafted from magic, what would he be like in this new one? When he did not need to pour so much of magic in a spell that mocked the living, what would he be like? That terrible thought gave Delex a chill. He knew Valash was stronger, but Delex had something Valash did not. He hoped it was enough.

A hand shot out of the darkness and slapped the barrier. This made Delex startle. A pleasant chuckle emitted from the darkness as the rest of Valash's face and body came into the dim light. He was clothed in beautiful robes of black encrusted in blood-red rubies, gold trimming and muted purples flames that scrolled across the fabric. It was him, but in his prime. His skin was tan and healthy. "Thank you for your blood yes? Now you can die knowing I will never die. I will keep your blood and rejuvenate whenever I wish. Yes? I want you to hear the beat of your blood in my heart as your final sounds. Soon the entire world will too. Yes, they will too." The voice was rich and deep. Delex could not prepare for how powerful Valash spoke in his new body.

Valash stepped back and blasted him with raw magic. It slammed into the barrier and made it glowed like hot metal until the barrier reacted and bounced the energy away. The beam of energy slammed into throne and melted a large chunk of the arm carving before it dissipated. Delex didn't stop to react. He continued to reinforce the barriers on the shield. Both shielding barriers, the surrounding one, and the sphere around the throne room ate up his magic with greedy delight. Valash didn't seem to notice. Valash shrugged. "Slowly die of thirst if you wish." The beat of the heart continued, it grew louder, faster, and stronger. Valash stepped back into the darkness. His ragged chuckles echoed from the darkness.

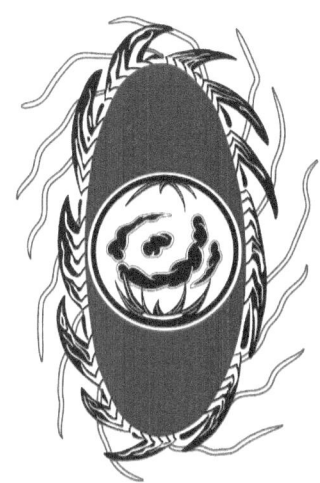

Chapter 21: The lonely Throne

D elex could feel Valash's power, it amazed him. Yet, something continued to shift inside him. It gave him an ever growing well of power beyond his understanding. He didn't feel sick. Delex didn't feel weak. He reached across a barrier that didn't rule him. He got to his feet and studied Valash as he wiped blood from his nose and eye. *When did I get a cut on my eye?* He shook his head. *No time to think, I have to watch for a sign, a time to attack.* Blood started to leak from Delex's ear, but he barely noticed. The rhythmic beat of Valash's heart boomed louder in the throne. Delex ignored it for now and grabbed more magic, Chaos magic, pure Chaos magic and poured it into the barriers. The barriers grew brighter. Small flecks of silver drifted in the thick walls of the spells.

Valash never felt so alive. He was alive! There was no pain, no fear. He felt powerful, stronger than he had ever before. His heart raced roared with excitement. He noticed the thick barriers full of Chaos magic. "I see you are powerful, powerful enough to foolishly toy with Chaos' magic."

"Maybe I am the god of Chaos." Delex smirked. He drew more

energy, all the magics, Earth, Fire, Water, Nature, Air, Spirit, Void, Chaos.

Valash laughed, not a mocking laugh, a real hearty laugh. "You are no god. I know they are not here. Chaos, is not here." Valash became serious as he looked at Delex. "We would know." A chill shuddered down Valash. It even made Delex shiver.

"Perhaps I am a godling?" Delex continued to smirk, but deep inside he doubted. Something might be wrong. He still dripped with blood, more blood than he thought his wounds could account for. *Did I get more cuts?*

Valash noticed as well. "Gods do not bleed, even the lesser ones." Valash flexed his hand and cut his palm with a sharp fingernail. No blood came out. "I will be one of them, then one day I-" Valash touched his chest. His heart beat was fast, maybe too fast. He started to feel dizzy. His head pounded with a sudden pain. "What is happening to me?"

Delex shrugged. "Earth knowledge. You may not know of adrenaline. Once, I accidentally drown in a pool and was not responding to CPR. They gave me epinephrine to start my heart." Delex pointed at Valash. "You have it coursing through your blood, maybe half a liter. I spiked your punch! It is not a poison, so I doubt your limited knowledge would feel it as such. Too much and..." Delex stood tall and folded his arms with a look of resolution as he waited.

Valash tried to talk but his whole body shuddered and had refused his commands. Valash tumbled to the ground like a broken puppet. He tasted sound, and smelled the ground from his finger tips as his nails scrapped against the rock. Valash twisted and seized as he screamed, but even this turned into a froth that poured from his mouth. He tried to think, to cast a spell, but his mind locked in shock. His magic run rabid out of his control. His magic tore from his body in ragged arcs. The magic twisted around him random weaves as it slammed into the ground, air and throne. It bounced off Delex's barriers and rebounded back at Valash. *Spells, hate, survive, stop blood,*

Doran and Zelexi, need to, blood spike, magic, purple farg ride, my tether, save carrots! His thoughts splintered into uselessness, like a broken kaleidoscope pieced back together by a blind man. Valash felt the adrenaline light up every part of him with overflowing power, then it all went out. The body made one final breath and stopped twitching. Blood poured from Valash's his eyes and mouth. Pink fluid, tinted with blood, bubbled out of Valash's ears. Valash was dead, again.

Delex felt sick. He never wanted to watch, and felt no pleasure in it. He killed a man, one of his own. He was the last true sorcerer and heir to an empty kingdom of one. Delex cried. He let loose all his pain and grief in those simple tears. He won, he killed a man. He lost, he killed his own. Delex could cry away his burdens, but it would not change the weight he carried on his soul. He only shed a few tears. Exhaustion overpowered any thoughts or emotions.

Delex sighed as his legged gave out. He took several deep breaths and prepared to release the barriers. He felt something stir within the corpse. The ground around the corpse rumbled as the corpse split open. Delex grabbed his hair and tilted back his head. "You got to be kidding me!" *That is it! I am done feeling sorry for this guy!*

It was the spell, it had not fully surrendered. It tore itself from the corpse and flung the body at Delex. The corpse slapped the barrier and hung there. Delex tried to move back but the wall was in his way. The corpse hung within arm's reach. Its dead eyes looked at him with dull hate. The silver light from the barriers weakened. The room grew darker as a black cloud formed and flickered with inner lightning. It hovered in the room as it extended a tether to the spike. The tether bounced off an invisible wall. It was Delex's barriers. The tether bore downward again, but once again bounced off the barrier. A moan emitted from the cloud as it slammed into the barrier itself. Red and purple lightning flashed as it smashed over and over into the barrier shields. The shields held firm.

Delex gave a small sigh of relief. The practice that Delex had with barriers made them much more powerful than his attacks. The relentless practice in Moraphen's care had benefited him beyond imagination.

As the cloud of magic slammed over and over Delex reached out and seized the corpse and dragged in through the barrier. If he was right, the bones of Valash were still within the body. Delex held his throat closed as he brought the putrid corpse through. It was covered in spittle, vomit and other fowl fluids. Delex gagged and brought the attention of the cloud of magic.

The cloud changed tactics and slammed its magics towards Delex. The barrier held. He didn't know for how long. The concentrated will of an ancient dead sorcerer crashed into Delex again. The cloud slipped past and around him, but did not touch him. Again and again the cloud roared and pushed. Several of the layers failed. If Delex died, his barriers would shatter. He continued to pour his life force into them. The layers of shielding stopped shattering. He couldn't muster the power to rebuild any, but he could hold what remained.

He just needed them to last long enough. He could feel the cloud weaken, but it was still strong. Below the spike of magic came to life. It reached up and slammed into the outer barriers. It too did not penetrate, but with each hit, the layers shattered. Delex strained even harder. He felt pain, real pain in his body. Delex tore something inside himself. He didn't have time to examine the damage. It was either push harder, or die with the planet. Time after time the cloud and spike hammered into the barriers. Sometimes together into the outer barrier, sometimes the cloud into Delex and the spike into the outer one.

The world shook. He knew the tunnels that lead to Valash's hidden lair had collapsed. He took a moment to quest with his senses. Several layers of barriers broken when he did. No one would come in time to help. He was alone, with over half the barriers he built, gone. Delex lowered his head to his chest and breathed heavily. The magical rhythmic crash of magics and his heavy slow breath played in his world. Time held no meaning. His mind drifted as his concentration focused on one thought. *I have to hold my shields, maintain the barrier.*

∞∞∞∞

Delex couldn't talk. He was too tired. Delex estimated twenty percent of his barriers remained. The spike had grown dormant, its limited animation could not hold without a recent command. It was a lucky break for him. He knew time passed, but how much? He heard chisels and hammers echo through the rock, but he could not guess how long it would take. *If I freed those prisoners, maybe they could have helped.* Delex sighed.

Another set of screams echoed from the other side of the throne room doors. A long time past since the last time he heard a scream. Delex thoughts drifted from the cloud to the halls and passages outside the throne room. He must had released *a creature during the battle. I guess the monster is not finding many targets left. Few servants left to roam the halls? It should be morning by now. I have to do something.* Delex tried to concentrate, but he suddenly felt weak, he lost consciousness for a brief second. At that moment he heard a cracking sound like crystalline glass. The cloud had quietly crept to the side and pressed on his barriers. Delex snapped back to wake in a rush of fear and adrenaline. His sudden burst of energy blasted away the magic cloud long enough to repair his barrier around him and the bones, and add a little strength.

The cloud hissed with laughter. "Mine, all mine," it whispered to Delex.

Delex ignored the taunt. It had done that for hours. It teased him with little words. *I can't just sit here and wait until my shields break. Let's see if this does something.* Delex placed his hand over the corpse and concentrated. Void magic and Fire. It ate away at the corpse. The cloud of magic roared. The air in the chamber resonated with pain. The spike in the center of the planet shuddered and shot towards him. It was not quick enough. As the corpse burned away, the spike did too. The cloud of magic screamed from a low growl into a high pitch shrill. Blood dripped from Delex mouth, but it still felt dry like sand. His body shuddered from effort, yet he still mustered up enough spirit to look at the magic cloud in defiance. "One down, just one to go. Your life is this tomb now. Nobody, not even bones. Your only source to sorcerer bones is me." Delex fell over on his side and lay there as he continued to pour his life force into the barriers. "They are currently in use." He laughed. The cloud responded with a hissed and slammed into the barrier over and over. Delex could feel it chip away a little each time.

Delex pulled in all the magic in the area and used it to replenish his magic. His body flowed with magical poison. He then poured even more into the barrier. This left him crippled with magical weakness. *Wonderful, I cannot move. First poisoned, and now weakened. If I try to do any more wizard or sorcerer magic, it will kill me. What is this other place? Does it have a limit?* Delex pulled magic from somewhere. It did not make him sick or weak, but he knew there had to be a cost somewhere. He did not have time to ponder it. He tried to pull harder, but its rich flow weakened as he bled Even poisoned, weak and bleeding, Delex lifted his eyes in defiance at the cloud.

The black cloud suddenly stopped its screams and engulfed the sphere of magic around Delex. Delex curled into a tight ball. Every time the cloud squeezed, the shields flared with light. Each flare of light seemed slightly weaker. He was not sure if it was the cloud that weakened, or his eyes. His barrier kept the air inside clean. He was smart enough to know that any outside air could allow the cloud to pass through. *Too bad I didn't make any air fresher too. I reek like last Tuesday as Jim would say.* His body trembled as tears welled up from inside. The sudden memory sapped at his strength. His concentration shattered as his power slipped from him. The shielding started to break away in layers from the onslaught. He tied off the magic of the inner and outer barriers as quickly as he could. They would not be as strong without his direct control, but they would last if he fell unconscious.

Delex huddled closer to himself and pulled the barrier tighter. He thickened them as they concentrated around him. Hot tears ran down his face into his hair. "Jim my dad, father, mother. I am sorry. I didn't become the man you needed." The sound of the onslaught slipped away as despair flooded his heart. Darkness like liquid shadow, took him into nothingness.

∞∞∞

Mercadio screamed as loud as he could. He yelled Delex's name over and over as he tried to wake the young man. They had to kill several more of the garrote spiders to get to the grotesque throne room, but they managed to make it alive. Blackus cut the massive doors off the hinges and then kept a look out in the darkness. Mercadio doubted they found all the spiders. After what seemed to be hours, Delex finally woke to his name. Mercadio whooped loudly with glee to see the young man stir. He cracked Soas heartily on the back and head several times with his staff as he cheered. Soas groaned as he defended himself from the sudden joyful attack. Soas brushed away Mercadio's apologies and grinned at Delex through the pain.

Delex looked around and saw a light at the end of throne room. It was Mercadio and Soas. They waved to him to come near. Soas jumped up and down excitingly. Delex didn't understand why they did not enter. His hearing ringed in his hears, so he couldn't understand much of what they said. They were pressed like two mimes against an invisible wall. Delex's outer barrier still held. He sighed in relief. He checked himself. Only three of the few hundred of his personal shields still held, but they were weak. The shields around the room looked to be in much better shape. The cloud had concentrated on him.

He was going to let them drop but Soas was frantically pointed at something. He saw movement in the corner of his eye. A small dark cloud flew off the throne and slammed into him and picked him off his feet. One of the shields shattered like glass and faded away. He could hear his friends scream out to him. The small cloud continued to press. He could feel another shield begin to crack. The magic cloud of Valash begun to pry at the cracks. He couldn't untie and feed more power to his inner barrier, he didn't have anything left. They would simply shatter.

Delex almost panicked, but his instincts took over. The shields around the room started to contract and pull inward. Mercadio and Soas stumbled forward. Delex continue to pull them in as the cloud attacked him. He pulled the shields closer until there was no room around him and the cloud. Delex took a step back. He passed through his shields. The cloud of Valash's essence beat against a highly dense prison of magic condensed down to the size of a tennis ball. The sphere fell to the ground with a solid smack like granite. It glowed brightly and shed light like a torch across the room. Delex poured his own shields into the magic prison and collapsed to the ground.

Mercadio rushed to his side. "Dear man! Are you okay?" Mercadio patted Delex all over, as he looked for hidden injuries. Delex felt bruises and fresh blood all over. He turned to his side and puked. Soas stood by the shielded cloud and poked it with a finger.

"Dude, stop doing that!" Delex croaked. His voice faltered. His mouth was full of acid. Soas shrugged and paced the room. He whistled at the extreme damage.

Blackus came in the room at that moment. He flicked some black ooze off his blades and slide them back into place. "No enemies remain. We freed the wizards."

Mercadio nodded and tired to pick up the globe of energy, with one good arm, but the sudden shock of weight almost tore his arm out of the socket. "Dear godly cracks!" Mercadio spun away and danced in place. He waved his arm back and forth as he tried to clear the pain.

Blackus came over and reached for the globe of magic. He grasped it and pulled. It scrapped slightly and chipped the rock from the ground. He gave an eyebrow of surprise. "Heavy."

"What it that?" Mercadio asked. "Where is Valash, are you okay? Are you injured? Can you walk? Is that his body?" Mercadio pointed to a burnt ash where Delex woke.

Soas came over and handed Delex a skin of water. Delex drank the water greedily. "We need to get out of here. This isn't over." Delex stood and cupped the shield cloud in his hands. It scored the ground as he moved it, but it lifted to his hand as lightly as a feather. Soas and Blackus gave each other a puzzled look.

Mercadio explained as they made there way through the under-vaults of Valash's lair. They had made it to the towers to find it in disarray. Most of the wizards that could be found had fought drethcon or used magic to keep the towers from being overtaken. The earthquakes had buried most of the catacombs and vaults. It had taken them two days to get into Valash's lair. Blackus organized help to get the prisoners out of the cells. Nova had reverted to a dragon to scanned the skies for other threats and clean up any last drethcon. Anyone found weak unable to recover, this was a good sign a drethcon was still loose. Delex was happy they had found her alive. It was one good news which made the heavy part of his heart lighter.

Soas and Mercadio pounded on the shields for hours. It had taken them two additional days to clear the monsters and reach him. They feared Delex would die from dehydration. The cloud had grown small by the time they arrived. They had witnessed several attacks on the wall shields. Yet, even unconscious Delex continued to leak power into them. That impressed Mercadio most of all. He called it an impossibility of magic. The cloud had sensed this and redoubled its efforts to attack Delex. Perhaps out of fear, or desire to take him. Mercadio had several theories on that as he started to go into one of his lectures. Soas made it loud and clear none of them wanted to hear his theories and voiced a specific and detailed route through Mercadio's bowels where the theories could be stored.

Blackus backhanded them both across the back of their heads before they started to bicker. "Focus children."

Mercadio growled but continued his report. The cloud seemed resigned to save its energy and wait for Delex to die as it watched the others pound away at the barriers that held it there and them without. They had encountered several garrote spiders. Soas explained what they were in garish detail that would make bards quiver. Mercadio actually was amused at the telling. He did enjoy a morbid story. After the prisoners escaped, Blackus was let loose within Valash's lair. The screams of pain the monsters echoed within the walls made even Mercadio shiver.

"What did you encounter?" Delex asked Blackus. He had not seen a single thing as he drew to the throne. He only encountered the horrid magical traps.

Blackus showed no emotion on his face. He looked to them all and whispered one loud word, "Work."

No one asked him anymore questions. That was all that had happened until Delex woke up.

Delex nodded to all of this as they made there way to the surface. Delex recounted the battle to them all. He left nothing out. He wanted to show bravery, but his clothes spoke a hard-pressed battle. Besides, Soas would more than likely recount to others a much more colorful story, with or without his approval.

The cloud begin to buck and fight even harder as they neared the light of the noon day sun. It started to scream, the tiny prison muffled the screams to almost nothing. As they walked away from the tower, the cloud shuddered violently and started slowly break apart.

Delex sighed. "That is what I thought. It could not survive away from the anchor. Valash's anchor was his bones. Without an anchor, it could not leave the location. This is what Valash created, a living spell, but it needs to hook itself to a source of magic." He pointed downward. "The core of the planet. It would bleed the planet dry, eventually. It is also tied to Valash's bones. It had to be close to the bones to restart the spell. I destroyed those, and the spike, and now the cloud." Delex gave a final shudder of relief. "I didn't fail after all."

Mercadio and Soas blinked in wonder as they watched. Blackus toyed with the bandage at his neck as the cloud made one final spark of blackness and dissipated. He pocketed the ball of empty magic. He figured he might try to find a use for it.

A roar above them made them all look up. A dragon glowed from blue and silver scales descended rapidly towards them. Several wizards scattered or screamed in fright. Nova skimmed over them and jerked to a halt in a blast of dust and wind. Everyone closed there eyes from the sudden gust of dirt. Delex opened his eyes to Nova in human form, wearing nothing, again! Here golden tan skin, almond eyes, and dark hair almost glowed in the light. She gripped Delex's shirt and planted a heated kiss on his face. Delex's body rippled with goosebumps from his toes to the top of his head.

Mercadio coughed. "It seems Nova had found a way to revert from her dragon body. Perhaps she will master it at will." He sighed with chagrin.

Soas groused. "Maybe she can magic some ashen clothes too. I don't mind the mental picture, but this sorely changes the nightmares I have of her dragon form catching me. My dreams are going to be confused."

Nova released Delex and looked down. She blushed and looked to the wizard with large purple eyes. "Please." She then looked to Soas. "Scoundrel."

Mercadio frowned and started to remove his outer cloak, but Soas reappeared at her side with clothing. She smiled and gave him a soft kiss on his cheek. Soas appeared mortified and scurried away into the crowd. "Justly served." She snickered at Soas as he fled. Nova dressed quickly as the men encircled her with their backs turned. "I am so glad they finally found you. I helped the wizards, but my mind could not stop worrying."

"It is so good to see you too Nova." His heart pounded from her kisses, and reeled from her voice. "Blooming ash I need rest. Let's go to Tower Port and settle in and relax."

"Oh? How would we relax?" Nova said in a rich, sultry voice. She giggled as Delex became visibility weak. "I jest, I jest. Let us recover your health. You look a bloody mess."

"I am a bloody mess." Delex was a true bloody mess. If he was in the woods right now, someone would mistake him for a drethcon and murdered him.

The wizards of the Tower of Magic were in a disarray. None of the party would have beds there tonight. Maltort came out to look for Narsis. Mercadio told him where he was and he was safe. Maltort sighed and organized the wizards with the help of the Mirimas Quickcast, Headstaff from the Tower of Record. They would recover the wizards in quick order. Mercadio reported as much as he felt necessary but still left out much about Delex. Maltort growled with displeasure, but Mercadio promised to come back with Narsis and give a full report to him and Mirimas directly. Maltort agreed and gave them leave to carry out with recovery. He gave one long careful look at Delex and tried to hold back the awe he saw. Mercadio doubted Delex's secret would last for much longer.

The group walked the few kilometers towards Tower Port. Delex told and retold the final battle with Valash as Nova questioned him. They were all in high spirits. He had to retell the story once again when they met with Narsis, Daylow, and a furious Jaxcel, who was still bound and gagged. Soas laughed and laughed as he saw Jaxcel. "Dear loving gods, have you been like this for three days?"

Jaxcel had his gagged removed. "I am going to gut you all like fish! You are going to pay for taking me from my own ship! Boom-a-lo-"

Narsis shoved the gag back into his mouth. "I hate Sparks so much." He looked to Mercadio. "He has been doing that every day. Trying to light things on fire."

Mercadio tapped his fingers to his mouth. "At least we know for certain what Aspect he is. We can rest here and eat a meal. Delex can have time to clean up."

Soas snorted. "That man looks like he needs a week to bathe and recover." He gave Nova a sly look. "Or maybe just one good night."

Nova glared at him but did not say anything. She had not let go of Delex since he was found. She was always by his side. She held his hand, or pressed near him. She turned away from Soas but a smile played on her face. "Thy tongue speaks a scoundrel's feast in words and deeds."

Narsis cast a simple spell to remove the blood and stink from Delex clothes. Delex still needed to bathe, but at least his clothes did not look like a murder. Delex vowed learn that spell from Narsis. Jaxcel muffled kissing noises from his gag and made obviously rude noises.

Narsis laughed as he leaned an elbow on Jaxcel's head. This shut up Jaxcel as he struggled to get the painful elbow off his head. "Aye, that will be a gift. I will happily teach you dear Heir." Jaxcel glared at everyone and everything.

They stopped for a quick meal with Narsis and recovered the cart and horses. Once again they had to recount the story again for Narsis and Jaxcel. Jaxcel actually stopped his struggles and listened in genuine interest. He could be a patient listener when he did not try to struggle against his bonds, or light people on fire.

They continued to Tower Port. As they walked, they noticed a few streaks of light in the sky. Delex pointed them out. "Look shooting stars."

Mercadio peered at them. "Seems overly bright."

The rest of the party stopped and looked up. At least a half dozen shooting stars arched across the sky as they exploded. They sent waves of color into the daylight.

"Interesting." Blackus said.

Mercadio cautioned. "No, they are not shooting stars of rock." He looked to the others. "Do you sense anything."

"I am not a wizard you rattle-hat." Soas mocked.

Delex and Nova shook their heads. They did not sense anything. Delex was too tired, and Nova's distractions hung at arm's length.

The party looked into the sky. A storm built over the ocean. A blanket of dark clouds quickly rolled in from every direction. Lightning tossed around and flash within the clouds while it chased each other like hungry monsters.

Narsis shook his head. "I do not either. Do you?" He asked Mercadio.

Mercadio nodded slowly as he looked into the sky. "I do now, I do indeed. I sense the Void, and Death."

Soas sighed. "Well, crap."

Continued in the Ter'Avan Series:
Storm of the Fallen

Thank you for reading.

You are the reason this world is beautiful.

D.C. Soas

First Look: Book 2

The First 1000 Words

A first look in the next Ter'Avan book:
Past Powers Trilogy, Book 2
Storm of the Fallen

Maelee sat at the docks and swung her legs over the salty ocean waters. Her dog, Slipshanks sat at her side. His head swiveled back and forth as he watched the sea birds zip over head. Maelee patted his head and watched for the vessel that would signal her father's return. Her father was a cargo runner for the Towers of Magic and made regular trips to ports all over the world to supply the towers.

An imp from his ship and delivered an earlier message. He would arrive after dawn, today. He would not leave for several weeks. Maelee squealed and placed her hands over her mouth. Her legs kicked back and forth in excitement. Slipshanks looked at her and cocked his head to the side. Maelee laughed and gave him another soft pat on the head.

Maelee stood up and gave a long stretch. She had woken up

early just to watch the sea. Sometimes father arrived early. She did not want to take the chance and miss him as he came to shore. Slipshanks gave a sharp yelp and suddenly bolted from the docks. Maelee called after him, but he paid her no attention. His bushy brown and white fur bounced up and down as his legs shot him towards the edge of Tower Port. Maelee stood to run after him when the low base tone of the sea-bell started to clank loudly from the lookout tower. The bell signaled a ship would soon arrive. Maelee scanned the horizon and even got on the tips of her toes.

"Father!" She screamed. The red and black sails of her father's personal colors crested the horizon. Father was home at last. Her imagination spun out of control as she pictured the next few weeks of happy memories they would make. The skies above seemed to shimmer with rainbows. Maelee looked closer, the skies really did shimmer! It was wonderful! She had been distracted by father's ship, but now a large commotion echoed over the docks. A second higher pitched sea-bell echoed over the town; this was the danger bell.

Maelee saw a shooting star streak over the sky and explode into another rainbow of colors. This one was much closer, and louder than the first. A warning shiver crawled up her skin. She looked down at her feet. Rats poured from under the docks and fled for the safety of the town and woods. No birds flew over head or cried from hidden nests. In fact, as far as she could tell, all the animals moved or already left. Maelee did not have long to contemplate the events. Her mother had come from the house and grabbed her by the arm. "Sweetheart, we need to go. The warning bell has sounded. We need to get back home."

"Mother! Father's ship is out there." Maelee fought against her grip. Her mother gripped her harder.

Maelee's mother spoke to her plainly. "I know dear, I was up in the tower when they sounded the arrival bell. We also saw the storm. He will be fine, he is still a long distance out."

Maelee wanted to argue that they needed to find Slipshanks

when another star screamed from above. The sound terrified her. It screamed as it fell, like it was attacked by sharks. The star did not just boom loudly or whistle with fire. It screamed, it screamed like a man. The star exploded above them and showered the sky with a rainbow. It would have been beautiful, if it was not for the shock-wave that blew them off their feet. The impact tossed them into the air and ripped Maelee away from her mother.

Maelee stood up to see the world flipped into nightmare. Houses blew apart like paper. Larger timbers scattered everywhere like twigs after a storm. Fires raged into numerous colors across the port. People lay shattered like leaves across the ground and in various states of confusion. The air shimmered in a prism of dust. Colors swirled in the storm that raged above them. Thick raged cloud rolled and chase multicolored lightning in the air. It was almost pretty. Her mother lay several meters from her. Her mother clutched her head. Maelee's mother screamed but the sound came from far away. Something wet leaked from her ears. She touched them and looked down at her hands. Her little fingers dripped with bright blood.

"Mama!" Maelee screamed. Her voice echoed in her head. The sound was flat like when she climbed the watchtower and yelled into the sea-bells. Her head hurt so much! Her mother staggered to her feet and fell again. Maelee tried to walk and go to her, but her legs could not hold her. She stumbled to the ground. She looked at her legs and noticed the sprouts of plants sticking out of them. Maelee tried to scream, but she could not. Her whole body started to sprout branches, leaves and vines. She choked and cough as she breathed. A clump of wet leaves slapped the dock.

She looked to her mother. Her mother floated above the ground and slowly spun in place. As she watched, her mother started to fall apart into a swirl of fog. The wind that blew from her mother whipped Maelee's clothes about her like sails on the high seas. Her mother dissipated into a cloud of fog and wind. Her mother's clothes flung away in all directions. Maelee tried to cry out to her mother but her face would not move.

Maelee looked to her legs once again. Only a small line of dirt and dust lay in a line were her legs once were. Around her others did the same in their own ways. One man walked by her numbly. He dripped fire from his veins as his clothing and skin smoldered. His face tilted towards her, but he had no eyes. They had boiled and dripped from his face. She knew deep down, she too, would die.

Appendix A: Timelines

The Timelines of Ter'Avan

Standard Lifespan of the Major Races.*

*Years are based in Ter'Avan cycles of 360 days.

<u>Humans, 100 Years</u> They are a healthy race known for cleverness and stubbornness.

<u>Wizards, 175 Year</u> Wizards are all Human. Other races have magic abilities but this does not increase their age.

<u>Warlock, 350 Years</u> A rare is a wizard that is also trained by a Sorcerer. Mercadio is considered a warlock but never refers to this title. 'Warlock' is used for the type of the training, not how they cast.

<u>Dwarves, 400 Years</u> Dwarves are a hard muscles race that speaks from their heart. They are also notoriously xenophobic and warlike. Even the merchants.

<u>Elves, 600 Years</u> Elves live long enough to have lasting relations with other races and especially the Sorcerer race.

<u>Sorcerers, 1200-1500 Years</u> Sorcerers live long lives and take a steady long looked approach like the elves, but are capable of cleverness and rashness like humans.

<u>Dragons, Unknown</u> Dragons do not die naturally. They have the ability to 'fade away.' They can also be reborn in what they call a 'shedding.'

A Year on Ter'Avan

<u>The Pace of a Year</u> A Year on Ter'Avan is equal to 360 Earth days. There is 8 months on Ter'Avan, each named after the aspect of each god.

<u>The Pace of One Month</u> There is 5 weeks in each month on Ter'Avan. All months have the same amount of days.

<u>The Order of Months</u> The months are: Earth, Fire, Water, Air, Nature, Spirit, Void, Chaos. The month of Earth, the most stable month, is the point where the moon begins the month furthest from the planet. The month of Chaos month, with the

most changing weather, moon distance and speed, is when the moon is comes closest to the planet.

The Pace of a Week There is 9 days in each week on Ter'Avan.

The Order of Days The days are: Stoneday, Flameday, Rainday, Windsday, Lifeday, Dawnday, Duskday, Moonday, Fadeday.

The Pace of a Day The pace of time is the same as on Earth. The day has 24 hour.

Birthdate of Delex Year 795 SP, Month of Chaos, Moonday, Day 17th. At the end of book 1, Delex is 24 physical years old, but 206 birth years old. Time travel is annoying on birthday cakes.

Timeline of History

Year (?) Godlings come to the planet and create themselves as gods. The god, Chaos is created by the combination of the other gods. The gods create various races, creatures, and laws that protect their creations and themselves.

Year (?) Chaos steals humans from Void and magic from the gods and gives the races the ability to use it. Chaos creates the Sorcerer race. Dragons begin recording history and create the term 'Antiquity Horizon.' New races and cultures emerge as the gods give birth to their imaginations. Races and cultures establish kingdoms.

History is not recorded, or the records are lost before this point. For more information, please refer to the Book of Dragons. Good luck finding it and surviving. The owners are not the borrowing type.

Year 10000 AH* *The Tower of Chaos.* Chaos offers god-level treasure in a tower his placed on the planet. Begins the World Greed War. Refereed to as ' WGW.' WGW consists of: 13 unique races made of 24 armies. 12 of these armies were human cultures.

Sorcerers refuse to enter the war. They battle all 24 armies to remain neutral. Sorcerers take heavy losses but destroy at 10000% efficiency. The battle rages for only a few sort months before the armies agree to the neutrally of the Sorcerer race. Sorcerers disappear within the next several years.

*Calendars are created. Before this time, is the Antiquity Horizon. (AH)

Year 9788 The WGW has raged for 212 years. The first race goes extinct from the World Greed War. The Pixie race dies from the world. Many races and cultures are close to extinction.

Year 9700 AH *The Laughter of Sorrow.* The WGW has raged for 300 years. At the top the tower, the treasure chamber is breached. The god-level gift from Chaos is rewarded, almost. The Tower vanishes in a massive explosion as Chaos laughs. WGW ends immediately. The world takes toll.

8 Human Cultures Extinct: Miner's Union, Pirate Nation, Hand of Flame, Green Children, Order of Faith, Chosen, Ascended, Worshipers of Nulx.

8 Non-Human Races Extinct: Troll, Minotaur, Efreeti, Awaken, Pixie, Undead, Neverborn, Fey.

4 human Cultures Survived: Maidens of the Feather, Eagle Riders, Mystics, House of Tricksters.

4 Races Survive: Dwarves, Sea Giants, Gnomes, Elves.

Estimated Death Toll: 1,006,925,300,000

Year 9700-7000 *Age of Lost Light.* 2700 years of recovering lost knowledge. House of Tricksters culture breaks down into separate thieves guilds. Sea Giants stop appearing near land and sea ports. Sorcerers reemerge as a race and establish the floating city.

Year 5000 AH The Gnomes are driving into the sea after a failed demonstration of gnome inventions leaves thousands dead. Mystics rediscover magic and re-brand themselves as Wizards.

Year 4890 Sorcerers disappear yet again. The floating city is locked down and barred from all access.

Year 4800 AH *The Rise of Scales.* Dragons emerge as a race. They are more powerful than sorcerers but limited in magical diversity. They are peaceful but also terrifying in appearance.

No one can match their power, strength or magic.

Year 4700 Sorcerer reappear. The floating city is unlocked. Wizards attack the floating island and battle sorcerers over magical dominance.

Year 4699 AH Wizards surrender to the sorcerers. The sorcerers do not request any terms of surrender. They release all wizards to just 'stop bothering us.'

Year 4699-3000 Sorcerers establish basic ruling laws and teach wizards greater magics. Sorcerers refuse any roles in leadership or government. Wizards us the new knowledge to begun construction on a wooden 'Tower of Magic.'

Year 2950 AH The wizards complete a single Tower of Magic. Wizards establish magical learning. Wizards invite Sorcerers to teach at the tower. The wizards learn sorcerer techniques to magic. The Sorcerer-trained wizards call themselves warlocks.

Year 2900 Wizards and combined armies of the nations battle the sorcerers for magical knowledge. They declare the right of free knowledge as the reason for the war.

Year 2898 AH The wizards and combined armies surrender. Sorcerers do not ask for any terms of surrender other than 'stop acting like children.'

Year 2897 *A Gesture of Kindness.* The wood 'Tower of Magic' show signs of deep wear. Thousands of sorcerers converge on the towers in a single night. They create two new 'Towers of Magic' as the wizards sleep. The new towers are near-impervious to the age of time, wizard level magics, and all but the most dangerous Sorcerer magic. Why? The sorcerers wanted to do something nice. Sorcerers do not ask for any compensation and leave after a humble breakfast.

Year 2897 AH Wizards declare a long-lasting oath of peace with the Sorcerer race.

Year 2180-2150 Long-lasting fears and superstitions are breed against dragons. The are feared as daemons. Dragons become hunted by the human cultures. Most hunts are rare and end with both sides having heavy loses and death.

Year 2100 AH Dragons evolve into armored creatures. Most hunts now end in failure.

Year 1800 *The Purge of Scales.* Wizards create magical armors and weapons to battle the dragons. The hunts almost always end in success. Dragons flee and go in hiding.

Year 1710 AH Dragons go to the moon. Nova remains to protect the rest as they depart. History records a green spot on form on moon shorty after. It is named the Eye of Chaos.

Year 1700-700 *The Millennia of Growth.* 1000 years goes by without any major wars. The wizards declare official victory over the daemon race called Dragons. Nova makes frequent appearances to the wizards until they stop making the declarations. Dragon hunts fade into memory and the knowledge becomes forgotten.

Year 700 AH *Consumption of Souls.* A darkness descends within the center of the Soul of Stars Galaxy, also known as Dragon's Eye. The lovable Valash is born.

Year 400 *Twin Stars of Change.* Delex's parents are born, Doran and Zelexi. Two flashes appears in the night sky, within the Soul of Stars.

Year 50 The Sorcerer race gathers. They debate on going to the moon to befriend the dragons and be taught under them.

History records the great attempt by the sorcerer race to leave Ter'Avan and live with the dragons on the moon to better enrich there magical learning and progression.

Year 0 SP* *Breathless Cries in the Void.* Calendars resets to SP. Sorcerers attempt to go to the moon. The city of the Sorcerer race is destroyed by the attempt. All sorcerers perished, the entire race, but three.

This point establishes a new calendar, the Sorcerion Pilgrimage. (SP)

Year 0 Three sorcerers are left behind. Doran, Valash and Zelexi.

Year 15 SP The three sorcerers finish building a government model for the world.

Year 16-900 *Age of Lasting Peace.* New kingdoms are established by the sorcerers upon request of disputing regions. The three sorcerer are known as the Triad.

Year 500 SP Selkroth is born, the friend to Doran and Mercadio.

Year 700 Mercadio is born as a wheat farmer. Doran and Zelexi marry and rebuild the city of the sorcerers as a city a single fortress and accompany grounds.

Year 750 SP Mercadio is accepted as a wizard and begins training. Skill and Will!

Year 770 Mercadio befriends Doran and studies magic under him.

Year 795 SP *Return of Lost Souls.* The Soul of Stars, the neighbor galaxy, reignites the light in the center. Delex is born. Valash begins to show signs of rapid age.

Year 798 Valash, creates knowledge of a secret spell.

Year 799 SP Valash finishes his spell and the world shudders.

Year 800 Valash and Delex's parents battle with Valash and lose.

Year 800 SP Mercadio hides Delex from Valash.

Year 801 Valash starts to build an army, keeps it secret.

Year 920 SP *The Discovered Doom.* Valash's army is discovered. War is declared a month later.

Year 930 All nations declare war on Valash, the last heir to the Sorcerer race. Moraphen is declared War Leader and his army multinational army grows tenfold. The Spinning Moon Army now enlists 70% of all free standing armies as a world policing force.

Year 932 SP Valash clashes with Moraphen. Both armies are defeated. Moraphen is lost with 40% of his army. The multinational army disbands. Blackus builds an elite mercenary army.

Year 995 *Rumors of Darkness.* Valash reemerges in secret. Sightings of Valash spread as his influence grows.

Year 1000 SP *Return of the Heir.* Valash is officially spotted. Our story begins...

Heir to Sorcery Timeline

WARNING: This section DOES contains vague story elements. It DOES NOT contain spoilers, which are terrible things made by terrible people.

Day 1 The Earthen Planet, Present

Today Mercadio and Daylow meets Jim and Delex. Jim stays at home. Everyone else finds a tunnel.

Day 1 Year 1000, Month of Chaos, Lifeday, Day 23.

Y1000 M8 D23 The party goes to Ter'Avan. Soas meets the party.

Day 2 Valash meets the party. Blackus meets the party.

Day 3 Foran, Mossa, and Wilor find the party and lead them to the elves.

Day 4 Party arrives at the elven village. Selkroth meets the party.

Day 5 Party leaves the elven village. During lessons of magic, the party is waylaid by a local storm.

Day 6 The wind settles down, Mercadio rests. Delex practices and enjoys a meal.

Day 8 (M8 D30) Delex finishes a lesson. Mossa meets Moraphen.

Day 9 Party arrives of Homgad, Mercadio meets Narsis. Delex meets Moraphen, Vex steals a finger.

Day 18 (M8 D40) Moraphen stops at a village. Soas contacts a friend.

Day 18 (Night) Blackus and Moraphen talk. Vex and Nova meets the party.

Day 19 The party walks away from the meeting area. Delex meets a girl.

Day 20 Jim lights a candle. Selkroth greets his daughter. Narsis talks to Maltort about Mercadio.

Day 23 Year 1001, Month of Earth, Stoneday, Day 1.

Y1001 M1 D1 Delex washes himself. The party talks about

history. Nova and Delex became friends.

Day 24 A stranger offers a hearty meal. The party is welcomed at Hilltan. The party meets N'Mora and discusses services for supplies.

Day 25 Jaxcel is encouraged to travel. The party performs a service at night.

Day 26 Blackus pays for a sword. The party depart from Hilltan and separates into smaller groups.

Day 31 (M1 D8) Delex has a dream of the past. Delex and Nova whistle to birds.

Day 34 Delex and Nova leave a valley. The birds Delex and Nova meet migrate from the valley.

Day 36 (M1 D13) N'Mora finishes harvesting in the fields around town. N'Mora heads off for other pastures.

Day 44 Daylow wakes Mercadio in Homgad. Blackus breaks a door. Narsis helps decorates a tree in front of a library. Maltort wakes from a nap.

Day 47 (M1 D25) Mercadio and Narsis collected books. Blackus tipped them over.

Narsis and Mercadio talk about travel. Valash can't find his friends.

Day 56 Mercadio and Narsis organize a burglary. It failed. Blackus adds new friends to his army. Mercadio encourages his behavior.

Day 65 (M1 D43) Narsis makes historic history by moving a cup.

Day 74 Year 1001, Month of Fire, Duskday, Day 7.

Y1001 (M2 D7) Narsis moves a cat. Narsis takes a forced catnap. People hide from Blackus' laughter.

Day 83 Narsis and Mercadio Craft jewelry.

Day 84 Mercadio, Narsis, and Blackus leave town. The party as a falling out. The party goes back to town, except Blackus.

Day 89 (M2 D22)Narsis and Mercadio discuss the past month. Narsis wants to milk a pet. Blackus visits the town of Hilltan.

<u>Day 107</u> Delex and Nova play with doggies. Blackus meets with Delex and Nova.

<u>Day 110 (M2 D43)</u> Blackus, Delex and Nova leave a forest.

Day 119 Year 1001, Month of Water, Duskday, day 7.

<u>Y1001 (M3 D7)</u> Soas meets everyone near the sea. The party has a party. Soas pukes on a doorway.

<u>Day 120</u> The party boards a ship leaving that day. A group waves goodbye at them. Jaxcel meets the party and likes Soas.

<u>Day 138 (M3 D26)</u> The boat wiggles in water. Delex's stomach wiggles like water. Nova is not invited to play games with Soas and Jaxcel.

Day 168 Year 1001, Month of Air, Flameday, day 11.

<u>Y1001 M4 D11</u> The party arrives in a dock. The party leaves town with a large wagon. Delex dreams again. Delex and Nova take a stroll. Delex plays with some dolls. Delex makes a friend. The friend leaves.

<u>Day 169</u> The rest of the party wakes up early and leave to find Delex and Nova. Delex and Nova trespass. Nova falls for Delex. Delex and Valash have a productive conversation.

<u>Day 171</u> Blackus and Mercadio Dig a hole.

<u>Day 173 (M4 D13)</u> The party meets back up near the wizard's educational retreat. Jaxcel is slightly upset. Narsis keeps Jaxcel quiet. The entire group travels back to the dock. Pretty stars violently explode in the sky.

End of Book: Heir to Sorcery.

Appendix B: Encyclopedia
Encyclopedia of Ter'Avan

Section 1 of 2: Creatures, Places and Things

A - B

Arcanic Sight: A limited secondary sight used by wizards to see magical flows of energy.

Aspect: A human with one uncontrolled aspect of magic. Also known as a 'poor man's sorcerer,' an aspect must be taught to control the magic inside or will eventually violently destabilize (explode). Most feared aspects for unchecked destruction are Chaos, Fire and Void.

Avanset: The direction which Earthen travelers would understand as "southwest."

Avanside: The direction which Earthen travelers would understand as "south."

Avanwise: The direction which Earthen travelers would understand as "southeast."

Absence Sense Spell: A spell used to locate a person or object based on the inability or blocking of magical senses.

Barlight: The Ter'Avan terminology for laser.

Bittle-Beetle: A magical toy created by famed gnome wizard Bittle Banecrafter. This creation failed as a toy, but succeeded as a feared and deadly weapon. It can wound sorcerers and kill wizards.

Broken Moon Army: An army of highly trained mercenaries lead by Blackus.

C - D

Colors: A set of names wizards give the aspects of magic, they are Spark, Quake, Strangle, Flood, Howl, Rapture, Curse and Thorn.

Craft and Cast: The title a wizard receives after being acknowledged as a master.

Daemon: A classification of creature know for its monstrous appearance, action or fearful demeanor.

Dragon: An ancient sorcerer that has transformed into a being of increased magic. With greater magic, it has higher knowledge of manipulation but less degree of precise spells. A dragon being able to breath raw mage-fire fuel by its own highly concentrated magical essence is better than any spell they lost.

Dragon Box/Dragonical: A device used for various experiments and turned sorcerers into Dragons.

Dragon-fire: The fire breath a dragon can spew forth. A magical essence that is akin to a *Terrica Lance*, but will not destroy magical essence, only the physical form.

Dreadwik: A city of bad reputation of minimal laws. Full of thieves, gangs and bandits. Avanside to a mountain range port city of Poht.

Dwarf / Dwarven: A highly territorial race native to Ter'Avan noted for muscular stature and strong wills, and easily angered with passive behavior. Angered with aggressive behavior. Angered by intellectual challenges. Delighted by physical challenges. A valued sign of respect is a total lack of etiquette.

Drethcon: A small daemon creature that copies the living and consumes their life-force. They also copy limited memories and can impersonate the host. If a drethcon becomes excited, it may resemble its natural red coloring and white eyes. It cannot copy magical abilities.

E – F

Earthen: The name Ter'Avan calls the planet Earth.

Elf / Elven: A long-lived race know for swiftness and ties to Nature. Highly magical race comparable to wizards. All elven children receive basic teaching in Nature magic. Elves with high levels of success and wisdom are encouraged to continue studies in magic.

Envenus Ritual: An Elven magic ritual which increases magical potency but is unpredictable. Dangerous, and may cost the death of the caster or attendant. Only taught by request. Failure to learn means exile from the community.

Farg: A loyal flying bat-lizard creature that can be trained as a riding mount that can fly for days without sleep. Not highly intelligent and incapable of learning more than basic commands. Prone to follow commands and disregard the safety of self or rider.

Filthy Harlot: The name of Captain Jaxcel's ship he cheated from the previous captain.

Fireheart Root: A black root with red veins. The leafs are poisonous. The roots give unending speed and endurance, but will degrade muscle, organs and nervous systems.

G-H

Garrote Spider: A silent hunter spider that removes the head of prey. It will ingest the prey's organs and uses the hollowed carcass to lay eggs. The spider silk is razor sharp and difficult to break.

Gediin: A godling that has become a full deity without gender. If a *gediin* chooses a gender, they are refereed to as a God or Goddess. In rare cases, the deity may still be refereed to as a *gediin* if they create a new type of gender.

Geotelology/Geotelograph: The Ter'Avan terminology for instantly transporting small items across a distance without the need to traverse the distance in-between. Refer to Teleport.

Gnome: A race of small humanoid known for inventions that are universally incorrect upon completion. Once land-based, now are sea-based after being driven away from other sentient races. Gnomes are considered happy, hospitable, friendly, giving, peaceful and extremely dangerous.

Godhood: When a godling becomes a deity. The godling also looses the previous powers and most memories of a godling.

Godling: A demigod of limited power. It can become a deity and take an aspect of reality. Godlings travel from unknown origin across vast distances in the Omniverse.

Good Harbor: A harbor town on the Avanside of the ocean. Near cities are Tolet to the Moonset, and Peht to the Moonwise.

Headstaff: Administrative title for the leaders of the Towers of Magic. Two Headstaffs run the Towers of Magic, one for each tower.

Hilltan: A small unremarkable village surrounded by hills, and farmland. There are no significant cities nearby.

Homgad: A large city which once protected the city of sorcerers. Now surrounds the floating fortress of the last sorcerers. The city headquarters of the Broken Moon Army.

Honorname: The surname given to wizards when they earn the title of a master wizard. This name is chosen by the other master wizards based on the abilities of the wizard.

Human: A average race knows for cleverness and stubbornness. Stolen from Nulx by Chaos.

Headless Hounds: An experimental monster created by dragons, which were later exterminated.

I - M

Imp: A daemon creature that can teleport and deliver messages. Limited intelligence.

Ledger-seeker: A wizard whim seeks knowledge in written and spoken form. Records and investigates significant moments of a magical nature.

Leadstaff: A wizard in charge of a group of three or more wizards.

Mage-fire: A magical fire that will burn on any solid or liquid surface. It will burn in a gas. Mage-fire is fueled by magical essence.

Magical Essence: The ambient magical residue found in all things. Magical essence can be used, manipulated, and store. Ambient essence and will recover in time.

Magical Poisoning: Drawing magical essence into the spellcaster. The poison effects the internal organs and nervous system at various levels of pain, until a critical level causes organ failure. The poison does not affect mental abilities or fine motor-skills. Magical essence will eventually leak out of the body and lower poison levels.

Magical Weakness: When a creature drains the innate

magical essence inside them. This emptiness effects the muscles, fine motor-skills and mental capacity. A critical level can cause muscular seizure and possible mental collapse and death. Innate magical essence will eventually recover without magical poisoning.

Magus Knife: An extremely rare dagger imbued with the ability to cut through simple barriers of magic. It can cut through more advanced spells but has the tendency to fail, melt and shatter.

Maul-storm: A series of skyrippers in one storm. It can cause massive destruction.

Meta-clairvo spell: A spell that uses clairvoyance to predict the outcome of reasonable scenarios.

Melthanna: A magical elven drink that has traveling effects near trees.

Mimi Bird: A Carnivorous bird that lures prey into nests for mass ambush attacks.

Mindscape: A mental landscape used by sorcerers to view and manipulate magic during deep focus and meditation.

Spinning Moon Army: A army tasked with policing the world for threats against life. The army has been destroyed and disbanded. This surviving army has been reformed into the Broken Moon Army.

Moonset: The direction which Earthen travelers would understand as "West."

Moonwise: The direction which Earthen travelers would understand as "East."

N - R

Nature's Gate: A renowned inn within the boarders of Homgad.

Omniverse: The name for all things in the universe, beyond, before, and will be.

Poht: Port city on Avanside of Ter'Avan. Closest city is Dreadwik. Moonwise and across the inlet on rival port city of Peht.

Quatll-kaat: A small, egg-laying warmblooded, colorfully

winged fox that forms groups known as 'Kingdoms.' Lead by a queen. Highly territorial and intelligent. A quatll-kaat will form life-bonds with fellow creatures that help protect them.

Reverse Tracer Spell: A spell used to guide a person towards an unknown location. Highly advanced form of tracking spell that is hard to detect.

Royalic: A hereditary surname given to royal families. Only royal families have surnames passed down by family lines. Not to be confused with a Honorname given by other wizards. Surnames do not change with marriage. Male children are born under the male's surname, female under the female surname.

S

Sask'a'roht: A dead elf spirit that died in horrific circumstances that seeks revenge until their magical essence expires or the revenge is complete.

Serridan Tree: A tree native to Ter'Avan, used in elven magical potions and housing.

Shaping: A term wizards and sorcerers use for casting a spell.

Skydream Leaf: A light blue leaf that slows the body and makes you sleepy.

Skyripper: A tornado on Ter'Avan.

Sorcerer: A humanoid race and that can naturally cast many types of magics.

Spark: An Aspect that is attuned to Fire.

Spellcaster: A creature able to manipulate magical essence on command to create magical effects. Not to be confused with passive or reactive abilities.

Spell-weave: A metal thread magically purified and thinned as fine silk. Crafted by magical means, it is not magical. It is naturally resistance to magical attacks and has the qualities of plate and chain armor. Spell-weave is as heavy as normal steel but as flexible as silk. Spell-weave is crafted into a cloth made of metal. This is crafted into cloth made from metal.

Staff: A human spellcaster that has finished training and earned a staff of the wizard.

Starscape: Another name for a mindscape. Refer to Mindscape.

T

Tempra: A magical tunnel that travels through space and time. As referred to as a portal. This is a temporary tunnel which exists outside space and time, but still within the Omniverse. The greater the distance and time, the greater the danger.

Tempra-beast: A creature that live within the tempra. It cannot travel outside the *tempra.*

Tempra-kin: A Collective term for the creatures, '*temprabeasts,*' in a *tempra.*

Tempra-lock: A time and place blocked from receiving or sending a *tempra.*

Tempri: The plural term for a *tempra.*

Ter'Avan: The name of the Planet and the god of Earth and Earth magic.

Terrav: The term for the common language of Ter'Avan. All sentient creatures known Terrav.

Terrica Lance: A spear of magic crafted from Earth, Fire, Spirit, Void and Chaos magic. The spell destroys magical essence, which also destroys the object it is represents. The *Terrica Lance* has a high amount of feedback. This can kill a spellcasting wizard by internal cooking. Sorcerers cannot use this spell, the feedback destroys them.

Terset: The direction which Earthen travelers would understand as "northwest."

Terward: The direction which Earthen travelers would understand as "north."

Terwise: The direction which Earthen travelers would understand as "northeast."

Tinder-box: A magical cube that converts a small magical residue from spells into a flame. This can also be used as a warning device.

Tower Guardians: High level wizards is charge with protecting the Towers of Magic.

Towers of Magic: The towers that wizards go to train and practice. Two towers exist. The Tower of Records and Tower of Practice.

Tower Port: The port town which supplies and transports the Towers of Magic with various good and services.

Tower of Practice: The tower that houses labs, combat areas, and experimental rooms. The tower for all spellcasting duels, practice and item construction.

Tower of Records: The tower that houses the library of magic, lecture halls and classrooms. The tower for classes, study, housing, dining and assembly.

W

Warlock: A wizard who has had advanced wizard training by a sorcerer. This is not a common term know by wizards accept by the highest levels.

Whistling Merecat: A simple inn within the town of Good Harbor. The inn is under renovations and cleansing. Soas has been temporarily banned.

Windcutter: A term Blackus named for his wind-based sword technique that requires no magic. This requires further study to find how 'Windcutter' manipulates the magical essence of wind with only speed, technique and Blackus' other worldly samurai style.

Wizard: A human which has mastered the ability to cast magical spells, rituals, and incantations.

Section 2 of 2: Peoples of Ter'Avan
A - B

A'orria: The goddess of Air and Air magic.

Augges: Boy from Hilltan that is a hawker, loud and talkative.

Bartlon: One of the assistants of Maltort Manycolor.

Bashor: A dishonest thief in Homgad. Probably a dead thief.

Bilden: Kid from Hilltan that Augges does not like.

Bittle Banecrafter: Gnome wizard creator of the Bittle-Beetle.

Blackus: Leader of the Broken Moon Army. Master of weapons.

C-F

Chaos: The god of Chaos and Chaos magic.

Chesor: Leadstaff of the Tower Guardians.

Daylow: A magically imbued black cat and familiar to Mercadio.

Delex: Last known sorcerer on Ter'Avan.

Doran: Father of Delex. Husband of Zelexi.

F-J

Frank the Tank: Delex's golem. A futuristic M1A5 Abrams.

Foran Darkwood: Royal son to an elven leader Selkroth Darkwood.

Forr: The god of Fire magic and Fire magic.

Jaxcel: Exiled royal knight of Rin. Captain of the filthy Harlot and Spark.

Jim Devoy: The human father on Earth that adopted Delex.

M

Maltort Manycolor: Headstaff of Practice. Also known as the five-color wizard.

Mercadio: Leader of the darker arts of the towers, and high council member of wizardry with four colors: wind, Void, Fire, Water. Few master wizards know him as a warlock.

Merlana: A wizard from Ter'Avan. Possibly 'Merlin' from Earth myths.

Mirimas Quickcast: Headstaff of Records. Known for casting up to four colors quickly.

Molty Marty: A nickname for Maltort Manycolor.

Moraphen: Once leader of the Spinning Moon Army. Now Valash's servant.

Mossa Darkwood: Royal daughter to an elven leader Selkroth Darkwood.

N

N'Mora: Mayor and blacksmith of the town of Hilltan.

Nerry Berry: A nickname for Narsis.

Narsis: Green wizard known for is abilities in Nature magic.

Has three colors: Nature, Spirit, and Chaos.

Neliea: One of two tower guardians under the command of Chesor.

Neroal: The goddess of Nature and Nature magic.

Nicklim Devoy: The fake name Delex gave the Tower of Magic guards.

Nova: Last dragon on Ter'Avan and once again, Sorceress.

Nulx: The god of Darkness, Death and Time. Now known as Void magic.

P - S

Penance: Blackus' great war horse, personally raised and trained by Blackus.

Pont: One of two tower guardians under the command of Chesor.

Selkroth Darkwood: Royal leader to one of elven communities.

Sepria: The goddess of Spirit and Spirit magic.

Seqoria: The goddess of Water and Water magic.

Soas: Merchants-of-lost-goods, friend to Delex and all around smart-mouth.

T - Z

Ter'Avan: The name of the Planet. The god of Earth and Earth magic.

Valash: A real big jerk. A sorcerer that has a hard time letting go.

Wilor: Life long elven friend to Foran.

Zelexi: Mother to Delex. Wife To Doran, and powerful sorceress.

Appendix C: Miscellaneous
Miscellaneous, phrases and Extra

Swearwords, phrases and Sayings of Ter'Avan*
*In Alphabetical Order

Curse words
Ash-head(ed), Ashed, Ashen, Ashing, Black-soot, By Nature's ashen breast, By Ter's testicles, Crack of the gods, Dox, Dox-in-pox, Dullard, Dust and breath, Flamed, Flaming, Graveled, Graveleye, Hedgerotten, Holy crapping Chaos, Lightmind(ed), Nullard(s), Soakface(d), Son of Nulx, Stone's teeth, Tower of testicles, Wind-whipped, Whispen, Zephwill

Insults
Addled like a baby rattle, Hedge magic, Rattle-hat, Settle your hat, Slow as uphill gravel, Son of a goat maiden, Stage-mage

Exclamatory Phrases
A trouble a triple, Arguing with a rock's shadow, By Fire, By the first scale, Darn Tootin', Right as tight, There is no bid that could purchase it, Toes and teeth, True teeth of the story, Unwise eight ways from straight, What in the orbs, Wisps of whispers, You can't teach a rock to roll uphill

Other Phrases
Any of ways, From mouth to word, I swear by the moon, To spear the point, truth to word, Skill and will, Stall my heart, Well and well, Well and ways, Well and wise, Without offense, Repeat?, Ready and right, Spreading the muck, Word is water clear and true.

Magic, Gods and Power Levels
Wizard Spellcasting

A wizard pulls magic essence from the surroundings and puts it inside them, then uses it to manipulates external magical essence and/or extrudes then magical essence to create magical effects. The wizard casting can cause magical poisoning. Wizard spell casting requires various spells diagrams, memorizing, and rituals to attune the body to receive and use magical essence.

Sorcerer Spellcasting

Sorcerers have large, innate levels of magical essence inside them. They do not require the wizard style requirements of spellcasting. As Sorcerer uses magical essence inside them, this can lead to magical weakness. A Sorcerer can recover magical essence faster by absorbing magical essence around them, but will cause magical poisoning. Magical weakness will lessen but not completely recover from this method. Only time can recover magical weakness.

Delex Casting

Delex has tapped into an ability to create magical essence and cast spells. It is still unclear where the source comes from, but it causes hemorrhage and blood lose. Further investigation is required.

Power Level of the Gods and Mortals

A godling has a specific power when they appear. Little is known why the power level is at a constant amount. Godlings do not speak about where they come from. They do not talk about the things they see on their travels. Gods are unable to change the level of their power without taking the power of another god. Godling powers cannot be taken. Mortals power levels are not like the gods. Power levels refer to the ease an ability to manipulate magical essences. Gods are the embodiment of magical essences they represent. They have complete mastery and control.

Ter'Avan *gediin* = 1, Nulx (Void) = 6, Chaos = 12

Godling* = 0.2 compared to a Ter'Avan *gediin*
Dragon Race = 0.1 to 0.18
Sorcerer Race = .05 to .15
Warlocks = .04 to .08
Wizards = .02 to .06
Other Race and creatures = .0001 to .08
*Special Note: When a godling becomes a god it looses all its previous power. Most godlings also loose a large amount of previous memories before the time they grasped godhood. Mortal creatures can improve there power levels through training and practice.

Power (PL) equation of the Gods:
N = Number of total Powers N > 1
X = total base power
$(NxX)-X=PL$

Power Progression of Nulx (Void)
God of Darkness = 1
God of Darkness and Time = $(2x2)-2 = 2$
God of Darkness, Time and Death = $(3x3)-3 = 6$

Power Progression of Chaos invested per God
Nulx = 3 powers(0.3) = $(3x0.3)-0.3 = 0.6$
Forr = 0.1 Power = $(4x0.4)-0.4 = 1.2$
Sepria = 0.1 Power = $(5x0.5)-0.5 = 2.0$
Ter'Avan = 0.1 Power = $(6x0.6)-0.6 = 3.0$
Neroal = 0.1 Power = $(7x0.7)-0.7 = 4.2$
A'orria = 0.1 Power = $(8x0.8)-0.8 = 5.6$
Seqoria = 0.1 Power = $(9x0.9)-0.9 = 7.2$
Chaos Blending = 0.1 Power = $(10x1.0)-1.0 = 9.0$
Unknown Source = 0.2 Power = $(11x1.2)-1.2 = 12.0$

The Book of Dragons

by
The Dragons of Ter'Avan

This is a recording of the world, accurate as we could find. We are the dragons, the precursors of knowledge and recording. We laid the foundations of understanding magics, art, war, dangerous knowledge, and forgotten secrets. We have seen conflict and compassion unlike any other creatures on Ter'Avan. We create this record of the life of Ter'Avan. We, the dragons of Ter'Avan, bare witness to this world for the future by recording the past.

This book, The Book of Dragons, has been crafted over countless years. It is in our own language, but also is imbued with powerful magics. For those beings of special gift, these words are crafted in archaic voice and read as written. Those of special gift can read the magics imbued. The magics within alter the meanings. You will understand the words more closely to your modern tongue. This is the way of the dragons, and the power of our arts. Read these word with caution. These truths are not the world's truths. These truths are not shared lightly to the world.

These truths are not the worlds truths. How utterly boring and pompous. You would think an ancient race of creature, self-made would have had a sense of humor. I guess it didn't translate. Hi. I am Soas. I am here to help make this book make sense. I hope you appreciate how much work it took to 'acquire' this book, and to hijack the magic to add my commentary.

Enjoy.

Thus, we begin, upon creation.

The suspense is murderous!

First Scale:
Birth of Deities

In the beginning like all things, creation was filled with the dark firmament. There was nothing that could disturb the darkness. Godlings ranged the open voids in exploration. Fore, within the firmament, creation was being born, and the godlings were curious.

Even the dragons do not know from whence the godlings came. They may have always been among the black. They do not speak of it. We can not force them. Not even the most mercurial of all deities we know, speaks of the measure and secrets before time, before the Antiquity Horizon. What we name godlings, is a word we dragons created to explain beings of mystery and powers unlike all in creation. They travel the limitless dark without need. They have seen wonders that will never be explained. Yet, for reasons unknown even to use dragons, they are drawn upon the makings in the firmament and are reborn as deities.

For uncounted measure, for there was no measure of things, this darkness was without form, seas of clouds touching, swirling, dancing. In this section of the dark, the clouds were abundant. They whispered to each other, they spoke of riddles yet completed, and answers yet made. Secrets were made in the clouds that would see no witness. The first of the godlings came upon the clouds and found the lure of those whispers appealing. It moved within the clouds. They greeted it, welcomed it, and whispered the gossip of the infinite emptiness. The first of the godlings took upon itself these clouds and became the first *gediin*, the *gediin* of Darkness. Thus, the *gediin* of Darkness was born.

The *gediin* of Darkness, sheltered within dark clouds, needed no name, for names gave birth to individuality. Darkness needed none. It was lulled by the whispers and secrets. The *gediin* of Darkness, lulled by the whispers, slept in shapeless slumber.

As the *gediin* of Darkness slept, the clouds grew heated. The whispers became thoughts, then thoughts into story, and story into notes. A note hummed into life, then another. The clouds quieted their whispering. The notes of creation increased. Clouds shifted among the notes and yearned to hear more. A crescendo flared and grew. The *gediin* of Darkness shifted in its sleep but did not rise.

What a heavy sleeper! A cosmic alarm went off, an ol' Darky Dark slept through it. I wonder if the first notes was the god farting in its sleep. 'Bramphf!' The first note of creation.

The sounds of creation flared again and within it a beat was born, a cosmic discord of rhythm. The clouds begun to dance upon the beat and musics swelled around them. They sang to the rhythms and formed many dances. The music grew, and in the music, light was created. The light was the heat of creation, the source of the music. The clouds swirled in there dance, making the music flare. The world of clouds spun upon and endless dance, upon an endless song.

I hear they started their own bardic troupe, The Cosmic Discord. It wasn't heavy metal. That wasn't created yet. Ha!

This is when the second of the godlings came. The light drew it much akin a moth draws to a flame. The godling saw the endless dance, upon the endless song and was moved. The beats and rhythms pleased the godling. The godling grew in need of the songs, of the beats. It brought balance to the song, and measure to the beat. The songs and beats became one and grew in harmony. Thus, the *gediin* of Time was created. The godling needed no name, for names never lasted as long as time.

The *gediin* of Darkness woke to a world unfamiliar, a world of music, movement and measure. The whispers were gone, for only the song remained. The *gediin* of Darkness fled from the clouds and the harmony of rhythm. It ventured out to the edges of the clouds were it found some whispers remained. There, the *gediin* of Darkness slipped back into slumber.

Real of story? This god went back to sleep! The god needs a breakfast or something?

The *gediin* of Time measured the beat of the music. It orchestrated the dance. It took measure of distance and the swirl of notes. The notes grew tight as they yearned to partner into song. The dance grew with the light. The beat grew louder with the music. The music roared in the clouds, the clouds of gas swirled and spun as the *gediin* of Time quickened the beat. It danced among the gas and clouds until the glowing shuddered. The dance inhaled a deep breath and exploded. Light flared far greater than ever before. The clouds were blown away from a singular light. A star was born.

The *gediin* of Time watched in amazement. The clouds of gas had ascended beyond all miracles, beyond the power of a deities and created true light. Within that light another godling appeared. Drawn upon the firmament, the godling rushed to the light. The godling could feel the power of all the clouds of gas made one, ever burning, a merger of song and beat, eternal flame of life.

The *gediin* of Spirit was born and took the sun as the symbol of all the eternal brightness of the soul. Within this brightness, the *gediin* of Darkness woke. It frowned upon the creation of the sun. It felt discord from the light. It had slept too long, and did not measure time for there was no measure whence it went to rest. Yet now the need was realized, and also, too late. The *gediin* of Spirit took no name, for names could not compare to the wonder of a soul.

I am starting to think these gods just didn't understand what a name was. Oh, look at me, I am beyond labels! If I could roll my eyes in this book, I would.

The dance continued but the sun pushed away the clouds and danced along with it. The clouds courted the sun, swirling and dancing within the light. Yet, the clouds did not come near. The *gediin* of Time and *gediin* of Spirit danced within the light, within the clouds, and within the dark. The *gediin* of Darkness watched but did not dance.

In measure, the clouds merged into dust, and dust into

rocks, for the *gediin* of Time willed a progression of order. Two godlings arrived together, friends upon the firmament. They watched upon the edges where rocks and ice danced within the darkness. They were moved by the song and felt moved into voice. The two godlings moved closer and raised voices in wordless song.

The rocks slowed the dance and listened in wonder. The dance faltered. Untold rocks within the firmament huddled together as the godlings soothed with voice and song. Rocks became stone, became boulders, became planets. Heat grew within the worlds and roared alongside the song of the sun.

The godlings sang voices into the rocks. Thus, the *gediin* of Fire and the *gediin* of Earth were born. The two deities took no name for they were engaged in merriment with the planets and forgot the need for names.

The *gediin* of Fire, and the *gediin* of Earth played among the planets. They tossed them at each other in jest and sport. The planets crashed and reformed forever at the desire of the deities. Yet, this brought much discord to the worlds. Some worlds cried out, for they were reduced to dust and small rocks and could not remember how to become planets.

So the gods were children throwing toys. That explains so much.

The *gediin* of Fire and the *gediin* of Earth ceased the merriment. The *gediin* of Earth sang to the rocks, and they were calmed. The *gediin* of Fire sang to the planets and embolden them with his inner fire. The planets settled around the sun as the *gediin* of Fire and Earth shepherd the planet into dances. Among the planets one emerged special from all others.

This planet was twined upon hip and backbone. Two great orbs, spinning and fused as one, joined in the firmament. It spun end over end, and rotated around the middle.

Ha, ha, ha, ha, ha. It was a peanut! A planet in the shape of a peanut! Did they make planet butter? Ha, ha, ha! Planet butter.

The *gediin* of Earth claimed the planet made from two. The *gediin* settled the planet into orbit about the sun and raised it above all others. Ter was named to the orb above, and Avan to the orb below. The *gediin* gave the same title as a name and became male. Ter'Avan thus named himself, as he would name the planet. He settled his essence upon the planet, and his power increased for he now had a home. Thus, the *gediin* of Earth became the god of Earth, Ter'Avan.

So he named himself after the planet. That will never be confusing. That was also sarcasm.

The *gediin* of Fire was moved by the god Ter'Avan. It settled upon the planet named after the god of Earth. The *gediin* of Fire took the name Forr and became male. Forr rested his mantle within the fires that burned at the center of the planet Ter'Avan. His fires mixed within the core, and the fires spun and danced. Thus, the god of Fire settled his home upon the world Ter'Avan and gained in power for he now had a home.

The other *gediin* grew curious. They all moved closer to Ter'Avan, even the *gediin* of Darkness, though it brought it much discord. As they grew curious, their came a greater pilgrimage of godlings. The godlings come from three directions. In their wake, they pulled upon the rocks and ice of the firmament. They came close to Ter'Avan. The curious ice and rocks followed.

The ice and rocks crashed into Ter'Avan making scars upon the world. The god of Earth, Ter'Avan wept for the suffering of his planet. Forr, The god of Fire, asked the great fires of the planet to melt the rocks and cover the scars.

"Why have you brought my world pain?" Spoke Ter'Avan. "Why have you wounded her?" His voice rippled through the rocks, dust, ice, and fire. His voice rippled through the light and the dark. Thus, Ter'Avan created language and spread it among the deities and godling. Thus, all deities and godlings spoke freely among each other. Ter'Avan gave purpose words and naming of things.

So before language, did they just grunt and point? Even I can make a polite conversation with a series of burps. It takes a cataclysmic world shattering event for a god to say "Hey, stop?" Im-

agine me shaking my head in disappointment.

The three godlings wept, for the rash movements upon the firmament had caused much sadness. "We are sadden. We had not intended such pain upon this beautiful world." Spoke a godling.

"We will repair this beautiful world, and make her better." Spoke another godling.

Wait, wait, wait. The world is a 'her'? The god, Ter'Avan, made a girlfriend version of himself? Last time I tried that, I was arrested by the city guard.

"I will be the first to correct this sadness." Spoke the last of the godlings. The godling brought ice from the edges of the firmament. The sound of ice whispered of healing and rest. It fell upon the planet Ter'Avan and soothed the scars. The ice melted and made rain. It cooled the fires of Forr upon the surface of the world and made the scars disappear.

The godling fell in love with the waves and rain it had created. The waters moved upon the world with great power and soothed the scars, as the ice held firm as armor. Thus, the *gediin* of Water was born and then become female. She named herself Seqoria, the goddess of Water. She grew tried of her works and slipped within the oceans to rest below the waves.

"I will be next to correct this sadness." Spoke another godling. The godling mixed the light with the rain, the fire with the water, and upon the world spread a mantel of Air. The Air sung of its own creation. It moved around the godling worshiping it. The Air loved the godling as a child would love a parent. Thus, the godling took the aspect of Air and become a *gediin*. The *gediin* decided to become female. She bathed herself within the Air and made rainbow clothing from it. She named herself A'orria. The goddess of Air was created. She flew across the world always moving, forever free.

So, she made clothing. The gods are all naked? Maybe she can make the others some clothes. At least pants. Please, or at least give my eyes a merciful death.

"I shall protect the world from the falling rocks and ice.

They will find great resistance and become lesser." She looked to the god Ter'Avan. "I promised for as long as my child, Air lives around this planet." The god of Earth forgave the goddess of Water, and Air.

The last of the godling watched with great wonder. It too wished to repair the scars of the world, but could not. "I have no gift to protect this beautiful world." It pondered with much discord.

The dragons love using the word 'discord' don't they?

Forr spoke to the godling. "We all have gifts, but not all gifts can protect. My fires would cause harm to the water, and pollute the air." He shrugged. "Yet, they bring warmth and keep the waters moving for Seqoria, and stir the air so A'orria may dance."

The godling looked at the deities and pondered. It ventured upon the grey rock and looked upon its beauty. It touched the waters that made the surface grey and brown. The godling looked upon the amber Air. The yellow sun shone upon the godling and whispered of the souls that created it.

The godling rest upon the world of Ter'Avan and sunk within the planet. It gathered the rock, and the water, and the air and the light. It sang to the elements and slowly they combined. A green essence emerged from the rock and water. A new *gediin* rose with the green and became female. The goddess of Nature arose from the dirt and water and stretched her arms towards the sun. She named herself Neroal. Neroal watched over her green children and gave it the ability to grow and evolve.

The deities of Earth, Fire, Air and Water rejoiced. The power of Nature spread over Ter'Avan and clothed the world in a soft green. Neroal's plants made the air sweet, and made the waters blue and clear. The air became clear and azure. The god, Ter'Avan, made soil so the plants spread easier. Forr the god of Fire, belched forth minerals so the plants may eat. This was the first life. All deities rejoiced in the wonder except one.

The *gediin* of Spirit took much discord with Nature. It did

400

not want to give up its light. The spirits of the sun was that *gediin*'s alone. It wanted Spirit to be eternal and without change. The *gediin* wanted souls to be perfect as they were. That *gediin* did not want the light to be consumed and made unto another. The *gediin* gave itself the name Sepria, and became female. She grew in power as she made her home within the light of the sun, which the planet Ter'Avan danced around. Sepria's light protected the Spirit of light and lessened the influence of Neroal. Sepria looked on the works of Neroal and begun to hate. Thus, hate was created among the deities.

There always has to be one. This is why we can not have nice things.

The light of the sun flared. The light had never harmed the world of Ter'Avan, yet now the plants suffered. Nature wept as her children grew fragile and brown. They screamed out in pain as they begged Neroal for protection. They suffered without end. Neroal begged Sepria for mercy. Sepria closed her mind to mercy, and Neroal begun to hate.

A blackness appeared on Ter'Avan among the brown plants. It grew first as a speck, then as a spot, then as a blemish of black. A *gediin* emerged from the rot. None had seen the godling enter, for they were wrapped in merriment. The godling had hid within the plants, and dirt and hidden places as it watched contently. Now it emerged from the plants as the *gediin* of Death. It did not name itself for Death would be more eternal than Time, and more lasting than Darkness. A name was a leash it did not wish to craft.

"What have you performed upon my children!" Neroal roared. "You have taken away there existence."

The *gediin* of Death shook its head. "No, I have given you a cycle. If there was no end to the cycle, your children would never become more. They would grow without end. In measure, they would bear no fruit, no children. All would become your children and nothing more." Death held out his hand. Within it, the *gediin* cupped a gift of dirt. "Do we quarrel here?"

Neroal looked within the dirt and beheld a wonder. Within

there was a seed. "My children are reborn, and are stronger." Within the dirt the seed grew into a new plant, green with health. It rejoiced within the light of the sun. Neroal bowed her head to the *gediin* of Death. "We have no quarrel here."

"Be warned, for this green should one day wither, and become old. Hark, I have given it the ability to die, and spawn children, each stronger than the last." The *gediin* of Death spoke.

Sepria, goddess of Spirit grew tiresome of the *gediin* of Death, but she grew with greater hate of Neroal. Thus, rivalry was invented among the deities.

This is why I do not go to family gatherings.

Ages past upon the world of Ter'Avan. The firmament became ruled by rhythm and peace. The firmament gave way to what we dragons call the sun system. Even the dragons do not know how many worlds are out in the dark. We are but a young race compared to the timelessness of the sun system. Yet we know there was a growing discord among the deities.

Much of the discord had been with the kinship of deities, and the matter of their magics. As the deities grew in power, the Spirit of the sun system became dormant. The rocks grew cold and silent. Water did not sing. Air did not whisper and laugh. Many deities blamed the *gediin* of Death for giving mortality to the rocks, water, fire, and all the things of creation.

The *gediin* of Death grew in anger. "I have performed nothing to the rocks, water, fire and all the things of creation." The *gediin* of Death raged into the dark. "We deities have stolen the energies and made of it our magics. Your power has grown at cost. The rocks will not sing, the waters will not laugh, fires with not cheer, but they are not dead. I have no power over them. You have crafted this upon yourselves."

The *gediin* of Death had only taken what was given by Nature. Its power was upon ending of things, not changing of things. Nature has the power to rebirth and change, but this was not her works. The deities created upon themselves inanimate life. The rocks grew simple, the waters moved without knowing. Wind blew without a dance.

"You have not lost your rocks, waters, fire, and all things of creation. You have only transferred life and made magic. You have the magic within. It was the final gift of all the rocks, water, fire, and all things of creation." The *gediin* of Death replied.

The other deities pondered upon the words of the *gediin* of Death. Forr was the first to test this. He spoke to the fires at the center of Ter'Avan. The fire did not reply to Forr. Forr poured his magics into the fire. The fire responded by dancing as Forr commanded. Forr not only had tied his godhood to fire, he had mastery over Fire. He could feel the connection. The fires of Ter'Avan were a part of Forr, and Forr was part of the fires. He had truly become the god of Fire.

He spoke to the other deities. They also reached out to the aspects of there godhood. It was the same for all the deities. Each deity tested and manipulated the firmament upon the sun system. The deities rejoiced knowing the rocks, water, fires, and all things of creation beat within their cores. Thus, ends to first scale.

They all dance and sang like happy little rabbits and birdies and settled around the sun for hot tea and a sleepover.

We the dragons speak of the creation of Ter'Avan and the histories. In the first scale, we spoke of the creations in the firmament, the sun system, the deities and the planet Ter'Avan. Unrecorded time within the Antiquity Horizon moved forward on Ter'Avan but did not change. The deities had powers but did not share them among each other. The deities grew in understanding. Each new increase of knowledge was shared with the other deities. They grew in speech and social understanding akin to children.

No, exactly like children.

Second Scale:
The Fall of Deities

The sun system had many deities, each crafted from their own aspect. The deities lived in relative peace. There was some discord among the deities. The goddess of Spirit and the goddess of Nature disliked each other. The god of Fire and the goddess of Water refused cooperation. Goddess of Air and the god of Earth openly mocked and chewed upon each others words. Yet, the *gediin* of Time ignored the petty squabbling. The *gediin* of Time kept the pace of the sun system measured and steady.

Of all the deities that bickered and quarreled, none compared to the *gediin* of Darkness. The *gediin* of Darkness hated the *gediin* of Death in amounts that could not be calculated. The *gediin* of Death ignored the hate and discord. The *gediin* of Death did not worry itself over the affairs of the living and the deities that ruled it. Yet, the *gediin* of Darkness did not rule over the things of the living and found quarrel that the *gediin* of Death existed.

The *gediin* of Darkness grew in hate and discord. It approached the *gediin* of Death and spoke. "Why do you exist *gediin* of Death? Is not the Darkness the death of things? Is not the Darkness the end of all things? Is not Darkness the path of all the living things of the sun system? Are you not useless?"

"I disagree. Darkness was the first of things, not the last. Death does not rest the living, but records how the living rest. You, the *gediin* of Darkness, are not Death. You were what was before. You were nothing, and in nothing you remain. You, the *gediin* of Darkness will always be the *gediin* of the useless beginnings." The *gediin* of Death rebutted. "I am the *gediin* of Death, I have the wisdom of hindsight. I have the hindsight of the living. You have the foresight of nothingness. Now leave me, *gediin* of Darkness, for I find this conversation as useless as your existence."

Ash and fire! Did the universe drop a degree, because the god of death slapped down some cold truth. Thus, offensive wordplay was invented among the gods. Thank you!

The *gediin* of Darkness was stunned. It did not move. The *gediin* of Death looked upon the *gediin* of Darkness and felt pity for it. The *gediin* of Darkness felt the pity and was enraged. The *gediin* felt a rage boil great like the core of a sun. The *gediin* of Darkness lifted its hand and swept it before it. The *gediin* of Death looked upon the hand with much curiosity. The hand swept downward and struck upon the *gediin* of Death. The *gediin* of Death recoiled from being struck and was rent open.

The firmament shuddered. The strike echoed upon the sun system and out into the dark and beyond. The *gediin* of Death screamed in pain. Its form spun, cracked and flew apart. The strike exposed the core of the *gediin*. The magics left the *gediin* of Death and twisted within the firmament. The *gediin* of Death died and left behind the aspect of its power within its corpse.

The *gediin* of Darkness watched in horror and wonder. The *gediin* of Darkness fled from the corpse of Death, but the corpse of Death pursued it. The *gediin* of Darkness grew with much fear but could not escape. The corpse of Death pursued and grappled upon the *gediin* of Darkness. The corpse of Death burrow into the *gediin* and clutched upon its core. The *gediin* of Darkness screamed in fear and pain.

Well kids, this is why you do not throw rocks upon a hornet's nest.

The corpse of Death combined with the core of the *gediin* of Darkness. The *gediin* of Darkness became the *gediin* of Darkness and Death. The *gediin* looked down upon its hand and grew in knowledge. The knowledge of theft, war, murder and pain was gifted to the deities. Thus, the *gediin* of Darkness and Death grew in power, and become twice as much as any deity.

Okay. I did not see this coming.

The deities shuddered. They gathered around the *gediin* of Darkness and Death. "What has happened? Where is the *gediin* of Death? What is this new knowledge that has come to us all?" The deities demanded.

The *gediin* of Darkness and Death cowered, its hands pressed upon its head. "I do not know. I quarreled with the *gediin* of Death. It mocked and slandered and challenged me. I struck upon it with my hand. The magics bore into my core. I have killed. I have murdered one of our kin!"

All the deities grew in shock and discord. The *gediin* of Darkness and Death wept for the lost of a deity. The other deities wept with him. They tried to bring forth the aspect of Death from the core of the *gediin* but could not. The aspects of Darkness and Death combined and were made one. There was nothing to separate.

The other deities surrounded the *gediin* of Darkness and Death and gave sympathy and remorse. They helped the *gediin* to recover and control the power which ragged within it. In measure the *gediin* of Darkness and Death became whole. The unity gave knowledge of family and it was gifted to the deities.

How sweet! Warm hugs for everyone. Let us celebrate the murder and death of a god with compassion, understanding, and complete lack of punishment or penalty. These gods have some weird family values.

The *gediin* of Darkness and Death retreated from the other deities to the privacy of the Darkness. The power within was made new, but retained the abilities of Darkness and Death. It was not the aspect of Darkness and Death, for there was no separation. The deities did not give this power a name.

The other deities returned to world Ter'Avan and discussed among themselves the events. The *gediin* of Time retreated into the quiet places within the firmament. It felt no need to socialize. The other deities feared being undone. The deities went among the sun system and touched all things within the firmament. They drew the powers of their magics out and made all things incapable of harming the deities. All the rocks, water, fire and all things of creation could no longer harm the deities.

As we dragons understand, the protection the deities created, made all deities invulnerable. This includes the *gediin* of Time and the *gediin* of Darkness and Death.

As the deities of Earth, Fire, Water, Air, Spirit and Nature made all things upon the sun system do them no harm, the *gediin* of Darkness and Death grew in discord. The *gediin* feared that the other deities were plotting it harm. It spoke to the Darkness and heard the Darkness agree and whispered back the same. The *gediin* of Darkness and Death knew the Darkness spoke secret, eternal truths.

I am pretty sure, we call it an echo, or insanity. I could be wrong. I am not, but I could be. Yet, I am not wrong. Gods are crazy.

The *gediin* of Darkness and Death approached the *gediin* of Time. "*Gediin* of Time, I come to you to bid your services. I need to see into the future and measure the harm to befall me."

"I have nothing to give you *gediin* of Darkness and Death. My powers control the stream of time, movement and measure. I merely record the past, and keep the beat steady and shape the course. Of all the deities I have the most potential but the least power." The *gediin* of Time spoke in a steady emotionless voice.

"Your words do me harm *gediin* of Time." The *gediin* of Darkness and Death threatened.

"Words do no harm to any deity. Do you wish to do me harm? If you wish, I will shape the course to harm you if this is your desire. I have no power to view my actions I have not done." The *gediin* of Time replied.

The *gediin* of Darkness and Death bowed his shoulders. "No, *gediin* of Time. I do you no harm, nor wish it upon you."

The *gediin* of Time turned his back. "Farewell *gediin* of Darkness and Death. Do not approach me again. For I-" The *gediin* of Time did not finish its words. The *gediin* of Darkness and Death rushed upon the *gediin* of Time. The *gediin* thrust forth its hand as one would a spear. Its hand ripped through the *gediin* of Time and broth forth the core of the *gediin* within its palm. The *gediin* of Time screamed in pain and fell apart. The sun system slowed and stilled. The firmament and all things upon it did not move. Thus, the knowledge of lies was gifted upon the deities.

Wizards have this wrong, one wizard in particular believes it was the god of Time which killed the others. This shows how useful wizards are.

The other deities rushed upon the *gediin* of Darkness and Death with great anger. "What has happened? We had asked of all things upon the firmament to never harm a deity. Hark! Look, for the *gediin* of Time is slain. What have you done *gediin* of Darkness and Death?" roared Forr.

The *gediin* of Darkness and Death pulled the core of the *gediin* of Time to its mouth and consumed it before the deities. The *gediin* gained the powers of Time and the firmament moved once more. "I am not the *gediin* of Darkness and Death, for I have the powers of Time." The *gediin* thus took the male form. "I am Nulx, the god of Darkness, Death and Time. I give this power the name of Void. I am the end, I am eternal and without end."

Dear gods, we all hear you. Your monologues are as bad as your stench, overpowering and unending. If I thought you were bad before you ate Time, now you are as repetitive as a waterwheel. Dry up already!

Sepria implored to Nulx. "We had asked all things to do no harm us deities. How have you done this!"

Nulx looked down upon his hands. He flexed his hands back and forth in front of the deities. "You ask me, how I have done this. You ask how the *gediin* of Time still fell to harm and nothingness." Nulx, of Void, held his head with one hand as he clenched the other in a tight fist. He looked up towards the deities under a hooded brow. "Did you ask us deities?" He smiled at the others.

The other deities moved back from Nulx. His power had increased. First, he was the *gediin* of Darkness, and as powerful as any deity. Then, he was the *gediin* of Darkness and Death akin in power to two deities. Now as they looked upon his smiling face, and his eyes shadowed under the hood of his brow, they felt his power. Nulx was as powerful as all the other six deities combined. Nulx was the god of the Void.

Thus, the knowledge of good and evil was gifted to the deities. Nulx grinned and chuckled in the knowledge. The other deities fled within the firmament and the sun system. Thus, ends the second scale.

That is how that monstrous disease of a god was created? Maybe the knowledge of loop holes should have been gifted to the gods.

In the forth scale we dragons spoke of the creation of sentient creatures, daemons and monsters. We spoke of the attack on the planet, 'The Great Rend.' The war of the deities created the First Oath, and the Walk of the Deities. We concluded, the sentient creatures look upon each other with wicked thought and deed.

Now we speak of the creation of the god, Chaos, and the moment Ter'Avan changed forever.

Once again the bore and snore of dragons penned out in words. Well and well. I hope to help translate this into something we can all stomach. Love, Soas.

Fifth Scale:
Creation of Chaos

A fter the deities had settled upon the sun system and the firmament, Nulx rested in the dark near Ter'Avan. The deities dared not leave the planet for fear Nulx would again feast upon the world. Nulx had gathered much power and could not be removed. The other six deities magics protected Ter'Avan and shielded the planet from the greater corruption of Nulx meddling. Yet his magics was also the magic of the world. They could not be forbidden.

The creatures grew and spread upon the world of Ter'Avan. Even as the creatures spread upon the world, the monsters of Nulx spread and grew. Yet, the abundance of creatures rally for their deities. They slay and war upon the monsters created by Nulx.

"You slay and war upon my creations! This violates the Walk of the Deities and the oath of our words." Nulx raged upon the deities sheltered within Ter'Avan.

"We have not violated the oath Nulx." Sepria spoke. "Our creatures slay and war, for your creatures prey upon them."

Forr spoke against Nulx even though he, of all deities, felt most akin to war and the mind set of Nulx. "They battle for we have given them the will to battle. Yes Nulx, they feast for war. A path of war can be walked in both directions."

"My creatures die and my powers diminish because of this! The oath is breaking." Nulx protested.

Seqoria took a deep breath. "This is war upon your will Nulx. We did not start the war of creatures and monsters. The oath is as strong as it has been upon creation. Your childish slander does not bend the oath, the oath will not sway to word, only deeds. I felt no violation."

"You have no tooth in this Nulx!" A'orria spurned Nulx. "Leave us, and this world. You lay the pressures of your magics against it. Your magics would end all that we have and you beg for relief. You are akin to the monsters you created."

Nulx raged against the godly protection around Ter'Avan. "This will not be the end of things. Fear my word, for I am the *gediin* of Time as well as Darkness and Death. I can see the future."

The god of Earth, Ter'Avan, laughed and smiled fondly to Nulx. "The boasting of immortals is much loved my friend. It is all boasting though dear Nulx." Ter'Avan looked bored upon the sun system. "Have we again heard these words? Yet, the oath is still immune to deception. Prattle, but prattle in a shadowed voice." Ter'Avan laughed and turned his back to Nulx.

The scream from Nulx could be heard through the firmament.

You could probably set a timepiece to it. Nulx is raging, it must be an hour past noon! Too early for tea?

Neroal raised her hand to settle the bickering of the deities. She looked upon Nulx. "God of the Void, if you do wish to change our minds, why not give your monsters more intelligence? They could live within the harmony of peace."

Nulx turned his back upon the deities. The oath that was given upon the creation of the Walk of the Deities has not been broken, for words and lies could not harm the oath. The oath would have broken upon its own.

Time past upon Ter'Avan without change to be recorded, except upon the time when a new godling appeared within the sun system and firmament. The godling was drawn to Ter'Avan but looked upon the system and sighed. "I am too late. For all has been taken and given." It mourned.

"Why do you gather upon this sun system godling?" Nulx asked with much pestering and discord. "Have you not the skill to see all has been taken and given."

The godling did not answer for it was deep within the grief of its core.

"Why do you not answer little godling of nothing? I am Nulx the greatest of all deities. You ignore my words upon your peril." Nulx threatened.

"Why should I answer. I am not mastered by you or any other deities. I am of my own mind and feel no allegiance or fear of reprisal. I am but a godling, and I will leave this place for another." The godling turned its back from Nulx and begun gathering upon its core to move away from the sun system and out past the darkness of the firmament.

Nulx gathered his powers and readied to strike down the godling. He raged within his core that a godling should show such disrespect. As his hands gathered power to slay the godling a thought formed. He moved close to the godling. "Godling of nothing, I know not of anything left within the firmament and sun system for you. Your core may not survive longer beyond the darkness. Meet with the other deities, and we will question them upon our knowledge. I, the great Nulx of Void may be able to grant you godhood under my apprenticeship, under my loyalty." The god of Void, the god of Darkness, Death and Time smiled at the godling as his eyes glimmered in their depths.

The godling agreed to follow Nulx towards Ter'Avan. It was amazed with the firmament and sun system. The other deities welcomed the godling as a friend. They questioned the godling whence it came and what wonders it had seen. The deities and godling talked of many things. Even Nulx seemed civil and respectable. The deities rejoiced in peace.

I hear Forr even did a fire juggling act.

The visit lasted for a time unrecorded until the godling sighed. "I must depart once again into the places beyond the darkness. I have to find somewhere to invest my core."

"Why do you not stay here with us?" Asked Nulx. The other deities looked upon him with much confusion.

"No aspect is left to have." The godling said in remorse.

"Yet, we can give from each of us, a small portion. Would you be able to fill your core?" Nulx asked.

"What is this madness Nulx?" Ter'Avan questioned. "What scheme do you play with us now?"

"I do not wish to see this godling leave. You know my words are true." Nulx retorted.

Forr barked. "But you never speak of all things. You will have us give of our core and you will remain aloft! This is your scheme. Your truth turns around unseen bends."

Nulx glared at Forr with much discord.

Are the dragons getting paid to use the word discord? I don't think it means what they think it means. Use another word!

Nulx magics gathered about him. The other goddesses stepped in to calm the male gods and their bolstering. The goddess of Spirit, Sepria, spoke for the female deities. "We goddesses spoke to each other why you males screeched and scratched." She looked at Nulx. "You speak truth, but hide your intentions. We parley that you shall be the first of us to gift of your core."

Nulx glared at Sepria. "How will I know if you shall honor this word?"

"We shall give oath upon the First Oath to do no harm. We will give of our cores a tenth amount. We shall recover and heal from this, but the godling will become a deity." A'orria spoke in a whisper.

"Please Ter'Avan, do this for me." Neroal asked of Ter'Avan.

Ter'Avan, god of Earth rolled his eyes but agreed. He looked to Seqoria. "Please Seqoria, Initiate the oath."

Seqoria nodded and brought forth the waters of her core. She whispered and placed her hands within. The waters grew with blue light. "All must place there hands within the waters." She looked to Nulx, "if you be true of word."

Nulx glared at them all and placed his hand within. The waters swirled with black. Forr was next followed by Sepria. The waters glowed with red and white. The deities placed their hands within the waters of the oath. The waters swirled in a prism of colors. All the deities spoke as one. "By First Oath, by safety from harm, we give our word."

Seqoria nodded. "It is agreed. Nulx, please go first."

Is it me, or have the gods become better at talking. I guess it only took several hundred millennia for the gods to master being social. Well done gods! I'll make you all a pretty little trophy. Just give me a few hours to digest my breakfast.

Nulx approached the godling with a raised hand. The godling moved back in fear, but the other deities whispered encouragement.

Its poo. The trophy is poo. My poo, mostly eggs, some corn and a little bread. I ran out of cheese.

Nulx touched the godling upon its form. Nulx placed a tenth of his power within the godling. "The deed is done. I have placed a tenth of my full core. The godling should now have a tenth of power. If we all share, this godling will have a seventh of our power of be a minor deity. It will be custodial Sheppard of the world."

Forr peered intently at new *gediin*. It was shuddering with the powers given to him by Nulx. "There is something wrong. The *gediin's* core has more power, it is not of a tenth scale from my gift." Forr moved towards the new *gediin* and placed his tenth within it, for he was bound by his oath. The other deities moved closer.

"Ah yes, I am the strongest. It has the strength of my three magics." Nulx preened with a smile.

"This is not the case." Forr roared. "It's core was six-tenths

upon your investment!" Forr looked down at his hands then back at the *gediin*. "And now the *gediin's* power is greater than my own."

The other deities hesitated. They had felt the *gediin's* power and bulked, yet the deities were compelled. "We must submit, yet as each of our cores are given, this *gediin* will gain upon the exponential!"

Who knew the gods were almost good at math! Thus, mathematics was almost correctly invented among the gods.

Nulx grinned. This was far better than he could have imagined. The *gediin* would grow and Nulx would have a thrall indebted to him. With the *gediin* under his command, he could finally remove the other deities and then slay this *gediin* and take all the powers of the deities for himself. Nulx mused as he watched the deities one by one place their hands within the *gediin* and invest into its core.

The *gediin's* power increased to twice, then three, then more until the last deities were the goddess of Water, and Air, Seqoria and A'orria. Both goddesses walked without hesitation and placed there hands upon the head of the *gediin*.

"Dear one, you are our child born of which we have all given. We welcome you with our hearts." A'orria said to the *gediin*.

"Dear one, you are our child given from our hearts. We welcome you as a deity." Seqoria spoke to the *gediin* with gentle feeling. Thus, the knowledge of love and family was gifted to the deities. Only Nulx refused this gift and cast it aside.

As the last of the cores within the *gediin* mixed, it glowed with a light which shimmered in a prism of colors. They spun and fought within. The *gediin* curled upon itself and clutching at its body. It screamed as the magics in its core fought against each other.

The deities, even Nulx, stepped back from the *gediin* as it screamed and raged in the firmament. "We could still kill this new deity and take back our powers. Its power is slightly more than seven of you lesser deities combined." He looked back to the others. "If but two of you assist, we can end it before it begun."

The gods Forr, and Ter'Avan looked to each other, then to Nulx. Ter'Avan glared at Nulx. "Was this your plan? You kill it and gain enough power to rival and overpower us?"

"Either you help me kill it and gain a fraction more power or let it live, and it and I will dominate you anyways." Nulx grinned at the other deities.

Before Nulx or the other deities could speak more, the sun system shuddered. A wake of energy pulsed from the *gediin* outward, penetrating to all corners. Just as quickly, the pulse of magics pulled back into the *gediin* with a resounding snap. The magics, within the new *gediin*, started to merge into each other. All nine magics from the seven gods converged into a single point and gave birth to a new magic, a magic which overruled logic and meaning. This magic twisted and contradicted itself yet this made it stronger. This new magic consumed the magics it was made from and hummed and flourished within its own paradox.

The *gediin* uncurled tall and bright among the other deities. The *gediin* took a male form. Now there was four gods of each gender.

Thus, the knowledge of group dating was gifted to the gods.

"By the firmament and all beyond, the birth of the tenth magic, within this eighth god has added to the other magic." Sepria stuttered. "His magic should not exist, cannot exist. It this not what you did Neroal?"

Neroal shook her head. "No Sepria, I took of the elements of the firmament and made my magic. This one took purely of the magic itself. He cannot exist."

"And yet I do." The new god said. It was shrouded in a cloak of shifting colors. "Yet I do indeed."

"You have taken form and name. Yet, your name is shrouded, how can this be?" A'orria mused. "This is new to us." The goddess of Air seemed humored by the event.

"He is strong, I feel it, I can feel my power within him." Forr added. He looked to Ter'Avan. "Can you not feel yours as well?"

Ter'Avan rubbed at his chin. "I can."

"We gave birth to a child, our own child." Seqoria had a brilliant grin. She gripped Neroal in an embrace.

Neroal laughed and pushed Seqoria off her embrace. "I understand your glee Seqoria, but we must consider what this means. We not only gave birth to a god, but to a new magic. What do we call it?"

"Chaos. You call the magic Chaos." The god within the shroud of swirling colors looked to each of them. "I take my power and core from the birth of the new magic. You can call me Chaos, for I am the magic. I am Chaos."

The god of Chaos, living magic of the combined magics, claimed his place among the gods.

Que dramatic music.

Nulx laughed. "And with that birth, you have sealed your fate, for my servant and I will subjugate you all." Nulx looked to the new god of combined magics. "Help me now, the First Oath prevents us from harming each other, but it does not prevent us from imprisonment."

Que dramatic belch. Way to ruin the mood Nulx.

The six lesser gods looked fearful. Seqoria looked at Nulx. "This is why you agreed to the First Oath. We could not harm each other, but imprisonment can be without harm. You are a pure monster." She said with bitter discord.

Nulx shrugged. "Imprisoned as you will be, your cores will wither and you will die in time." Nulx motioned to the god of Chaos. "Now help me capture them."

Chaos nodded and held out his hands. "I wonder Nulx, how long will they last within your prison?"

Nulx grinned, "Long enough to see us destroy everything they hold dear within this sun sys-" Before he could finish, a ray of colored light shot through his shoulder and into the firmament. He turned to see Chaos. He griped his wound, holding his magics from leaving him.

We dragons think Nulx was fortunate the gods had given birth the knowledge of armor during the war of the gods. Yet, this subject was covered in the third scale. Refer to the third scale for reiteration.

Breaking the fourth wall dragons! Interrupting the story, how rude! Oh, wait...

"But the First Oath, you cannot harm me!" Nulx ragged.

Chaos shrugged. "I do not remember any oath, numbered or otherwise. My magic was not birthed during this oath. I am new, this Oath hold no binding. I did not place my hand within the waters."

The truth of the words touched each god in unison. The became fearful, even greater than the fear of Nulx.

Nulx glared as he held his shoulder. Nulx made a seal over his wound before his magics leaked out. They all felt the god of Chaos's power. Within him burned the power of the nine types, plus the new power, a tenth power. This god was as powerful as all the nine original gods. "You are my thrall, my servant. You cannot do this!"

"Can I?" Chaos mused. "I am not going to destroy this place. My core would die. Perhaps not. Perhaps my core would live, for I am not tied to the elements." Chaos shrugged. "Yet, I am made of my parents. Perhaps I will. Should we test the theory not-father?" Chaos spun around once and looked at Nulx.

Ter'Avan turned to Forr. "His power, it is equal to nine strengths."

Forr nodded. "True, but together our power would rival him, twelve strength to nine."

Chaos held out his arms wide. "Care for a hug moms and dads?" Chaos chuckled. "Oh, my apology. That may aggravate your wound." Chaos pointed to Nulx's shoulder. "I would hate to cause more pain until you are," Chaos paused and gave a sly look, "able to shoulder the burden."

Thus, the knowledge of terrible puns was gifted into Nulx's shoulder.

Nulx turned to the other gods. "We must unite and kill this god! He is correct, he has not taken the First Oath, but he also is not protected!" He looked at each god as they turned away or cast down their eyes. "Why can you not see this danger! If we all combine, we can take this god! He can kill any of us at any moment!" Nulx pointed at them all. His face was twisted in an insane grimace. "One of us will lower our guard or be alone, and he will erase us. If he was to destroy any one of you, his strength would be 20 of ours!"

Well, the numbers check out! (11 x 2)-2 = 20. Nulx, you past first grade. Come get a gold star!

Neroal stepped forward for the gods. "We cannot. His is our child, we could never kill our own child." She folded her arms and glared at Nulx. "Furthermore, you just tried to kill us." The goddess moved away. "Lastly, even though we are more powerful with our powers combined some of us would fall. He would take that power and become greater."

Neroal shrugged. "Perhaps we could imprison him, it would take much less power. A single god could do this. That god must tend the prison and would be vulnerable to you. We gods will protect ourselves and build a protection from Chaos, and from you." Neroal glared at Nulx. "Your plans have failed god of Void. You have been the biggest of fools." She turned away from Nulx. The other gods moved away and back to the world, Ter'Avan. Chaos simply faded away.

Nulx raged at them and swore in words he created. He screamed out each of the gods by name. He poured his logic and fears into each word. The gods did not hear him. Nulx grew tired of his ranting. He had yelled and raged for an extended time and had nothing to show for it.

"I would love to say I am sorry you did not get what you what, but I am not." A voice appeared behind Nulx. Chaos had appeared by Nulx. His arm rested over the shoulders of Nulx in comfort and sympathy. "You also tried to kill me. I can forgive you, no harm done." Chaos squeezed the Nulx's wounded shoulder and vanished with a mocking laugh.

We dragons have recorded the echos of Nulx's godly scream that still bounce about the sun system. We have recorded it and are left stunned but the power and sicken by the echo of its pain. Thus ends the fifth scale.

Remind me never to annoy the god of Chaos. Oh, too late. Well and wise, not too much.

We dragons did not always live on the moon. In fact, we were not always dragons. Our tale has not come. Yet we speak now of the creation of the god homes and the moon. Ter'Avan was a peculiar planet, for its shape was two orbs pressed together upon a bridge and belt of stone.

The gods had lived upon the planet, yet they did not make themselves a home. They had taken places of the planet to rest. Now Chaos had been born, they needed places that were sheltered from his influence. The gods needed places that they have dominance. They feared the mischief Chaos would do as they rest.

Chaos was an unpredictable god and performed acts within the firmament, that before, were impossible We dragons do not know if this is due to his tie to all forces or his over all power. Even though Chaos was the combination of all the magics from all the gods, it was a new magic entirely. This magic was dictated by Chaos himself. At times the magic worked flawlessly or to a better degree than predicted. At other times the magic did not work or even resulted in disaster. Sometimes the magic did things completely unpredictable.

Chaos was just as unpredictable as the magic he came from. The gods were at the mercy of his cruel humor. Even Chaos himself was at his own mercy. He often played jokes on the other gods, and at times, on himself. Somehow he was able to surprise himself and even anger himself and amuse himself with mischief at the same time. Of all the gods, the goddess of Water and goddess of Air was his favorites. They mostly benefited from his gifts. Nulx was almost always gifted with the worse jokes Chaos created. Chaos also sometimes gifted him a great boon, just to make it interesting.

If the gods knew anything from Chaos, they knew to never

trust him. More often than not. Chaos lied. The other gods were unable to tell the truth from the lies. Chaos could lie at one moment, then make those words truthful after the fact. He could all tell the truth and then make it a lie by changing his mind.

Yet Chaos' magic was still bound to the laws of the firmament. He could not completely ignore the governing reality. He merely bent or used it to the best advantages. Thus, ends the fifth scale.

I bet he invented the headache. I wish that gift was kept to the gods.

We dragons wanted to make this clear before we continued to the next part of our histories. The creation of the moon was one of Chaos' most mocking jokes against the other gods, and one of the grandest gifts the world had ever received.

I am roasting the corn kernels. Start the chapter dragons!

Sixth Scale: Creation of Sanctuaries

The gods decided to build shelters against the unpredictable works of Chaos. All the gods performed acts against the other gods to different degrees. It was a game of sorts. An endless dance of minor acts that allowed the gods to gain a larger foothold on Ter'Avan or prevent others from doing the same. Yet Chaos did not seem to care. He played a game all to himself.

So the gods looked at ways to block him from harming them as they rested or wished for solitude. Ter'Avan was the first of the gods to build this protection. He gathered the earth about him. The Earth did his binding, swirling about. A grand mountain rose from the crust of the planet. Ter'Avan pressed his fist upon the peek of the mountain with great force. The peek pressed down and pushed out at all sides splitting into a series of ragged wedges that made a great ring of mountain peeks.

Was not this the god that was crying over a few rocks hitting his planet? Here he is punching it. This is planet abuse.

Water erupted from one of the jagged peaks. The spring water poured down the side and into a small waterfall. The great depression in the middle of the mountain ring filled with spring water. Ter'Avan gathered plants of all types from around the planet and the creatures that lived within them. He planted the growth within the great ringed mountain and later placed the creatures. He spent and unrecorded time crafting and shaping the plants and animals within. Without the power of natural he had to shape the plants by normal means, allowing many years to make a single change. After he was satisfied, he called for the goddess of Nature, Neroal.

She came to Ter'Avan. "Dear god of Earth, why have you asked for my presence?" She smiled fondly at him.

Ter'Avan blushed. "I have made a thing for you. It is but a small trifle that I hope you would like."

"Oh, have you made a creature for me?" She asked. She chuckled at his embarrassment. The god of Earth was strong and boisterous, yet around her he was a simple giant of a man with the deepest caring heart she had ever felt.

"No, I have stolen from your plants and animals and crafted a thing from them."

"You did what to my plants and animals?" Her voice dropped an octave as she leveled accusations at Ter'Avan.

Ter'Avan looked downward. "Perhaps my words are wrong." He pointed at the ragged and terrifying mountain range. "Look within, your plants and animals lay with the palm of that ring of rock."

Neroal gasped at the monstrous rock claw that had been pulled from the earth. "What have you done under my eye? Why was this hidden? What terrible cage have you imprisoned my children within!" Before the god could answer, Neroal rushed to the ring of mountains to save her beloved plants and creatures. Her eyes fell upon the wonder that Ter'Avan had created.

Within, he had made a paradise. Nature was entwined upon rocks and dirt. A lake shimmered with emerald depths so clear the bottom could be seen. The sand around the lake swirled in many colors. The plants lay upon the round valley, verdant and healthy. Flowers were in full bloom and boasted a rainbow of petals.

Well played Ter'Avan. You are going to get some sweet goddess affection. I am making kissing noises and inappropriate gestures.

Within the plants, creatures ate from the plants or hunted

each other in an endless circle of life. It was a perfect balance of nature. She looked at Ter'Avan with tears streaming from her eyes. "Why would you do this? Why spend so much effort and time?"

"We needed a home, a shelter from Chaos and the other gods. We have all spoken or made plans, yet none had dared. We needed a home, and I wish to craft it from my own hand, for you."

Neroal nodded, "Yes I can bless this shelter as a home." She gasped, "Wait, you said we?"

Ter'Avan moved close to her and gently took her hand. "I did. I wish to bless this as a home for us both. I am but an empty rock without you, a geode without the beauty inside. You are my heart of stone."

Neroal could not answer him. Her words would not come. So she answered with a kiss. At that moment, the paradise glowed with light. The first home of the gods was blessed, and Ter'Avan and Neroal lived within the first sanctuary.

The other gods, had settled down to a semblance of peace, even the god Nulx. Nulx started to refused references to his powers as Darkness, Death and Time. He only referred to his powers as Void. The other gods did not care. For them it was easier than saying the god of Darkness, Death and Time. They still did not trust him, but he was predictable. They were getting use to his schemes. Only the god of Chaos was still feared and loved by the gods.

In short order, the other gods and goddess created homes for themselves. Sepria, the goddess of Spirit created a temple of marble resting on top a plateau of basalt. The plateau stuck out over a grassy plain protected within a formidable frozen mountain range.

Forr, god of Fire created a great tooth of stone filled by a waterfall of fire and lava drawn upwards from the core of the planet. The entrance to his home was surrounded by ragged peaks that held no life.

A lot of those gods are making homes in mountain. I guess the land was cheap? Maybe they just do not like guests. How deeply antisocial.

Seqoria, goddess of Water, made her home deep with the depths of the ocean. Her castle was created from the sands within the sea and traveled along the ocean floor. Her entrance has yet be to discovered by the dragons.

A'orria, goddess of Air, dug her home from the highest peak on the tallest mountain upon the planet. Great holes in the sides of her home allowed the wind to come and go from all directions.

Nulx, god of Void. Made his home within a vast deadly swamp. Even though he spent most of his time in the darkness around the planet, he wanted to make his presence known. He left it open for any creature or monster to wander in. Most did not wander back out.

He is a colossal buttock.

Chaos wandered near the homes of each of the gods. He even spotted the hidden home of Seqoria. He amused himself by entering their homes and leaving gifts and graffiti. The gods grew upset with Chaos.

What a wonderful day, the dragons didn't use the word 'discord.'

The had thought the shelters they made were impenetrable to the works of Chaos. They were wrong. Chaos was still able to enter their homes, even though he could not carry out more minor distractions within the shelters. It seems the protections worked to a strong degree, but it was imperfect. Even the mutual home of Ter'Avan and Neroal was unsafe. Chaos would toss defecation from the various animals within the home, into the waters of the lake.

Chaos tossing nature-anchors in the bottom of perfectly clear lake. Now, that is funny!

His favorite target was Nulx. He would place flowers in the swamp and paint the colors of trees and waters in soft welcoming colors. Nulx would destroy them as the cropped up, but his anger was much harder to stamp down.

I swear, I was near the swamp once and saw a grove of pastel colored weeping willows.

The gods gathered to discuss the problem. Nulx was the most upset. "We cannot abide this desecration! He comes within our homes and disrupts them. We must kill Chaos."

Ter'Avan sighed, "Oh not this again." He pounded his fist into his hand. The other gods nodded. "This is not why we are here. We fear our homes are not safe from his minor occurrences, but what if he tries more?"

Is it me, or are the dragons finally figuring out pronouns? They can travel to a moon, but it took this long to improve grammar. Dragons, if you read this, thank you. Idiots. Love, Soas.

"Like, take your home for my own, leaving you vulnerable?" Chaos said as he appeared between them all. The gods stepped back from him. He paced about, his hands folded behind him. "I could, I think. I could try, but I have a better idea." Chaos lifted his face to the stars. "Ah, it is arriving now."

The gods looked up to see a monstrous rock hurtling towards the planet. The size of the asteroid was so massive, it had become a sphere. It was not an asteroid, it was a planetoid. The rock held its own gravity. The gods screamed at Chaos and even a few of them readied to strike at him.

Chaos held a hand up to the gods, "Wait your attack and watch." The miniature planet started to veer off course and slow. It spun around the planet several times and settled into an orbit. He pointed to the moon. "There is my home."

Seqoria cocked her head to the side. "Where, I do not see it, which part?"

Chaos smiled to her fondly. His face was a mask of amusement. The smile slipped from his face as it become suddenly stern and serious. This was never a good look for Chaos. The gods were nervous because he acted like a petulant child, but feared him when he was serious and focus. "All of it. The whole of the moon is my home." Chaos' eyes become deadly as he spoke is a welcome. "You are welcome to visit. I love guest." Chaos vanished without another word.

It is so nice to see he didn't go to large. Nice and humble. I am rolling my eyes right now.

The gods and goddess spoke to each other about the change. They tried to examine the moon from afar, but were rebuffed. They tried to pull it from away from orbit, but it would not budge. The home of Chaos was permanent. None of them dared to visit. They were not sure if Chaos jested or as serious. If words spoke kindly, yet his eyes spoke danger.

As they watched, they noticed the moon would spiral closer to the planet as it orbited, then would shoot outward again. It kept this spiral dance at a regular pace. We dragons have witness this spiral over many years and found it has never faltered. The gods feared the moon at first, but found the moon was one of the greatest gifts ever created. The moon regulated the spin of the planet, even as it ventured closer and farther away. This defied everything we dragons knew of the laws of the firmament. The moon made the waters shift and the winds move and brought more life to the planet from the rains it produced.

The moons shifted the plates of the planet and made volcanoes roar, bringing minerals to the surface. The moon helped sheltered the planet from rocks and ice of the firmament. Chaos named the moon The Eye of Chaos.

We dragons mentions in the first scale, the planet spun end over end and twisted about its middle. The god of Earth stopped the planet from flipping end over end. The Eye of Chaos helped settled the axis into a single plane of orbit and removed the duty from the god of Earth's constant care. The seasons became mild and located by the area of the planet.

The variation came from the moon and became incredibly predictable. This surprised the other gods most of all. Chaos merely shrugged and laughed as he spoke "It was the one thing you least expected."

The planet became in harmonic balance and allowed the creatures and monsters that struggled on its surface to survive and adapt in greater comfort.

The gods and goddess finally accepted Chaos as one of their own. All thought they have to tend with his tricks and jokes, when they thought back, he had never harmed them. Nulx was the only target of physical wounding and still touched his shoulder in remembered pain.

Thus, all the gods had homes and the moon of Ter'Avan settled into her orbit. Thus, ends the sixth scale.

Chaos should have put a big arcing crack in the moon. It would be funny to see a large floating backside spinning around the planet.

Excerpts of The Book of Dragons will continue in book 2.
Once again, thank you dear reader.
Thank you for reading.
D.C. Soas

Mercadio

Daylow

Delex

Soas

Valash

Vex

BlacRus

Moraphen

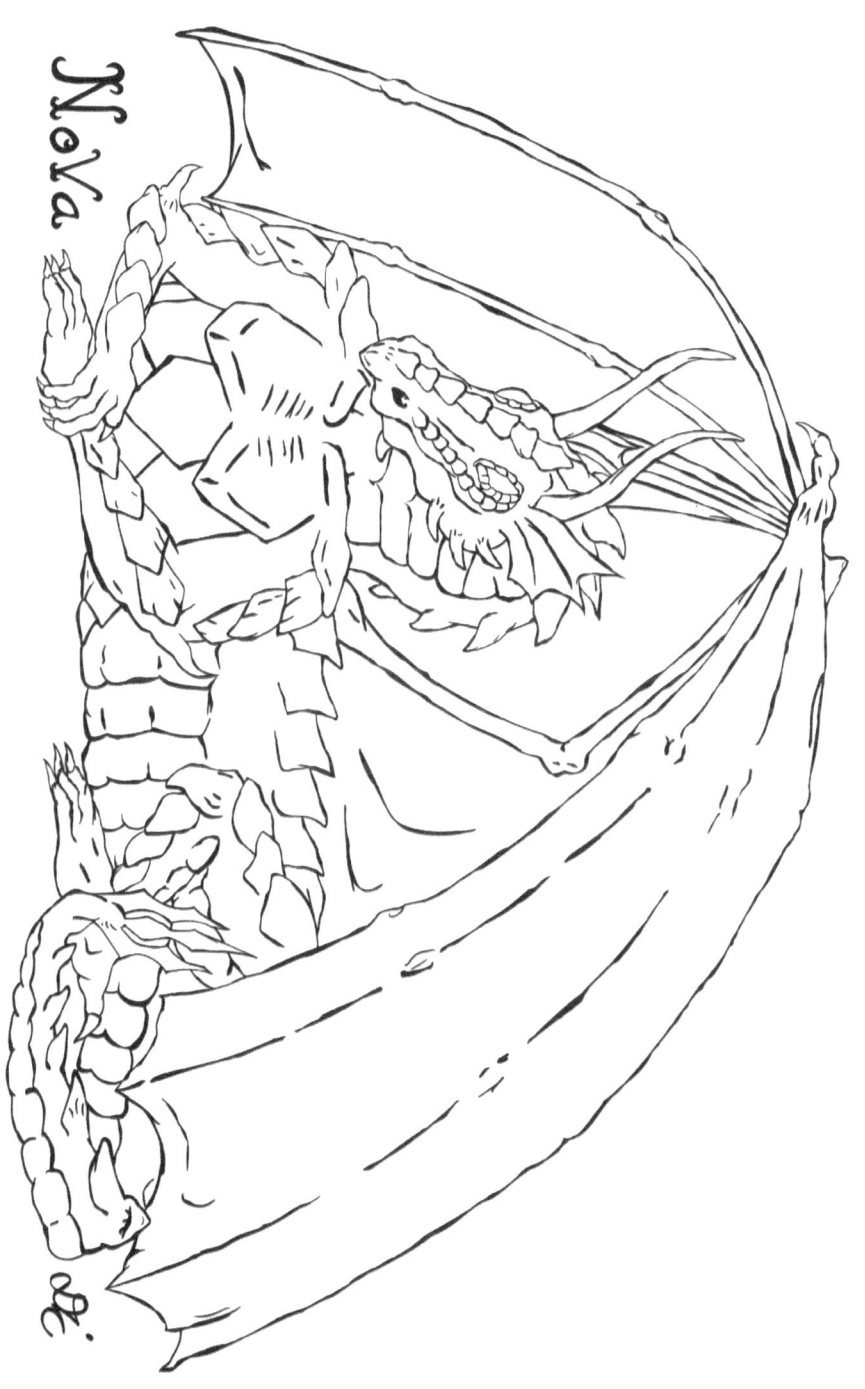

Nova

NoVa

About the Author

D.C. graduated in the top 1% and as the No. 1 science student of his high school class. He had already begun college classes in chemistry, biology and calculus with an emphasis in biochemistry and astronomical physics. D.C.'s love of science was parallel with his passion for art, drama, and debate. *Yet, he couldn't craft a musical score if he had a gramophone sticking out his backside.†*

He continued his study into college when his world changed dramatically when a personal life event spurred his soul into service of the US military. He left his campus behind and stepped into an unknown world which demanded a person unlike the one he had ever been. *More alpha wolf, less betta fish.†*

D.C. excelled in training, witnessed a country tragedy, and in short order, D.C. was given orders overseas, and left his first-born child of two weeks old in his memories for 14 months. He came back permanently wounded, physically and mentally. *Granted, the boy always been the wrong marble. Good lad though.†*

Years later, D.C. met Soas. Their passions echoed each other and with Soas as his mentor, D.C. took the reins of his imagination and brought it to life. Soas gave him a deeper understanding of the literature world, and a humor of a crazed hermit. D.C. gave Soas the energy and imagination to share their vision Without Soas, D.C. would not be half the writer he is today. *That's our kid, decent boy. I'm almost ashamed for tossing stone at his 'About the Author' page, almost.†*

† Soas' comments.

Soas declined to add his past and experiences. He remains the mentor and friend to D.C.

www.ingramcontent.com/pod-product-compliance
Lightning Source LLC
Chambersburg PA
CBHW031943260626
47157CB00017B/2093